# Life
## after
### Ted

*For Donna*
*And in memory of Dr Bill Feneley (Dad)*

# Life after Ted

R. D. Feneley

echo
PUBLISHING

*echo*
PUBLISHING

An imprint of Bonnier Books UK
4th Floor, Victoria House, Bloomsbury Square
London WC1B 4DA
www.echopublishing.com.au
www.bonnierbooks.co.uk

Copyright © R. D. Feneley 2023

Echo Publishing acknowledges the traditional custodians of Country
throughout Australia. We recognise their continuing connection to land,
sea and waters. We pay our respects to Elders past and present.

This is a work of fiction. Names, characters, businesses, places, events,
locales and incidents are either the products of the author's imagination
or used in a fictitious manner. Any resemblance to actual persons,
living or dead, or actual events is purely coincidental.

First published 2023

Printed and bound in Australia by Griffin Press

MIX
Paper | Supporting
responsible forestry
FSC® C018684
www.fsc.org

The paper this book is printed on is certified against the
Forest Stewardship Council® Standards. Griffin Press holds
chain of custody certification SCS-COC-001185. FSC®
promotes environmentally responsible, socially beneficial
and economically viable management of the world's forests.

Editor: Lauren Finger
Cover designer: Nada Backovic
Page design and typesetting: Shaun Jury
Front cover image: Close-up of blue wren perching on cable,
Australia, by Borja Perez Dopozo/Getty Images; Australian
male superb fairy-wren, by Douglas Cliff/Shutterstock

NATIONAL
LIBRARY
OF AUSTRALIA

A catalogue entry for this book is available from
the National Library of Australia

ISBN: 9781760688240 (paperback)
ISBN: 9781760688257 (ebook)

 echo_publishing
 echo_publishing
 echopublishingaustralia

## ABOUT THE AUTHOR

Rick Feneley was born at Bulli, NSW, in 1962 and has lived for most of his adult life at Bondi, where he and his wife, Donna, raised two daughters. He has been a journalist for four decades and currently works for the *Sydney Morning Herald*, where he has held editing and writing roles. His first novel, *Sly*, was published in 1995. This is his second novel.

**Praise for *Life after Ted***

'I envy readers who are still to discover Rick Feneley. What a treat you have in store. In this fresh, touching and wise novel, Feneley deals with secrets and drama – the biggest drama, family drama – with a light touch and a true feel for the love that flows between wives and husbands, mothers and fathers, children and friends. *Life after Ted* is also really funny, its humour poised on that tender nerve between horror and hilarity. Like its title character, this book is both sweet and salty, and wholly lovable.'

MALCOLM KNOX

*… what do righteousness and wickedness have in common?*
*Or what fellowship can light have with darkness?*

2 Corinthians 6:14


*Life has loveliness to sell … Spend all you have for loveliness …*
*And for a breath of ecstasy / Give all you have been, or could be.*

From 'Barter', by the American poet Sara Teasdale, in her
Pulitzer Prize-winning collection, *Love Songs*
(The Macmillan Company, 1918)

# THE EMAIL TRAIL

**Friday, 5:16 p.m.**

Dear Seb,

Given the scene that confronted you this morning, I thought I should make contact before you leap to too many conclusions. You must have no doubt that I adored your father, that I will never stop loving him.

I'm overwhelmed with grief, as I know you are. I'm not ready to attempt explanations. I can, however, understand your shock and, I imagine, your eagerness for answers. In good time I will be able to tell you things that will give this morning some perspective. They will, I hope, cast me in a less harsh light. I ask you to bear with me.

Love, Mum

**5:21 p.m.**

Mum,

Need I remind you that Dad's funeral was three days ago?

Sebastian

**5:22 p.m.**
No, Seb, you needn't.

Connie Blunt slurps her third G & T through crushed ice. It's no better than her first. What was it that Ted did to give them so much zing?

She's alone in his little study under the stairs. The glum, blue glow of her dead husband's computer screen is her only light. It conjures a creepy reflection in the federation window; her silver helmet of hair floats facelessly in the night outside. Her spare stethoscope, strung up on the wall behind her, is out there too, hovering in the night, and it somehow amplifies the unreality of this long, hot Friday.

'Christ it's hot.'

And ridiculously late. It's 11:23 p.m. and still this day is a stinker. Connie goes to the window and opens it but there's not the whiff of a breeze, so she returns to the desk and drains the last of the G & T. She wants it to taste of nostalgia but supposes it can't. Not this soon.

She should go to bed, she really should, but she carries on reviewing this afternoon's email exchange with Seb.

**5:24 p.m.**
Or need I describe the 'scene' that confronted me barely five hours ago? You use that word as if the scene were a culpable third party.

**5:25 p.m.**
Please, Seb, I only ask that you give me a little time.

**5:27 p.m.**
You certainly wasted no time. Spare me the wailing-widow performance. At the very least you might answer me this: who was that?

**5:29 p.m.**
How dare you question my grief? As I said, I understand your shock, but you have no idea. You can be horribly self-righteous, Seb. I used to blame those Pentecostal pests but, no, I tend to think it's just you.

Connie stops reading. Why go through it all again, the escalating rancour? It doesn't surprise her but it does upset her, this widening gulf – the mutual incomprehension – between her and her only child.

He's hardly a child now, though it's been going on since he was, if she really thinks about it. This time, though, she fears it will be irreconcilable, and Ted would be sad about that. It was only last month that he challenged her about another of her email ping-pong matches with their son.

'Why don't you just walk the five doors and talk to him?' Ted asked.

'Five doors and five million light years.'

'You could shout from here.'

'I'll keep it civil.'

'You know what I mean,' Ted said.

She did, and she does. She's dwelling upon it now, but she can't see a way through it. Their long civil war has been, in the main, *civil*. They've kept a lid on it for the sake of the family, for the grandkids, but after today she anticipates open hostility. It's a pity because today had been going so well. Despite this hellish heatwave, it had been sublime, beyond sublime, until Seb barged in.

Connie looks to the wall and her husband's little photo gallery, the trio of frames taken over three decades or more. In each Ted is surfing the same red longboard with a child on his shoulders: first Seb at five, then Seb's kids – Gracie and Mack – at the same age. On the facing wall is Ted's favourite picture of Connie, the one he took in Manhattan. She's wearing high boots, a mini, a midriff and mad hair, as she tended to wear it when she was twenty-eight.

Connie grips the computer mouse. It's strange that email remains her main mode of communication with her son, two decades after both became early adopters. Now it seems quaintly formal. Texts or snapchats, as she corresponds with her granddaughter, would be warmer, chattier.

She flicks her forefinger over the mouse's hump and the rest of today's email trail scrolls by in a blur. It bounces at the bottom, at her final exchange with Seb.

**6:03 p.m.**
WTF, Mum? What the actual f--k? For the love of God, you're 70.

**6:04 p.m.**
You're almost 40, Seb. Grow the fuck up!

Once she'd sent it, it was too late. There was no retracting an email, she realised. Connie can't understand that – why they haven't invented an email 'dump' button, as for radio, a seven-second delay for the intemperate correspondent. It could have its own key: UNSEND!

# 1.
# ODD SOCKS

It is almost eighteen hours earlier, well before the dawn of the same day, when the widow wakes at 5:17 a.m. Neither the exhaustion of eight days' grief nor benzodiazepines have been able to break this forty-year habit. Connie welcomes the first murmur of the day, the metronomic thrum of the ceiling fan and its breaths of cooling air. It's already too warm outside, though the kookaburras don't seem to mind; they're making their hilarious racket in the gum by her window. Connie listens for the smaller, less bombastic birds and is rewarded with the Morse code soprano of the eastern spinebills that shelter in the low thicket she's cultivated for them.

She has to think: this will be the ninth day? Yes. It's Friday, so yesterday was her eighth complete day alone, if she counts Thursday last week. It was the longest day, after all. That morning, Connie had been stirred from sleep about this time, not by the birds but by the routine departure of her husband of forty-two years, Ted McCall, for nearby Bondi Beach. As always, she felt Ted's lips on her forehead. *Way down in the Congo land,* he sang, as he had on any given day, *lived a happy chimpanzee. She loved a monkey with a long tail (Lordy, how she loved him!)* Ted was a creature of the chirpiest habits. 'Hooroo,' Connie would sigh, then roll over and occupy his side of their king-size bed, what they liked to call its western suburbs. She'd hear him skipping down the stairs, in fuller voice by now, singing that dippy show tune, his reveille … *Baba, daba, daba, daba, daba, daba, dab / Said the monkey to the chimp* … Then she'd doze for five minutes – fifteen on drowsier days.

This morning Connie has woken to find herself already on Ted's side, burrowed into his pillow, ingesting his sweet saltiness. Or is it his salty sweetness? She'll change their sheets this morning, once and for all, but she has a little time now. The smell of him is so vital he could walk in from the ensuite bathroom, in his uniform for his morning drill: his Speedos, and not a stitch more than those budgie smugglers. She loiters here to imbibe the last draughts of Ted.

★★★

Seb McCall's eyelids open like cash registers at 5:29 a.m., a matter of heartbeats before his scheduled alarm at 5:30. His God-given body clock has performed this daily synaptic miracle for most of his adult life. Muscle memory propels his left hand to disable the bedside alarm before it chimes. At this ridiculous hour, Amber reasons, he can have his wife as Sleeping Beauty or Waking Ogre.

Last night, though, Seb hadn't set the alarm that never rings. That was because today was meant to be the rarest of days, a sleep-in followed by a weekday off work from Surfside Hardware, the business his father established in 1981. It's two blocks back from the beach – not quite surfside – but nobody quibbles. On any other day, Seb would now alight from his bed, slip on his togs and leave Amber sleeping while he crept downstairs to look in on Mack, their six-year-old son, being careful not to wake him, then head out back with no more cover than thongs on his feet, a towel over his shoulders and swimming goggles around his neck. Until Thursday last week he walked daily from their backyard into the rear lane and, five houses along, met his father – identically attired – at the gate of the house where Seb was raised.

'The son also rises,' Ted often greeted him.

6

As they'd jaunt off in the pre-dawn, down the old dunny carters' lane dividing the houses of Banksia Avenue and out on to the street and past their front gates, they'd anticipate the daily salutation of old Mrs Visser, who'd be watching from her veranda for their lanky silhouettes.

'You're still taller, Ted,' she announced the last time father and son passed, and Seb happily conceded that his dad, in his eighth decade, had a good inch on him. Mrs Visser has been quieter since. When the shorter silhouette passed yesterday, alone, she'd said only: 'It's too sad, Sebastian.'

Since his father's passing, and more especially because of it, Seb hasn't missed a dawn at the beach with their swimming crew, the Odd Socks. This is what Ted, as their founder, would expect. To soldier on. He christened the Odd Socks thirty-six years ago when he corralled his first pod of ocean swimmers, an informal little club drawn mostly from the ranks of Bondi's volunteer lifesavers, but which, ever since, has welcomed anyone willing to assemble on the beach at dawn to run two laps on the sand as a warm-up, then swim two laps – point to point – seven days a week, if they're keen, winter no exception for the keenest. Ted suggested Odd Socks because anyone silly enough to rise in winter's dark might be unlikely to arrive wearing matching socks, but also to characterise the strange bedfellows who assembled, for most of the year not in socks but in thongs or barefoot. There were tradies, firefighters, police officers, lawyers, a couple of judges, accountants, schoolteachers, doctors (though never Connie Blunt) and, of course, the hardware merchants. The swimmers have come and gone over the years and the numbers continue to rise and fall, but it's still a reliably miscellaneous mob.

Seb won't be among them today. They won't begrudge him this one day of rest, and nor would Ted. God knows Seb needs it.

It was Simmo, God bless him, who recognised Seb was struggling.

'Take a breather,' he told Seb yesterday.

'Simmo' is Tommy Sim, founding member of the Odd Socks, co-owner of Surfside Hardware since 1983, and Ted's dearest friend. They were crewing surfboats together when Ted invited Simmo, then just twenty-three years old, eleven years his junior, to take a stake in the business, though not in the real estate. Tommy is fifth-generation Australian–Chinese, and since his first days at the surf club has been known as Dim – as in Dim Sim – to the Bondi lifesavers. He's always copped it sweet but Ted never liked it, so he came up with Simmo, hoping it might catch on. It never did, other than for Ted and his family.

'You need the break,' Simmo told Seb.

'Don't we all,' Seb protested.

Simmo could use some bereavement leave himself. Still, Seb relented. His plan had been to sleep until nine, but his internal clockwork has performed as always and here he is, awake. He's not irritated by this biological curiosity; it's proof of the hand of God and he counts it as a blessing, so much that he wonders whether he might be safe to dispense with the alarm from this day on.

No, it would be arrogant to put his Saviour to that test. God wakes those who wake themselves.

Seb rolls to his left and watches Amber sleep. She is facedown, rag-doll limp. Only children and drunk teenagers sleep as unabashedly as his wife. She has just turned twenty-eight but looks younger this morning. She looks no older than Gracie, Seb's daughter from his first marriage, who is twenty-one. This thought is both gratifying and disconcerting.

Amber snores musically, a bubble of drool inflating and deflating at the corner of her mouth, and she's wondrously pretty. And for all of this Seb gives praise.

★★★

Connie reaches for her phone on the bedside table. The slightest touch of its screen throws an orb of light around her pillow, and she finds this halo vaguely amusing. She goes to her log of videos and scrolls to the recordings of their Christmas Day singalong, just seven weeks ago. There are half a dozen entries from that day, most identified only by Ted freeze-framed at the upright piano in the family room downstairs. She's been playing them randomly. She selects one now and taps play.

Ted tickles the keys and starts to croon: *Why do I do just as you say / Why must I give you your way* … 'Yes!' someone coos off camera. A few voices fall in behind Ted. Some stumble on the verses but they're all good for the chorus: *It had to be you* … Connie watches to the end.

At the top right of her screen is the outside temperature: it's 25 degrees Celsius in the pre-dawn. It's going to be wretchedly hot. Again.

She plays another Christmas video, the only one featuring her and Ted. They're swing-dancing barefoot to Dean Martin's 'Let It Snow'. Christmas was another heatwave and the phone-cam captures the sweaty backs and summer frocks encircling them while Ted sings it as if pleading.

Connie stops the video. She scrolls instead through her call log. So many callers in the past week, screen after screen, some identified, many not, an unrelenting stream of condolences and expressions of disbelief that Ted McCall – the man behind the counter for four decades at Surfside Hardware and, more notably, stalwart of the Bondi Surf Bathers' Life Saving Club and legendary sweep of its surfboats – was dead at seventy-three. Ted McCall, the Peter Pan of lifesavers, dead.

He would've surfed until his hundredth year, they said. Yes, Connie agreed, he would have.

Ten or more screens deep, she finally arrives at Ted's phone number. It's the only document of their last call. It came at 6:52 on the night before his final morning. Ted must have called Connie at the surgery. She must have answered because there's no recorded message. She has no memory of what they discussed. Groceries, most likely. That night's dinner.

Connie's thumb hovers over his number. It twitches there until, magnetically, it makes contact with the glass and summons Ted from the satellites. It rings. Connie raises her thumb over the end-call button.

Stop it, she's thinking.

But she doesn't. She presses the speaker icon and lets it ring and it peals through the room. It rings five times before his voice is delivered from the cosmos: 'You've reached the phone of Ted McCall. Unfortunately, or fortunately if you happen to be Ted – that's me, by the way – well, I'm out of range right now. That no doubt means I'm on the beach and my phone isn't. I find they don't mix. These smart phones, they get between the grains of sand and then the beach doesn't work so well. Anyway – after the beeeeeep! – you know what to do.'

Ted hadn't changed his hokey message in four or five years.

Connie waits for the beep, then takes her cue. 'No, Ted, I don't know what to do.'

She says nothing else for a few seconds, aware of her silence. She's comfortable with long pauses. Her frequent messages for the living Ted, from her general medical practice on Bondi Road, were much the same. He never bothered deleting old messages and only yesterday Connie recharged his phone in the study and listened. 'Hi, Ted. Insane here today. Summer flu. Yes, white fish, now that you're asking. Flathead, if I'm not too late. [Connie's pen drum-rolling on a prescription pad.] Tiring of salmon, must say. [Pen tinging on teacup.] Put that pinot gris in the freezer about six-thirty. [Ting-ting-ting!] Okey-dokey. Hooroo, my lovely.'

'So here I am,' she tells him now, holding her thought awhile, 'lying in our dirty sheets.' She hums to fill space. 'You'd be horrified.

You'd have changed them a week ago but, you know, housekeeping was your department. Never my thing.' Connie bunches the top sheet and presses it to her face. 'Always loved the smell of you.' She inhales deeply. 'Sandalwood.' Another whiff. 'And salted caramel.'

She laughs aloud. 'I haven't lost the plot, Ted. I know you're not listening.' She runs the sheet's silky trim between her fingers. 'It's just that it's a bit of a thing, apparently: women calling their dead husbands. I've obviously got far too much time on my hands, all this googling around, but they reckon it can help. It's hardly peer-reviewed stuff but, y'know, what have I got to lose? As long as we keep this between you and me.' Connie laughs blackly. 'I'm banking on your incapacity in that regard.'

The trim tickles the V between her fingers. 'There's this one woman, an artificial-intelligence geek. *Bereavement in the Digital Age*. I think that was the headline. Anyway, she's taken all her dead husband's text and voice messages over the years and she's programmed them. Truly, she's built this algorithm to create a neural network. And now she's turned him into a chatbot – that's what they call it – and he talks back to her. She swears it's just like him. It's just text messages for now but one day it'll do voice and they could even make an avatar of him from their home videos and she'd have him as a hologram, y'know, hovering there in their lounge room. Hooley dooley! I won't do that to you, Ted. It was spooky enough seeing you sing at your own funeral.'

★★★

Amber drools on Seb's pillow. He could lie here for an hour, just watching her sleep. Perhaps he will.

He makes a mental note: reschedule her birthday bash for Saturday week. That's tomorrow week, just eight days away. It's tight, but do-able. The party had been planned for last Saturday, an evening gathering of thirty in their backyard. Seb and his father had practised a surprise. They were to perform 'It Had to be You' and 'Gimme a Little Kiss (Will Ya, Huh?)' under the stars. Ted had coached Seb to deliver the latter more like the jovial original by Whispering Jack Smith, less like Dean Martin's lecherous pining. Amber wouldn't have known one from the other, but she would have loved it. It never happened, in any case. Her party became instead a pre-funeral send-off for Ted.

She deserves a celebration. She'll say there's no need but Seb will insist and it will do them good. Or perhaps he'll surprise her. And he'll still sing for her, without his father, though this worries him. Seb can hold a tune but his dad was the real singer. Ted's harmonies made anyone sound good, with the exception of Seb's mother. They all agreed, even Connie, that she couldn't carry a note in a bucket. Gracie, too, poor thing, struggles. She's inherited her grandmother's flat pitch. That and her sharp tongue.

These hard feelings about his mother and her partner in crime, his daughter, have kept resurfacing since their antics at the funeral. Seb wishes they wouldn't because, even without their input, it's been eight days of hell and a succession of sleep-deprived nights since his father's ... accident. The first five days, the funeral preparations, allowed Seb no time to stop and grieve, not even on the nights when he shuddered awake at one or two in the morning and lay thinking until dawn. On the first night he woke with wet cheeks and realised he'd been crying in his sleep. What an odd comfort that was. He wanted to go on crying quietly to himself and relive his water-coloured days with his dad: surf-club days, kick-the-footy days, back-lane-cricket days, church-choir and music-hall days, hymn book and Handel, Gilbert and Sullivan, Rodgers and Hammerstein, father and son, Ted and Seb. A sob might have done him good.

Once awake, however, Seb had been incapable of tears, consumed instead by his duty to worry his father's funeral – Ted McCall's final production – into being: the death notice, the choice of funeral director, the newspaper obituary, the selection of hymns and readings, the artwork, the scouring of photo albums for images, the soliciting of condolences from politicians – local, state and federal – and the invitations and service booklets, the commissioning of a professional printer and the choice of fonts, the photographer, the videographer, the mustering of Ted's choirs, not one but two – church and secular – and the guards of honour, not one but two – the lifesavers and the choristers – and the highly sensitive decisions about who should stand where in the hierarchy, and who should be the pallbearers.

Seb found archived film and video of Ted's glory days at the helm of the Bondi surfboats and arranged for their urgent conversion to digital format. Thank God for Robbie Watson, Seb's brother in Christ. Robbie shoots and edits corporate videos for a living, and Seb oversaw his artful editing of this footage so it could be shown at the funeral service and the wake, requiring the hiring of two giant screens, one for the church, another for the surf club.

Then came the choosing of caterers, the options for canapes, the selection of beers, wines and spirits, the recruiting of waiters. Seb budgeted for three to four hundred mourners but could never have reckoned on the seven hundred who rolled up and spilled from the church and club.

'Your father would've been happy with a sausage sizzle,' his mother said.

That was her contribution. That and her intervention concerning the coffin and hearse. Given the paucity of choices, she complained, both would have to be white – coffin and hearse.

'I quite liked the rosewood for the coffin,' Seb told her.

'It's morose,' she said.

'It's a funeral,' he reasoned.

'It doesn't have to be drab. He'll haunt you if you make it drab.'

'You don't even believe that,' Seb said.

'What?'

'That he'll enter an afterlife from which he might haunt me.'

'No, Seb, I don't, but you do, and that's how he'll haunt you. It'll all be in your head.'

His mother's only other efforts were to ad-lib a eulogy to white-ant Seb's – after insisting she wouldn't give one – and to conspire with Gracie to convince Ted's secular choir, the Surfside Singers, to sneak 'Aba Daba Honeymoon' into the church service. There was no consultation, none with Seb or the church choir or the rector. It was no excuse that his father sang it daily or that he'd sung it with the Surfside Singers or that he would perform it with them, as it turned out, at his own funeral. A video of Ted in action with his choir played on the big screen as a backdrop to the live choristers and their hedonistic chant – *Aba daba daba daba daba daba dab.* It was never meant for a church. They could have saved that party trick for the surf club but, oh no, that wouldn't have done for Gracie and her grandmother. That would have been no fun at all.

How they relished their little rebellion. Outside the church, Seb seethed. While accepting condolences from queues of mourners, he quietly told them that their stunt had been an act of sacrilege and, if that meant nothing to them, of sabotage. They've been giving him the silent treatment since.

Which hasn't helped with Seb's sleep.

He turns his thoughts to the big paddle-out, which he has scheduled for Sunday week. That's the day after Amber's party. It'll be fine – an action-packed weekend. On the Sunday morning, he is expecting a hundred or more locals to assemble with their surfboards on the Bondi shore, from where they will paddle out the back and form a ring around a surfboat for the last of Ted's hurrahs as Seb – taking his father's position as sweep – dispenses with his ashes.

Seb will need to prevail again upon Robbie Watson to cover the spectacle with two or three cameras. The drone shots will be spectacular. So might be the budget. These events are exhausting in the conception, let alone the execution.

But having today off is a huge help. God bless you, Simmo.

★★★

The sheet's trim triggers a memory from Connie's infancy, when she'd suck her thumb while caressing a silk blanket between the splayed fingers of the same hand. The fingers of her other hand twirled her hair into curls. Connie wonders whether she really remembers this or merely her mother Valentina's recollections of it. Val's death-bed recollections, when Connie was thirteen years old, were desperately vivid. They've been coming back to Connie since Ted's sudden exit.

*Exit?* Don't you start, Connie. It was his death. Sudden *death*. She supposes *exit* is at least less equivocal, less mealy-mouthed, than *passed away* or, worse, *passed*. Why can't people just say the thing? When you're alive one minute and not the next, it's hardly a passing. It's a wrenching.

'I know you're just dead,' she tells Ted's phone now. 'Plain old dead.'

She sings a bar of his morning gibber, *Aba daba daba* …

'I told Penny she'd have to mind the fort for a month, but I'm already thinking I need to get back to work. All this googling will do my head in otherwise. Yesterday I fact-checked your crazy story about kangaroos. Turns out you're right: they really do kill more people than sharks. But you neglected to mention that almost every person killed by a kangaroo was in a car at the time and the poor old roo ended up as roadkill, too.'

Connie checks the time and hardly fifteen minutes have passed since she woke. Days are longer now. Minutes are longer. She spreads her arms and legs – starfish. 'This bed is ridiculously huge for one.'

Minutes are becoming bloated with concerns that her workday

routine has never accommodated. Routine is good like that. Connie thinks of her schedule for today. Dawn will come at 5:59, a minute before the pool gates open. She'll be poolside well before that. Apart from her swim, she has only one real commitment – back here at 10:15 for Simmo. It strikes her as curious that she hasn't mentioned this in her voicemail to Ted's phone. Not that he's listening, but she registers it as a conscious omission.

'You know what, Ted? I'm yet to shed a single tear. In the past eight days, not one. Do you reckon that's a bit off?'

She leaves that thought to float.

'I'm absolutely shattered – of course I am – but I don't know about the tears. I asked Penny and she said it was okay, that this bereavement thing is different for everyone. I know that, of course. It's not like I haven't seen a few in my time. Deaths. Kind of an occupational hazard. Still, the way some of the old clubbies carried on bawling at the funeral, it was like no one had ever done it before. As if you'd invented it. That's your line, I know, or a variation of it. Seriously, though, it was as if Ted McCall invented death and you scared them shitless. If you could die, they all could. You were fitter than the lot of 'em put together.'

Connie repositions her head and Ted's pillow exhales him. Sandalwood, yes, but also, bizarrely, horse saddle. Ted last rode a horse in his late thirties, when he took young Seb for a gallop on Burrabogie, the McCall family's sheep, wheat and barley property just outside Tocumwal, on the Murray River. It's hard to even picture Ted on a horse now. Connie sees him as he was the last time she saw him, dressed, or undressed, as he had been for much of the past four decades.

'I wanted them to put you in the coffin in your budgies. You always looked so lovely in them. I thought Seb might back me up, but he went with the funeral directors. They put you in your suit and tie. I felt claustrophobic for you.' She snorts. 'Imagine if they heard me now. I'd be struck off. They'd schedule me, lock me up.'

*Seriously,* she's thinking. She lies here attempting to summon an ordinary, sane thought.

'My neck's playing up again. I could use one of your massages. That woman around the corner is too hard. Tried her the other day and she triggered a migraine. Won't go back.' Connie bumps the phone screen. 'Oh, look, your time's up, Ted.'

She ends the call to her dead husband. She gets up and strips the top sheet. It billows towards the fan. She strips the fitted bottom sheet, then the pillow slips, then bundles the dirty linen into a pile on the floor. She'll see to it when she returns from the pool.

Connie defaults to her morning drill. She collects her phone and ambles to the bathroom, shedding her nightie as she goes. It falls as lightly as ever. Grief has made things strangely leaden, so she takes comfort from its familiar drift to the floor. A-tisket a-tasket.

Naked, she places her phone on the bathroom vanity and grabs her toothbrush from the old tea mug that still holds Ted's as well – his and hers – and she squeezes a glob of toothpaste onto the worn bristles and with her free hand takes her one-piece navy swimmers from the shower rail and suspends them at an angle that invites one leg at a time, and she slithers into them like a second skin. She's foaming toothpaste into the basin by the time the Lycra straps clasp her shoulders. She takes a pair of belted white shorts from a hook on the back of the bathroom door, slips into them and fastens the buckle.

It's been this way for most of her married life, one seamless movement, here and beyond, a daily glide from bedroom to bathroom to stairwell – headphones swept from the bannister at the foot of the stairs – and through to the open-plan kitchen and family room and out the sliding door to the back garden where she scoops her goggles and towel from their hooks, and wires herself for sound before she walks to the rear lane and along the old dunny-carter's path to Banksia Avenue, past the front of their home and Seb's place, and across the street to wave to Mrs Visser, then up to Bondi Road for the march seaward.

Except this morning Connie has paused before the bathroom mirror to inspect the woman behind the glass. Every day is a new day in Ted's absence, but she knows today will be the newest. In preparation, yesterday, she took herself into town where, for the first time in her life, she had her legs waxed and her eyebrows tinted. She's quite happy with the legs but not so sure about the tint. Too dark. Connie had suggested Annie Lennox as a guide but the beautician was too young to know who that was.

Connie steps in close to the mirror to study her darkened brow. More like Vampira. She takes a step back to consider the whole package. She attempts to regard her reflection with detachment. How does the woman behind the glass shape up? Willowy? Lissom? Sun-glazed? Oh, Connie wishes, but she is grateful that this is how her contemporaries see her, and envy her. They've told her so. She's the lithest of them all, they say. And sexy. *For seventy*, they mean.

Still, they mean well.

Connie also knows how her granddaughter's contemporaries see her, and admire her. Gracie's university friends tell her, if not Connie directly, what they reckon, and Gracie passes it all on. Jaunty, they say, as if it's a compliment. Jaunty, nimble, perky and – *kill me now*, Connie's thinking – sprightly. One of them said handsome. Truly, whoever calls a woman handsome except as consolation for her being old?

The patronising little witches.

Connie adores these kids, she really does, but she could spank them when they *ooh* and *ah* about her bone density and muscle mass, for fuck's sake. They marvel, too, at her vinyl collection – her Velvet Underground, Patti Smith, Television, Stones, Iggy Pop,

Bowie, Ramones – as if they can't possibly be of a grandmother's vintage.

'I'm younger than all of them,' Connie told the girls. 'Especially the dead ones.'

When was that? Barely two weeks ago. And the kids loved it: Gracie's foul-mouthed gran with the awesome soundtrack telling them, ever-so-nicely, to go fuck themselves.

It was four days before Ted's last, now Connie thinks of it. She and Ted watched as Gracie and friends spent that hilarious Sunday afternoon in their living room, choosing tracks alternately from his and her polar-opposite vinyl collections, which are demarcated by a kitsch ornamental monkey – hear no evil – on a six-metre shelf that runs the length of the living room. The girls played one tune from Connie's collection, east of the monkey, then the next from Ted's to the west, and so on … Ted's choristers and crooners and Broadway showstoppers in mortal combat with Connie's rockers and punks and protopunks. Sinatra's 'Drinking Again' versus The Ramones' 'I Wanna Be Sedated'.

'Patti's "Piss Factory" shits all over the rest,' Gracie declared.

Ted was only three years older than Connie yet aeons separated their musical appetites. Connie explained their filing system to Gracie's mates. The nearer an album to the monkey – Nina Simone, some Bowie, Springsteen and Dylan – the more likely that both she and Ted liked it.

Connie has so much time for the kids, but this morning – before this unforgiving mirror – she hears only glib condescension in *perky* and *handsome*. She can't abide it, not today. Time will have its way with them, just watch. It will catch up and ravage them, gouge crows' feet and laughter lines into their peachy skins and daub them with age spots.

Connie touches an evolving spot as big as a twenty-cent coin on her upper left chest. It brings her eye to the craggy crevasse in her shoulder. She pans from here to a chasm of chest bones that once paraded as décolletage. Gravity has pilfered the once-ample bosom that provided cover for that pronounced breastbone. Wherever did her boobs go?

She wishes she wasn't feeling so crotchety, so insecure. She's spent much of her adult life counselling women to repel apparitions of beauty – the female patients who account for almost two-thirds of her practice, her small network of local friends, particularly Miranda, Simmo's wife, when she was alive, and now Jean Amos, and Gracie and her gang, a generation both blessed and afflicted by its perpetual connectedness, emergent women with the world in the screens in the palms of their hands, group-selfies streaming in to assure them they are imperishably young yet confirming they are not always so beautiful as the next girl. Connie worries for them. Be yourselves. Be happy with your *selves*.

And yet she's not sure she can do the same today. Today Connie wants to be beautiful, or as near beautiful as she once was. She peers into the mirror. Might she be desired?

The woman behind the glass twirls and looks over her shoulder and inspects Connie's backside. That's where your boobs went, Concetta Blunt. To your arse.

Only her Italian mother called her Concetta, sometimes as a reprimand, usually to poke fun.

When Connie was young she had wanted a rump instead of the scrawny, hollow-cheeked spare ribs that passed for her buttocks. She supposes she should be grateful at last for the extra heft. In any case, she can do nothing about it. And it's too late for stage fright. Today is the day. It's decided. And her bum is indeed better for the ballast.

She picks up her phone, leaves the bathroom, rollicks down the stairs and collects her headphones. She passes a melee of wilting funeral flowers in the living room, so ripe they're rancid. She'll need to turf them and open up the house for a good airing when she returns from the pool.

The sliding door, never locked, is slightly ajar. She opens it wide and steps barefoot into the back garden, her lovingly neglected native tangle. It's still dark out here. She's running later than usual but she should arrive at the pool before first light.

Her husband's beach towel hangs from its hook to the right of the door. She takes a whiff for another blast of Ted. Some details are lost in the blur, though. Did she return the towel to its place or was it Seb? Likewise Ted's swimming goggles, which hang from the next hook, and his size-twelve rubber thongs, which are back by the potted lime tree that bore the fruit of his famous G & Ts.

Connie takes her towel and goggles from their hooks. She puts on her headphones and thumbs the face of her phone for playlists until she arrives at 'Gracie's kick-arse mix for Yeah-Yeah'. That's what her grandkids call Connie — *Yeah-Yeah*. Gracie might have been fifteen when she curated this mix. She's made many more since but, as Connie recalls, this one's a cracker.

It's 5:43 a.m. Connie hits play and is instantly accosted by a ruckus between her ears, and she succumbs to the erratic pulse of drums and a dirty walking bass. A punk diva wails above the mix. Connie checks her screen. The track is listed as 'Holy Sick' by WAAX. It launches Connie into a canter down the dunny-carter's lane to Banksia Avenue, past a smiling Mrs Visser, who seems vicariously animated this morning by the music streaming through her doctor's ears. It propels Connie down Bondi Road and through Hunter Park and down the steps to Knotts Avenue, where the Icebergs Club teeters prettily on the southern headland over Bondi Beach. Painted white, the club descends four storeys from street level, like a stack of ice cubes over the pool deck. The fifty-metre ocean pool is somehow luminous before the first peep of sunlight.

The music spurs her down yet more stairs to the club's locked rear gate. She grips its vertical steel bars, plants and secures a toehold on its waist-high horizontal rung and hoists herself up, then presses her palms into the top of the gate, a fulcrum for her full body weight. She throws her left leg over, swivels to bring her right leg with her, then leaps to the ground. Connie is a paid-up swimming member but the daily thrill of this illegal entry is its own reward. She sails down yet more steps to the pool and goes to its deep end. It's 5:57, later than usual, but she's still beaten the hordes who'll start coming through the turnstiles in three minutes. They've given up asking how she got in.

Anyhow, Connie won't rush into the water this morning. She'll watch the dawn. As advertised, it arrives at 5:59, reticent golds bleeding magenta. The Cowboy Junkies then the Stones seem perfectly scored for the lightshow. The dawn arrives well before the sun rears its head. Twenty-five minutes pass before the dome squints over the horizon and its violet figments give the sea a blue-velvet sheen. If Connie snapchats it, nobody will believe she hasn't photoshopped it. Nevertheless, she climbs back up the stairs to get some perspective. The pool by now is reliably turquoise in the foreground. She snaps the panorama and posts it – too good to be true – knowing Gracie will wake soon and it will make her happy and Connie's friends envious, which is the whole point of Snapchat, isn't it?

★★★

Amber sighs and nuzzles the edge of Seb's pillow. The distance between his wife and his daughter, despite their closeness in age, saddens Seb. When he met Amber, she was a year younger than Gracie is now. His and Amber's first meeting was virtual, an online prayer group. Even with a dodgy Skype link, the connection between them was instant and incandescent. Their laptop screens were split into eight panels, one for each brother and sister in the conference call. While the others prayed, eyes shut, Amber caught Seb peeking at her. He supposed she was peeking at him, too.

Soon they met face to face at the Praise Symposium in Sydney, for which Amber flew down from the Gold Coast where she worked for her father, a residential property prospector. Seb caught sight of her on the other side of the auditorium. She lit up the place. Their greetings were blushing and she repeatedly said 'awesome' and Seb echoed that adolescent refrain. They joined worshippers in a chain of hands and, upon this first touch, an electrical charge passed between them.

Later, Seb drove Amber to her hotel. The motor idling, she began to open the car door when she turned to farewell him. He kissed her. It was inappropriate, and kinetic. Seb explained, between their kissing, that – technically – he was still married, but it was over, he was sure it was, because Kimberley, the mother of his child – oh yes, he had a daughter – anyway, Kimberley had confessed to a fling with their carpenter – his name was Parvis Husseini, another member of their Christian fellowship – and while Seb had wanted to give Kimberley a second chance, he had come to believe she could not put Parvis out of her mind and, frankly, Seb told Amber: 'I don't think I'll be able to put you out of mine.'

'We've just met,' she pointed out. 'You have a daughter?'

'Yes – Gracie. Did I mention Gracie? She's thirteen.'

'Thirteen? Already?'

Yes, already. He'd become a father at eighteen, Kimberley a mother at sixteen. He'd been seventeen – and Kimberley fifteen – when he got her pregnant.

'That's illegal,' Amber noted.

'Nobody wanted to involve the police. Her parents were Christians, born-again. They encouraged us to have the baby, to keep her, to raise her together.'

Kimberley Wyman's parents also introduced Seb to their church, the Congress of God in inner-city Waterloo.

'They left it long ago,' Seb told Amber. 'They stopped believing, just like that, but I'm still there, thank God. Otherwise I'd never have met you.'

Amber was overwhelmed. She was twenty, single. Seb was thirty-one, almost thirty-two, and almost single. His marriage — he could suddenly rationalise it — was floundering at best. Until now he had fretted that its collapse would offend God. Certainly it would be an affront to his and Kimberley's church community. He had told no one of her infidelity because he did not want the humiliation, not for himself nor for Kimberley. She, however, had stopped attending church services, as had Parvis Husseini. Seb attended alone and the faithful noticed. He found their concern for Kimberley — Is anything the matter? — excessively solicitous.

What might they have made of Seb and Amber? He followed her upstairs to her hotel room. Afterwards, both were confused, elated but guilty. Seb went home to Kimberley and announced the marriage was over, after all.

She took it well, remarkably well.

★★★

At the pool's edge, Connie adjusts the volume to slightly above her pain threshold. She unbuckles her belt and unzips her shorts and they drop to her feet. There's an odour of damp. She must remember tonight to launder her togs. But for now she refocuses on the noise between her ears, the gorgeous delirium. She headbangs, four emphatic nods, then removes the headphones.

And silence.

The silence is searing. Connie loves this part, her daily rush into the void. It's her transcendence, this divine *nothing*. The trick is to make the music, whatever it is, extremely loud. Her ritual emerged from an accidental discovery in 1968 when Connie was fifteen and home from boarding school, bored rigid during a hot, dry spell in small-town Tocumwal. Her father, Mick Blunt, the local stock and station agent, was on the road. Her brother, Clem, was away droving. Her mother, Val, was two years in her grave. Connie was home alone, minding the phone for her dad's business.

There were few escapes from the heat. There was, however, her father's magnificent Magnavox record player. The stereo was the widower's refuge, and on this day his daughter's. She put on her dad's big-eared headphones and surrendered to his collection of swing, blues and rockabilly, and she stripped down to her bra and undies and lay on her back on the coolest surface in the house, the linoleum floor by the fridge. She played Lead Belly, Little Walter and Gene Vincent. Soon she became fixated on Vincent's 'Be-Bop-A-Lula' and she played it over and again, rocking on her bare back.

She didn't hear the knocking on the front door or the tapping on the window. She didn't hear the fly-screen door whining open and banging shut. She didn't hear the footsteps in the hall or the hollered inquiries: 'Anybody home?'

He found her soon enough, near naked and fitting in silence on the kitchen floor, her head wrapped in a strange vice, her eyes shut. She kept writhing and he kept watching. He followed the wire that snaked from her head to the record player in the next room, and gathered this was the source of her convulsions.

Ted McCall, then eighteen, had come with a message from his father to hers, but he couldn't bring himself to disturb her. He turned to leave.

Connie felt movement beneath the lino, the floorboards rippling sticky against her back. She opened her eyes and saw the back of him. Tall, broad, he filled the door frame, sweat drenching his blue work shirt. His thatch of straw-blond hair brushed the architrave. On so many Sundays he'd been a beacon, head and shoulders above the faithful at St Peter's Catholic Church, a dozen pews ahead of the Blunts. As townies, the Blunts knew their place. The squatters occupied the pews closest to God.

Mick Blunt knew all the graziers and grain farmers well enough, and he knew the McCalls better than most, but Connie had never uttered a word to the taller and more princely of the McCall twins. They were nominally identical, Ted and Lochie, but not to Connie. Ted was aloof, yet by all accounts sweet. Lochie was stockier and, although technically as handsome, was conceited and cocky, and his breath had stunk of beer and tobacco and peanuts when, a year earlier, on the riverbank, he'd attempted to kiss Connie. He'd been seventeen to her fourteen. She'd fled into the water, which had made his friends laugh. Lochie, humiliated, had declared her a scrawny little scrag.

She would have been happy for the attention of Lochie's twin. Ted had been among her first memories. He might have been six years old to her three the day he kicked the footy into the sun and she had squinted to watch for the ball to come down. It never did. The infant Connie was convinced it never did.

And now he was in her home. He was majestic. But he was leaving and she was incapable of calling his name or saying a word to stop him. She couldn't breathe.

She removed the headphones, just so she could. Breathe. She inhaled the silence and it was immense. She remained paralysed in that crescendo of silence. How long had he been watching her in her underwear?

For a while, she hoped.

She would die there wondering, sweating on the lino, incapable of moving. She listened for the sounds of his exit – the banging of the fly-screen door, the ignition of his starter motor, the opening and shutting of the gate, tyres whirring on the cattle grid – but mainly she heard the relative silence that had displaced Gene Vincent.

For the rest of the afternoon it spun on the turntable at forty-five revolutions per minute. On each completion the automatic arm returned the needle to the start. It would play forever, or until Connie intervened. For hours she didn't. Rather, she put on the headphones, took them off, put them on, took them off. It became a relentless fugue of counterpoint: glorious noise, staggering silence, glorious noise, staggering silence, until she didn't know herself. Or perhaps she was just coming to know herself. She couldn't be sure, but she liked the feeling.

Fifty-five years on, she still likes the feeling. At the Icebergs now, silence subsumes glorious noise and it's a happily dissociative state. Before the hard light of day arrives and flattens all in its path, the morning begins with these curves of a softer lustre and sonic immersion. Every day can have this lovely warp.

Connie stretches her goggles over her skull until they rest on her forehead. She walks to her perch over the swimming lane closest to the surf. She peers over the pool's edge. Waves lap the rock shelf that abuts the bottom of the pool wall. It's low tide, unlike Ted's last morning. She looks across the bay to the horizon, over which the sun levitates and ripens to apricot. The sky is lightening to lavender and shapes are emerging from the ocean's surface – a pod of swimmers. A few hundred metres away, they're ploughing a path towards Connie. The Odd Socks.

At this time eight days ago, Ted was among them. From this same perch, following her twenty laps in the pool, Connie watched him leave the surf with Seb and Simmo and their fellow Odd Socks. Then she watched Ted re-enter the water on his stand-up paddle board. Though he'd retired from the surfboats, he was still the awesome oarsman.

On any other day, Seb – preferring a regular surfboard, whether long or short, conditions dictating – might have paddled out with his father before work, but this time he was called home. The tiler had arrived and Amber required Seb's urgent decision regarding the feature tile for the kitchen renovation. So Connie watched Ted paddle out, alone, standing tall on his bulk carrier, hoeing his plot of ocean, up and over its lumpy swells. The country boy had spent more than half his life, the better part, at this city beach.

27

Connie's toes are suspended over the pool's edge. She replays her final visions of her husband: Ted, directly across the bay from her, perhaps a pool's length away, advancing effortlessly through the breakers and towards the line-up, until he turned and paddled to catch a fat, glassy, two-metre swell and scrawl his cursive signature on that long last wave.

Connie watched it all from the Bergs while waves crashed over the edge and rolled across the pool. High tide. She kept watching as Ted's wave chugged past her vantage point and swept him towards the beach, as he disappeared then reappeared, head and shoulders above the crest, and carved from trough to curling lip, trough to curling lip. She watched him gather pace as that wave churned into the shallows. With each bounce off the lip, he disappeared then reappeared, disappeared then …

The board darted into the air without him. She watched it recoil on its legrope and spear back into the whitewash.

She kept watching. Ted didn't reappear.

Something was wrong, horribly wrong, but she couldn't see what was happening. She ran along the pool's edge, ignoring the incursion of waves, skidding on the slime, to get a closer look. Still she couldn't see him, but she could see there was no one in the surrounding surf and no one on that stretch of beach to help Ted. No lifesaver for the lifesaver.

Connie estimated it might be a beeline swim of one hundred and fifty metres to reach Ted, should she dive in from the pool wall. She almost did. Connie, however, had never put a toe in the ocean. She'd always stuck to the pool. While she'd swum the Murray all her childhood, and it could be treacherous, the river contained no sharks. She knew Ted was right about the ocean, that her shark phobia – given the statistics – was irrational. She'd watched often enough as the Bondi shark alarm emptied the bay of its bathers yet she'd never witnessed an attack.

Sharks, in any case, were not at the front of her mind then.

Connie calculated she'd be quicker to reach Ted by running the few hundred metres, up the stairs and out of the Icebergs, up Notts Avenue, down the steps to the beach park and to the promenade, and down the ramp to the sand and onwards to the shore. First she had to dash back along the pool's edge to collect her phone and dial triple-0. Swimmers arriving at the Icebergs sidestepped from her path as Dr Connie Blunt barked into her phone for an ambulance. 'Man likely drowning, Bondi Beach, south end.'

She'll never know if she might have reached him sooner by water. She can only console herself that it would have made no difference. By the time she got to Ted a surfer had found him facedown in the shallow water and was detaching his legrope and hauling him to the sand. Blood eddied in the swash. Connie dropped to her knees and inspected Ted's wound. His skull had been caved in by his board. She shook him and cried 'Ted', but got no response.

She tossed her phone to the surfer – 'Call the ambulance again. Where are they?' – while she rolled Ted on his side and watched too much of the ocean drain from his mouth. She rolled him to his back and started pumping his chest – thirty compressions – then two ventilations, mouth to mouth. Thirty and two, thirty and two ... until the ambos arrived and zapped him with a defibrillator, and again, and still no response, until they all agreed – Dr Blunt included – there was no use.

Ted was gone.

She had woken at 5:16, his wife. At 6:58 she was his widow. That was the time they agreed for the coronial report. Ted was no doubt dead before that, Connie keeps telling herself. Whatever, he was taken from her in a relative instant amid the irresistible routine of their fortunate lives. Not by a shark, as she had fretted, nor a kangaroo, nor a bus, nor a falling branch from their backyard gum. The widowmaker, Ted had called it.

But the widowmaker had been his paddle board. A fucking

surfboard. Absurd. What were the chances? Google holds few clues about 'death by surfboard'. Connie has found anecdotes – of concussions, of the odd death – but no hard stats. What can anyone do or say about this kind of random, shit-happens death? A slow decline, a cancer, a creeping, painful death, might at least yield some meaning. Death-bed confessions, apologies, affirmations. But not this way. Not with this pointless liquidation by happenstance.

Connie checks her watch. It's 6:22 and the Odd Socks are closing in, perhaps fifty metres off. The sun casts them in a corridor of silvered light that distorts their forms and gives them watery mass. She often fancies them as amniotic sacs on the tide, limbs thrashing to break free of the brine. She can't place Seb or Simmo yet, but they'll be among them. Then there'll be Brad Wiseman, Meg Richards, Marty Ratcliffe and Bertie van de Boor. They're the core of the Odd Socks. One by one, Connie identifies them, until she realises they're a man down this morning. Her son is not among them. It's most unusual.

The swimmers make their turns ten metres before the rock shelf, but Marty Ratcliffe stops and wades and raises a flabby arm to salute Connie.

He hollers: 'Glorious morning, *Mzzz* Blunt.' He beams, bald and goggle-eyed. Marty is another veteran boatie, same vintage as Ted, though he's let himself go. He's never tired of his *Mzzz* joke since discovering twenty-nine years ago, when Connie put up her shingle on Bondi Road – Dr Connie Blunt – that she hadn't taken her husband's name. Marty has called her Mzzz Blunt ever since. Never Dr Blunt. Never Connie. He means no harm, but she never tires of finding him tiresome.

She nods in greeting. He waves and proceeds to swim back, if it can be called swimming. He waddles as might a punctured floaty. This thought amuses Connie. Her crueller diversions have not abandoned her in this period of grief, and for this she is grateful.

What might have waylaid Seb, though?

She does worry about her son, more than he'll ever suspect. Mainly she worries about his worrying, about his constant need to *help*. It's some kind of saviour complex and it all amounts, Connie is sure, to his desperation for accomplishment.

To accomplish what? Something. Anything.

It's anxiety – diagnosable anxiety.

The Oddest Sock, she once called Seb. She wishes she hadn't. It was a long while ago, twenty or more years. It was a private joke between mother and father, an aside to Ted when he'd become concerned that Seb, at nineteen, was singing songs of praise while walking the aisles with customers at Surfside Hardware. Ted and Simmo considered having a quiet word to him but they let him be. Connie's wisecrack – the Oddest Sock – was an expression of sympathy with her husband, gently mocking of their son, but never meant for his ears. Ted, however, was so amused he burst into the shop and shared it with Simmo, not realising Seb was crouching under the counter. To Seb it had sounded savage, he'd later told her. It had hurt that his father had found it funny, but the savagery was his mother's.

Connie pulls the goggles over her eyes. She positions herself over the line on the pool floor. This black line will convey her for a kilometre, twenty laps in as many minutes, during which she'll think of nothing but her next stroke. And the next. To propel herself forward she must pull water backwards, and these simple mechanics will require so much of her bodily attention that all other thoughts will be flushed. Swimming becomes an inertia of the mind. It was Miranda Stanhope who'd explained it to her in the early 1980s, who'd made it sound so alluring, and Connie had repaid her by introducing her to her future husband – Simmo.

Connie rolls her shoulders back and forth. *Here we go, Ted.*

★★★

Sunlight plays mosaics on the bedroom wall and it dawns on Seb that he's been lying here for an hour, perhaps longer. Time seems to have no shape today and this, he supposes, is a welcome change. Duty and schedule form the contours of his days: the burdens of family, business and church. He is thankful, of course, that he's a man who is relied upon by the people he loves. Seb can think of no worse curse than to be a man free of obligation, a man such as Brad Wiseman, his fellow Odd Sock. Wiseman is an independently wealthy stock-market speculator, a bachelor in his early middle age who eats and drinks and fucks what he pleases, but whose every day, following their sunrise laps of Bondi Beach, is surely a marathon of diminishing purpose.

Surely.

Seb offers a small prayer of thanks for his blessed burdens.

Amber, without waking, lifts her head from the wet patch she has left at the corner of his pillow and nestles into hers. Her pink summer nightie is hitched in such an awkward twist it's barely a ribbon for her exposed rump, which moons her husband. It's quite something.

The years since their first meeting have not treated them equally. Seb is keenly aware of this. Soon he will be forty and Amber will remain stubbornly in her twenties. Yet God wanted this for Seb – and for Amber. So Seb makes a prayer of beholding his wife. The sun catches the natural highlights of chestnut in her brunette hair, which flops over her cheek and curls under her chin. The fine line of her neck merges with the curve of her shoulder and her extended arm, which rotates gradually until her inverted hand is propped on her backside. Her fingers curl upwards, sculpturally, as if mounted on a plinth. Seb dwells at last on the curve of her thighs.

He's tempted to rouse her, to wrestle with the ogre. It's a lovely thought, but he'll leave her sleeping. Is it a perversion, he wonders, to be a voyeur of your wife while she sleeps?

A noise downstairs – *tharump, tharump* – interrupts Seb's self-interrogation. It's the new day calling Action Man to duty. Seb knows his son's drill. Mack is trampolining on his bed. Soon he commando-rolls from the bed with a thud and opens fire on the snipers roosting atop his cupboard. *Kerpow!* Seb has been caught in the crossfire, so he knows the sound effects. Action Man scampers out of his room and down the hall and hurls a grenade – *pkworrrhhh!* – into the stairwell, accounting for more snipers. He advances to the kitchen and dispenses with still more of the enemy.

Seb can hear Mack heaving open the pantry door, climbing on the stepladder, shaking the Cheerios box for proof of contents, climbing down and pouring the cereal – mostly, hopefully – into a bowl. The fridge door opens. Mack is getting the milk and pouring it – mostly, hopefully – into the bowl. Seb can hear him carrying his breakfast down the two wide steps to the open-plan family room, no doubt losing more Cheerios and milk overboard. He'll be sprawling on the Monet rug in front of their new television with its two-metre concave screen. It devours Mack, who wants to be consumed. The TV comes on loud and Seb is impressed by the oomph of the surround sound. Amber's snoring changes tune momentarily, but she doesn't stir.

Cartoon villains go *mwahaha*. They always sound more fiendish when Seb can't put faces to the voices. Should he really be leaving them to babysit his six-year-old? Seb hears Mack mimicking them. It's remarkable the way he drops an octave to malevolent, flicks the switch to dastardly. He has a great set of pipes, like his pop.

Seb takes his phone from the bedside table, inserts the earplugs and scrolls to one of the videos from Christmas Day. It's his father, Mack and himself singing 'The Marvellous Toy'. Ted reckoned the smartest thing a smartphone ever did was resurrect Val Doonican doing 'The Marvellous Toy' on YouTube. He and his grandson could watch it all day. Somewhere on the high shelf in Ted's study, where he kept all his reel-to-reels and old videos, there's footage of Seb as a lad singing the same song with his dad. 'Two Little Boys' was always their favourite, though. It distresses Seb to think Rolf Harris was jailed for molesting four little girls. He wishes he could play that reel for Mack, but it would seem icky.

Seb becomes aware of a faint beeping downstairs. Mack has left the fridge door open. This is probably his cue to go down and *mwahaha* with his son, yet something keeps Seb in bed. He's on a roll of thought. His song for Amber's party ...

He scrolls through his phone and finds another file, Gracie's hand-held video of his and Ted's only practice session for the event. Ted is seated at the piano, Seb standing at his shoulder. Ted plays it by ear, feeling his way through the chords, humming until he divines the melody through the fingertips of his right hand. Then he sings – *It had to be you* – and Seb falls in, a third higher. Not too shabby, he realises now. In the second verse, Seb takes the lead while Ted switches to the harmony. They alternate lead and harmony throughout. Seb is overwhelmed by the resonance of his dead father's voice via the puny device in his palm. Ted's phrasing is so assured. It adds some drama and heartbreak to the sweetest of melancholy melodies. No matter the song, Ted is a bit Frank Sinatra, a bit Ray Charles, and he borrows a little fragility from Billie Holiday. But so what? It's all Ted.

Seb has an idea, an audacious idea. Why not another posthumous performance by his father? Beyond the grave, ladies and gentlemen, the late, great Ted McCall. If Seb's mother and Gracie got away with it at his funeral, why not for Amber's party? Seb decides he'll rehire the big screen and speakers. He and his dad will sing their duet, after all.

He climbs out of bed and collects his shorts and T-shirt from his chair, and steps into the hall and pulls them on. He treads quietly on the stairs. He wants to surprise Mack. In the kitchen he finds a trail of Cheerios and spilt milk. He leaves the fridge door open for now. He stands at the precipice of the family room and watches his son spread-eagled on the rug, absorbed in the cartoon, unaware of his entrance. Mack contorts his body to the shape of a raptor on the screen. He caws and rasps.

Now Seb caws and rasps with him. Mack looks up. He finds his father balanced on one leg, making a grotesque face and clawing at the air with talons. Mack smiles, almost sympathetically.

'That's silly, Dad.'

'Why?'

'You look like a stork.'

'Oh, I thought I was doing a raven.'

'It's an eagle.'

'Eagle? How can you tell the difference?'

'Eagles are deadlier.'

'Pardon me. You really know your raptors.' Seb lowers his right leg. 'I stand corrected,' he says. In case Mack missed it, he adds: 'That was a little joke. I *stand* corrected.'

Mack rolls his eyes. Seb joins him on the rug. He lies on his back, yawns and looks wistfully at the ceiling. Mack studies his father's face, then picks up the remote control and turns off the television.

'You're not swimming,' Mack observes.

'No, not today.'

'Are you too sad?'

'No,' Seb says, then finds himself conceding. 'A bit sad, yeah.'

'Me too.'

'Come here, Mack Mac.'

It was Ted who first called him Mack Mac, his diminutive for Mack McCall. It's stuck. Mack crawls on top of his father and lies facedown on his chest. He adjusts his position for optimum comfort and burrows his head into Seb's unshaven neck.

'You're prickly.'

'I'm a porcupine.'

Mack burrows deeper and cuddles his father. 'It's okay to be sad,' he says.

And this does it. His boy's innate compassion taps the source of Seb's un-cried tears. Suddenly he is weeping a flood. Mack, with his face still in his dad's neck, hasn't noticed. Seb can see that Mack is looking to the wall and the dual portraits of his pop: Ted, in his budgies, strikes an identical pose in the side-by-side vertical frames, hugging the same longboard, the first shot in 1985, the second in 2015. Two metres along the wall is a cluster of three photos: Ted riding the same longboard, first with a young Seb on his shoulders, then Gracie, then Mack last year. Seb had them all framed as a matching set and ordered a second set for his father.

'Dad?' Mack asks.

'Mmmmm?'

'Could Pop ...' But Mack is distracted by the moisture slithering between his face and his father's prickly neck. He props himself up on Seb's chest to investigate. His dad's tear ducts are geysers. Plump pearls cascade down his father's cheeks. Seb can feel the itchy rivers in his stubble. He tastes the saline at the corner of his mouth and through a blurry film of tears he watches his son watching him cry. Mack uses the back of his hand to wipe his father's face. 'It's okay to cry, Dad.'

'Thanks, mate.'

'Mum said.' Mack burrows back into Seb's neck, into its dampness.

Father and son carry on for minutes in silence, except for their breathing. Mack rises and falls with the filling and expiration of Seb's lungs. They could be a single organism. Seb becomes giddy with the intimacy.

'Dad?'

'Mmmmm?'

'Could Pop rise today?'

'What?'

'Like Jesus?'

'No.'

'It's the third day.'

Seb attempts an explanation. 'But that was only for Jesus.'

'Why?'

'Jesus is the son of God.'

Mack rests with that answer for a moment. 'We're all God's children,' he says. 'You always say that.'

'I know, but ...'

'God shouldn't have favourites.'

What is Seb to tell him? He blunders instead into the arithmetic of the third day. 'I suppose this is the fourth day, anyway.'

Mack doesn't get it. 'What?'

'Well, if Easter Sunday was the third day, counting from Good Friday, then the Friday must have been inclusive, like' – Seb counts the days on his fingers – 'Friday, Saturday, Sunday. See? Now, if we include Tuesday for Pop's funeral, then count forward to today, Friday' – he counts them again on his fingers – 'we get Tuesday, Wednesday, Thursday, Friday. Four days.'

'Oh yeah.' Mack whimpers.

'And, technically, Good Friday was the day Jesus died, not the day of his funeral, so this would be the ninth day for Pop, not even the fourth.'

Mack looks hugely disappointed. 'It's too late.'

Seb feels his pain. He wishes he hadn't gone and done the sums. 'Don't worry,' he assures Mack. 'Pop will live forever – in Heaven.'

'But I can't see him in Heaven.'

'You will. One day.'

Mack holds this thought, then says: 'When I'm dead.'

Seb flinches. 'Yes,' he answers at last, 'but that'll be a long, long time away.'

'That's what I mean, Dad. I don't want to wait a long, long time.'

'Me neither, mate, but we have to. We have to be patient. And then we'll see Pop in Heaven, where we'll all live together forever because Jesus died for our sins.'

Seb can almost hear his boy processing it all, until he asks: 'Yours too, Dad?'

'What?'

'He died for your sins, too?'

'Yes, mine too.'

Mack takes it on board. 'Dad?'

'Mmmmm?'

'I've never seen you sin.'

Seb smiles meekly. *Oh yes you have, Mack Mac.* But he can't possibly discuss his sins with a blameless child. How might he speak of the banal venalities, the new Range Rover Sport outside, the false gods in surround sound on these very walls, the adulterous thoughts and, let's face it, the downright adulterous act that led to Mack? Seb still struggles with that one.

'It's God's will,' Seb told his parents at the time, just as he had following the conception of Gracie fifteen years earlier.

His mother reacted sarcastically. 'Blessed are the fornicators!' – precisely as she had when Seb broke the news regarding the pregnancy that resulted in her granddaughter.

How can he forget? Her ridicule. She apologised, and she said it came from a loving despair, but he remembers it as one of her incidental brutalities.

He's expecting Mack to grill him about the details of his sins, but his son lets him off the hook with a less curly question.

'Will I sin one day?'

It hurts Seb to even think about it, but at last he sighs and confirms: 'Yes, mate, you will. We all sin. We're only human.'

# 2.
# STAGE FRIGHT

It is not yet seven and Connie, having swum her laps, calculates she has an hour or even two to fritter away. She'll just need to spare some time to tidy up for Simmo.

Anticipation of this appointment, however, is causing her some anxiety. It is manifesting as butterflies, which she recognises as mild gastric distress. She decides this is not urgent and might best be allayed by lying poolside and listening to the rest of Gracie's eclectic offering, her Kick-Arse Mix for Yeah-Yeah. But her phone emits a high-pitched click, the Snapchat notification. Gracie has messaged in response to Connie's dawn snap.

Love it!

*Thanks. And I'm loving Holy Sick. Who is it again?*

A thought bubble pulses on Connie's screen. Gracie is typing her reply.

Blast from my past

*Since when were you old enough to have a past?*
*Who is it?*

WAAX

*WAAX, hey? They're sick!*

Yeah, great

*You're up early.*

Worms to catch. Love ya Yeah-Yeah

*Yeah-Yeah* was Gracie's doing. Connie had opted for 'Yiayia' soon after Seb − not yet eighteen, still in his final year at high school − came home and confessed he'd got Kimberley Wyman pregnant. 'She's almost sixteen,' he said. Her being *almost legal* was as helpful as her being a little bit pregnant. It was carnal knowledge, no less.

Despite the options Connie immediately articulated, Seb and Kimberley insisted they would keep the baby and raise it together.

'You're kids,' Connie pleaded. 'You don't need this responsibility.'

'It's God's will,' Seb answered.

Seb had only recently become acquainted with God, so it was galling for Connie to hear him sounding so certain. Yet Kimberley's parents, Phil and Di, agreed: 'God's will.'

'Oh, for Christ's sake,' Connie said, 'and blessed are the fornicators.'

She immediately wished she hadn't. At the time, Phil and Di were born-agains and it only incited their righteous indignation and their determination to save Seb by inducting him into their church, the Congress of God, and to endorse the kids' plan to marry, once they'd completed school, of course, and just as soon as Kimberley turned eighteen.

Kimberley, the year below Seb, had been young for her grade when they'd met at a Christian camp promoted by their separate, single-sex schools. The consummation and conception happened concurrently or thereabouts, not at the camp but upon their return to Sydney, in the back of Ted's hardware van while it was parked, bearing Seb's P-plates, on Bondi's northern headland, Ben Buckler.

Connie blamed the happy-clapping proselytisers. She hadn't wanted Seb to go on that camp in the first place. Nor had she wanted him to attend his Anglican school, St Barnabas' College, but she'd relented to the switch the previous year because, well, it was where Ted and Lochie had boarded, as had their father, Cliff, and because Connie and Ted had been worried that Seb was smoking too much weed and they hoped – wrongly, as it happened – a more conservative school might be the circuit-breaker he needed.

Initially, Seb showed no interest in religious instruction at St Barnie's, and why would he? His religious influences at home had been, at best, ambiguous. Connie, though raised Catholic in Tocumwal, had renounced God as a teenager in the years after the Lord had forsaken her by claiming her mother. Ted and his twin, meanwhile, had been raised Catholic in the same Tocumwal church and primary school, St Peter's. The twins' mother, Irene, had prevailed on the question of baptism. Her husband, however, had been raised as an Anglican and he had prevailed on the selection of senior school.

When it came to Connie and Ted marrying, they chose St Peter's. Connie, not yet a militant atheist, cared less about the venue or the rites than she did for Irene. Back in Sydney, after they were married, Ted sought membership of a church choir, not so much for devotional purposes, but because choral music elevated his spirits. He found the Catholic choir in Bondi to be a discordant rabble; the Anglicans up the hill, meanwhile, could sing. He jumped ship.

The Anglicans, however, could not stop a teenage Seb smoking pot. His new classmates at St Barnie's had more pocket money with which to score drugs. It wasn't until Seb's life-changing experience at the Christian retreat that he discovered Kimberley and God in the same breath, and promptly lost interest in spliffs and bongs. That retreat, though encouraged by the schools, was an outsourced evangelical operation. It changed everything about Seb. He came home declaring he'd been redeemed.

It was devious and cynical, Connie told Ted, to beguile the

kids this way, to let loose a bunch of hormonal boys and girls from segregated schools to romp in the fresh air. No wonder they were vulnerable to indoctrination. Connie has long wondered what might have become of her son without this intervention, whether he might have weaned off the pot in any case and studied science at university as he'd indicated he might. Failing that, Connie has wondered – in her more honest moments – whether she might have preferred the company of a godless stoner.

She was forty-eight when Seb announced Kimberley's pregnancy. She was to be a grandparent before fifty. The child would be Gracie, the light of her life, but at the time Connie was far from ready. She certainly was unready to be called Grandma or Nanna, or even Nonna as a nod to the Italian half of her parentage. She had no Greek heritage, but Yiayia sounded cool and once removed from the impending reality of grandmotherhood. Among the first words uttered by an infant Gracie was an attempt at Yiayia. It came out as *Yeah-yeah,* which was twice removed and all the better for it. It was the rock'n'rollest name the mother of a parent could wish for, and Connie owned it immediately. She wrote it down. She found it typographically more pleasing to capitalise both Ys.

Grandmotherhood, as it happened, came more naturally to Connie than motherhood, perhaps because it was only ever meant to be a part-time devotion. Again, in her more honest moments, she can't recall doting on the infant Seb the way she did with his daughter, although in the case of Gracie she wasn't studying day and night to establish a medical career. Excuses now seem as pointless as regrets, yet Connie can't suppress either. And she can't help thinking her shortcomings as a mother largely explain Seb's decades-long rebellion: his strident faith.

That was how it seemed from the outset, from his declaration of Gracie's conception. He was making a big statement. Connie's teenage son, born again, had no need for his birth mother.

Less bitterly, as Connie saw it, Seb was rebelling against Ted, too. While he was still seventeen and on the brink of fatherhood, it became Seb's first rite of passage to step outside his father's coil. He left Ted's parish choir and its necessary accessory, the unassuming local church, and entered the immensely flashy converted warehouse that was the Congress of God. Seb then announced he would not accept the financial support his parents had offered to allow him to proceed to university from school. Rather, he would go straight to work to support his young family, a decision Phil and Di Wyman described as noble. 'Well thank you, Phil and Di,' Connie said, not to the Wymans but in another aside to Ted.

On the question of employment, however, Seb arrested his flight from his father's coop. He requested work at Surfside Hardware and his dad did not hesitate to recruit him.

'You're enabling him,' Connie protested.

More than two decades later, Seb is still there in the shop. Connie has given up mentioning it because he'd only respond that he's fulfilled in his faith. He's unaware that his mother knows his secret: his unfulfilled ambition to become a full-time lieutenant of the Lord, a preacher.

Gallingly for Connie, Phil and Di Wyman left the fold within six years of inveigling Seb to join. No one confirmed why. There were murmurs of a scandal. The Congress of God pastor at the time, to whom the Wymans had been close, was soon removed from his ministry without explanation. Phil and Di moved to the coast and lost all interest in the promise of salvation. Connie soon extracted these bare details from Kimberley, who had promptly lost all faith in her parents. She stopped talking to them and denied them access to their granddaughter, citing 2 Corinthians 6:14: 'Do not be yoked together with unbelievers. For what do righteousness and wickedness have in common? Or what fellowship can light have with darkness?'

It was to Seb's credit, Connie had thought, that he told Kimberley this estrangement was too harsh. But it was only after the breakdown of her marriage to Seb that Kimberley reconciled with her parents. Connie supposed Kimberley had discovered the many shades between darkness and light. Gracie, re-yoked with Phil and Di, reported to Connie only last month on her journey north in the week between Christmas and New Year to visit her 'second-favourite grandparents'.

Connie reviews her Snapchat conversation with Gracie and smiles at her granddaughter's lack of punctuation. This niggles, even in an informal text exchange that will vanish in twenty-four hours, but she is confident Gracie will grow out of it. Connie stretches out on a lump of rock smoothed by generations of sunbathers. There's already the slightest sting in the sun. It'll be a scorcher, all right, but the early rays warm her bones in lovely synthesis with the stream of sound between her ears. She particularly enjoys some of their old Sunday arvo favourites, Gracie's indie rock and alt-country induction, much of it from her early teens. Gracie had a precocious musical palate, although Connie realises now that most of this playlist was recorded from her collection, east of the monkey. Mazzy Star's 'Fade into You' is an opium lullaby ...

Connie wakes to the sound of nothing but waves lapping. She checks the time and it's almost half past eight. Still on schedule. She will listen to some more of the playlist. There's something interesting from someone called FKA Twigs, a Gracie thing, and there are blasts from Connie's past: Velvet Underground, The Smiths. She listens to quite a few until 'This Feeling' by Alabama Shakes, another opium dream, tempts sleep, so she skips to the last of twenty tracks, 'Avant Gardener' by Courtney Barnett. Gracie was barely fourteen when it came on Yeah-Yeah's car radio. Connie had been doing her regular Friday afternoon school pick-up, for which she closed the surgery early. She and Gracie were stuck in a jam outside the school gates. Cocooned in her little sedan, they discovered the song together and soon they were caterwauling the chorus – *I'm having trouble breathing in* – like nobody was listening. Half the school was.

'They're just jealous,' Gracie told Yeah-Yeah.

Swaddled now in the melody of that loving memory, Connie feels the sun on her shut eyes. It plays psychedelic tricks of purple on the underside of her eyelids. There are splotches of mauve and blue, and the abstractions of light and infusions of sound are so pleasurable she smiles from plugged ear to plugged ear as she sings the refrain tunelessly – like nobody's listening. *I was never good at smoking bongs / I'm not that good at breathing in* ...

Several Icebergs regulars are listening.

'Dr Blunt!'

Connie stops singing. She opens her eyes and squints at the peculiar shape silhouetted between her and the sun. She immediately recognises it: the three tractor tyres of fat on tent-pole legs can only belong to Nadia Kovac, a long-term patient. Mrs Kovac is a diabetic in her early fifties who might pass for sixty-five on her better days. She is wearing a Spandex swimsuit that Connie assumes she bought for its slimming qualities. Mrs Kovac's incorrigible gluttony has persisted despite recent lap-band surgery, against which Connie advised. She has also warned Mrs Kovac that dog-paddling for a single length of the Icebergs pool, a few days a week, does not begin to account for the exercise she needs to compensate for her over-eating. Connie would put it still more plainly if she weren't constrained by the expectation of a bedside manner. She has long considered it an overrated quality for a GP, but she has learned to keep a professional check on her preference for brutal truths.

'Dr Blunt!'

Connie's eyes adjust to the light and she can make out the expression on Mrs Kovac's jowly face. It is a look of disapproval.

She is judging Connie and her verdict is that this is no way for a widow to behave three days after the funeral for her husband, the universally revered Ted McCall. Connie resents the presumption, although it seems Mrs Kovac may not be alone. A further three Icebergs regulars are scrutinising Connie.

*Rubbernecks!*

Only now does Connie remove her ear plugs.

'Are you all right, Dr Blunt?' Mrs Kovac inquires. 'Is there anything I could do?'

Connie notes the hypothetical *could*. If she really wanted to help she'd say *can*. Connie might respond: *Yes, Mrs Kovac, you could go and stick one of those foie gras feeding tubes where it fits. That would console me enormously.*

'I'm fine,' she tells her, 'thank you.' Connie stands, gathers her things, farewells her patient and climbs the stairs to leave the Bergs. She reaches the top step as Jean Amos arrives in her path.

'How about now?'

'Ah?'

Jean is a friend, the closest of Connie's casual catch-up Bondi friends. She is a little younger than Connie, mid-sixties, and some months ago she took a redundancy package from the university where she'd been a professor of anthropology. Consequently, Jean has a load of time on her hands and has discovered belatedly that she'd prefer to spend less of it with her long-retired husband. She'd like some more of Connie's time and the feeling is mutual. They get along famously, but Connie has explained she has no particular plan to retire or phase down at the surgery, so she's not sure when, apart from during this period of mourning, she'll find more time for Jean than she already manages. For the past two days she has resisted Jean's attempts to snare her for coffee.

Connie checks her phone for the time. It has got away. It's almost 9:15 and she has nothing prepared at home.

Jean perseveres. 'Five minutes.'

Connie weakens.

'No,' Jean confesses, 'you don't get off that cheaply. Ten.'

They take their usual seats at the outdoor cafe, high over the pool, where the barista spots them before they can order and delivers their coffees forthwith.

'You've done something,' Jean tells Connie.

'What?'

'I don't know. What is it? You're different.'

Jean is examining her face. Connie will wait to see if she spots it.

'I know,' Jean says. 'The eyebrows.'

'They're too dark, aren't they?'

'No,' Jean says, though a little too equivocally. 'I think I like them. Good on you, anyway. They are bold, though.'

'I did suggest Annie Lennox to the girl but she was born the day before yesterday. Meant nothing to her.' Connie repeats her other thought: Vampira. 'Who was that actress?' she asks.

Jean shrugs. 'They're not that bold. Morticia Addams, possibly.'

'Which would be fine if I had black hair. On me they look like racing stripes.'

Jean has a big horsey laugh that makes everything funnier. When she settles, she narrows her gaze at Connie. It's a real quizzing. *Why? Why get them tinted now?* Connie can only imagine this is what her friend is wondering, but they are not yet as close as they hope to become and there's plenty Jean Amos doesn't know about Connie Blunt. Jean is a woman of impeccable manners and wouldn't consider the impudence of putting Connie on the spot.

'Enough about my appendages,' Connie says. 'How's yours?'

'Keith?' Jean says, instantly deadpan. 'He could do with a makeover.'

It's a cute twist on a running joke between them.

'I'm sure the man could boil water for himself before I retired. But not now that I'm home.'

'Don't even begin to spoil him,' Connie says.

'Too late for that.'

'It's never too late.'

Jean seizes Connie's hand and becomes suddenly teary. 'I was hoping you'd say that.'

'Oh, Jean, are you okay?'

Clearly she isn't. Connie feels guilty for not having given her some time sooner. But Connie is also realising that drinking this coffee has been a terrible mistake. It's playing havoc with her innards. She can feel it roiling through her gastrointestinal tract.

Jean becomes despondent. 'It is too late to leave him altogether – when he's this old.'

'I beg your pardon. He's sixty-nine! That's a tinted eyebrow you see me raising.'

'Sorry, I know that's not old if you're Connie Blunt, but if you're Keith Noble it's bone-creakingly old. He's so gloomy. I thought he might brighten up – you know, make an effort – with me at home, but it's as cheerless and loveless as ever. I should have done it twenty years ago.'

'You'll say the same twenty years from now.'

'Dear Lord, he won't last that long, will he?'

'You want a prognosis? I'm not his doctor.'

'He might last five years, but I'm not sure I can survive twelve months.'

'It sounds like you've answered your question. It's not too late.'

Jean smiles, clearly grateful for Connie's encouragement, but both know this discussion is hypothetical. It is every time.

'I'd never find anyone else, of course, but I'd be better company on my own. Nothing could be as lonely as sharing a home with Keith.'

Connie needs to make a break for the toilet but doesn't want to leave Jean after this. She persists. 'Didn't your pal have some success on that dating app? Amelia …?'

'Adelio.'

'Yes, Amelia Adelio. Sounds like a stage name. Is it for real?'

'Yes, that's it.'

'She mentioned her e-Harmony date. He was a keeper, wasn't he?'

'She thought so, but then she couldn't afford him. He wanted an ATM, not a partner.'

'Shame,' Connie says, smiling apologetically. 'Now, Jean, I'm afraid I have rats cartwheeling in my gut.'

'Beg yours?'

'Rats. It's the caffeine. It stimulates the bile that propels these acrobatic rodents in my belly.'

'You're hilarious.'

'I'm about to become less so. Honey, you'll have to excuse me for today.'

★★★

Connie takes fragile steps to the swimmers' change rooms and toilets. In a cubicle, her emergency becomes reekingly irksome, and she fears it will take far too long to resolve. She wonders whether it's a parasite rather than stage fright. Whichever, she could do without the interruption. It's 9:29 already. She makes a mental list of all she needs to do at home before 10:15: shower, make bed with new linen, discard dead and dying funeral flowers, and – if time – remove dirty dishes from sink and hide them in dishwasher. There's more, much more, but that'll have to do.

Connie runs her palms over her waxed thighs. Lovely and smooth, if she says so herself. She's surprised Jean didn't notice the legs because she doesn't miss much, yet it's a relief because the waxing would have taken a lot more explaining than the eyebrows, and she and Jean aren't on those terms yet. It's a point of considerable regret that she hasn't developed a single friendship to fill the void left by Miranda. When Miranda was alive there was nothing Connie wouldn't tell her. She misses their women's business. She certainly wouldn't have hesitated to tell Miranda about something as trivial as a leg waxing, although there'd have been no waxing if Miranda were still alive.

Connie cringes at the pong she's making. She can hear women shuffling and muttering on the other side of the door and she's embarrassed. It makes her think of Ted on the bog at home. He'd hear her climbing the stairs and he'd cry: 'For Christ's sake, Connie, don't come any closer. It'll be marriage-ending.'

She laughs aloud at the thought, then stifles it. They'll be wondering who let the bag lady through the turnstiles.

But it makes Connie think, too, of the 'Diphthong Song'. Ted never considered toilet humour beneath him and his 'Diphthong Song' was his most sublime offering of the genre. He was just a year out of school when he wrote it for a university review to lampoon a pompous professor who'd marked down students whenever they strayed from Oxford to American English. Half a century later, it remained a standard at the McCall-Blunt household's high-spirited gatherings. Connie realises she'll be committed here for quite some minutes, so she scrolls on her phone to find the finale of their Christmas Day singalong. She inserts her earphones and presses play and Ted's ragtime revelry – a shameless aping of Tom Lehrer – comes alive.

All their guests recall the chorus and sing it with Ted:

*I must say I still prefer*
*A diphthong in my diarrhoea*
*Oh yes indeed I do prefer*
*A diphthong in my diarrhoea*

The shaky phone-cam pans the festive warblers: Seb and Amber, and there's Simmo, who hasn't missed a Christmas with them since Miranda died six years ago, and then there's their daughter,

Vanessa, a few years younger than Gracie, and the girls are arm in arm, singing, and there are a few regulars from the Surfside Singers, José Diaz, June Westerbrook and Jimmy Tran, and then there are Ron and Anna Antrim from up the street. And they all know the refrain. Even Mack is singing it alongside his pop.

*Oh yes indeed I do prefer*
*A diphthong in my diarrhoea*

It's a riot. Only when Connie takes off the earphones does she hear herself snuffling. She makes an effort to regain her composure. When she finally opens the door, Nadia Kovac is gawping at her.

'Dr Blunt.'

'Mrs Kovac.'

★★★

Something stirs Seb. He wakes and finds his son sleeping soundly, rising and falling on his chest. He takes a moment to get his bearings. Ah yes, they're still on the Monet rug. Seb shuts one eye to read the kitchen wall clock. It's 9:52 a.m., for heaven's sake. Even so, how lovely it is to have submitted to his weariness. He lies here thinking only this thought – *how lovely* – until he hears the latch catching in the front door, then movement in the foyer. He assumes it's Amber, back from the shops, but his wife enters the kitchen in her pink nightie, yawning, well ahead of the sounds at the front of the house. Seb frowns.

Gracie? It must be Gracie, though this is surprising given their standoff since the funeral tensions. His daughter appears suddenly behind Amber, startling her.

'Sorry,' Gracie says. 'I knocked but no one answered. It's foul out there – this heat – so I let myself in.'

'It's okay,' Amber says. 'Our home is your home.'

Seb winces. That she needs to say this proves it isn't true.

Gracie's trek to university would be easier from Bondi, but she chooses to live with her mother on the North Shore. Seb fears Gracie might bite at Amber's remark – she has form – but she's treading warily today. She smiles at Amber.

'Day off?' Gracie asks Seb, who's still pinned to the floor by his sleeping son.

'Yeah.'

'Want me to take him?'

'Sure.'

Gracie descends to the family room and lifts Mack from Seb. Mid-lift, Mack shrieks with glee.

'Do it again, Gracie! Do it again!'

'You were faking, you little monkey. You weren't asleep.' Gracie lifts him three more times. 'Are you bludging again, Mack Mac?'

'Yes,' he squirms. 'No school all week.'

'Least you're honest.'

Seb intervenes before Amber can. 'He needs some time. He's sad for Pop.'

'Of course he is,' Gracie says. 'I was kidding. No one needs to explain.'

Amber changes the subject. 'Shower time, Mack, then pancakes.'

Mack is elated. He dawdles in his sister's company as Amber leaves the room to go upstairs. Seb notes the visible transformation in Gracie upon her exit. His daughter's shoulders drop a couple of notches. She strokes her brother's hair.

'Dad,' Gracie ventures, 'can I borrow fifty?'

Seb is crestfallen. So much for the olive branch.

'Until payday?' she adds.

'That's why you're here?'

'No, I wanted to talk to you.'

'For a change.'

Mack frowns at them.

'Run up to Mum,' Seb says.

Mack waddles off comically, adorably, his attempt to leaven the atmosphere. Seb and Gracie don't speak until they hear him reaching the top of the stairs.

'I thought you might have come to apologise,' Seb begins.

'Whatever for? Pop loved that song. It was the highlight of his funeral.'

'It was vulgar and gratuitous. It offended the rector.'

'It wasn't the rector's funeral, and it wasn't yours. We chose it because Pop and Yeah-Yeah both loved it – together. Couldn't you let her have that much?'

'Couldn't you have at least mentioned it to me?'

'You would have vetoed it.'

'You're not wrong there.'

Gracie starts to leave. Seb goes to the kitchen bench for his wallet. He extracts a fifty-dollar note and hands it to her. She hesitates before taking it.

'Thanks.'

'You couldn't ask your mum?'

'It's okay. They're not charging me rent.'

'I should hope not. I'm not worried about the money. I was just wondering.'

Gracie doesn't want to engage on this point.

'Look,' he says, 'go easy on the paid work. You need more time for study, and the pub doesn't pay enough.'

'It's not bad.'

'We'll pay better.'

'You know that won't work, Dad. I'm not coming back.'

'It's only pride,' Seb tells her.

'Mine or yours?' Gracie pockets the money. She heads towards the front door, then about-faces. 'I actually did come to talk to you. Can't you bury the hatchet with Yeah-Yeah? It's no time for, y'know ...'

'No,' Seb agrees, 'it isn't. I was thinking of dropping by today.'

'Don't think. Just do it.' Gracie can see he remains unsure. 'It's only pride,' she tells him.

She has some nerve, and Seb can't help but admire it. He grins and asks: 'Mine or hers?'

'Yours.'

He stops smiling. Gracie sees he's stung.

'And hers,' she concedes.

★★★

Connie is striding down the dunny-carter's lane when something makes her double back. She looks over her front gate and, as she anticipated, more home-cooked meals have arrived from patients. Bless them. She goes to the doorstep and picks up two sealed plastic containers brimful with frozen casserole. She hopes she can make room in the freezer for this lot or it will go off before she can eat it.

As always, Connie left home this morning without a key. She carries her deliveries back down the dunny lane and around to her rear gate. She's in a lather of perspiration – it must be mid-thirties and rising – when the phone vibrates in her bum pocket. It's on silent and she doesn't want to answer it, but she fumbles to check the screen and sees the caller is Penny Amarta, her locum. Penny's been minding the fort at the surgery since Ted's death. It's unlike her to trouble Connie unless it's pressing. Connie cradles the food in her left arm so her right hand is free for the phone.

'Penny?'

'Connie, I have Dawn Driscoll with me.'

'Uh-huh?' Connie walks through the gate, which is permanently ajar because it's wedged on uneven ground. It's little wonder Penny is calling. Dawn Driscoll can be a handful.

'She's come in this morning with a swollen tummy,' Penny explains. 'She has some pelvic and lower back pain.'

'Oh? She'll need a scan and some bloods.'

'That was my plan, yes, but she's getting on a plane for Los Angeles first thing tomorrow morning. She says she has no time.'

'She'll need to make some. Can't she move her flight?'

'She says not.'

'Penny, give me a few secs.'

Connie paces through her garden to the outdoor shower. She places the food offerings on the paving. She returns her towel and goggles to their hooks, then puts the phone on speaker and places it on the edge of the potted lime. She turns on the tap and rinses herself for only the requested few seconds because she'll shower again upstairs, but the removal of salt and sand before entering the house is a discipline adopted from Ted. Just as she turns off the shower and moves to collect the phone, she's stopped in her tracks by a tiny flash of blue in the thick undergrowth by the fence.

It can't be.

It is. It's a superb fairy-wren, a breeding male. After all these years, now of all times, he makes his return. He's foraging under the tea tree. Connie momentarily loses sight of him but then he reappears, dazzling. It's more than fifteen years since the fairy-wrens abandoned her garden. To attract them she had created an undergrowth, a fortress of paperbarks and the local sea-cliff scrub and grasses, and the sandstone banksia and the honey myrtle, and the climbers and creepers. And the fairy-wrens had made her garden their empire. Whenever she saw a blue one – only the male breeders are blue – she had thought of Ted in Manhattan on the night of their first real meeting in 1980, when he wore his superb blue shirt. It became a running joke between them, or it did until Rollo Costa moved in next door with his three murderous cats and the kingdom of the fairy-wrens fell. Any that survived the slaughter left in search of more secure fortification.

Some months ago, Rollo buried the last of his cats, and it seems the superb fairy-wrens have taken note. They're back to reclaim the empire, although this little showstopper has made it a brief performance. He's vanished again into the understorey.

'Connie?' Penny is waiting.

'Okay,' Connie says. She hauls open the unlocked sliding door and drips a trail across the family room, which stinks of the dead and dying flowers.

Penny suggests: 'If I send her for the tests, I thought you might have a better chance requesting a quick turnaround, and maybe you could call in a favour with a specialist to squeeze her in.'

'Good thinking. What time's her flight?'

'Seven-fifteen in the morning.'

'Cutting it fine. How important is this trip?'

The festering flowers are overwhelming.

'She's the keynote speaker at a five-day seminar,' Penny says, 'followed by a week's skiing in Aspen.'

They truly are fetid. Connie's thinking she should have noticed sooner, even while she's thinking through the Driscoll case.

'Let me think, let me think,' she's saying as she climbs the stairs, wet footprints in her wake.

Dawn is fifty-nine, at the height of a second-wind career in what she calls *conferencing*. Her verbing of the noun irritates Connie, who nevertheless understands it to mean that Dawn has found a way to profit from seminars such as the one she's about to attend. If she's the keynote speaker, it must be a conference about *conferencing*.

Dawn is recently – and, she keeps telling Connie, happily – divorced. Not as happy, in Connie's estimation, as Dawn's ex-husband, Simon, who is also a patient. Soon before they split, Dawn was still describing their union as a 'satisfactory marriage'. She was damning it with faint praise, of course, but Connie didn't feel at the time that it was conscious. Perhaps Dawn needed to say the word *satisfactory* often enough before she heard the silent prefix, *un*.

'First things first,' Connie tells Penny. In the bathroom, she uses her free hand to unbuckle and unzip her shorts. They drop to the floor. She steps out of them and begins to peel off her bathers. 'I think you need to persuade her to take a later flight.'

'She refuses. She'd miss her address.'

Connie checks her watch. She has thirteen minutes. 'Penny,' she whispers into the phone, 'you're not on speaker, are you?'

'No.'

'Here's what you need to know about Dawn Driscoll: she's a pain in the arse. Always has been.'

'Er.'

'What? She didn't hear that?'

'Possibly.'

'Christ almighty. Look, order the tests. Stall her for a few minutes. I'll call back.'

Connie ends the call, turns on the shower, steps under its fountain and furiously lathers herself in liquid soap. She's had possibly the two greatest pains in the arse on her list, Nadia Kovac and Dawn Driscoll, in the one morning. Connie takes a shampoo bottle from the rack. She upends it, then rethinks. She leans out of the shower, grips the corner of the vanity unit for support and inspects her hair in the mirror. She attempts to run her fingers through it but it's stiff with saltwater.

'Bugger!'

She turns off the shower, wraps a towel around her and slides on the soapy tiles. She recovers her balance, picks up her phone and proceeds, dripping, to the walk-in wardrobe that forms a corridor between bathroom and bedroom. From a row of coat-hangers she selects two outfits, a blue pinafore frock and a bright-yellow skirt with a cream blouse. On her way to the bedroom she hits redial on the surgery number and again puts the phone on speaker. She tosses it on the bed and listens to it ringing. She steps in front of her tall mirror and assesses the blue frock in her left hand and the skirt-and-blouse combo in her right while she weighs up the life-and-death scenarios for Dawn Driscoll, with precisely – Connie hovers over the bed to check the time on her phone – eleven minutes until Simmo's scheduled arrival.

The phone rings twice more on the bed, then Penny answers. 'Connie?'

'Yes. Why don't you put Dawn on speaker?'

Connie listens to the beeps as Penny, unfamiliar with the surgery comms system, fumbles for the right buttons. Connie uses this pause to hold the hanger with the blue frock alone in front of herself. She vacillates. There's a long and loud beep and the sound quality from the surgery becomes echoey. Connie can hear Dawn grumbling faintly in protest. And just now the doorbell chimes.

'Hang on, Penny. That's someone at the door.'

It can't be Simmo this early. He wouldn't be so ill-mannered. Whoever it is, she'll pretend she's not home.

'Don't worry. Let's keep going.' She hurls the frock to the bed then clumsily arranges the skirt and blouse at her waist and chest for cursory inspection. 'Dawn,' Connie bellows, 'can you hear me? Because I need you to listen.'

'I beg your pardon?' Dawn says.

Connie knows that Dawn begs nothing of the sort.

'We need to get you some blood tests and a CT scan today, at the very least. And I'm going to call Dorian Metze and plead with him for an urgent appointment. That also means today, well before your flight tomorrow.'

'Dorian who?'

'Metze. He's the best gynaecological oncologist I know, and he's just up the hill in the Junction. And I'll ask him to plead with the radiologist to email your pictures as soon as they have them, even if they can't manage a report in time.'

'Oncologist?'

'Yes. He has a two-month waiting list, so you'll be a lucky woman if he agrees.'

A brief silence.

'Lucky?' Dawn says. 'You're speculating about cancer?'

'I never speculate. That's why we conduct tests.'

Dawn keeps her waiting.

Connie perseveres. 'It's mine and Penny's job to think of the worst thing this could be. You might be fine, but we plan for the worst while hoping for the best.'

Still Dawn keeps her waiting.

'No,' she says at last.

'What do you mean, no?'

'I can't possibly. I'm still writing my speech. I have too many loose ends …'

The doorbell peals through the house once again.

'Trust me, Dawn,' Connie says. 'You have no end as loose as an undiagnosed pelvic mass.'

This shuts her up. Connie lets Dawn stew while she frowns at the garishness of the yellow skirt in her hand. Whatever was she thinking? She discards it along with the blouse and settles on the blue frock. She untucks the towel at her chest and drops it to her feet. She takes a moment to grimace at her body in the mirror, then pulls the frock over her head and watches it fall.

'Are you still there, Connie?' Dawn asks.

'Yes, still.'

'This could all wait a couple of weeks, surely.'

'Possibly,' Connie replies, 'but not surely. I can't give you certainty, I'm afraid. Unlike you, Dawn, I don't have an MBA.' Connie fears she's overdone the sarcasm.

Eventually Dawn replies, almost humbled. 'I didn't mean to suggest I knew better.'

The doorbell chimes a third time.

'Who the hell?' Connie mutters. 'Dawn, have you eaten in the past couple of hours?'

'Not since seven.'

59

'Good. Now listen. I have someone at the door, I'm running late for an appointment, I have a house in chaos and I have a dead husband, so I'm going to tell you straight: get the tests, get to the specialist, get on your plane and break a leg in Aspen if you must, but if there's something serious going on here, the sooner we know the better.'

There are beeps on the line. Someone's trying to call Connie. She inspects herself once more in the long mirror. She does like the way this frock falls, the way it splays just above her knees. She likes the intensity of its blue and the softness of its cotton. She strokes two ripples at her ribs, to flatten them. She can hear Dawn muttering under her breath to Penny.

Connie has a moment's doubt. Is it too young for her, this frock?

Of course it is. That's the entire bloody point.

'Still thinking, Dawn?' Connie asks.

'Yes, one minute.'

Leaving the phone on the bed, Connie returns to the bathroom and rummages in a drawer for lipstick. She rarely wears it, but she applies it now – sultry red – and instantly wonders whether it's too much. Is it try-hard? Probably. She leaves it.

Back in the bedroom, she looks at the bundle of dirty sheets on the floor. She scoops them into her arms and contemplates where she might hide them. She could take them into the walk-in wardrobe and stuff them into the space above Ted's shoes, but there's no time. She dumps them in the armchair by the bedroom door and picks up the black lace underwear she bought yesterday, still in its wrapper.

'Is that a *yes*, Dawn?'

At last Dawn confirms. 'Yes.'

'Hooray!' Connie says. 'And hooroo.' She goes to end the call. 'Hang on, Penny. I'll call Dorian while you order the tests.'

Just as Connie picks up the phone from the bed and ends

the call, the doorbell rings for the fourth time. She drops the underwear on top of the dirty sheets in the armchair and marches barefoot out of the bedroom and down the stairs and along the hall towards the front door. The phone rings in her left hand and she answers it – 'Yes?' – as she opens the door with her right.

'Hello,' says Simmo, on the phone and on her doorstep.

She looks at the phone. 'Simmo', it announces. 'Has that been you ringing the whole time?'

'Um, yes,' he confesses.

'You're still seven minutes early.'

'I'm sorry, I ...'

They're still holding their phones. Both terminate the call.

'I would've waited,' he explains, 'but it's so bloody hot our here. See, I've got all sweaty.'

'I'm not ready,' Connie says. 'Nothing is quite ready. I've had an interruption from the surgery. You'll have to come back.'

'I'm not going back out in this heat. You look amazing.'

★★★

Amber looks delectable. Her new Lycra bodysuit is a vibrant lemon and Seb is glad he took the gamble and bought it without consulting her. She and Mack are dragging their mini-trampolines to the middle of the Monet rug. They will bounce together, as they often do, and Seb has promised Mack he'll watch, as he rarely does.

'Are you sure you won't throw up?' he asks Mack. 'You've had a lot of pancakes.'

Mack has had four to Seb's one and Amber's none. Her pancakes are always a triumph with Mack. They've been a welcome distraction for Seb while he's been warming up to visit his mother. She isn't expecting him, and he has no reason to suppose she will be heartened by his arrival.

Seb needs to put an idea to her. It's something he's been

formulating – that he and Amber have been formulating – for some time. A real estate proposal. It could change their lives, all of their lives, for the better. As did their last proposal. That's what he'll tell his mother, but it's sensitive. Seb begins to stack the dishwasher.

'Stop, I told you,' Amber says. 'For once, just relax.'

Seb abandons the washing-up and returns to the couch to watch. Amber plays with the TV remote control while commencing a low bounce. The sound arrives before the picture. It's a familiar doof-doof beat booming through the new speakers – a dance party, electro-pop, soul kind of groove. Or Seb thinks so. Amber and Mack bounce on the same beat. They know precisely where the vocal track kicks in, and they sing on cue:

*M-m-messiah, t-take me higher*
*M-m-messiah, t-take me higher*

On the TV screen a troupe of performers appears: men and women with big, shiny hair, gorgeously backlit. It could be a shampoo commercial. They chant the same lyric throughout the song, and Seb sings along for a few bars.

He will have to consult Simmo, too, about this property proposal. It involves the shop. Seb imagines Simmo will be more amenable than his mother, though he might prefer prospective business deals be set aside while they're in mourning. In a trance induced by the bouncing music, Seb finds himself praying for his father's best friend – 'Lord, comfort him in his quiet sorrow' – because Simmo's never been a man to make a song and dance of his grief. He carries on. He's a coper. He nursed Miranda through the ravages of motor neurone disease until her death, and all the while he was a rock for their daughter. Vanessa wasn't quite thirteen, a cruel age to lose a mother. Seb's mother was that age when she lost hers, and he has wondered at times whether that explains a lot about her maternal shortcomings.

Simmo was practically a kid himself, not much older than Vanessa and Gracie are now, when he and Ted started crewing surfboats together in 1981. Ted soon employed him at his fledgling hardware business and, a couple of years later, brought him in as a partner. For Seb, growing up, Simmo was more the uncle than his blood uncles in Tocumwal.

But Seb, having been an early starter in the marriage and fatherhood stakes, beat Simmo to it by a couple of years. Simmo was already into his forties when he met Miranda, and Seb never quite understood why he'd taken so long to find love. He was entirely lovable.

Until eight days ago, Seb and his father and Simmo took turns opening Surfside Hardware at eight-thirty while the other two dawdled in the surf or on the sand or in the surf club gym or getting coffee. Later, the three of them shared duties throughout the day, keeping shop, ordering stock, taking deliveries, staying on top of the bookwork and, critically, sustaining the chatter with customers.

'The chatter is our least idle task,' Ted reminded Seb, often. 'We'll never be as cheap as Bunnings, but they'll never out-charm us.'

Seb has always had to work harder at the charm than his father and Simmo. No doubt Simmo is charming the customers, as ever, this morning. Seb decides he'll return the favour tomorrow and give him a breather.

'Not so high, Action Man,' he tells Mack. 'You will – you'll throw up!'

'I won't.'

Seb's attention drifts from the trampolinists to the kitchen and the new tiles and, in particular, the feature tile, which Amber already treasures. Seb sees it as a nondescript wisp of blue on white but apparently it isn't white at all. It's *alabaster*. It was for this tile that Seb left the beach in the prelude to his father's last wave.

It had been Simmo's turn to open the shop. Seb was waxing his longboard, preparing to paddle out with his dad, when Amber called to say the tiler was mixing his grout, so could he please whizz home to offer his urgent opinion on the feature piece. Seb can't look at it now without thinking what might have been had he stayed at the beach. 'If you love it, Amber, you know I will.' That's all he'd needed to say. Everything that transpired from that point would have been different – because that is the way of things.

When the music stops, Amber ceases bouncing and returns to an ambling clean-up in the kitchen. Mack continues bouncing without accompaniment and he keeps down all the pancakes. Seb continues his pretence of slacking on the couch, but he's twitching. Always a fidget, sloth has never been Seb's sin. He thinks about what he could do next rather than confront his mother. He could take Mack to the park and kick some up-and-unders, or they could take their softies to North Bondi for a surf, or they could ride their skateboards down to the bowl in the beach park and shred away the hours.

The kitchen clock says 10:28 and if Seb wants to spend a few moments with his mother this morning – he remains equivocal at best – he anticipates she'll leave home in the next thirty minutes. He knows her movements, if not by his years of observation then via Amber, who's been looking out for her over the past eight days. His mother has had her swim. On most days in the past week she's returned from the pool but left home again late morning, although she has no pressing reasons to go out; her surgery is in good hands; she could feed battalions with the food supplied by patients. The only thing compelling her to leave home is to escape the absence of Ted.

This thought arouses in Seb an alien sympathy for his mother, and its oddness makes it all the sadder.

There is another, more pragmatic, consideration for Seb: she tends to be less combative in the mornings. If they are to reach anything resembling a détente, it is unlikely to be in the afternoon, when she is most irascible.

Seb leaves the couch and contrives to loaf up the two steps to the big island bench in the kitchen, where he finds Amber alphabetising the spice rack. He walks two laps around the island. He stops and pretends to admire the feature tile, hoping Amber is noticing because she needs to know – really she does – that he doesn't blame her or the tile in any way. He blames himself for leaving his father to surf alone so he could offer his token opinion on the stupid thing, twenty centimetres square, which Amber would have chosen regardless. Had Seb stayed at the beach, he and his dad would have shot the breeze on the way to the surf and entered the water slightly later than Ted did alone. It is unlikely his father would have taken off on the particular wave that became his last. Even if he had, Seb might have dropped in and hustled him off it in the typical prankish contest between father and son. Or if Ted had won that duel and ridden the same wave in the same fashion and wiped out as he did and was concussed as he was, Seb would have been there to save him.

Seb knows it's pointless churning it over again. It doesn't stop him. He knows it's not his fault or Amber's fault or the fucking tile's fault. It is what it is.

He moves on, another lap of the island, and begins to hum a tune, 'It Had To Be You' … until he remembers that this is to be Amber's surprise. He worries that she's recognised it. Then he worries that she hasn't. He hasn't got the melody quite right. He needs to practise, but not now.

'Damn,' says Amber, 'I forgot the marjoram.'

'Mmmm?'

'See, I've filled all the spots to wasabi and white mustard but now I've found the marjoram at the back of this shelf.'

'Just stick it at the end. No one will notice.'

'I will. I'll have to fix it.'

Seb jiggles the frothing arm on the coffee maker. He couldn't stomach another coffee. He lurks over the unwashed pancake frying pan. He dabs at the crusty residue around its edge and delivers a sticky crumb to his tongue. It's the best bit, but Seb leaves it. He has no instinct for gluttony. That's never been his sin, either.

He concludes that Gracie is right. Pride is the only thing keeping him here, and this makes him deeply ashamed. Pride is Seb's sin.

'I won't be long,' he tells Amber. 'I'll just pop over to see Mum.'

'That's nice.'

Mack stops jumping to ask: 'Can I come?'

'Next time, mate.'

'Are you going to fight?'

'No,' Seb says, defensive. Why would Mack even ask? 'No!' he says again, in case he's left any doubt.

'Will you discuss the shop?' Amber asks.

Seb hesitates, before saying, 'Yeah.'

'Are you sure?'

'Sure.'

He doesn't sound sure.

# 3.
# STINKER

Even at a tentative stride, no more than twenty seconds separate
Seb's backyard from the rear-lane entrance to his parents' garden.
This gate has always been preferred by the family to enter the
house in which he was raised from infancy, and which remains,
more than his house, *home*.

He'd never admit this to Amber, who is rightly proud of the
home she has made for them over the past five years. She found it,
as she has since found their six investment properties; her inherited
radar for a real estate deal is never switched off. If it weren't for
Amber they'd still be in the heavily mortgaged two-bedroom flat
at North Bondi that Seb bought with the meagre proceeds of his
divorce settlement with Kimberley. Seb and Amber lived in the flat
with Mack for his first year, but it was always Seb's dream to move
back to Banksia Avenue, even though it would be pricey and the
street's owners rarely sold.

But Amber had asked Seb about number nineteen, the most
rundown of the street's old terraces.

'Worst house, best street,' she said.

'No off-street parking,' Seb said.

'That's okay.'

'But it's Verna Trembath's. She's been there all her life. She'll
never sell.'

67

Still, Seb wanted something closer to *home*, closer to his father. His emotional detachment from his mother would be no different, he confessed to Amber, whether they bought in Banksia Avenue or in Kazakhstan.

'We wouldn't be buying in Kazakhstan,' Amber said.

'You know what I mean.'

She didn't, quite.

Yet Amber could surprise Seb, and she did. She kept her ear to the ground. When Verna Trembath died suddenly at sixty-seven it was a shock to Seb and his parents, but not so much to Amber because she hadn't been relying on her husband or parents-in-law for her intelligence. Instead, she'd been keeping in touch with the neighbours either side of the Trembath house.

The property market was in a short-term dip at the time. It was to be a deceased estate. Without telling Seb, Amber made a solid offer before it went to market. Her offer was accepted and, on her calculation, they picked it up for half a million under its high-market value.

'She's mercantile, isn't she?' Connie said when Seb reported the good news.

'That's unfair,' he said.

'Mercantile? How is that unfair?'

'You meant mercenary.'

'Are you and your father and Simmo not mercantile? You're all merchants, aren't you?'

Seb wouldn't let her snarkiness go unremarked. Since then, he and Amber have easily doubled their money on the place. Seb can't help thinking of Mrs Trembath's five adult children and their paltry inheritance once the estate was split between them, as he approaches his parents' gate. The subtext for this visit, after all, is real estate, and yet he shouldn't be distracted from his goal. He should be mulling over his tactics, his opening gambit with his mother. How to even broach it?

It is a good plan, and that is why he knows his mother will oppose it. Not because the numbers don't stack up – Amber has run them, and they all know how good she is with running the numbers. Seb will be able to demonstrate that shutting Surfside Hardware and selling the property will yield a far greater return than holding it and persisting with the shrinking business. Even at low interest, the return on the proceeds of the sale will outperform the shop's meagre profits. It should be a no-brainer for his mother and for Simmo. Ted was the one sentimentally attached to the business. Now he's gone, selling would be a bonus for all parties.

Seb will propose, however, that they do not put the shop on the open market. He will invite his mother and Simmo to sell their shares, instead, to him and Amber. At market price, of course. This would allow Seb, after seven years' part-time study at the College of Divinity, to fulfil a quietly held aspiration to convert the shop into a non-denominational church, his breakaway Christian ministry.

He can imagine his mother's reaction. *You want to what?*

Today's prickly heat won't help. If the forecasters are right it will climb to 40 degrees Celsius shortly. Perhaps Seb should retreat and return with more favourable weather.

That would be a cop-out. If he's going in, he shouldn't procrastinate out here in the heatwave, yet he needs some time to consider the right form of words.

The truth is, Seb has long had misgivings about the Congress of God. The scandalous rumours involving Kimberley's mother and their former preacher, Jim Albion, aside, Seb has never been happy about the direction of the church under the leadership of Jim's replacement, Pastor Pat McWilliam. The place has become overrun by social climbers, and Pastor Pat panders to them, encouraging them to count their financial blessings as God's reward for their piety. All the while he banks their generous tithings.

Not for a moment has Seb suspected Pat is lining his pockets.

Rather, he's an empire builder, which still amounts to corruption in Seb's mind. Pat is a shameless populist, a purveyor of the prosperity gospel and gormlessly literal readings of the Bible. He has turned their church into his vanity project. He's invested in cinema-sized screens, light and sound equipment, two drum kits – apparently they need not one but two drummers on stage at any one time. It's smoke and mirrors.

Seb is determined his new little church will not resort to such conjury.

He began studying theology soon after he met Amber and separated from Kimberley. The more deeply he read the Bible, the more distant he grew from Pastor Pat. On occasion, early on, Seb had taken Pat aside and attempted to engage him in debate, to ask him to consider the Bible's more bloodthirsty passages, the prayers for vengeance in Psalm 137 and Isaiah and their implication of divine licence to plunder, rape and slaughter, and to dash babies' skulls against rocks. Seb also took Pat to Book of Numbers and the Lord's instruction to Moses to vanquish the Midianites as vengeance for the Israelites, to kill every male among their children, to ravish their wives and murder them along with any female who'd known a man by lying with him, but to spare the virgins – thirty-two thousand of them – because they would make fitting rewards for God's righteous warriors.

'Are all the scriptures God-breathed?' Seb asked Pastor Pat. 'Or do we accept that much of it was written by psychopathic mortals? Otherwise God is the psychopath, and I don't believe that.'

Pat, oblivious to Seb's plans for a rebel church, responded that every word indeed was God-breathed. It was not for them to cherry-pick the Bible. Pat did not attempt to defend it line by line because, Seb decided, his pastor was – and remains – a lightweight. Only months ago the preacher informed his congregation that a plant geneticist had uncovered irrefutable evidence concerning Adam and Noah. Both had lived well beyond nine hundred years.

So might we all today, Pat claimed, if not for the terrible and mysterious impact of the great flood.

This was the final straw for Seb.

He is confident that he's equipped to launch his ministry founded on a rational reading of the New Testament and its promise of salvation for believers in the life, miracles, crucifixion and resurrection of the Lord Jesus Christ. Yet he knows this will not wash with his mother, who scorns the miracles as sorceries. 'It's of little consolation,' she emailed Seb – what was it, four years ago? – 'to discover you no longer believe in Old Testament fairy tales while you persist with your New Testament fairy tales. I'm relieved you're not a young-Earth creationist, but you still believe in virgin births, the transfiguration, the ascension. Once entirely gullible, you've become selectively suggestible. Should I call this progress?'

Seb emailed in response: 'As always, Mum, you are fervently faithless, which makes progress in these debates difficult.'

'Fervently faithless?' she replied. 'Love it! If I wasn't, I am now.'

Now, outside her back gate, he anticipates her implacable opposition to his proposal, that she will sabotage her financial self-interest to spite her son and his faith. Perhaps today's visit is best approached as an icebreaker, an attempt to establish a truce, while leaving the subject of the shop for another day. Amber would be disappointed, but Seb must tread carefully, strategically. There's so much at stake.

The maddening thing is that he'd had a heart-to-heart with his father about it only in November, on the night of Seb's graduation ceremony. His mother made her excuses and didn't attend, but Ted was there to cheer on Seb at the divinity college. Emboldened, Seb took his dad for a late supper and told him all about his dreams for the shop. He took him through Amber's numbers and Ted did not doubt them. Seb explained his plans had been evolving since soon after the news of Mack's conception.

'That's when I heard my calling,' he said.

'Right,' his father said.

'This is what I'm thinking: the hardware shop becomes — wait for it — the DIY Church.'

'Right?'

Seb explained he would keep the hoarding and the signage: SURFSIDE HARDWARE. 'The shopfront would hardly need to change.' He'd get a signwriter in merely to tweak the kicker. 'Your DIY Specialists' would become 'Your DIY Church'.

'Meaning?' Ted asked.

'Meaning the whole philosophy of our independent church will be this: come build your own bridge to God. Pastor Seb will be able to lend a hand, give you some tools, but if you want to get closer to God, you'll have to do the hard yakka yourself through good works in our community. Prayer alone won't cut it. Put in the elbow grease.'

'Doing what?'

'Helping wherever help is needed. The elderly, the homeless, the street kids, whoever. They'll be our everyday mission, Dad.'

'How many are you expecting to join this congregation?'

'Once we clear the aisles, lay out the fold-up chairs, I estimate there'll be room for a couple of hundred.'

'That wasn't really my question. How many do you reckon will choose to sit on those chairs?'

'I'll fill it, Dad. Just watch.' This was Seb's belated coming of age. He was telling his father that he was ready to strike out, to be his own man at last.

Ted looked worried.

Seb remained upbeat. 'This is an opportunity for you,' he told Ted. 'Year after year the business is declining. It's beyond us to change it. We can't possibly stand up to the majors. This way you'll make more money not working. It's a logical step.'

'I suppose,' Ted said, 'but I don't know, mate. For now we can afford not to be governed by the logic. I still like showing up for work each day. This is what I do. I'm not ready for retirement.'

'You're seventy-three. What age were you thinking?'

'I've never given it much thought. How about I let you know when I'm ready?'

Seb realised it was time to back off. 'Of course.'

'And when Simmo's ready,' Ted added. 'He's well under retirement age.'

'Whenever you're ready,' Seb said, though he dared to venture: 'You could surf all day, the two of you.'

'We already surf morning and night. We'd only get melanomas.'

The take-home message for Seb, nevertheless, was that his father was not outright opposed. It was a question of the timing.

'There's no need to mention it yet to Mum,' Seb said, to which Ted agreed.

Now Seb wishes he hadn't made that request. He wishes he had encouraged his father to at least fly the kite with her. Now he'll have to do that himself.

But not today. He's firming up about this. Today would be a mistake.

He pauses here in the relative privacy afforded by the lane and looks both ways to confirm he is alone. He shuts his eyes and raises his hands, palms to the sky, in supplication. He prays for God's guidance and for a modicum of His grace. It becomes quite a long prayer, although Seb meanders between devotion and cogitation. This is his way. He loses track of what is invocation and what is angst, but that's okay. His prayers are conversations, as much with himself as with his Maker.

He concludes this prayer and opens his eyes, only to be startled by the presence of Rollo Costa. Rollo has emerged from the gate next door, armed with a familiar bottle of weedkiller, and he is glaring at Seb with a familiar loathing. This is because he knows what Seb is up to. Rollo, a Catholic, has had a single conversation with Seb about his Pentecostal church. 'It's a cult,' Rollo told him, some years ago. Without a word now, Rollo crouches with his bottle of poison and sprays a beard of weeds creeping under his fence from the lane.

★★★

Seb passes through the narrow opening of his parents' unclosable gate and into their ill-attended garden. Ted McCall was no gardener and Connie Blunt is no pruner. He stops here momentarily and looks for movement in the living room. He can see none from this distance. She may be in the study.

Seb decides he will approach her with determined humility. Whatever happens, whatever his mother says to provoke him, he will not bite. He has inherited her propensity for haughtiness – he knows it and she knows it – but he won't lower himself to it this morning. Seb is coming in peace.

He begins to move along the overgrown path. The garden is a verdant tangle, as his mother prefers it, apparently immune to any runoff from Rollo's weedkiller. Seb has not taken six steps before a large frond lances his cheek. He dabs the wound, just under his eye, and finds that it has drawn a little blood. This damned palm, encroaching on the path, has been a hazard for months but she won't listen. Seb is tempted to snap the frond and discard it in the green-waste bin by the back fence, but that might be an incitement. He gently bends it off to his left. As he forges ahead, the frond rebounds and swats the back of his neck. It stings; he feels a hot itch on his skin. He inspects the injury with his fingers, but this time finds no blood. He steps over a perilous gum root that has broken through the paving. The trunk of the towering gum is half as wide as the house. In a strong wind one of the high limbs could break and demolish the back rooms, upstairs and down. The *widowmaker*, his dad called the gum, though he never did a thing about it.

Seb arrives at the glass sliding door. He peers inside and confirms his mother is not in the living room or kitchen. He becomes distracted by his father's rubber thongs, still in their place by the potted lime. Seb hovers over them.

'I'll never fill your thongs, Dad.' That was a line from Seb's eulogy. It got the laugh he hoped it would, and now it provokes a fond memory: his infant feet swimming in his dad's big thongs. There's a photo of that somewhere.

Seb kicks off his size-elevens and nudges his dad's size-twelves. His toes explore the craters that his father's heels wore in the rubber. Seb steps fully into them. His feet still swim in them. He never will fill them.

He steps back into his pair. He clasps the door handle and gives it a shove and it slides to a one-metre opening. He thinks about security. He'll make a time, not today, to suggest to his mother that she start locking it. Would she even know where to find the key? Seb recalls that he has a spare in his kitchen drawer. He looks to the unsecured back gate, which has never had a key. He could at least do some repairs on that. One thing at a time.

Seb is about to step inside when he hears a whimper overhead. He takes a backward step and looks up to his parents' opened bedroom window. It was a faint sound but, unmistakably, it came from his mother. And now, once more, she gasps. It is hard for Seb to imagine her crying, even this soon after her loss. But he is sure this is what he's hearing: the sound of his mother in her private grief. He shivers at the realisation.

It's as shocking to Seb as it was to witness old men in tears at the funeral. They had thought Ted was certain to be the last man standing of their generation, and to outlive many from the next. His dying confronted them with their mortality and they cried like little boys. Even as she comforted them, Seb's mother didn't shed a tear, or none that he saw. She had appeared impassive if not cold, he thought, and this seemed to be in character. He might have been kind and interpreted it as stoicism, but on the day he thought it betrayed her as an emotional vacuum.

It makes him all the more ashamed now to be standing here, beneath her window, eavesdropping on her sobbing.

He takes a breath and steps inside. He walks through the family room and is overcome by the smell of putrefying funeral flowers. The room collects so much sun from the north and west in the summer that the flowers are rank. This provokes another odd feeling of empathy: his mother must be unmindful of the smell because, beneath her hard façade, she is so consumed by grief that her senses are failing.

A condolence card dangles from the shrivelled stem of a white lily: 'Connie, we pray that you can face the coming days and months with the courage we know you possess.'

He wonders whether his mother can accept their prayers. He prays she can. He decides he'll gather all the dead flowers on his way out and toss them in the green bin.

He hears her again, sobbing. As he arrives at the foot of the stairwell it becomes louder, more distressing. He hears her yelp, a high-pitched keening.

'Mum?' he calls softly.

She mustn't have heard him.

He tries again. 'Mum?'

Still no reply.

Seb climbs the stairs and the timber creaks underfoot. She'll hear this, he gathers, and he's having second thoughts. She won't want him to see her in this state. She's proud, too proud. It's not fair to intrude, perhaps wiser to retreat.

No. He at least needs to see her, to confirm she's okay.

As he reaches the landing, she emits a low, guttural, mournful wail. It's the saddest thing Seb has heard; she's in the throes of an emotional breakdown and this breaks his heart. He clasps the handrail and pauses briefly to summon courage, then advances towards her opened bedroom door. She shrieks. It's an odd sound. In another context it might be mistaken for laughter.

Seb steps over the threshold into her bedroom – and finds that she is indeed laughing.

She is yet to see Seb, who stands motionless, attempting to make sense of the spectacle in the matrimonial bed of his barely departed father.

His father's widow is not alone. Her back is arched over pillows, her breasts exposed, her eyes cast to the ceiling. Seb cannot identify the interloper, whose feet and ankles protrude from the end of the bed. Otherwise he is shrouded by the sheet, a grotesque, hump-backed figure. Seb studies the contours of the sheet. The stranger's head, evidently, is ensconced between his mother's thighs.

'Mum?'

'Shit!' she says.

The bed shudders with the sudden movement of the intruder, but she seizes his head and holds it firmly where it is.

'Mum?' Seb asks again, but she has nothing to say.

Seb moves to leave, then halts. He sees the old bed linen bundled in the armchair by the door, then the dazzling whiteness of the sheets on the bed. He becomes fixated on these sheets, crisp with factory creases.

'They're new,' he says.

'What?' Connie asks.

'The sheets. Brand new.'

★★★

Simmo remains frozen, huddled on his knees on the bed as they listen to Seb thundering down the stairs. Connie hoists a leg over him, wrangles the top sheet and wraps it around herself, and leaves the bed to take up a position by the window in anticipation of Seb's exit.

Simmo rolls to his back and they listen to Seb stomping through the living room directly beneath them. Connie watches him emerge and pound along the garden path. He stops abruptly halfway along. She frets that he might turn back.

'Do you think he knows it's me?' Simmo asks.

Connie shrugs.

'You should probably go after him. You know, to explain.'

'Explain what?' Connie asks. 'Which part?'

'All of it.'

'Hell no. I'm not ready for that.'

Seb has not moved on. He is standing before the frond overhanging the path. He is deliberating. Suddenly he grabs it and yanks it. It's his mother's soft tree fern, the one Seb mistakes for a palm. He twists the frond back and forth and kicks its stem with the heel of his thong. It snaps free of the trunk. He's in a terrifying rage. Seb carries the dismembered limb towards the four wheelie bins against the back fence. Connie keeps watching as he stuffs it into the green-lidded bin. He moves to leave but when he reaches the gate he stops and doubles back to the bins. He hovers over them as if making a calculation, then chooses the blue-lidded bin for paper and cardboard. She watches him fossick in there until he pulls out a sheath, the packaging that wrapped her new linen. He reads it.

'Unbelievable.'

'What?' Simmo asks.

'He's going through my rubbish.'

Seb takes his phone from his back pocket and aims it at the wrapping. He photographs it.

'You are kidding.'

'What?' Simmo asks again.

Connie watches her son reading the detail, every word about the one hundred per cent pure linen flax grown in the Netherlands. He takes another picture.

'Exhibit A,' she says.

'Hey?'

'He's gathering evidence.'

'Of what?'

'My premeditation, I can only assume.'

'Do you want me to go?'

'No,' Connie says, her back still to Simmo. *Hell no!*

She turns to him. He's not looking at her. He's sprawled, flat on his back, hands behind his head, watching the rotations of the fan. This pose eliminates his slight paunch and accentuates the definition in his pecs, biceps and thighs. He's fit. He's in indecently fine shape for a man of sixty-two. She watches him while he's not watching her.

She turns back to watch Seb. At last he leaves.

'Gone!' Connie declares. She faces Simmo and spans her arms as wings. This opens the sheet and exposes her rangy nakedness.

He smiles, but she can see he's anxious.

They came close three days ago, on the night of the funeral. It was after eleven when the last of the festive mourners left the surf club, and Connie told Simmo: 'The widow's a bit merry. Just as well I didn't bring the car. Too pissed to drive.'

'Me too,' he said.

Simmo walked her home and it was only there, on her doorstep, that he cried for Ted. He bawled in her arms. Connie still couldn't, but Simmo wept until he was out of tears. Then he stroked her hair, which she wasn't expecting. It sent currents right through her. She felt ecstatically alive when he did that. He didn't say anything – just ran his fingers from her scalp to the nape of her neck and back again, and she didn't want him to stop. He didn't for quite a while, but when he did he moved his face closer to hers and his lips brushed her cheek, which tingled numb, and the ticklish swarm migrated to her spine and it made her woozy – she was wobbly enough on her feet as it was.

She tilted back her head, as if offering her mouth, but instead she spoke. 'This is a bit weird.'

'It isn't,' he said. 'You know it isn't.'

'It's a bit soon.'

'Sorry,' he said. He stepped back. 'Yes, it is very soon. Sorry.'

'How about Friday?' she suggested.

'Friday? You mean this Friday?'

'Is ten-fifteen okay?'

'In the morning?'

'Yes.'

'Here?'

'Yeah.'

Simmo laughed out loud. 'I have a ten-fifteen appointment with Dr Blunt. Will I get the Medicare rebate?'

His joke made Connie cackle, so loud she feared the neighbours must have heard. The merry widow, indeed. Simmo, apparently quite pleased with himself, chuckled his way up the street. She stayed on the doorstep and watched him cross Banksia Avenue and she kept watching until he turned the corner into Bondi Road. He was a bit wobbly himself.

*Pissed,* she was thinking. *Both of us, pissed. It'll be different sober.*

Because Simmo would wake up to himself. Because he's a young sixty-two – he might pass for mid-fifties – and Connie is irrefutably old. She is eight years older. The same age difference separated them when they met, of course, when she was not yet thirty to his twenty-one, but then those eight years were an allurement for a young man barely evolved from his adolescence. Now, in the cold light of day, he'd surely discover their age difference was cause for repulsion. Connie knew this was the cruel and lopsided truth about years, the inequivalence of young years and old years. She'd spent her career observing the vital signs of ageing, so she knew it, empirically. She expected Simmo would call in the morning and apologise. 'My mistake,' he might say, and they'd leave it at that.

He didn't.

'You're seven minutes early,' she barked at him this morning on her doorstep. 'You'll have to come back.'

It was thirty-eight degrees and the poor bugger had been cooking out there. What was she thinking? He refused to leave merely so he could return in seven minutes. He followed her down the hall and into the kitchen as she explained she'd been interrupted by a call from the surgery so she hadn't emptied the vases of their rotting flowers or cleared the dishes from the sink or moved the lump of laundry from the couch or stacked away the litter of sympathy cards on the dining table. She hadn't made the bloody bed.

'See,' she said, lifting the packets from the kitchen bench, 'the new linen I bought yesterday.'

'That might've been a lot to cover in seven minutes,' Simmo suggested.

'I know, ridiculous.'

'The bed? I wasn't sure you'd want to move so fast.'

'Sorry,' she said, 'was that presumptuous?'

'No.' He started gathering dead flowers. 'I'll get rid of these, then help with the bed,' he said. 'The rest can wait.'

'So can the flowers. I'll do them later.'

'They're pretty whiffy.' Simmo collected perhaps a third of them in one big bundle, sneezing as he went. She watched him carry them through her jungle, down the garden path to the back fence. He stuffed them in the green bin then brushed the pollen and desiccated petals from his shirt. He looked nice in that mauve shirt as he moved back through the garden, the gum-filtered light dappling his shiny black hair and his tanned skin. His shirt and his fawn shorts were freshly ironed. The colours suited him. His leather sandals, completing the ensemble, passed for smart–casual in Bondi. He'd made an effort.

'That's enough,' she told him. 'The rest really can wait.'

He conceded, then stood at the kitchen bench and undressed the linen from its packaging. The sheets fell to the floor, as soft and white as a wedding dress. Connie gathered them up, then the pillow slips and the quilt cover, and she began to head for the stairs. She stopped when she realised Simmo wasn't in her trail. He was gathering the packaging and heading outside. She watched him distribute the paper and plastic into the correct bins for recycling. It made her laugh. He was so like Ted – never one to leave today's mess for tomorrow. So unlike Connie.

Simmo followed her upstairs to the bedroom. It was hers now but it was still his and hers: Ted and Connie's. Simmo seemed to note the dirty old sheets in the armchair and Connie was embarrassed that she hadn't hid them. He looked from Connie to the king bed, which was stripped bare but for its cotton mattress protector, upon which lay the ghost of Ted. Years of his perspiration had impregnated the cotton. His yellowed shape survived him as morbidly as a chalk outline at a crime scene. It was incontestably Ted.

Connie took the fitted sheet from the pile of new linen and flung it high over the bed. It ballooned and parachuted down. Simmo helped her wrap the corners over the mattress, and Ted was gone. He flung the top sheet and it hovered then floated to the bed. Connie went to her side and began to tuck it in, amused when he took over and patiently folded hospital corners. She knew he was a fastidious housekeeper – Miranda always said so – but still she was surprised.

He sat on Connie's side of the bed rather than Ted's and began feeding her quilt into its new embroidered cover. It was hot work. Connie watched rivulets of perspiration run down his brow and neck and dampen the back of his shirt. She switched on the fan and it throbbed and instantly she felt puffs of air prickling cool on her dewy skin. Flumes of air found nerve-endings through her pores.

He was yet to touch her. What was he waiting for? He was stuffing the quilt into its cover and patiently buttoning it, as if they'd be using the stuffing thing at the height of summer.

'Shit,' Connie said.

'What?'

'I forgot to make a call. Sorry, I have to do this.'

'Sure.'

She took her mobile from the hip pocket of her frock. She called Dorian Metze, the oncologist.

'Dr Blunt speaking,' she told his receptionist. 'It's urgent. Could you put me through? He'll understand.'

Connie could see Simmo was surprised by her casual authority. You could know someone most of your life and still surprise him, and be surprised by him.

'Connie!' Metze's big growly voice projected from her phone.

'Dorian, I know this is a big ask but I need you to shoehorn in an extra case today. Dawn Driscoll's her name. She's getting on a flight to LA tomorrow morning but my locum has just seen her for a swollen tummy. It's quite a pelvic mass. We're getting the scans and bloods now but I'm hoping you can hurry them up so you can see her this arvo.'

'There goes lunch,' said Metze.

'How late was your lunch?'

'Late. They do a great deal at the leagues club on Fridays, as long as you order before three-thirty: ten bucks for a cheeseburger and fries.'

'Your cardiologist will be elated.'

'My marriage counsellor won't be. I was meeting Anna.'

'Apologies to Anna. So, what time can I tell Dawn?'

'Three-thirty.'

'You're a legend.'

Connie texted the confirmation to Dawn Driscoll and Penny Amarta. Then she watched Simmo sitting there on the bed, buttoning the never-ending quilt. So many fiddly buttons.

'Had enough of your foreplay?' she said.

It made him laugh.

It felt odd being so familiar with him, but how else was she meant to be? After four decades of friendship, it would be odder to be coy. Yet she couldn't be gamesome, either. Seduction was beyond her. She was a bundle of nerves and the cartwheeling rodents were back in her gut and she wanted Simmo to make all the moves. Simmo, she gathered, was as reticent as she was.

She walked to the edge of the bed and stood close. He dropped the quilt to the floor and stared at her, eyes narrowing.

'You've done something.'

'What?' she asked, though she knew what.

'I don't know. Wait. Eyebrows.'

'Too dark?'

'No. A little, maybe.'

She repeated the joke she'd told Jean Amos at the pool. 'I asked for Annie Lennox and got Vampira.' She didn't have another line.

Simmo reached for her hand and drew her to him. Still standing, she bent at the waist to deliver her mouth to his. She feared the sun and saltwater had dehydrated her lips but upon contact they melted agreeably into Simmo's. All the apprehension dissolved on his lovely lips.

It went on and on, this prolonged kiss of teenagers, until Connie became aware of his hands at the backs of her thighs – because she was standing and he was sitting and where else could he hold her? – and she remembered what she was about to do before she went downstairs to answer the door to him.

'I forgot my knickers,' she said. 'I was about to put them on when you rudely interrupted.' She went to the armchair to retrieve the unwrapped lingerie from atop the dirty sheets, then returned to him. 'Will I put them on?'

'Just so I can take them off?' Simmo's hands advanced to her bare buttocks. 'That's not such a bad idea,' he said.

'Okay,' she said. 'Give me a tick.'

Connie needed an excuse to go the bathroom, anyway, because Simmo's early arrival had interrupted the remainder of her preparation. Her shopping expedition yesterday included a detour to a pharmacy in Paddington, where neither the chemist nor his staff knew her. While she hadn't accounted for dry lips, she had for vaginal dryness. She found a suitable lubricant on the shelves, feeling like a schoolboy buying condoms, which she thought was both funny and irritating. She knew it was stupid, but she waited for the chemist to leave the counter before taking her purchase to the girl. Then she took the bus home. She would have driven, but she hadn't since Ted died because he was the last to use the Mazda and she couldn't think where he might have parked it. It could be streets away.

At the bathroom mirror, Connie lifted her dress and applied the gel. She unwrapped the lace undies and pulled them on. She lifted her dress again to inspect them and she imagined them on her thirty-year-old self, and thought how silly it was to be playing the coquette at seventy, and how bizarrely exciting. She puckered her lips at the glass for closer examination and, yes, they were cracked and dry, so she rummaged in the drawer for some balm and she applied that, too, and she smacked her lips together and thought about Simmo kissing her and her kissing Simmo and how it made up for all the times they hadn't, all the times in all the years – the pre-Miranda years – that they might have.

She could have cried. Connie watched her lips tremble in the mirror and thought she might do it now, at last. But if she started she mightn't stop. Simmo was waiting.

What was too soon? Three days after the funeral? Three months? Three years? Would she love Ted any less if she waited three lifetimes?

'Let me see,' Simmo said when she emerged.

She went again to the bedside. He lifted her frock to see her lace undies.

'Worth the wait,' he said.

'Do you mean just now, or the full forty years?'

'Both,' he said. He let the frock fall. He turned her around so she faced away from him. He stood and wrapped her in his arms and kissed the back of her neck, right where it excited her most, and this ignited a chain reaction. He fluked it, obviously; he couldn't possibly have known. No one but Ted had done that particular thing, kissed her at that precise ignition point: C2. It triggered a series of detonations today as it did then, in 1980.

Yesterday's detour to the pharmacy proved to be a wise investment.

★★★

Connie holds her winged posture before him, the fan making the sheet billow behind her.

'Has he definitely gone?' Simmo asks.

She checks the window again. 'Seems so.'

She laughs strangely and this appears to disturb Simmo.

'I suppose it was a nasty shock for him,' he says.

'I know. It's a terrible mess, but what else can we do?' She laughs again as if to demonstrate: what else but laugh.

'I can't,' Simmo says.

'Yes you can,' she says, and she attempts to make him. 'Now, Sebastian, if you must know, that's Simmo down there under the sheets, making the ultimate sacrifice, because your poor old mum's a bit out of practice with this horizontal-dancing caper and, frankly, it's a bit of a pain in her whosie-whatsit.'

Now Simmo does laugh.

'Very sporting of you, by the way,' Connie says.

He winces laughing. He sighs and sprawls flat on his back and his little paunch does its disappearing trick. She notes that his cock is at ease.

She might have to see about that.

Connie still fears he'll come to his senses any moment and see her for what she is, for what she's become. Old. She has grown, must have grown, manifestly unattractive to the man who, in his youth, secretly admired her. She knew then that he did. It was innocent enough, other than on the one occasion Connie attempted to make it otherwise. Simmo soon put paid to that. Perhaps now he's seeking to refire that long-ago suppressed desire, willing himself to covet the widow as he once coveted his best friend's young wife.

That was all years before Connie introduced him to Miranda. After they married, Connie occasionally caught Simmo looking fondly her way. It was flattering. She refused to regard it as carnal. Yet today it has been. And now – while she stands here watching him – he smirks at her and it strikes Connie as a sincerely lustful look. He's looking at her as if she's thirty again, or as if it doesn't matter whether she's thirty or seventy. And now his cock budges of its own accord, or by some telepathy. What a trick! It jigs in his lap.

'What?' he says.

'Stand-up comedy.' Male arousal is hilariously transparent to Connie.

Simmo looks at its progress and shrugs. What can he do?

He's uncircumcised, unlike Ted. She watches its head emerge and its frilly neck unripple till its taut. There's no disguising it, no faking. He desires her. He's horny and this makes Connie horny. She goes to the bed and straddles him.

'Again?' he asks.

'Again.'

She likes these staccato bursts in their conversation. She manoeuvres on him until she feels his hardness pressing into her. She might need another interlude in the bathroom.

'Too sore?'

'Quite possibly.'

But she squirms onto him, little by little, and it becomes almost narcotic. She wants to hold this feeling. She clenches every muscle around him and rides him in twitches, little tremors, while he just lies there, still as a plank, watching her twitch until they're done.

'Woo!'

'Yep!' he confirms.

She rolls off him and catches her breath. 'It's been a while, Simmo.'

'Me too.'

They watch the fan rotating.

'Should we have done this way back?' she asks.

'Probably not. It would've destroyed everything.'

She doesn't disagree.

'Is that why you introduced me to Miranda?' he asks.

'Possibly. I don't think I ever thought of it in those terms – not consciously. But possibly, yes.'

Simmo plays with her earlobe and she quivers. He traces a line from here to the deep crevice of her collarbone.

'But have we left it too late?' she asks.

'No.'

'You're not so old. Soon I'll be quite old.'

'I'm not worried by any of that.'

'Not yet.'

★★★

Seb won't go home. He's still pacing in the rear lane, back and forth between his gate and his mother's. It's so insufferably hot but he can't go inside to Amber. He should at least pick up his hat and sunglasses then take a walk, even in this heatwave, to collect his thoughts. Each time he approaches the threshold to his yard he thinks better of going inside. What is he supposed to tell his wife? I've just caught Mum in bed with a stranger?

Amber wouldn't comprehend it – that Mack's seventy-year-old grandmother might be so wanton, three days after Pop's funeral. But she isn't incurious. She'd ask questions.

'Who?'

'I don't know. I couldn't see him.'

'What do you mean?'

'His head was beneath the sheets.'

Seb could hardly say it explicitly: 'Whoever it was, he was going down on my mother.' He would never say such a thing to Amber. She's so wonderfully ingenuous. She always assumes the best of people, even when they don't deserve it. His instinct is to say nothing at all.

He walks past his mother's gate and down the dunny-carter's lane to Banksia Avenue. He crosses the road diagonally and takes shade under a big wattle. From here he can watch his mother's front door. Yellow wattle flowers rain on him in a fine shower that makes him itch and sneeze, but he endures this to maintain his stakeout. At some point her guest will have to emerge.

★★★

Connie watches Simmo drift into sleep and wishes she was a napper. She slips quietly out of bed and, when she reaches the door, turns back to confirm she hasn't woken him. He looks sweet asleep. It reminds her of lingering to watch her grandchildren in their beds. Seb, too, when he was a boy. 'Stop watching me,' he told her once, when he was a pre-schooler. 'Go away!' he said. Seb wouldn't remember it but Connie hasn't forgotten. He would never have said such a thing to his father. His mother did as he instructed.

With Simmo, though, it seems oddly proprietorial to watch him sleep, and it strikes Connie that this is unlike her. She contemplates what people might think of it all. What if everyone knew even as much as Seb now knows? They'd be appalled, as Seb is. But people have no idea. Really they don't.

She pulls the door to.

She goes downstairs to the study and plonks in Ted's chair. His mobile phone is in the in-tray where he left it, still plugged in. She lowers the volume of its ring tone. She picks up the receiver on the landline and dials Ted's number. Soon his phone vibrates in the in-tray.

She has no one else to tell.

★★★

Mrs Visser on her front veranda and Rollo Costa on his have Seb's post under the wattle flanked. Seb is about to abandon it, lest they start thinking he has his mother under surveillance, when his daughter enters Banksia Avenue. He takes cover again and watches Gracie's approach. The neighbours watch him watching her. Gracie opens her grandmother's gate, climbs the two steps and presses the doorbell. She waits. She rings again.

Not even her granddaughter's grief, it seems, will interrupt the widow's tryst. But Seb can't tell Gracie. She adores her grandmother and who is he to disillusion her? Seb is so scandalised he doubts he'll tell anyone. Not even Simmo, with whom he spends more waking hours than any other person, Amber included. Seb can't begin to imagine the form of words he might assemble to broach the subject with Simmo. He'd be shattered. Simmo, above all, stands for common decency.

So while Gracie waits patiently at the door, Seb is confronted with the realisation that there is no one on the planet he can confide in regarding the matter of his mother's depravity. He's almost forty and he has no one to share this load.

He watches Gracie pull a notebook from her backpack. She presses it against the door, writes something, rips out the page

and bends down below the fence line. Soon she leaves, looking
forsaken. Seb waits until she has left Banksia Avenue before he
crosses the street and opens his mother's gate. The note is wedged
under the door. He crouches and extracts it, unfolds it and reads
her scribble.

*Was thinking of you Yeah-Yeah then thought how marquee moon
blew our minds on the sand last time Came round to do it again
but your not home no rush but found lost splitter so we can share
whenever you want*

*Love Gracie*

Seb notes the lack of punctuation and the grammatical error.
His mother, in her priggishness, will inform Gracie of these, but
she'll do it with encouragement, not in the schoolmarmish way
she browbeat him as a teenager. Seb reads the note again with a
terrible pang of envy. He can't decode it. He has no knowledge
of their experience on the sand or to which lunar event it refers.
Gracie's cryptic shorthand is clearly familiar to his mother and he
begrudges it because their easy attachment, as much as anything,
demonstrates the depth of their bond.

Seb paces down the steep fall of Fletcher Street, T-shirt drenched
with perspiration, to the headland park that separates Bondi and
Tamarama. At Marks Park two young mothers push infants on
swings, all of them wearing sensible hats. The sun burns the back
of Seb's neck and its glare makes him giddy. He goes to drink from
a water bubbler but it's not working. He forges on to the treeless
expanse of lawn and becomes aware that he is the only person
occupying it. He is suffocatingly alone.

He is also short of breath.

Seb is fit, he knows he is, but he's hyperventilating. He recog-nises what is happening – it's a panic attack. He has never had one, but that is what this must be, and he knows what he must do, or mustn't do. He mustn't panic.

He looks north over Bondi Beach and south towards Tamarama. He considers which way to go. In Bondi he'd bump into locals. That's the privilege and the inconvenience of being the son of a local legend; Ted loved a chat, and everyone expects Seb to be as chatty. He tries, he really does, but he can't face his father's people today. They'll know something is wrong.

Seb feels physically ill. He keeps seeing what he saw – his mother's grip on those crisp white sheets. It's nauseating. The ground is shifting. He has an urge to vomit, but doesn't.

Time, too, is shifting. Soon he arrives at north Tamarama with no memory of his trek along the cliff-hanging path. He steps out on the bald-rock headland, all the way to the cliff, and he heaves over the edge. Nothing comes up. He wishes it would. He heaves again and again, dry-retching.

There's the slightest puff of a breeze rising from the ocean and he's grateful for it. He looks to the horizon.

'Are you okay, mate?'

Seb turns. His inquisitor looks vaguely familiar. A customer? He looks worried. Which is nice, Seb supposes. It's what people do these days. They see a man in distress at the edge of a cliff and they assume he's suicidal and they intervene. It's sweet that people care, but Seb is not suicidal. Nor is he okay, but there is nothing this kindly gentleman can do for him so Seb nods – yes, I'm okay – and waves him on.

A customer? A clubbie? A patient? Seb is hopelessly preoccupied with putting a face to the ankles that jutted from his parents' bed. Those ankles were suntanned. He remembers no other peculiar feature or blemish. Who in the surf club, for starters, doesn't have suntanned ankles in this, the last month of summer? A process of elimination, on the ankle test alone, might exclude only Noel Farrelly, the fairest of them all. In any case, Noel is a mad punter and Seb's mother detests gambling. So who in their midst might be a backstabber? Who could be so treacherous?

'G'day, buddy. All good?'

Seb about-faces and finds two policemen, a slight one and a burly one, striding onto the cliff-top. Seb is not quite present. What does that mean: *All good*? The officers step into positions either side of him. He's not anticipating their moves. The burly one lurches at Seb and envelops him in a bear hug.

'You'll be okay, mate,' he says, hauling Seb back from the edge, then all the way to the path.

'What are you doing?' Seb demands.

'Calm down, sir,' says the slight one.

'I am calm. You're the ones who need to calm down.'

Thirty metres along the path is the informant, the man who asked Seb whether he was okay.

'This is absurd,' Seb cries. 'Let me go.'

'Easy, mate.'

'I'm not your mate – and I'm not suicidal.'

'You were on that cliff for forty minutes.'

'Unless you're alleging I'm homicidal, I suggest you release me.'

The burly one releases him. 'Can we have your name, please sir?'

'Whatever for?'

They don't respond.

'Sebastian McCall, if it's absolutely necessary.'

'Ted's son?' asks the burly one.

'Yes.'

'Sad to hear about Ted.'

'You'll find I have a clean record.'

'Have you been in an altercation?' asks the slight one.

'Altercation? No.'

'There's a cut under your eye.'

'Oh, that. My mother's palm.'

The officers look sceptical.

'Silly,' Seb tells them. 'This is just silly. Am I free to leave?'

They step back and he huffs away, muttering and laughing, which they will interpret – Seb can only assume – as derangement.

★★★

The old landline receiver is slippery in Connie's hand, its arc glistening with her perspiration.

'So there you have it, Ted. We're not going to die wondering, Simmo and I.' She hangs up.

She watches Ted's screen as her message drops into his call log. She fondles his mobile and scans its photo roll and video bank and marvels at how much of Ted's life it contains. The urn that will contain his ashes will hold less of him. It will deserve no more reverence, if she thinks about it. And she does – because the urn will be ready for pick-up any day. Connie could check in with the funeral directors but decides she's better to leave that to Seb. If she were to collect the ashes without consulting him, it would only be another thing to piss him off.

Connie climbs the stairs. 'Simmo?' she calls.

'I'm awake.'

She opens her bedroom door. 'Don't you need to get back to the shop?'

'Yeah. I just texted Vanessa to let her know I won't be long.'

He rolls over and Connie sees there's a sheen to his eyes.

'You okay?' she asks.

Simmo smiles sadly.

'You're missing him.'

He shrugs, yes. 'You really should talk to Seb,' he says.

'I know.'

'Sooner would be better than later.'

'Probably. Give me a few days.'

94

Seb walks back along the cliffs and into the valley of Bondi. He checks his phone and it's just after two. He keeps losing whole hours from the day. He can't account for most of the past hour, but he's still not ready to face Amber lest he blab to her. Or, worse, tell her fibs to cover up the ghastly truth.

He arrives at Surfside Hardware at 2:17 p.m. From across the street he can see Simmo at the counter, serving a customer. His daughter is alongside him, serving another. Seb has done the rosters so he knows Vanessa isn't scheduled to work today. Simmo must have called her in for back-up, which is not like him. He must be doing it tough.

Seb isn't ready to face them. He's fragile, dehydrated, weak. He leans against a power pole for support. He looks skyward and contemplates the lovely ascent of the flats, rising four storeys above Surfside Hardware. They're a consoling diversion: the clean lines of steel, ironbark and glass, and the distinguishing curve of the eaves over the balconies and the spectacular green waterfalls of hanging gardens that elongate the vertical drops. This was Amber and Seb's project, completed a couple of years ago. They had taken the proposal to Ted to build into the airspace above the old, single-storey shop. Amber's back-of-the-envelope calculations had been compelling: they could average $1.8 million for each of the six two-bedroom units, and as much as $6.5 million for the sprawling four-bedroom penthouse with its panorama of the beach and headlands. That'd be as much as $16 million for an outlay, at a rough estimate, of $5 million. It was a no-brainer. The banks would throw the money at them to fund the development, Amber advised. This kind of development was the way Amber's father had made his fortune on the Gold Coast, and he had shown his girl the ropes.

Ted accepted the reality: the hardware shop was a business in gradual but terminal decline. They all understood the futility of a small, independent operator attempting to compete with the hardware chains. Ted and Simmo – Ted, mostly – were still very attached to the shop, but now they could make some real money out of the thin air over their heads.

Impressed with Amber's figures, Ted did a few sums himself, which he attempted to explain to Seb. Ted had bought the building, empty, for a quarter of a million in 1981. A couple of years later, Simmo paid him $40,000 for a half-share of the then growing business, though not of the bricks and mortar. In those days, you'd pay decent money for the goodwill in an expanding business. Forty years on, with the incursion of the chains, the goodwill was worth precisely nothing, of which Simmo owned half. He had nothing to sell so he would walk away with nothing whenever it came to Ted's inevitable decision to sell off the real estate and shut up shop. Simmo was also a late-comer to superannuation and, even then, he had diverted a large chunk of his contributions to managing the decline of Miranda. He spent a bucket making their home wheelchair-accessible, then another bundle on a live-in nurse for her final months.

Ted called a family meeting. He ran his thoughts by Connie and Seb and Amber. What if each of them, Amber included, were to borrow $1 million for the development? What if they invited Simmo to do the same to make up the $5 million for the rebuild? And what if they split the profit five ways? They could each clear $2 million, possibly more.

Connie looked at Ted for a moment as if he were mad. He'd mortgaged that property himself and paid off every cent. He could show this same proposal to the bank and raise the funds to proceed alone, then take the full $10 million profit and run. He wanted to split it five ways? He wanted to give away most of their nest egg?

'Splendid idea,' she said.

Seb baulked. 'Simmo,' he pointed out, 'has no equity in the existing building.'

'Neither do you,' Connie said.

'Yes, but ...'

'Yes, but one day you'll get the lot,' she said. 'Eventually you'll get whatever's left of the proceeds of our home and my surgery and our combined superannuation and shares. For now, you'd get two-fifths of the hardware development while having invested, based on your rough estimates, what?' She scratched out the equation on paper. 'Two-fifteenths of its eventual worth. Ultimately, you'll also get Dad's and my two-fifths. Or would you prefer to argue the toss and hold out for a four-way split, thereby leaving Simmo destitute?'

'That's a bit rough,' Seb said, looking to his father for support. 'That's not what I was suggesting.'

'What were you suggesting?' Ted asked. His father was clearly unhappy with this squabble over the spoils of their hypothetical fortune.

'I don't know, Dad, but I thought you could at least have the building valued as it stands, then hive off that amount before accounting for Simmo's share.'

'But not your shares?' Connie said.

Seb again looked pleadingly to his father.

Ted's support was not forthcoming. He asked: 'Just how rich do you need to be, Seb?'

Seb had no answer. He felt instantly mean and shabby. Only his father had this power over him. Ted had rarely deployed it. In his next breath, he appointed Seb as their project manager.

Seb now watches Vanessa kiss her dad goodbye and move towards the door. Simmo stops her, opens his wallet and hands her cash. This is odd. He doesn't need to use his own money; he should pay her from the till. Seb checks his watch. It's 2:35, which is also strange. It doesn't match the finish of the usual shift or half-shift.

Simmo's clearly struggling. He needed Vanessa's help and he considers this his problem, so he's covering the cost. It's not fair, but Seb can't even raise it without letting Simmo know he's had them under observation.

Seb is parched, delirious. He crosses the street to Reggie's, the cafe next door to Surfside Hardware, and joins the queue on the street at the takeaway window. Beth, the gorgeous tattooed barista, is framed in the window, busy at her espresso machine. She sees Seb advancing in the queue and, as always, greets him with her toothy smile. She's wearing one of her dresses with the plunging necklines that show off the crimson florets tattooed on the crescents of her breasts. Sometimes Seb wishes she wouldn't. She's mid-thirties and 'involuntarily single', as she protests with captivating self-deprecation.

'You all right?' she asks.

'Yeah,' he says. 'Why?' He instantly wonders whether he sounded too jumpy.

She points under her eye, then to his.

'Oh, that,' he says. 'I went a couple of rounds with a palm tree.'

'Likely story.' Beth laughs.

She really lights up when she laughs. Seb's father used to tell her: 'That's a two-hundred-and-forty-volt smile.' Ted could do that, pay a young woman a compliment and never sound grubby or sleazy. Seb wouldn't attempt it, mainly because – he has to be honest – he's had some fleetingly grubby thoughts about Beth. She's beautiful, in a muscular, earthy way. He's probably been misreading her, but she does seem flirty with him. He beats himself up about it. Just waiting in the coffee line each morning can be a trial. But he doesn't want to think about it now. It's too hot and he has less frivolous concerns.

'Bit late in the day for you,' she says. She goes to make his usual – macchiato, extra hot.

'Actually, I'm dying of thirst. Could you make it a berry juice, plenty of ice?'

'Mmmm? That's controversial. There'll be a demarcation

dispute if I attempt that. Laz, could you fix that for Seb: berry juice, plenty of ice.'

Larry goes to work on the juice. Seb steps aside to allow the next in the queue to order. Two men step up to the counter – both locals. They're familiar faces but Seb knows neither. One is perhaps fifty-something, the other late-sixties. Both wear shorts and thongs.

Seb finds himself inspecting their ankles. Neither man's are unlike the ones in his parents' bed. Both are tanned. He scans for others. There are half a dozen men milling on the footpath, waiting for their takeaways. All wear shorts. If this were a line-up, Seb could rule out only one of them – because he's Black. It's a pointless pursuit. It's madness. He knows it is.

He decides he should see Simmo, after all. He needs the company of someone of sound mind and, among the living, he knows nobody with a sounder one. He pays for his juice and leaves without farewelling Beth.

The electronic security bell at Surfside Hardware goes ding as Seb passes the threshold. He and Simmo might hear it a hundred times on a good day, but today Simmo appears strangely startled by Seb's entrance.

'Seb?'

'Just need a few things for home,' Seb bluffs. He places his juice on the counter and heads directly to the middle of the shop's three aisles and makes a show of looking for something. He turns back to Simmo, fearing he's been rude. 'You okay?'

'Yeah,' Simmo says. 'But what about you? Have you been in a scrap?'

'What?'

Simmo touches his cheek, just beneath his eye.

'Oh yeah,' Seb says. 'No, Mum's palm ... never mind.'

There are mirrors for sale at the top of the first aisle. Seb goes to one of them and checks his wound. It's swollen, purple and a sliver of blood has congealed in a magenta crust.

'It's just that, Seb, I've had a phone call from Tamarama surf club.'

'Oh?' Seb walks to the counter.

'They said you were arrested.'

'I was not arrested!' Seb smacks the counter. 'The police spoke to me briefly, but I was not arrested. I was not taken into custody. I mean, it was nothing. This is ludicrous.'

'That's good to hear. What happened?'

'Nothing happened.'

'Okay then.'

'Nothing at all. Zilch.'

'Good. Don't worry then. I'll call the Tama lads and tell 'em it was a misunderstanding.'

'Would you, Simmo? Please.'

'Of course.'

'Because this has gotten way out of hand. I mean, a man looks at the view and they call in the wallopers.'

'They said you were near the edge?'

'Guilty! I was near the edge! Hundreds of people approach that edge every day. To look at the view. You know that. We all know that.'

'Sure. I'll set 'em straight.'

'Great. Tell 'em it's a complete furphy. It's fake news, people!'

'No problem. You might want to message your mum and let her know you're okay. When I couldn't get through to you, I checked in with her to see if she'd heard anything.'

'Oh?'

Seb checks his phone and sees Simmo's missed call, one from his mother and a further three from Amber. He must have bumped the ring tone to silent. He fixes it. He sees his mother has also texted: 'Please call!'

'Maybe you could let Mum know,' Seb suggests.

Simmo nods, sure.

'There's a nice swell building,' Simmo says. 'I thought you'd be out amongst it. You don't want to waste your day off in here.'

Just the way Simmo talks modulates the mood in a room. He's so reassuring. It eases Seb's anxiety.

'Yeah, I might get out there. I just needed a few things for home.' He's almost of a mind to tell Simmo everything, here and now. His mother doesn't deserve his silence, but Simmo is Seb's main consideration now. Simmo is doing his best to carry on. The news of her appalling behaviour would be crushing. In the middle aisle, Seb feigns interest in picture hooks. He fumbles about before taking three small packets. 'Zenith hooks,' he says. 'Can't get enough of them.'

It's an unconvincing ruse. Seb knows that Simmo knows he has more than enough at home. But the older man nods in agreement. Seb goes behind the counter to complete the charade. He rings up the sale on his private account. Nobody at Surfside Hardware – not the staff, not the bosses – gets free merchandise. They all pay wholesale. It's a rule Ted imposed from the outset. It keeps the books in order.

'Simmo,' Seb says, 'I'll cover for you tomorrow.'

'That's all right, mate. No need.'

'I insist. I can't tell you how grateful I am for today.'

Simmo bows his head. He looks suddenly unsettled.

'Are you all right?' Seb asks. 'You look unwell.'

He really does. He's shaky on his feet. That's how crippled with grief he is, Seb realises.

'I'm fine. Just tired.'

'Get some rest. Your turn for a breather tomorrow.'

Seb leaves the shop mollified. Perhaps his father was right: there's something unceasingly cheerful about the hardware business. 'It's the quiet purpose of the place,' Ted always said, 'the nuts and bolts of it.' Even while confronting its falling profitability, simply being there was enough for Ted – a life among the instruments of utility, the power tools and spanners and the sixteen grades of sandpaper and the nails for every occasion – for hardwood and softwood and plaster board and brick – and the light bulbs for every fitting and the plumbing supplies and kitchenware …'People come in with a problem,' Ted said, 'and we send them home with a solution.'

The only time Ted ever really roused on his son was when Seb was eighteen and grappling with parenthood. Seb was indifferent about a future in hardware, despite having requested the job, but arrogant enough to think he understood the business. He had sent a young family away with twelve hundred dollars' worth of materials but hopelessly ill-equipped and ill-advised to assemble a DIY kitchen. They'd mismeasured it all, so the boards they cut were good for nothing and they came back pleading to Ted that they couldn't cope, that they needed a builder. 'They came in with a problem and you sent them home with a bigger problem,' Ted told Seb. 'That's not what we do here. If you didn't have a young family yourself, I'd take it out of your wages.' Ted refunded the couple and wore the cost.

Of all the transgressions that deserved his father's rebuke – in earlier years, his pot-smoking, or his drunken theft of a surfboat, which he and his mates scuttled on the rocks, or even his carnal knowledge of Kimberley Wyman – it was this cavalier treatment of customers that really upset Ted. Seb learned his lesson. It never happened again, and Ted never raised it again.

★★★

Under the shower, Connie composes and recomposes the email she will send to Seb this afternoon. He has not responded to her phone messages and apparently he doesn't intend to. Simmo has just called her to inform her of Seb's visit to the shop and the offence he has taken at the reports of his arrest, and of his obliviousness to Simmo having been the man in her bed.

Connie is worried. Seb seems unstable. She knows he'll at least read an email, at some point, if she sends one.

'Seb,' it might begin. But no, that's too abrupt. She imagines a 'Dear' before his name, but this is too formal. In her mind she replaces 'Dear' with 'Hi'.

'Hi Seb ...'

Yes, this seems about right. The first line hereafter is a challenge. 'I know what you must be thinking but let me assure you ...' No. This is too defensive. 'When you burst in this morning ...' Too militant. Seb is in distress, clearly. Connie needs to choose these words carefully. She tosses around ten or more first lines. The main point is that Seb saw what he saw and he cannot *unsee it.* That's an expression Gracie likes to use. It seems to have some currency.

Connie selects a loose house dress. In the kitchen and living room she is confronted by the dirty dishes and the remainder of the stinking funeral flowers. It is tempting to be diverted to these tasks, but first she must deal with Seb. With this in mind, she puts the kettle on the boil and makes preparations for a pot of Mum-tea.

At her worst, Connie is inclined to act or react in haste. A strong cuppa gives her pause. It can be her wisest counsel. She still has the Royal Albert cups and saucers and matching teapot that her father, Mick, bought for his new bride, Valentina, in 1947. Val had not long immigrated, the daughter of Italian fruit growers, the Mariottis. She soon converted to Mick's preference for tea over coffee. Val developed quite a taste for it. Mainly she enjoyed life's pauses and conversation over a pot of tea was an excuse to pause. She called it Mum-tea because she was Mum, never Mamma, to her children. She was an integrationist. She never spoke Italian in the home because she wanted only one vocabulary for her family, nothing to confound it. She joined the Country Women's Association and she knitted a cosy for her Royal Albert teapot.

Connie takes the tea cosy from its hook. She pets its wool before she slips it over the pot. All her mother's tea-making paraphernalia is older than Connie, who salvaged it from the dresser in the living room at Tocumwal before they moved her dad to the nursing home six years ago.

The kettle whistles. Connie waits for it to stop hissing and bubbling before she pours the water. 'Don't scorch it, Concetta. Now leave it to brew.' This ritual of tea-making has always been a kind of thanksgiving for Connie. It's not a spiritual thing, but it is an act of remembrance of her thirteen short years with a mother. She pours her first cup. She takes it black, as her mother did. She sips it. It's too hot to drink fast, which is why it should be hot. It is not to be rushed. She clasps the cup to draw on her mother's warmth. No mother since Val has doted so much on her children, or that's the mother Connie remembers. She knows she idealises her, that no mother could be so perfect. Or Connie prefers to think so.

★★★

Seb has climbed the hill for home and he's entering his back garden in a better frame of mind. He's primed himself to mention nothing to Amber about this morning, and nothing that might corner him into telling a white lie to conceal those events, because that would only lead to lies upon lies. Seb steels himself with Proverbs 12:22: *The Lord detests lying lips, but he delights in people who are trustworthy.*

Amber sees the blood under his eye. 'You're injured!'

'It's nothing.'

'You've got a shiner, Dad,' Mack says.

'It's just Yeah-Yeah's silly palm.'

'It'll get infected,' Amber says.

She goes to the bathroom and returns with Betadine and cotton buds. She sits Seb on the couch and tends to his wound.

'And look at you – sunburnt! Why were you out in this heat

104

without your hat? Get me the aloe vera, Mack. Do you know that jar?'

Mack runs to the bathroom and returns with the correct jar. Amber rubs the cream into Seb's neck, forehead and cheeks, then his arms and legs.

'You'll have sunstroke.'

'Dad,' Mack asks, 'who were you waiting for?'

'Mmmm?'

'I saw you, from the window upstairs, under the tree. Waiting.'

This is news to Amber. She frowns at Seb.

'Dad?'

'Well, mate, Yeah-Yeah's had so many kind visitors that she's a bit tired, so I was just asking people to come back another time.' Seb detests his lying lips, as does the Lord.

'I didn't see anyone come.'

'I need to catch up with some accounts.' This, too, is a lie, but if he stays down here a succession of intolerable truths might tumble from his lips.

In his study, at his desktop computer, Seb is not doing the accounts. He's staring at his screensaver, a dove's wings spanning over a silhouetted crucifix. Above this image, in bold capitals, is the assurance that CHRIST IS RISEN. Beneath it is the assertion that SIN IS BROKEN.

The same screen has welcomed Seb for years, without provoking a moment of internal controversy. Today it seems to mock him. Who in God's name wrote this mindlessly glib catchphrase? Seb wonders why he ever fell for its puerile sloganeering. Who sincerely believes, more than two millennia after Christ was risen, that sin is broken?

It is not broken. Sin is having its renaissance. Sin is in rude health.

It's just after 4 p.m. It is normally later, after putting Mack to bed, when Seb retreats to the study and leaves Amber downstairs with the television. Recently she asked him: 'When will we have some quality time watching dumb telly?' Which he thought was clever, both funny and derisory. She isn't prone to be either. He chuckled and kissed her as if this might suffice as an answer, but she persevered: '... like normal couples.'

For most of their marriage, Seb has had the excuse of his academic commitments, his preparation for his religious vocation, but now his studies are behind him and he continues to withdraw to read or to surf the web for spiritual inspiration or to join Christian discussion boards. He cannot bear to trifle away valuable hours, but he knows that he owes Amber her quality time.

Now he can't face her.

Seb consoles himself with the verse from Proverbs that immediately follows the lying lips: *The prudent keep their knowledge to themselves, but a fool's heart blurts out folly.* On this adjudication, he is right to withhold his mother's abominable behaviour from his wife. And yet he hears it jarring with the preceding verse, despite knowing the Bible is a rich source of contradictory aphorisms, ready for plucking to suit the moment and absolve the sinner.

Sin isn't broken. Seb is.

The screensaver continues to taunt him. To supplant it, he clicks on the email icon. The tedium of his inbox is momentary relief, yet soon it also taunts him. It prods him to consider emailing his mother.

He types 'Blunt' into the search bar and brings up the record of his correspondence with her. The log of their exchanges now fills three screens, which is not so many when he considers their emails date back more than twenty years, and that they barely communicate otherwise. With each new computer or operating system, Seb has archived their emails. He's not sure why, and he is less sure why he subjects himself to re-reading them. He does it again now, nonetheless.

Their correspondence has tended to come in sporadic bursts.

In any given year there are clusters, most notably in the aftermath of Christmas Day. Their first skirmish, in fact, was on the evening of December 25, 2001, when Gracie was a few months old. Seb had taken offence at his Christmas gift from his mother, a Richard Dawkins book, *The Blind Watchmaker*, in which the evolutionary biologist ridiculed the notion of a divine creator.

'Why,' Seb demanded in his first email, 'would you choose Christmas Day, of all days, to rubbish my family's faith and the entire Christian story?'

She replied: 'Because it's a story, nothing more. What better day? In any case, I'm not rubbishing anything. It's an attempt not to mock but to start a discussion.'

At Christmases since, Seb has unwrapped an inevitable oblong from his mother to find another tome by another bellicose atheist – Hitchens, Hawking, Harris, Sagan, Stenger, Dennett, Grayling and, again and again, Dawkins – and their antagonistic titles, *God Is Not Great*, *The End of Faith*, *The God Delusion* …

At Christmas eight years ago Seb decided on a strategy of resistance, and so his mother opened an oblong gift from him. It was *The Language of God: A Scientist Presents Evidence for Belief*, in which the geneticist and reformed atheist Francis S. Collins claimed to reconcile the facts of evolution with his rediscovered Christianity. Seb scrolls to his mother's email from that Boxing Day. The record shows it arrived at 11:52 a.m. How many times has he done this – reopened this of all emails, this particular wound? He has read it and the ensuing email trail most years since, and many times in some years. It's a doozy.

> Dear Seb,
> Many thanks for the book. It's hard-going but I promise to finish it if you'll do the same with mine, or even one of the books I've given you at Christmases past. You never do tell me what you think of them. I hope your gift signals that

you're open to a debate. It is our common interest, in many ways, and god knows (ahem!) we should connect more often.

I should have told you long ago a story about Val, the grandmother you never knew. I suppose I want you to understand, at least, where I'm coming from, and this may help. Val was a believer, or she certainly wasn't a doubter. I think there is a distinction, by the way. To not doubt the god of your indoctrination is not quite as conscientious as *believing* in him, as I know you do. In any case, when Mum died, I initially spent no time doubting that she had gone to our capital-G God. I also did not doubt that God had taken her. The Almighty had taken our mother from us, and for this I blamed Him. I did not doubt God. I disowned Him.

A few years later, when I was sixteen, I was home from boarding school one evening when the parish priest came knocking. I eavesdropped while he and Dad drank beer on the veranda. He was worried. He wanted to know why Dad had stopped coming to Mass. Having been away at boarding school, I was unaware he'd stopped going, but I listened as Dad explained why. I was surprised to learn he felt much as I did. He told the priest, in words to the effect: 'I prayed to God and let him know I was mad at Him.' (I recorded this in my diary at the time, so it's a reasonably faithful recollection.) 'But it's become clear to me,' Dad said, 'that God hasn't been listening to a word of my anger. That's not because He doesn't care. It's because He isn't there. I've been praying to thin air. Accepting that, finally, has made it more bearable. Cancer isn't a punishment. It doesn't choose those who deserve it. It chooses the good with the bad, no God about it. So it's pointless being mad at Him, or being mad at all. I can't stop being sad, but it's better than being mad.'

Nothing the priest said could dissuade him. And all at once it became bearable for me, too. I could stop being angry.

Of course, this story does not disprove God. I don't expect it to persuade you of anything, only to give you some context for my faithlessness. I do, however, hope you'll be open to more compelling points of persuasion, particularly from science.

I don't have to remind you how much it saddened me when you came home from summer camp, still a boy, to announce you'd been redeemed. Still, your dad and I thought you'd work it out for yourself. We thought the born-again thing would be a phase, that you'd grow out of it, but I despair with each year that passes. I fear you are irredeemably 'redeemed'.

That probably offends you. I suppose I do write it to provoke, but not to offend. I want us to be closer, so I need to be honest with you about what I was thinking then and what I'm thinking now.

I wish you'd study something. It's not too late. Science was always your strength. It's fascinating that Gracie is already leaning the same way. She tells me she's reading Hitchens. Chewy stuff for a 13-year-old. It won't do any harm if she reads some authors on your side, either, as long as she's reading and thinking, challenging herself. Kids can be impressionable, otherwise. I could pass on Collins to her when I'm done.

Love, Mum

Seb responded at 1:46 p.m. that same day:

Hi Mum,
That's interesting background about your dad and the priest. Sad.

You're right: irredeemably 'redeemed' does offend me, the ironic quotation marks in particular. I share your concerns about Gracie's impressionability, so please do pass on Collins. I hope you'll read him with an open mind, which is how I've read all of yours. Yes, ALL of them. Just because my mind isn't changed, it doesn't mean it's closed.

**2:11 p.m.**
I'm impressed, Seb, that you've found a bona fide scientist in Dr Collins, leader of the Human Genome Project, no less. I'm still struggling with his leap of faith – that the God of the Bible is also the god of the genome. He dismisses intelligent design on the one hand but believes in miracles on the other. He accepts Darwinian evolution but also paranormal poppycock.

If he takes Big Bang as a starting point for creation (he seems to), why would the Almighty have been patient enough to spend the next ten billion years stroking His beard and waiting around for the first sign of single-cell life to emerge, then the better part of four billion more years for a solitary species to evolve with a brain capable of imagining that He might exist? (I could say "She" but I'm less patient than your Darwinian God, so I can't be fussed, particularly when we consider it was the human patriarchy that created Him in its image in the first place.)

You might recall Carl Sagan on this question of human existence. He imagined all known time – the 13.7 billion years from Big Bang to the present day – compressed into a single year. On that scale, the dinosaurs don't arrive until Christmas Day and primitive humans finally appear on New Year's Eve. Someone else, I can't recall who, compresses it further, into a single day, in which case humans don't arrive until four seconds to midnight. We're nanoscopic in the grand scheme of things. If we're God's chosen ones, why would He have troubled Himself with all that primordial soup palaver and the rest of it?

As I said, I'm relieved you've progressed to Dr Collins, but that still leaves you worshipping alongside all the young-Earth creationists who reckon God pressed the start button just ten thousand years ago. Don't you want to scream at them? Dingbats!

By the way, a belated bravo to Kimberley. Tell her this year's Chrissie pudding is her best yet. I'm having leftovers as I read Dr Collins, trying not to share any with him.

Yours, Mum

**2:25 p.m.**
God is indeed patient, Mum. Keep reading and you'll come to Collins's reasoning that God need not be bound by our human construct of space and time. It is reasonable to ask what or who brought about the conditions that preceded Big Bang. What made the primordial soup possible? It's not reasonable to ridicule people because they haven't grasped the complicated science.

(Re Kimberley, best not to mention the pudding. She ran out of time this year and bought this one from Kmart.)

Seb

**2:29 p.m.**
Re mocking young-Earth creationists: sorry, but that's the fun bit. Don't be such a killjoy. Re space and time: I always wondered where He found the time to keep tabs on all of us, so maybe Collins is onto something. Re the pudding: Kmart, you say? Really!!!? Mum's the word.

**2:31 p.m.**
Thanks re the pudding. Re the Lord watching over us: He would hardly be an indifferent God.

Reading it back now, Seb wishes he could have enjoyed this jousting with his mother. She clearly wanted him to. He also wishes he had the patience to explain to her the complexity of his belief – that it is not a blind faith but an endlessly questioning one. He did not need a science degree to make it so. Since this correspondence, nothing has made Seb interrogate the Almighty more than his years of biblical studies. The more he has read and cross-referenced the scriptures, the more he has excused God of their authorship. Rather, they are the record of fallible mortals striving to understand His will, and this is no reason to dismiss them.

Seb accepts the eternal mysteries. Where he looks to the stars and sees trillions of divine sparks, his mother sees only the brutal physics of a universe of setting suns, expanding to its inevitable death. He reads on.

**2:34 p.m.**
This is exhausting, Seb. Why would the Creator of our abundant universe care any more about, let's say, your church attendance than the salvation of a solitary amoeba on a barren planet seven hundred light years away? That amoeba might be the only potential ancestor of future life forms that could one day evolve into creatures capable of calling themselves God's children. That lonely little smudge of life might yield billions more souls – ten billion years from now, let's say. Wouldn't your patient, omniscient God give a bigger stuff about its survival than your menial, venial sins?

**2:37 p.m.**
I think you're overthinking this, Mum.

**2:39 p.m.**
I think you're underthinking it, Seb. (By the way, is everything okay with Kimberley? She did seem distant yesterday.)

**2:40 p.m.**
Everything's fine.

**2:41 p.m.**
Okay. Hooroo.

It still hurts Seb to read these last lines. Everything was far from fine with Kimberley. Seb, at the time of writing, had no idea this would be his last Christmas with her, or that she was in the early stages of her affair with Parvis Husseini, their builder and brother in Christ. It's not that Seb still yearns for Kimberley or that her infidelity can still hurt him. He doesn't. It can't. It's that he was so trusting and pathetically clueless.

He's feeling the same humiliation today with the exposure of his mother's mysterious affair, and he's feeling it on behalf of his father. This is the worst part – that his father, too, was an oblivious cuckold.

★★★

Connie sits before the completed draft of her email to Seb. She reads it one more time, adds one comma and replaces another with a full stop. She is ready to send it at 4:44 p.m. when her phone rings. It is Dorian Metze.

'Dorian?'

'Bad news, I'm afraid.'

'Oh dear.'

'Pathology was sky-high and, sure enough, the scan reveals a pretty big ovarian tumour.'

'Any spread?'

'Not that I can see.'

'You've told Dawn?'

'Yes.'

'How is she?'

'She's a tough one. Still refusing to cancel the trip, so I've booked her in for surgery the day after she flies in.'

Connie calls Dawn, who says: 'I'm quite sure. This trip is my biggest moment, frankly. If my time's up, more reason not to miss it.'

Connie sits and muses on how much she suddenly admires Dawn Driscoll, for the very reason that she's a pain in the arse. How gutsy.

She thinks she might postpone this email to Seb. Enough upheaval for one day. And yet it's still here on the screen before her, and she can't help but review it one more time. She is satisfied that it strikes the right notes. She spellchecks it. She moves the mouse to the top of her screen and hovers over the word 'Hi'. She clicks on it, then says aloud: 'Hi Seb … Dear Seb … Hi Seb … Dear Seb …'

She replaces *Hi* with *Dear*. It's more respectful. She moves the mouse to the top of the screen and clicks the send button. It is 5:16 p.m.

★★★

She was right eight years ago, Seb is thinking. No matter how much his mother enjoys them, their email exchanges are exhausting. He scrolls up and down on the old Boxing Day trail and resolves that, no, he will not write to her today. When the time comes for it, he can ill-afford sloppiness in the wording. He'll need to invoke his father's prudence and humility because he will be writing that message as much on Ted's behalf as from himself. Seb is quite settled about this course of action – that he'll hold fire – when a notification flashes at the top of his screen. A new email has dropped into his inbox. It's from his mother.

Dear Seb,
Given the scene that confronted you this morning,
I thought I should make contact before you leap to too many conclusions. You must have no doubt that I adored your father, that I will never stop loving him.

I'm overwhelmed with grief, as I know you are. I'm not ready to attempt explanations. I can, however, understand your shock and, I imagine, your eagerness for answers. In good time I will be able to tell you things that will put this morning into some perspective. They will, I hope, cast me in a less harsh light. I ask you to bear with me.

Love, Mum

Seb reads it, and re-reads it. She has some pluck. He reads it twice more. It gets worse with every reading. He imagines letting loose with a screed. At 5:21 p.m., however, he sends a one-line response:

Mum, need I remind you that Dad's funeral was three days ago?

Sebastian

**5:22 p.m.**
No, Seb, you needn't.

**5:24 p.m.**
Or need I describe the 'scene' that confronted me barely five hours ago? You use that word as if the scene were a culpable third party.

**5:25 p.m.**
Please, Seb, I only ask that you give me a little time.

**5:27 p.m.**
You certainly wasted no time. Spare me the wailing-widow performance. At the very least you might answer me this: who was that?

**5:29 p.m.**
How dare you question my grief? As I said, I understand your shock, but you have no idea. You can be horribly self-righteous, Seb. I used to blame those Pentecostal pests but, no, I tend to think it's just you.

**5:32 p.m.**
Seb? Look, it's the heat. It's oppressive and I imagine it's not helping either of us. Please, just a few days. That's all I ask.

Mum

**5:34 p.m.**
Oh, the heat! That explains everything. All is forgiven. At least you had the presence of mind to plan for the stinking heat. Who'd have known – the cooling qualities of Dutch linen? That blurb was an education.

**5:37 p.m.**
And your father would have been so proud to see you head-first in our bins like some tabloid muckraker. What on earth were you looking for? A little Christian compassion, perhaps? Or did you find something else to incriminate your mother?

**5:44 p.m.**

I hardly needed to look. I'd seen it with my own eyes. Who was it? I can still hear your eulogy from Tuesday. What a cruel fraud that was. For all its absurdity, I had believed you were at least sincere when you described Dad as the love of your life. You proceeded to stand in the church where he worshipped and attempted to claim him, posthumously, as a fellow unbeliever. It was madness. Nobody challenged you because we all pitied you. We were heartbroken for you.

You took us all for fools. This morning I saw it. I don't want your explanations or excuses because there can be none. You allude to some background that might absolve you. Really? You'll concoct your absolution by defaming Dad? Clearly you don't have your story straight yet, hence the delay in telling all. You have dishonoured the most honourable man you or I will ever know. God forgive you.

This seems to shut her up. Seb watches the minutes pass in the top right corner of his screen. Ten minutes, twelve. It is unlike her to cease hostilities without a parting shot. She has to have the last word. Seb is waiting for it. He considers leaving the room for a toilet break when she returns fire.

**5:57 p.m.**

Seb, it's you, with your toxic moral certainty, who dishonours your father. He never liked that about you – your creepy sanctimony. It probably shocks you to read this now because your dad was always too kind, or too benign, to tell you. He told me, though. He hoped you'd rise above it one day. You never have, but you know your dad: eternal optimist.

Actually, you hardly did know him. This was in abundant evidence in your self-serving eulogy. I only changed my mind and spoke on Tuesday to bring a little reality to the occasion.

Whatever you think, I am grieving and I can't deal with this now. Rest assured I will.

**6:01 p.m.**
Don't attempt to make this about me. Don't attempt to make it about Dad. It's all about you, Mum. I mean, WTF?

**6:03 p.m.**
WTF, Mum? What the actual f--k? For the love of God, you're 70.

**6:04 p.m.**
You're almost 40, Seb. Grow the fuck up!

They sit five houses and five thousand light years apart, reading and re-reading their radioactive emails.

Late in the night, Connie is drawn back to Ted's study to read them yet again. Three less-than-satisfactory G & Ts prolong the exercise. They don't take the edge off, as she expects they might. She and Seb have said what they've said and none of it can be unsaid. There is no unsend button. It will always be there for the record, the inerasable email trail.

# 4.
# THE DAY AFTER

Connie wakes in the pre-dawn, on Ted's side of the bed. The fan throbs, the kookaburras cackle. Ted is still dead.

Is it Saturday? Usually Saturdays feel cheerier, readier for action. Ted's eagerness for the weekend always mobilised her. This is his second Saturday dead. At some point she'll stop these tallies, she's sure.

Connie checks the time on her phone and finds she's woken unnecessarily early. It's not quite 5 a.m. She needs more sleep, much more. There is nothing to stop her sleeping in if she so chooses, nothing but her wakefulness. Perhaps she'll skip the pool this morning, stay here in bed and at least give it a crack. She remains lying, imagining sleep, knowing it won't happen.

She types a search into her phone – the words *email* and *unsend*. Shit! There is such a thing, after all. Better than a seven-second delay, it gives you thirty seconds to unsend. That would've been ample time, if only she'd known.

Too late now.

She rises, goes to the armchair, retrieves a sheet from the bundle of dirty linen and returns to bed. She snuggles her face into its griminess and Ted still smells good and earthy and alive, much as he always had.

Their first time was in Manhattan. Autumn, 1980. She had

been nursing in London for close to a year, and she and her closest Londoner friend, Trish Mayer, a fellow nurse, had just arrived in New York for a two-week break. On their first night, while on a bar crawl – and at the peak of an acid trip – they stumbled into a cosy little gin joint. Connie, who'd just turned twenty-eight, had never experimented with LSD until then, but she was not displeased by its disembodying effects. As they entered the bar, she became aware of herself speaking loudly and of Trish, louder still. They were turning heads, Connie realised, partly because they were boisterous, but largely because Trish was so astonishingly sexy in her high boots and higher mini.

'Connie Blunt of Tocumwal! Is that you?'

She turned and it was him. 'It's you,' she said.

'Clem told me you were in London,' he said.

'I am,' she agreed, then faltered and corrected the record. 'Not now. Now I'm in New York.'

'So I see. And you're nursing?'

'Yes, but not here. In London.'

'Crazy!' Ted McCall said.

'Crazy?' she asked.

'What are the odds?' he said.

'Odds?'

Time oscillated strangely along with her senses, which seemed to flit between her flesh and the space beyond the mirror behind the barman. The mirror contained Connie Blunt and Ted McCall of Tocumwal and she watched them talking amid a dazzling array of bottles of coloured intoxicants, one of which, or two of which if she counted its reflection, matched precisely the gun-metal blue of Ted's lovely shirt. Connie was thinking, *This is the first time in their lives that Connie Blunt and Ted McCall have had an actual conversation*, and she had this thought in the third person because she was a bystander, watching them while tapping her foot to the music.

'You know,' he said, as if it was an adjunct to something he'd just uttered, though Connie was certain too much time had elapsed, 'two kids from Tocumwal just happen to walk into the same old speakeasy on the other side of the planet.'

'Kids? Yeah, crazy.'

Ted was thirty-one. In Tocumwal years, Connie was a spinster at twenty-eight. Mrs Oxley at the bank in Deniliquin Street had told her so the last time she was in town.

What were the odds? In fact, they were more than reasonable, given that bumping into Ted in New York had been the singular purpose of her Transatlantic crossing.

Clem, Connie's only sibling, had recently visited her in London and mentioned his stopover in Manhattan where he'd caught up with Ted, his old footy teammate from the Tocumwal Bloods. Clem had explained that Ted was in New York for a few months before deciding on employment options in Sydney, after having resolved he would not return to work on the family property. He was leaving Burrabogie for his twin to run. Lochie, the brother Connie had rejected, was to inherit the earth.

Clem's intelligence concerning Ted's movements had shaken Connie. Never had she contemplated returning to live in Tocumwal, not even, in her silliest dreams, for the delicious Ted McCall. But now he was moving to Sydney.

Connie had rifled through her brother's luggage while he showered and found a receipt for Henley's Hotel in SoHo. She'd made a note of the name – working on the flimsy assumption that her brother had booked into the same hotel as Ted – and as soon as Clem left London, Connie dropped everything. She pleaded with Trish to accompany her to New York. It was a scramble but they both managed to arrange leave.

They couldn't afford Henley's but Connie imagined she would watch the hotel until Ted emerged. She would stalk him, if need be, until she could stage a footpath collision. In the busiest city in the world, it would be a made-for-Hollywood, serendipitous, meant-for-each-other collision.

Within hours of landing at JFK she decided this strategy was too tricky, too sneaky. She'd opted for a more upfront kind of subterfuge. She would tell Ted that Clem had mentioned he was in New York and – while she happened to be here – she thought she might as well look him up. So Connie went directly to Henley's and asked the receptionist to put her through to Ted's room.

'I'm sorry, madam, he checked out this morning.'

'No.'

She had missed him by hours, so Connie and Trish walked the streets of SoHo and beyond in the vain hope of seeing him, head and shoulders above the multitudes. They didn't. In her funk, Connie drank bad wine with Trish at an al fresco bar, where she persisted with her futile vigil until they were pestered by a toothless street dealer. Connie tried to shoo him away but Trish was amenable to sampling his wares.

'Two tabs,' said Trish, who seemed to know what she was buying. 'It'll be a blast,' she assured Connie.

They dropped the acid and synchronously, as they liked to recall it, experienced Manhattan as a funfair.

At the bar, Connie watched Connie Blunt asking Ted McCall a question in the mirror. 'Am I talking too loudly?'

'Not at all,' he said.

'Are my eyes dilated?' she asked.

'Have you taken something?'

'No, we didn't take it – we paid honest money for it.' She snorted at her joke. 'Didn't we, Trish? We paid an obscene amount for two teeny-weeny thingamies.'

'We did,' Trish said.

'Forgive me. Trish Mayer of Hackney, this is Ted McCall of Tocumwal.' Connie snorted once again. 'Did you notice how that rhymed? McCall of Tocumwal. Did you also notice, Trish, how his gorgeous shirt is exactly the same blue as that bottle of, er ... bartender, what do you call that liqueur? Mmmm? Beg yours? Did he say Blue Curuçao? In that case, we'll have three Blue Curuçaos to match the gentleman's shirt.'

The barman got to work and Connie carried on. 'You probably hadn't thought of this, Ted McCall of Tocumwal, but this is the first time in our lives we've actually had a conversation. Or did I say that already? Did I? I think I did. Am I talking too much? A bit too loudly?'

'You did say that already, but you're fine.'

'I'm fine,' Connie agreed, tapping her foot to the beat. 'I am indeed *fine*. I love this tune. Do you like this tune? I want to dance to this tune.'

'What tune?'

'Bartender, what do they call this tune?'

'Which tune?' the barman asked. 'Is there a tune?'

'There's no tune,' Ted informed Connie.

'Really? Are you certain?'

'Yes.'

'Then I think we should drink our blue curiosities and go in search of a better class of establishment.'

They found bars with tunes they could all hear and Connie threw herself at Ted as the trio danced in the dives of his adopted neighbourhood. Connie wondered all the while why Ted chose to dance mainly with her and paid little attention to Trish.

'She's a total sex bomb, isn't she?' Connie asked him, and he confirmed she was.

When Ted's dancing partners finally came down from their trip they could not find their hotel. He took them back to his room, more affordable than the one he'd vacated that morning. Ted tucked them into his bed then lay on the couch.

'Too kind,' Connie told him. 'Trish will be happy on the couch.'

'Deliriously happy,' Trish agreed.

And Connie added: 'She's English, did you notice? The English are very polite.'

But so was Ted. He wouldn't hear of it.

They slept it off. Trish left before Connie woke. When she finally came to, Ted made Connie coffee and a fancy mushroom omelette. It was already afternoon. Soon she felt human, then elated to be in his company. They washed their plates at the sink, where she threw herself at him once again, sober this time. He was reticent, polite.

'Sorry,' she said. 'You don't want to?'

'No,' he said. 'No, I mean yes. Yes, I do.'

He kissed her briefly, lips closed. She kissed him, open-mouthed. He was slow on the uptake.

'Lochie always fancied you,' he said, interrupting. 'I thought you'd go for him.'

'Why?' she asked.

'I don't know. He was always more confident with girls.'

'That's why I didn't go for him.' Connie told Ted about her teenage encounter with his twin by the river, when Lochie attempted to kiss her to show off to his friends. 'He seemed to hate me for that, for running away from him. He didn't tell you about it?'

'No, but we've never been close. Not all twins are. Lochie's never told me much about anything.'

'But he did tell you that he fancied me?'

'Not me so much. He told Mum when I happened to be there, but this was years later. We were in our early twenties, both working on the farm. Mum was asking us about girls of potential interest, and Lochie told her there were only two who were marriageable in all of Tocumwal: Connie Blunt and Tory Denning. In that order.'

'What do you mean "in that order"? That's terrible.'

It was terrible because back in Tocumwal, Lochie was already dating Tory. It was terrible because Tory had been Connie's closest childhood friend. It was terrible because only six or seven years earlier – while Connie was studying nursing in Sydney – she'd had another encounter with Lochie during a trip home. Drunk at the pub, he'd been emboldened to remind her that she owed him a kiss. She'd ignored his advance and this had provoked him.

'Still stuck-up,' he'd said. 'Still too good for a Tocumwal boy.'

No account of this had ever before reached Ted.

'Not so stuck-up now,' Ted said.

'Hey?'

'Here you are in Manhattan, with a Tocumwal boy. His identical twin, no less.'

'I wouldn't be here if I saw you as identical. To me, you're opposites.'

Ted kissed her again, more fulsomely this time. Connie couldn't know then how deeply affected he was by her declaration that she had always preferred him. He became playful. He waltzed her in a circle by the sink. She laughed and he kissed her with a sudden hunger. They undressed with urgency and made love. He became focused on Connie and her every response to his touch, fascinated whenever he chanced upon the spheres of her arousal: the back of her neck, for instance. Who knew that one? Not Connie.

Afterwards, watching the liquidambar leaves float by his bedroom window, she nuzzled his armpit.

'That's brave,' he said.

'Fearless.' He smelled amazing – sweet, woodsy, malty, tangy, salty. All at once. Then she licked his armpit, if only for the shock value.

He writhed, duly shocked.

'You smell amazing.'

'You're mad, Connie Blunt.'

'Only about you.'

He went quiet. She instantly regretted saying it. She'd come on too strong. Too keen, too soon. Nonetheless, she couldn't sustain her fraud and she confessed everything – that her trip to New York had been an elaborate ruse. She told him of her childhood fascination with the boy who had kicked the footy so high that it never returned to planet Earth. She told him of her and Tory Denning's mutual infatuation with him, and how Tory had used the spike of a geometry compass to etch it into the desk in Connie's bedroom: TD & CB ♥ TMac. They coloured the letters in blue ink and the heart in red.

Connie also told Ted of the time she was riveted to the kitchen floor, in her undies, immobilised and unable to speak, as he left her house without saying a word.

'I couldn't bring myself to interrupt,' he explained.

Connie worried that her honesty would spoil it, but she couldn't be slippery with him. He responded with open-heartedness. Candour seemed effortless between them and this chemistry bonded them over the next fortnight. They included Trish Mayer in some outings but she gave them space. Connie dragged Ted to see bands he detested, Television and The Cramps. He was marginally less affronted by Patti Smith and he adored the sweet-sweaty soul of Mink DeVille. Ted dragged Connie to Broadway shows.

On the night before Connie's return to London, Ted became suddenly earnest. On Lafayette Street he asked: 'Could you see yourself married to someone like me?'

Connie pretended to be calm. 'Is that a hypothetical question or a proposal?'

'I suppose it's the latter.'

'Then don't suppose. Ask me properly.'

'I don't want to rush you. This is very soon, and I don't have a ring or anything.'

'Go ahead and rush me.'

Weeds sprouted from cracks in the pavement. Ted found one long enough and plucked it.

'Connie Blunt, will you marry me?'

'I suppose,' she said, teasing.

'Don't suppose.'

'Okay,' she said. 'Yes, Ted McCall of Tocumwal, I will marry you.'

He knotted the weed around her ring finger. They both knew this was absurdly fast. They found Trish to celebrate and they feasted and discussed whether they had acted rashly. Yes, they all agreed. And they danced.

Later, Ted and Connie considered some practicalities. He had some money from his father, a $30,000 severance payment, for which he had agreed to forfeit any further inheritance. They couldn't subdivide the farm and sell Ted's half because anything smaller wouldn't be viable.

'That doesn't sound fair,' Connie said.

'No, but thirty grand isn't an inconsiderable sum.'

It wasn't at the time.

In his brief stint at university, Ted said, he'd felt more at home in the city. He was relieved to be leaving them.

'What will you do?'

'I wish I knew. I'll buy a small business somewhere, something that doesn't require too much knowhow. As long as it's by a beach, I'll be happy. What about you?'

'What about me?'

'You were meant to do medicine, not nursing. That's what Clem said.'

'You've discussed me.'

'A little. Is that what you'd still prefer to do?'

'I suppose so, but I fell short on the marks.'

'You went close.'

'Within a whisker.'

'You could try again.'

'I haven't given it much thought.'

'You should.'

Ted sounded like her dad. Nobody but her father, until now, had told her that a second shot at medicine might be a good idea. Ted hardly knew her, but Connie realised he understood her and already he didn't doubt her, and because of this she felt she wasn't being rash about marrying him. Though she still thought Ted was being rash about marrying her. She could only hope time would confirm the wisdom of his impulse.

In any case, it was decided. They discussed their plans until dawn. They would return to Sydney. They would rent a flat and Ted would hunt for a suitable business. Connie would find the surest path to enrol in medicine, even if that meant repeating her school leaving certificate. And they would plan for their wedding. Ted conceded it would have to be in Tocumwal.

His widow watches herself in the mirror, curled foetally on their bed, where she has made a pillow of their old sheet. Connie gets up to open the curtain. It's still black outside. She collects the rest of the dirty linen from the armchair and takes it through to the walk-in wardrobe and stuffs the lot on a low shelf, into what little space remains above Ted's shoes and boots. Onward.

Togs, teeth, phone, earplugs.

At the bottom of the stairs she looks momentarily left, towards the front door, where something catches her eye. She walks along the hall and finds a piece of paper tucked under the door. She bends to pick it up, unfolds the page and reads the scrawled message from Gracie. Connie notes the lack of punctuation and the grammatical error.

She texts her granddaughter.

I'm sorry I missed you yesterday. If you're free tonight,
Marquee Moon on the sand at sunset would be a treat. How

about the Pavilion at seven? PS: To be pedantic, you should have written "you're not home". Love, Grammar

Gracie replies:

> *See you then Grammar. Just to be pedantic – that pun's so groaning Pop's ashes would blush*

Connie is about to leave when she remembers the stockpile of meals from her patients. She finds a supermarket bag in the pantry and fills it with six containers of assorted stews, frozen and unfrozen. She steps into the garden and takes her goggles and towel from their hooks. On her way out she stops to inspect the undergrowth but finds no sign of the blue fairy-wren. She crosses Banksia Avenue to Mrs Visser's. She's there, faithfully, in the glow of her porch light, drinking tea. Connie opens the gate and its rusty hinge whines.

'Nice surprise,' Mrs Visser says.

It shames Connie that her visit is surprising. 'Some casseroles for you. I'll find some space in your freezer.'

'I'll have to call Michael over to help me,' Mrs Visser says.

Michael is her son. He's sixty-ish, never married, though Mrs Visser has never abandoned hope.

'Bring yourself a cup,' Mrs Visser says. 'I've just made this pot.'

Connie returns with a cup. 'Just half,' she says. 'I'm on the run.'

'You're right to keep moving. The days are long when you're still.' Mrs Visser's days have been still since a blood clot killed her husband thirty or more years ago.

They look to the street, the tilting shadows of its trees and the shades of black that give gothic charm to houses that soon will be rendered ordinary by daylight.

'Love this time of day,' Mrs Visser says.

'Me too.' Connie stands to leave.

'That's the way. Just keep moving.'

The sun climbs from the horizon through crimson rungs. Simmo, who's limbering up a few metres from the shore, seems entranced by this trick of light. Seb recognises in this moment something he's always known about Simmo. He's the kind of man who stops to count the smallest blessings. It's not a religious thing for Simmo, not in the least, but as they limber up, rolling their shoulders back and forth, Seb senses a shared gratitude for intangible gifts. He prays that one day Simmo will acknowledge them as God's beneficence.

They're barely a metre apart yet they haven't spoken this morning. They needn't. So much of their communication at the shop is unspoken, a reward of so many years in proximity. Only Ted would have had more time with Seb. In any event, Seb's focus this morning is not on Simmo but on their fellow Odd Socks – Brad, Marty and Bertie – and, for the moment, their ankles. Which is crazy. Seb knows it is. He shouldn't be giving a moment's consideration to the possibility that his mother might be sharing her widow's bed with any of these three, but he is casting the net wide. A process of elimination is all he has.

The three men are stretching and star-jumping while sustaining an animated discussion about a fresh scandal at the Roosters, whose newly recruited halfback has tested positive to an as-yet-undisclosed party drug. Seb would normally pitch in with his analysis of this controversy, but he can't get interested today. He really can't.

'You ready, Dim?' Marty Ratcliffe asks Simmo. 'Seb, ready?'

The Odd Socks jog along the shore. Closest to Seb in the pack is Brad Wiseman. Brad is an infamous root-rat but he's almost half Connie's age and he's known for bedding women half his. First eliminated. Next is Marty, who'd be up for it, yet Seb can't believe his mother would be up for Marty. She's regarded him with condescension, at best, for too many years. Of this unlikely line-up, Bertie van de Boor is the most probable suspect. He's the silver fox of the surf club, as fit and as handsome, arguably, as Ted was. And a tad younger. Bertie is not quite seventy. After their point-to-points each morning, he works out in the club gym then preens himself in preparation for an hour's sunbaking and try-hard flirting with promenading divorcees.

But Seb strikes out Bertie, too, after falling behind the trio on the return lap on the sand and making another pointless inspection of their ankles. His memory of the impostor's feet is not photographic, but, as he recalls, the ankles looked older than Brad's, younger than Marty's and Bertie's, and more suntanned than all of them. Possibly.

Whoever's ankles they are, he must be living in their midst. Seb's mother has never had the time, nor made the time, for a secret life outside the daily cycle of her Bondi existence. Seb knows the pattern of her days. He always has. Even a son who has become as emotionally distant as he has knows his mother's comings and goings when she lives five doors away. His mother's life is as routine as his. Her footprint is confined almost entirely to the 2026 postcode, between home, pool, surgery and the odd diversion to a restaurant, bar, cafe or club, all local. His parents took occasional excursions to the city for the theatre or cinema, and his father had his Rotary meetings on Tuesday nights, just up the hill in Charing Cross, but otherwise their Bondi realm provided all they required.

Seb casts back, trying to pinpoint a single absence for which she might have required an alibi. There were the annual medical conferences, but she stopped those five or six years ago. Otherwise, nothing.

Perhaps she used her unsuspecting practice manager, Rhiannon, to rearrange patients' appointments around her assignations. Or was Rhiannon a witting facilitator of her boss's infidelities?

The Odd Socks approach the surf via the rock shelf at the north end. The moss is slippery underfoot. Bertie skids and teeters, and Seb braces his shoulder to set him straight. They all hunch down for balance against the surge and suck of the tide and they edge forward in the foam. They time their dives, each waiting for an upswelling glut of water lest they gnash their bellies on the ledge. Seb watches the backwash sweep his crew like corks into deeper water.

He's the last in. He puts his head down and swims at pace to catch up. As he gains on them he sees their feet aflutter just below the surface, none connected to the nameless cad who's screwing his mother.

Soon Seb is out in front, leading the pack. Ted had always led them and Seb typically followed right behind him. That seemed to be the natural order of things. When Seb joined the Odd Socks in his late teens, he wasn't as strong a swimmer as his father. He learned then to stay close behind Ted, to stalk him so he could ride his slipstream. In the past ten years or so, Seb might have been the stronger swimmer for no other reason than his relative youth, and Ted could have hitched a ride in his wake, but they never tested it. It's never really been a race for Seb, or not against his father, at least. Truth be known, he'd have been disappointed to beat his father at anything.

Swimming for Seb is not competitive, but purgative. It clears the crap from his head. Fifty metres in and he's typically thinking of nothing but his next stroke and the beating of his feet and the roll of his body and the timing of his breathing, and so it goes for almost two kilometres, two lengths of the bay, almost every day of his life, each stroke, kick and breath as meaningless and profound as a meditational mantra, and as cleansing for a cluttered mind. It's a prayerless exercise and that's fine because Seb's prayers come later.

This morning Seb's mind cannot be stilled. It keeps churning with a rollcall of names: the clubbies, the choristers, his mother's fellow medicos, the husbands of her friends and acquaintances ... Warburton, Boysted, Pune, Methers, Klein, Chisholm, Barnard ... and none is likely. None is, prima facie, the special kind of cunt it must have taken to occupy his father's bed while his body was still warm. Seb hears himself thinking this thought and it is jarring. That's not a word he uses. He consoles himself with his father's thinking on the subject, that it's a perfectly appropriate word when used judiciously.

'It should be reserved exclusively for cunts,' Ted said.

Seb was a teenager when his dad said that. Jim Mercer, a spivish local carpenter and aspiring developer, came into the shop in a spitting rage. He'd made a big order via young Seb – the entire window schedule for a block of flats he was building. The contract joiners had delivered almost forty cedar-framed windows to the building site, and fewer than half fitted the cavities awaiting them.

'Your kid's fucked up the measurements,' Mercer said. 'You can wear it, Ted.'

Ted brought out the order book. Stapled to the requisition form was a page torn from a mini Spirax notepad. On it were written the measurements, and all in Jim Mercer's hand. Ted used his pen to tap the notebook in Mercer's breast pocket.

On his way out, Mercer kicked over a tub full of shovels.

'Cunt,' Ted said, loud enough for the cunt to hear.

Almost twenty years in the business by then, Ted had never had cause to curse at a customer. It upset him. Seb remembers it as a kind of initiation, Ted deciding his son was sufficiently grown up to hear him at his worst. Seb hears the word now in solidarity with his dad.

Whoever it was beneath his father's sheets, his affair with his mother must have predated Ted's death. Seb's reasoning for this is painful. It was his mother's laughter – her casual hilarity – as he walked in on them at the apparent height of her ecstasy. She'd hardly be so blithe, so familiar, with a new lover.

Perhaps the more salient point, for Seb, is this: senior citizens don't go down on their first date. Surely not.

Seb's arcing right arm slams into rock. He has blundered past his turning point and crashed onto the rock shelf at the south end, beneath the Icebergs. A lapping wave has run him aground on the shelf and he's sprawled in a few centimetres of water. His wrist and chest have drawn blood.

He sees his fellow swimmers are twenty metres and more into their return lap. None has noticed his gaffe. But now Seb looks up to the pool, to his mother's domain, and there she is at the rail, in her bathers, watching him from the deck. She holds his gaze for a moment, then pulls her goggles over her eyes and dives out of sight.

Seb picks up the pace to catch his crew. He attempts to think only of this mission – to swim harder – but he is consumed by his calculations of the likely duration of his mother's affair. It could have been going on for many years, perhaps decades. Seb can only speculate.

He wishes he could stop speculating.

Even if it began after Ted's death, Seb can imagine no scenario that absolves his mother. Yet he is open to considering circum-stances that may mitigate the culpability of the man involved. It is possible, for instance, that he had been secretly admiring his mother from the sidelines, innocently, for a long time. For half a lifetime, for all Seb knows. That kind of attraction, never acted upon, happens. Such a man, in the privacy of his daydreams, might even have imagined the ways in which Connie Blunt might one day become his: that Ted might leave her, that she might leave Ted, or – more conveniently, given the unlikeliness of those eventualities – that Ted might die, as people do, of natural causes. Nobody's fault.

But why then the indecent haste? A decent man would have waited a respectable time before offering the widow companionship. Seb could have understood that.

It's not as if he has always been pure of thought. In the immediate aftermath of his first face-to-face contact with Amber, following the prayer symposium, he drove home to Kimberley, sick with guilt about the excitement he was feeling and with anguish about how he would break the news to his wife: that their marriage, which only months earlier he had pleaded they should salvage, was over in any case. On his approach to Bondi, Seb had worried that he was incapable of this task, that he would chicken out, and he had two appalling thoughts about how he might escape it. The first involved his death – a ghastly car crash. The second involved Kimberley's accidental death – a misplaced foot at the top of the stairs. A terrible fall, terribly fortuitous. Seb was so revolted by this diabolical fantasy that he entered their home with trepidation, fearing he would indeed find her at the base of the stairs – that this would be his punishment.

She was not by the stairs. He found her in the shower. He waited long enough for her to towel herself dry. Then he confessed all to her: that he'd come to realise he could never forgive her for Parviz, so he could not love her wholly, and – this part was difficult – he had also met someone.

Kimberley's reaction remains a painful memory for Seb. She was so relieved she reciprocated with cathartic honesty in a sequence of what sounded like well-rehearsed dot points: she had not stopped seeing Parviz; she had been with him that afternoon (hence the shower, Seb had to assume); she loved Parviz, not Seb; she doubted she had ever loved Seb; their thirteen-year marriage had been founded on a faith she no longer shared, and, finally: 'We don't need to involve lawyers, Seb. A clean fifty-fifty split will be best for both of us.'

It annoys him that this memory can still hurt him, given his much happier marriage to Amber.

Seb stops swimming. He dogpaddles to get his bearings and, good heavens, he has swum way off course. He's out past the headland, beyond Ben Buckler. The others are leaving the surf via the boat ramps, a hundred or more metres closer to shore. Seb experiences an intense tightening of his chest, a shortness of breath.

Dry land looks too far away. He attempts to slow his breath but senses a constriction in his windpipe. For the first time, he feels unsafe in the water. He doubts he can make it.

★★★

'Better make mine tea,' Connie tells Jean Amos. 'Discretion's the better part of valour.'

She and Jean are perched again at the cafe over the pool, where Connie describes her toilet emergency yesterday. She recounts the whole episode and the horror on Nadia Kovac's face when she emerged from her cubicle. Jean's laughter escalates as Connie's story, in its embellished retelling, becomes more and more farcical. Mrs Kovac, who is poolside again today, looks up to investigate the disturbance. She catches the merry widow in cahoots with her friend. Connie and Jean see that she has caught them in the act of being amused, which makes it funnier.

'I've asked Amelia to come along this morning,' Jean says. 'I hope that's all right.'

'Of course.' Connie wishes she hadn't. She really isn't fond of Amelia Adelio. 'I can't stay too long anyway.'

Jean makes a show of drooping her lower lip. 'You're always running away.' But she moves to weightier matters, namely her unsatisfactory marriage. She seems eager to cover some ground before Amelia arrives. 'I feel so suddenly claustrophobic,' she says. 'In all these years together, we've never had so much time in the same space.'

'You need a hobby.'

'I need six, but that wouldn't be fair to Keith. He's been waiting for this, my retirement. I don't know what he was expecting. We've never had a common interest. Maybe he thought we'd just sit around moping together, and that'd be an improvement on moping alone. If only he could be fractionally less miserable, that might resemble contentment.'

'I wish I had an answer for you.'

'Never mind. Just telling helps.'

Jean can tell Connie anything. Connie could reciprocate but doesn't. Today she will certainly mention nothing of consequence that happened yesterday. If Connie started with yesterday, where might she stop?

Amelia Adelio's arrival spares her this dilemma. The woman talks without drawing breath. Connie would like to tell Jean her friend is a bumptious old hag, but she resolves to sit quietly for a few moments before excusing herself and heading home.

★★★

On his walk towards the shop, Seb passes wellwishers. They're still making an effort, nine days later. He might also have died in the surf today, so soon after his father, so this evidence of human kindness is reassuring.

He joins the takeaway queue outside Reggie's Cafe. Beth looks up from her espresso machine and smiles at him as he advances in the queue. How flattering it has been since Beth started working here – what is it, six months ago? – her daily, innocent flirtation, but how sad it is that nothing seems so innocent anymore.

He takes his mobile from his bum pocket and checks the time. It's almost seven-thirty. He dials home.

'Hi,' Amber answers.

'I won't make it back for brekkie, sorry. I don't want to miss the early rush.'

It will hardly be a rush – they both know – but an early start on Saturdays can catch some extra business, the builders and local DIY crowd who'd otherwise head to Bunnings.

'Don't work too hard,' Amber says.

Seb can work no harder than his customers demand, but he knows what she's trying to say: Don't stress.

'I won't.'

He will stress. He knows he will, not least about his lying to Amber. She's been so understanding. She knows when to give him a little space. Seb will make all this up to her.

'Hi,' says Beth.

'Morning.'

'New shirt?' she asks.

'No. Don't wear it very often.'

'You should. That blue suits you. It's like one of your dad's.'

She really pays attention. It is identical to his dad's because Ted bought one for each of them.

Beth points to her cheek, just under her eye. 'Your war wound's coming good,' she says. 'Not so gory today.'

Seb nods. He feigns interest in a big new picture on the wall behind Beth. It's a drone photograph of Bondi Beach. A sunbather on the sand and a longboard rider in the surf are each wearing canary-yellow cossies and they are cropped into identically sized rectangles of almond beach and blue water.

'It's nice, ay?' says Beth. 'I know the photographer. She can do prints if you like.'

'Good to know.'

Beth grinds fresh coffee beans. She gives the coffee plug a whack to empty it, then refills it, and she twists it into its socket in the espresso machine. This action tightens her forearm flexor, where a black spider is tattooed to her honeyed skin. She flicks a switch and the machine purrs quietly and dribbles coffee into Seb's cup. She's in command. His macchiato will come extra hot, so it won't go tepid while he's serving customers next door. She presses her palm against the metal milk jug to gauge its heat. She froths his milk. Seb wishes she wasn't so hot.

For a change she's wearing a V-singlet today rather than a dress. The crimson florets on the half-moons of her breasts are still exhibited. Seb tries not to look but she keeps looking his way. It's pissing him off. He rubs his face to show off the ring on his finger. She must see it. It's been there every time he's extended his hand to take a coffee from hers. Amber doesn't come this way for coffee, so it's possible Beth has never seen her, but she can't have missed his wedding ring. Maybe it doesn't trouble her.

It troubles Seb.

For most of his twice-married life he's not noticed other women noticing him, but in the past couple of years – in his approach to middle age – he's been noticing. He gets looks he never got before. Or did he fail to notice before? It annoys him that he's so easily flattered, his vanity so easily indulged.

Seb catches a sideways angle of himself in the mirror to the left of Beth. *No poster boy*, he's thinking. *Not like Dad.*

Amber did tell Seb last month he was getting better looking with age. It was such a wifely thing to say. Seb can't really know.

While he waits he is struck with self-revulsion. Because women, per se, are not suddenly noticing him. He's aware of only two, now that he does a reality check. A grand total of two. There's Beth and there's Kerry Waldren, from church. Kerry is the wife of Ant Waldren, another of Seb's brothers in Christ. Seb suspects Kerry, Amber's closest friend, flirts fruitlessly with him only because her husband is so desperately dull. This is an un-Christian thought, but not untrue. The most interesting thing about Kerry's husband is the contraction of his name from Anthony to Ant.

'Here you go,' Beth says.

Seb beholds her: the outstretched arm, the paper cup suspended at the end of it, the spider on her flexor, the florets adorning her chest, the ineffaceable smile. He takes the cup, nods his thank-you and turns away.

'Seb,' Beth calls.

He turns back.

'People still come in every day and tell us what a champion your dad was. I wish I'd gotten to know him better.'

'Thanks, Beth. I really appreciate that.'

'He was such a cutie.'

'He sure was.'

As he departs, Seb has a jaundiced thought. Beth is not much younger than he is. Her body clock is going off. It has nothing to do with Seb, in particular. It's biological. That's all it is. For all Seb knows, she'd put out to any gainfully employed, sperm-bearing biped.

He's been with two women in his entire life – and married both of them. The only wild oats he ever sowed resulted in Gracie and Mack. His inexperience, Seb is thinking, explains his prolonged adolescence, his juvenile engrossments. It's biological for Seb, too. Beyond his control. *Don't beat yourself up, Seb.* He will, nevertheless.

★★★

It's 8:20 a.m. and Seb has had six customers. Not a bad start. He's sold a drill set, four metres of sixty-grit sandpaper, a garden irrigation hose, three bags of potting mix, a jar of Spakfilla, a trowel, and twenty bags of ready-mix concrete. He's done it all on autopilot. Now he's cutting four keys for two young women – university students, he's guessing – who are excited about occupying a rental property this morning.

'So you'll be flatmates?' Seb asks, an attempt to show interest.

'Yeah!'

But he's not as encouraging as he should be, as Ted would have been. The key machine chews at metal.

'Pardon?' says one of the young women.

'Mmmm?'

'You said something.'

Did he? Seb can't imagine what that might have been. He uses a wire wheel-brush to shave the gluey edges from the keys.

'That'll be seventeen-sixty, thanks.'

*Senior citizens* … that's what he was thinking. The young women are leaving the shop, giggling. Did he even take their money? He checks the till and, yes, he did. *Senior citizens don't go down on their first date.* He was thinking it, but Seb can't have thought it aloud. Or might he have?

He is troubled as much by the banality of his thought processes. What would Seb know, anyhow, about the sex lives of senior citizens? His mother and her generation were there for the sexual revolution. Why would they have any taboos now?

He remembers his younger mother well, and there's that picture of her in his father's study, in her mini. Connie Blunt must have appealed to men other than his father. And still does, apparently. Seb dials Gracie's number.

'Dad?'

'Do you want a couple of hours?'

'When?'

'This morning. Ten-ish.'

'Er?'

'Forty an hour.'

'Whoa! You don't have to ...'

'It's okay. I'm doing Simmo's shift, but I've just got a few things ...'

'Okay, okay. Ten.'

★★★

Connie returns from the pool and is about to enter her back garden when she looks along the lane to Seb's gate. She has an urge to see him. They'll have to deal with it sooner or later. She's not ready for full disclosure but she knows it's Seb's Saturday off, so she has this window. She doesn't know what she'll say but something, anything, will be better than nothing.

His gate, unlike hers, is fastened. Familiar palpitations of music escape from inside. Connie hears squeaky voices, Amber's and Mack's, singing over the mix. She puts a hand over the gate and unlatches it. She nudges it open and peeks inside. The bifolds are wide-open and Amber and Mack are bounding on their mini-trampolines in the back room and singing at the television: *'M-M-Messiah, t-take me higher / M-M-Messiah, t-take me higher.'* It goes on interminably, a chorus bereft of a verse. Amber's Lycra body glove is as lurid as the music.

Connie can't see Seb. She decides she'll fall back and leave them to jump with Jesus.

'Yeah–Yeah!' Mack has spotted her.

'Yeah–Yeah!' Amber echoes, still jumping.

Amber always calls Connie *Yeah-Yeah*. Connie wishes she wouldn't. It's cute from the kids but she is Amber's mother-in-law, not her grandmother. She's never said anything, and how could she? Amber is so gormlessly unsuspecting. Connie knows Seb senses her aggravation – most of their irritations are perversely vicarious – but they have never discussed this one.

Connie arrives at the threshold to the back room.

'Jump with me, Yeah-Yeah.' Mack reaches to her in invitation, singing: *'M-M-Messiah, t-take me higher.'*

Connie smiles but doesn't move forward. 'Wow,' she says, 'you've learned *all* the words.'

'You're teasing,' Mack says.

'Possibly. What do you call this kind of music?'

'Pop music.'

'Really? Popular with whom?'

'She is,' says Amber. 'She's just teasing.'

Connie shrugs: perhaps. 'I thought Seb might be home.'

'He's at the shop,' Amber says, puffing. 'He's giving Simmo a break today.'

'Oh? That's nice.'

Simmo hasn't mentioned this to Connie. She backs out, waving to the trampolinists. The refrain follows her down the lane – *M-M-Messiah, t-take me higher* – and Connie catches herself humming this bilious earworm.

Seb arrives at his observation post under the tree in Banksia Avenue about 10:15 a.m. Golden wattle drops on him like dandruff. It's tricky, being a Saturday, because the neighbours are on the street, coming and going. He pretends to read messages on his phone and he natters to anyone passing: 'G'day Gordon ... Hi Di ... It's warming up, ay? ... Swell building this arvo ... How'd you go, girls? ... One goal! That's too bad.'

Half an hour passes. Seb needs to urinate but he doesn't want to go home and alert Amber to his absence from the shop. He has no way of knowing how long this stakeout might take, or whether or not his mother is entertaining today. Her guest might arrive tonight. He might already be inside. How can Seb possibly know? Around-the-clock surveillance is hardly feasible.

He considers that he might do better by watching the rear lane – the family entrance. It irks him, the very idea of her lover coming and going by the back gate. Somehow that would be a greater trespass.

'How're you getting on, Seb?' asks Ron Antrim. 'Anything we can do?'

'We're all good, thanks, Ron. Appreciate your thoughts.' He wishes he could ask to use the Antrims' toilet, but that would be weird. He jigs from foot to foot, hoping Ron isn't noticing.

'How about your mum?'

'I think she's battling on okay,' Seb says, 'but I suppose it won't hurt to ask her. I think she's home now, if you want to knock. It's no problem to knock.'

'Oh, I'll keep that in mind. I have to run now, though.'

Pity.

Seb watches Ron climb into his car, parked rear to kerb. He has no doubt Ron will knock on his mother's door as soon as he possibly can. Because Ron is ceaselessly thoughtful – always has been. He and his wife, Anna, have been in Banksia Avenue for close to fifty years, and Seb was at primary school with their daughter, Christine, and he's friendly enough with her younger brothers, Graeme and Steve, both tradies and regulars at Surfside Hardware.

Six years ago, Anna suffered devastating renal failure. Ron wanted to give her a kidney but they weren't compatible. He sold his electrical supplies business and became her full-time carer throughout her dialysis. Ron and Simmo – two great pillars, in Seb's mind – became a support for each other as they conferred on the challenges of caring for a sick and dying wife. Miranda's MND was certainly terminal but so was Anna's condition unless they found her a donor. A month after Miranda died, they found Anna's match and saved her life.

A sudden and frightful thought possesses Seb. As Ron drives out, smiling in farewell, Seb is thinking his mother is much more than the Antrims' GP. She was their neighbour, friend and emotional support throughout the trial of Anna's long illness. Anna was terribly frail. Perhaps Ron and his mother, united in their despair that Anna would certainly die, made their own connection. It saddens Seb to even consider this possibility, but such connections do happen. It's possible.

Seb experiences a cold, nauseating flutter. Because – no – it is not possible. That cannot have happened, and it was monstrous of him to give it a moment's thought. Ron Antrim is a paragon.

Just after eleven, Simmo strides into Banksia Avenue. He's coming at a cracking pace from Bondi Road, carrying a dazzling bunch of orange orchids. His entrance takes Seb's breath away and he shrinks behind the wattle. He watches as Simmo nears his mother's gate. What else can Seb do but hide, considering he's supposedly covering for Simmo at the shop?

Poor Simmo, though, has no idea. He has come to comfort his best mate's widow and, for all Seb knows, she has her lover with her now. Where might Seb begin to explain it all to Simmo?

But he must. He steps out from behind the wattle. He has no time for equivocation. He has to catch Simmo before he rings the bell. He dashes across the road. Simmo is through the gate and climbing the two steps to the front door.

'Hey!' Seb calls.

It gives Simmo a fright. 'Seb?'

'Sorry.'

'Er, who's got the shop?'

'Gracie's covering for a couple of hours.'

'Oh, goodo then.'

'Yeah.' Seb hovers.

Simmo watches him jig. 'You okay?' Simmo asks.

'Yeah,' Seb says, 'it's just ...' He hovers.

Simmo frowns.

'There's no easy way to say this ...' Seb begins.

Simmo stares at him and waits.

Finally Seb spits it out. 'My mother has a lover.'

Simmo doesn't react. He doesn't say a word. He's incapable of reacting, Seb realises. The poor man is speechless.

'I know, I know,' Seb says, 'it's ridiculous, but I caught them yesterday – in Dad's bed!'

Seb allows Simmo a breath to take in this detail.

'I know what you're thinking – three days after we sent him off. It's deplorable. Unbelievable.'

Simmo is frozen. Seb can't keep still. He needs to piss. Now his phone rings in his bum pocket. He pulls it out to check who's calling. Amber's face fills the screen. Seb goes to decline the call, but Simmo can see it's Amber so Seb decides to answer.

'Can I ring you back, honey?'

'It's me.' It's Mack on his mum's phone.

'Hi, mate.'

'Why aren't you at work? Why have you been hiding?' Mack's voice carries.

'Hey?' Seb asks.

'I saw you, from upstairs. Why were you hiding behind that tree again?'

'I wasn't.'

'Yes you were. Like yesterday. Hiding.'

Seb looks to Simmo, defensive.

'Hey, Mack Mac, I'll be home in a tick, okay.' Seb ends the call. 'I didn't want to tell you,' he tells Simmo. 'It's just, y'know, it's possible this bloke's in there now, as we speak.'

Simmo himself is yet to speak.

'What are you going to do?' Seb asks him.

Simmo finally answers. 'Your mum's expecting me for a cuppa. I suppose I'd better go in.'

'Of course, of course. If she's expecting you.'

'She is.'

'So he mustn't be,' Seb says. 'Inside, I mean.'

Simmo nods.

Seb backs out of the front garden and closes the gate behind him. He watches Simmo over the gate and slowly backs away as he rings the doorbell. One house up, he hears his mother's welcome and is puzzled by it. But Seb can't think. He really needs to piss.

★★★

Connie finds Simmo sprouting orchids on her doorstep.

'What a lovely surprise!' she pronounces.

Simmo puts a finger to his lips to shoosh her. She is puzzled. She leans into him and kisses him on the mouth. Simmo recoils and shooshes her again, then pushes her inside and closes the door behind them.

'It's Seb!' Simmo tells Connie. 'He's just outside.'

'Oh?'

'He told me all about yesterday. He has no idea it was me.'

'Good.' She kisses him again, longer this time.

'Why is it good?' he asks. 'We'd better tell him.'

'We will,' Connie says. 'Just not now.'

'I don't want to lie to him. The longer we leave it, the madder he'll get.'

Connie doesn't say when.

'Soon?' Simmo pleads.

'Soon-ish,' she offers.

'Soon,' he presses her.

'Orange orchids!' she says, and takes them from him. 'I don't think I've seen them orange before. Great timing. I was just getting started on all those dead flowers.'

★★★

On his front doorstep, Seb frets that he'll wet himself. He's about to put his key in the lock when he decides this deviation will arouse Amber's suspicion. He prolongs his torture by walking back down the street, along the dunny lane and around the back.

Amber, at the kitchen bench, frowns at his arrival.

'I'm busting,' he declares, and makes a beeline for the downstairs toilet. He has no time to shut the door behind him or to raise the toilet seat.

His heavy flow alerts Mack, who appears at the door.

'Who were you hiding from?'

'I wasn't hiding. I was just texting some people.'

Mack's look is reproachful. Seb is ashamed. His excuse is so lame it sets off a six-year-old's bullshit detector.

'That's a long wee, Dad.'

'Yeah.'

Amber appears and takes one step into the confined space. 'You shouldn't hold it so long,' she says.

'I know. I was just …' Seb isn't sure what he wants to suggest he was *just* … he shakes off and zips up his shorts.

Amber and Mack watch without really watching.

'Who's at the shop?' Amber asks.

'Gracie. Just a couple of hours.'

'Give her the whole day.'

Seb washes his hands. He has a thought – something plausible to tell Amber. 'I was just chasing up the video from the funeral.'

'Is it ready already?' she asks. 'He's quick.'

'Not quite. He'll send us a rough cut, on email. Tonight maybe.'

'He's so clever, our Robbie. So generous.'

Seb dries his hands. 'I'll insist he take some payment.'

'Pat says he won't.'

Robbie Watson does Pastor Pat's productions free of charge, and now it seems Ted's funeral.

'Don't want to stretch the friendship,' Seb says.

Amber goes to the toilet-paper roll, breaks off two sheets and wipes Seb's dribble from the seat. She flushes away the paper.

'Sorry,' he says.

She goes to the vanity unit, dispenses liquid soap into her palms and washes her hands.

'I was making chicken salad,' she says.

'Nice.'

'Can we go for a surf tonight, Dad?'

'Sure.' Seb squeezes past them and heads for the stairs. 'I'll be down in a bit.'

He goes to his study and quietly calls Robbie Watson, to establish his alibi in retrospect. Robbie did say something at the funeral about having a rough cut ready by Sunday, so Seb is merely following up.

'How about tomorrow arvo?' Robbie suggests.

'No rush. Whenever.'

'After church.'

★★★

Simmo and Connie remove the last of the stinking funeral flowers from the house. He fossicks under the sink and finds a deodorising spray, which he squirts in thick jets about the living room. Connie puts Simmo's orchids in a tall vase before she begins to head upstairs. She is on the final step before she looks back to him, still at the bottom.

'We don't have to,' she says.

'No, we don't, but let's.'

Under the whirl of her fan, Connie watches perspiration evaporating on his skin. She runs a finger along his arm, smudging a film of moisture before the fan can do its work.

'Still feels weird,' he says.

'What?'

'Sweating in Ted's bed.'

'Don't worry. I told him.'

'Who? Ted?'

'I left a message on his phone, about us.'

'I don't think he's checking his messages.'

'No.'

'That's a bit wacky, Con.'

'I know.'

They giggle, which sounds like music to Connie.

'He'd be happy for us,' she ventures.

'Do you think?'

'I do. And Miranda, too. I think she'd be happy.'

'Now, possibly,' Simmo says. 'A few days after her funeral? Probably not.'

'It was me who told her how wonderful you were. I wouldn't have introduced you otherwise. I told her everything.'

'I know you did.'

'She'd be expecting this.'

Connie reaches for her phone. She scrolls through her videos and finds the various takes of their Christmas Day singalong. She holds it up so Simmo can see the screen, then presses play on another clip of Ted at the piano. He's tinkering while chatting to someone just off camera. Cutlery clinks on plates and conversation rises and falls in the background. There are exclamations of endorsement for the pudding, which prompt Ted to request a mouthful. A hand enters the shot and delivers a spoonful to his opened mouth. Cream glistens on his lips while he keeps rambling and running through a rapid chord progression.

'Sinatra always made it sound so simple,' he's saying, 'but this is really tricky because he has to manage so many crazy chords into each phrase. See ...' Ted plays and hums and mumble-sings to demonstrate. 'That's four chords for five words: F-major-seventh, D-minor-seventh, G-minor-seventh and C-seventh, see! And then F-major-seventh to F-sharp-seven-diminished. That's mad!'

Connie hits pause on the video.

'Mad!' says Simmo.

'Obsessive!' says Connie. 'Who's his victim?'

'Not sure. José from the Surfside Singers? He's the only who'd appreciate the music lesson. He carried on like this in the shop, as if I had the slightest interest.' Simmo smiles at the memory, then asks: 'Did he tell you all about his special fetish for diminished-seventh chords?'

'Oh yes. The *drama* of them.'

'The drama! We had a quiet Friday arvo a few weeks back and he spent the whole time telling me how he'd discovered, quite by accident, after all these years of playing diminished-sevenths, that there were actually only three of the bloody things on the entire keyboard. He'd been playing them up and down the piano – a diminished-seventh beginning for every note, or so he thought. Then one day he was messing around with these chords and suddenly he got it. So many of those chords sounded the same, regardless of which note he started with. And then he worked it out by ear: you got the same combination of four notes whether you started with an A or a B or a G or whatever – I can't remember the actual notes – and he goes, "Bloody hell, Simmo, it's taken me half a lifetime to figure it out: something that seemed so complicated had been very simple all along." He felt so stupid. He's going, "There are only twelve notes. That's not so many to get your head around. What was I doing all these years?"'

'Torture.'

'For Ted or me?'

'You.'

'Sometimes when he gibbered on like that, I'd pull down a rivet gun from the shelf and hold it to my head.'

Connie shrieks.

'He got the message. But mainly I let him gibber.'

They watch the fan turning.

'I'm missing his gibber,' Simmo says.

'Me too.'

Simmo pulls the sheet to his chin. It seems suddenly cooler, which is a relief. Connie takes the remote control from her bedside table and lowers the fan speed.

'I'm not sure I want to carry on without him,' Simmo says.

'That sounds drastic.'

'The business, I mean. It'd be quite a deal to give it up, but you know how it was with Ted. Even when business was good, we were never really in it for the money. We were there for the life, for the beach, for the friendship. Now it's a shitty little business and he's not here, I don't know why I'd stay in it.'

'There's Seb.'

'I like working with Seb, I really do. But his heart's never been in hardware.'

Connie sits up. 'There might be a way out,' she declares.

Simmo frowns.

'I'm not supposed to know this,' she says, 'but Seb wants us to sell our shares to him.'

Simmo doesn't react for a long interval, then says: 'You knew?'

'What do you mean, *you knew*? Of course I knew, but you knew, too?'

'Ted told me, but he said to say nothing.'

'You too? What else did he tell you not to mention?'

Simmo shrugs.

'Did he tell you why Seb wanted to buy us out?'

'Because he wants to turn the shop into a church.'

'Right,' says Connie. 'Well, I suppose we both needed to know.'

'Ted and I thought there was no way you'd ever agree – y'know – to a church.'

'Did you just?' She's peeved they never put this theory to her. 'Well,' she says, 'I still mightn't.'

'You just said there might be an easy way out.'

'*Might.* I said *might.*'

Simmo suppresses a laugh. She can read him. He's amused that she's indignant.

'There's no rush,' he says.

He's good at reading her, too, she realises. He won't push her into a corner.

'Do you think that's all it is between you and Seb?' he asks.

'What?'

'The churchy stuff.'

'I wish that was all.'

Simmo awaits her elaboration.

'His first memories, if you asked him, would have to be of Ted, not me. I don't doubt it. Ted was so good for all those years I was studying. He effectively raised Seb without me, so I could cope. You know that. You saw it.'

'It wasn't that bad.'

'It was. Apart from expressing gallons of milk, I was absent. Ted put you on bottle-feed duties, too.'

'On occasion.'

'And still I only scraped through medicine. I had to put in stupid hours just to get over the line. Ted made it possible. You, too. Ted was a natural and I wasn't. It didn't take Seb too long to sort it out – who mattered most to him. Ted could see this was becoming a problem, so he suggested I do the bedtime story at least a couple of nights a week, and I agreed. You remember how that went, don't you? Seb wasn't even three. What a performance. "Daddy reads the story!" And he was right: Daddy always had. Why spoil it? I can't begin to describe how humiliating it was to go *ee i ee i oh* to your infant son while he refused to be amused. *With a moo-moo here and a moo-moo there.* "Not funny, Mummy."'

'He didn't know any better.'

'Of course he didn't. I'm not blaming Seb. I blame myself. I'm just saying, if you're asking where this all began, it goes way back before the God thing.' Connie hits play on the video. 'I'm glad we're making up for lost time, you and me,' she says, 'but I fear it's too late with Seb.'

'You've got loads of time.'

'Easy for you to say. I'm old and you're not.'

'I told you, none of that matters.'

'It will in five or ten years.'

Simmo goes silent. Five or ten years? Connie realises she's got way ahead of herself, but she's said it now.

'I know it's only been a couple of days,' she says, 'but I'm not muckin' around here, Tommy Sim.'

Simmo props himself on an elbow to look at her. With his free hand he traces the contours of her face. It makes her quiver.

'Neither am I, Connie Blunt. Neither am I.'

★★★

'Here we go, Mack. This one's ours.'

In the last hour of daylight, towards the south end of the beach, they're in a cluster of forty surfers competing for the remains of a nor-east swell. A clean two-footer shapes up for father and son, who are paddling the same longboard. They're at the head of the line-up and Seb paddles hard to secure their position. A young punk attempts to hustle them for it.

'Oi!' Mack cries, calling the teenager off the wave.

Seb is shocked by his son's gall, and surprised when the punk concedes the wave to its rightful claimants. It peaks into an A-frame. Seb and Mack feel the ocean's pull and they pop to their feet as one, as if wired to the same command system. They bear right, Seb steering from the back, cruising in the same easy style preferred by Ted. Up front, Mack makes a light-footed show of walking the plank.

★★★

Connie spots them from the promenade, where she's weaving a path through the crowd towards her 7 p.m. meeting with Gracie at the Pavilion. This could be awkward. She doesn't want to bump into Seb tonight, not even with the kids as a buffer. She watches his and Mack's wave. A feathery wisp of white trails their languid turns. Connie is struck by how similar this scene is to Ted with young Seb, thirty and more years ago. It's sweet, of course it is, but Connie can't understand why they're not wearing helmets so soon after Ted's accident. She can see that just one surfer in the pack tonight is wearing one, but Seb should know better. These longboards are lethally heavy. And yet, had Ted survived his bump, she knows he wouldn't have listened to her. He'd be out there now with the boys, no helmet.

'Yeah-Yeah,' Gracie calls.

Her granddaughter is sitting on the steps to the sand. At twenty paces, they light each other up.

'You look better,' Gracie says.

'Better than what? Than crap?'

'I just meant you look good.'

'I know you did. You're too nice.'

Gracie stands and throws her arms around Connie, who responds by holding her unusually tight.

'I'm not embarrassing you?' Connie asks.

'Never.' Gracie perpetuates the hug. 'I found the splitter,' she says. 'See? We can both listen.'

The gadget is attached to Gracie's phone. Her earphones are already plugged into it. Connie's earphones are loose around her neck and she plugs into the second port on the splitter.

'Ready?' Gracie says.

'Yeah.'

They hold hands and cross the sand to the shore, shambling to a one-two bass and trilling electric guitars. Connie skews left towards the north end, away from Seb and Mack.

★★★

'We'd better head in,' Seb tells his son. 'Mum'll be hungry.'

'Angry?'

'Hungry, but that can make her angry.'

'One more!' Mack pleads.

Seb yields. 'One more.'

He can hear his six-year-old self pleading with his dad. Always one more. Ted was a pushover, too. It was Mack who insisted they share the one board tonight. Seb had been strapping their short-boards to the Range Rover when Mack requested the longboard.

They paddle back towards the line-up. A wave rises thirty metres ahead of them and they paddle harder in an effort to climb the peak before it breaks. Mack is meant to suppress his impulse to kick when they're on the longboard, but now he kicks hard and his heel collects the wound under Seb's eye.

'Ah!'

'Sorry,' Mack says.

'It's okay.'

Mack swivels to look. 'It's bleeding,' he says.

'Don't worry,' Seb says. 'Paddle.'

They paddle hard but they're too late. The wave breaks on them and throws them off. Soon they surface and they're bobbing in the whitewash, and Mack panics.

'The blood!' he cries.

'We'll be right.'

'Sharks.'

'It's okay, mate. That's just Yeah–Yeah.'

Mack clambers onto the board and shrinks into the middle. He looks over the side for sharks.

'Get on, Dad, quick! Let's go in.'

Seb slides on from the back.

'Paddle!' Mack commands. 'Paddle fast!'

Seb does as he's told.

'Faster!'

Mack doesn't put a limb in the water. Seb picks up a little wave and leaps to his feet and rides the whitewash.

Mack stays on his belly and cries: 'Get down! It's not funny. You're bleeding.'

'We're fine, buddy.'

Seb rides it till they're beached. Mack runs off the nose of the board onto dry land. Seb dawdles in the shallows, wrapping the legrope around the board.

'Get out, Dad. Get out!'

Seb carries the board to Mack and offers him his free hand. Mack clings to it and sobs in spasms and shivers as they trudge across the beach.

'You shouldn't do that. You're still bleeding.'

'I'm sorry.' Seb regrets he wasn't more sensitive so soon after Mack lost his Pop to the surf.

'Look!' Mack says.

'What?'

'Yeah–Yeah and Gracie.'

Seb looks and they're quite a distance to the north, hand in hand and dancing at the water's edge.

'They're silly,' Mack says. 'Let's surprise them.'

'They're listening to their music. Leave them be.'

'I want to hear.' Mack takes off at a sprint.

Seb stays put. He watches Mack creep up behind them and go *boo*! They jump out of their skins, or they pretend to. Seb watches his mother and daughter take turns hoisting Mack from the sand. Then Gracie shares one earphone with Mack. The three of them hold hands and sway to whatever it is that Seb isn't hearing.

It's a long tune. Eventually Gracie instructs Mack to go back. She waves faintly at her dad while Mack scurries towards him.

'They've played the same song five times,' Mack reports. 'It goes ...' He plays air guitar and sings the riff: *Diddle-diddle-diddle-diddle-it.*

'Can't say I know that one,' Seb says.

'It's Television,' Mack says.

'It's on television?'

'No, it's a band called Television.'

'That's a funny name.'

'That's what I said. Later it goes ... *Diddle-diddle-diddle-diddle-it ...*' He's got the rock 'n' roll swagger.

Seb enters a Google search on his phone, the words 'band' and 'Television'. And now he twigs. This is their *Marquee Moon*.

Tonight's moon is not one of those. It's an unexceptional pale sliver over the water, but Gracie and his mother have resumed their baying at this humdrum moon.

157

★★★

Connie squeezes Gracie's hand.

'I told you this story, didn't I? When I dragged your pop along to Television in New York.'

'You did, more than once. Tell me again.'

'Of course I did. He really, really hated them. "That bloke sings like he's being garrotted." And I said, "That's why he sounds so good." For my penance, he made me sit through *Ain't Misbehavin'* on Broadway. I pretended to barely tolerate it, but it was wonderful. I was so besotted, I'd have enjoyed *Disney on Parade* in his company.'

They're still squeezing hands.

'Let's get takeaway and watch your wedding,' Gracie says.

Connie stalls. 'I don't know. It's such a performance – digging out the video and that old VHS player. Do we even have the plug to connect it to the old telly?'

'Yes, you do.'

'Such a rigmarole.'

'That's the fun of it,' Gracie says. 'I'll do it.'

Connie hesitates then says, 'Okay.'

They put their earphones back in. Connie feels rueful to be so exhilarated. She knows she has no cause to be guilty. She is and she isn't. The last splinters of daylight leave her and Gracie ankle-deep and singing flat. A swimmer passes, apparently amused by their off-key reverie.

★★★

The bride alights from an immaculate mint-green FX Holden. Her wedding gown is a halter neck. No trail, no veil. No frills.

Gracie has found the video on the shelf in her grandfather's study and reconnected the VCR to the old television in her father's boyhood bedroom downstairs. They lie on his bed and eat takeaway noodles from cardboard boxes. Connie watches her twenty-nine-year-old self proceed, on her father's arm, towards the vestibule of St Peter's Catholic Church, Tocumwal. She's satisfied that, if she had her time again, she'd choose the same no-fuss dress and endure the same ribald asides about its off-whiteness. But she wouldn't agree again to a church ceremony. Ted wanted the whole shebang and, at the time, she wasn't fussed to argue. She was faithless by then, but not yet zealously so.

The picture is jittery, the sound tinny. Connie remembers her dad buying the newfangled video camera in time for the wedding. It was quite an investment. She recalls the untrained camera operator, recruited for the occasion, getting too close for comfort with the hulking lens, even at the altar.

The exchange of vows is mainly inaudible, nonetheless. Outside the church, the shaky camera captures wedding guests clustering according to blood ties and other affiliations. Lochie, the groomsman, resists the cameraman's attempts to corral him into the frame with his twin, the groom. Lochie is already unsmiling, stockier than Ted and a couple of inches shorter. If they'd ever been identical they weren't by now.

The Tocumwal footy clubhouse scrubs up for the reception. Extravagantly arranged flowers gladden the drab hall.

'Pop-Pop's so young,' Gracie says.

That's how Gracie and Mack distinguish their great-grandfather from Ted. Mick Blunt gets two Pops.

'He'd be fifty-two, maybe fifty-three.'

Mick's speech is short and sweet and almost unbearable. 'My only sadness today,' he says, voice cracking, 'is that Val can't be here to see her girl so happy.'

'He'd already been alone for a long time,' Gracie says.

'Almost fifteen years.'

Clem Blunt, Ted's best man, is more handsome than Connie remembers her brother. Ted wasn't so close to Clem at school but they became closer when Ted returned from university and both played for the Tocumwal Bloods. Clem's speech recounts

Connie's connivance with Trish Mayer, her London nursing mate, to 'chance upon' Ted in New York. Trish, having travelled from London to be maid of honour at the wedding, speaks briefly after Clem and adds adornments to this story.

'Why wouldn't Dad have used all this great material for the eulogy?' Gracie wonders.

Ted speaks next. He thanks Trish for her conspiracy with Connie in New York.

'I'd never met *the one* – the woman I thought I could make a life with. I think I knew that night: Connie was *the one*.'

Gracie swoons at this, as ever, but it's always the toughest part for Connie – rewatching Ted's speech and hers. Hers is longer than the others'.

'That the bride should be speaking at all,' she begins, 'has become a matter of some controversy in Tocumwal. I'm reliably informed of this by Mary Oxley at the bank. She filled me in on the chatter yesterday. "Connie," she said, "I'll be frank with you. I couldn't care less. I'm just relieved you won't finish up a spinster, after all." Well, Mary, thank you for that lovely thought. We're only sorry you can't be with us today. We had to draw the line somewhere with the invitations.'

Gracie snorts. 'You were so sassy.'

The bride recounts that her groom had paid her no attention when they were kids in Tocumwal.

'It's not that he never looked in my direction. He did on the odd occasion. It's just that he looked straight through me. I was invisible to him. Until Manhattan.

'Which brings me, strangely, to my mum, who never went to Manhattan. Val was thirty-four, not so much older than I am now, when she died. I was only thirteen, but old enough to remember her well. Clem and I used to watch Mum and Dad dancing in the kitchen, Dad grinning like he was the luckiest bloke on the planet. The way he looked at her – wow! I remember thinking:

One day I'll marry a man who looks at me the way Dad looks at Mum.

'Then the years passed too quickly, and soon enough I was in my late twenties, thinking: Maybe not. Maybe that can't happen to everyone. And it can't. Of course it can't.

'Then, Manhattan. Four or five nights after our first meeting there, Ted and I were on Bleecker Street. We'd seen a show. The traffic was thick so I was watching where I was walking, eyes straight ahead. We came to a don't-walk sign, and we stopped. I was watching the sign, waiting for it to go "Walk", but I somehow became aware of Ted's eyes upon me. I turned and I caught him, just looking. And I thought, that's it. That's the way Dad looked at Mum.'

The bride raises her glass. 'And here we are,' she says. 'Please be upstanding and raise your glasses. To Mum and Dad. To Val and Mick.'

Gracie cries. 'Gets me every time.'

Connie, dry-eyed, doesn't mention the parts she omitted from this account, not even the part that had featured in her speech at Lochie and Tory's wedding a little over two years later, but which they had edited out of their video. Connie wishes she could tell Gracie the rest.

# 5.
# SABBATH

Six hundred voices lift Seb's spirits. For all of his reservations about Pastor Pat's church, he is roused by the united exultation of its fellowship. Seb sings along.

*We'll follow Him*
*Day and night*
*We'll honour Him*
*His power and might*

Amber and Mack, too, sing the rocking hymn, as do their friends Kerry and Ant Waldren and their kids Aaron and Luke and Jemimah, a row in front, as they are every Sunday in this vast assembly hall, the Congress of God Church. The congregants are on their feet and the chorus is led by Lakepi, a Tongan giant at centre stage with a Madonna mic latched to his ear, whose soulful tenor is leavened by his wife Avoca's lilting harmony, a third higher. The six-piece band behind them, with its two full drum kits, is going full-tilt boogie. A skipping bassline spurs the legions to dance on the spot, and upon each repetition of the word *power* the dual kick drums impel them to jump as one.

Seb wonders, as he often does, where he'll find such fine singers and musicians for his DIY Church. When the time comes, this may prove to be his greatest hurdle. Without a solid house band it will be difficult to recruit worshippers and harder still to keep them, particularly young ones.

Seb jumps on *power*.

From the rhythm section up. That's how he'll build his band. Find a great drummer and bass player and the rest will come. But nothing so showy as this outfit. One drummer – snare and cymbal – will suffice.

Seb wouldn't dream of attempting to poach Pastor Pat's players. Not that they'd defect. Seb's looser interpretations of the scripture are a harder sell than Pat's gospel truths. The DIY Church will appeal to a different constituency.

Only now does Seb hear the sounds coming from his mouth. He's adding sevenths to Avoca's thirds, and he's turning heads because it sounds sweet. He's been doing it inadvertently because it's a gift – from his father and from his Heavenly Father – and he gives thanks because it's infectious and voices around him are following his lead, and Lakepi can hear it welling up from the floor. He gives Seb a thumbs-up and they all rejoice.

*We'll follow the path that Jesus paved*
*The only path to be saved*
*We'll never stray, we'll follow His light*
*We'll honour Him, his power and might*

Kerry Waldren turns and smiles at Seb to acknowledge his influence. She turns back to the stage, raises her arms and jumps with the kick drum and shimmies to the cymbals. Her firm glutes quiver under her dress. She wears it like Glad Wrap. It's skin-tone this week, or a match for her fake tan, but she has a seemingly endless supply of these Sunday-best body-huggers. The colour changes but all are cut to cling to the body that she sculpts at the gym where she works out with Amber.

Amber sings with her eyes shut. Kerry turns again and smirks at Seb, because she knows – or it seems to Seb she knows – that he's looking at her arse. Why else shake it at him, Sabbath after Sabbath?

He invokes Matthew 5:28 – *I tell you that anyone who looks at a woman lustfully has already committed adultery with her in his heart* – but he can't deny the swelling in his loins.

Amber's eyes remain mercifully shut, as do Mack's. Seb's son is mimicking his mum, God bless him, and they both sing in veneration.

Seb tells himself he didn't ask for the distraction of Kerry's arse. Which is the voice of Satan, he knows it is. The Devil wants him to make excuses. The Devil knows that Seb, in the rankest recesses of his mind, is lifting Kerry's dress and fucking her. These images occupy milliseconds but they recur, even as Seb prays to be chastened. He's fucking Kerry, the wife of Ant, his brother in Christ. It's subliminal. He does not ask for it or encourage it, but he and the Devil and the Lord Jesus Christ know what's happening. Satan would trivialise it as a thought crime. Seb agrees that it is, yet what greater blasphemy than to allow such filth to colonise his mind and body while his family worships alongside him?

Seb hears a gear change in Mack's voice, then Amber's. They, too, are following his pitch. He glances sideways and Amber nudges him with her elbow and smiles. *Listen to us,* she's saying. *Aren't we magnificent together?*

All sing. All rock and sway and jump – in a singular spasm – to the kick drums, and all chant *power!* With each cycle of this incantation, the euphoria mounts. Seb observes it. It works. Mass hysteria works. Amber and Mack are as rapt as the rest.

Seb, too, can be a sucker for a tune. But his voice fades. He senses its retreat. And he resolves that his church will do without the hocus-pocus. There'll be music, yes, but none of this trickery.

Seb turns to his family. Amber jumps and on landing her

buttocks quiver under her dress, much like Kerry's, and he has an impulse to look behind him. He finds Jeremy Digby, another brother in Christ, looking in the direction of Amber's arse. Seb can't be sure he's looking at it though. Jeremy looks elated, yet inscrutable. But don't they all? Almost every face under this roof has that look. Who is pious and who is perverted? They can't all be leching after the piece of arse in the next row.

The hymn gallops to its final chorus.

*We'll never stray, we'll follow His light*
*We'll honour Him, his power and might*
*We'll follow Him, every hour*
*We'll honour him, his might and power*

All jump again on *power,* but this time the song ends abruptly on this word: singers, guitars, keyboard, bass and kick drums all come to a synchronised, heart-stopping finish, and the lights go out. Which leaves the faithful suspended in darkness, in ecstatic silence, in readiness for Pastor Pat's sermon. Pat appears from stage left under a roaming spotlight. It follows him as he struts to the absent beat, to which the congregation keeps rocking on its feet. They know this routine and they keep time, counting down the silent beat, until Pastor Pat gives the cue and the kick drums shatter the void and he leaps and proclaims with them all: 'Power!'

'Oh yes, oh yes, oh yes,' Pat exhales into his Madonna mic. '*Power!* We know all about it, don't we? We know power, good and bad. Many of us have been on the receiving end of power in the wrong hands: the bad boss, the power-hungry team leader, the violent husband. If you've had some of the power some of the time, you'll know it can be used for bad, but also for good.

'Today I want to tell you a story about a greater power, the power that can be yours whenever you need to call upon it, no matter where you are or who you are, no matter your age or your rank. I don't care if you sweep the factory floor. I don't care if you're dumpster-diving for your next meal. The power that will lift you is the power of the Holy Spirit. What did I say?'

All respond: 'The Holy Spirit!'

All but Seb.

'What'd I say?' Pastor Pat demands again.

This time Seb answers with the rest: 'The Holy Spirit!'

'So let me tell you a story about that power,' Pat says. 'Just last Monday, I arrived in the city for a long-planned meeting with some fellow preachers. We'd come from far and wide to exchange ideas, swap notes and, y'know, tell some war stories. We're only human. We like to talk shop, we preachers, so I was looking forward to our pow-wow. But I was not ten metres from entering that meeting when I was stopped on the street outside. An old man with a long grey beard and a dirty overcoat had taken up residence on the footpath. And he was laughing at me.'

Here we go, Seb is thinking. Another of Pat's fables. They're always crowd-pleasers, his homilies, but he's never been one to let facts get in the way of a good sermon.

'This broken old man was there with all his worldly possessions … a swag, a large plastic bag containing nothings but packets of potato chips – y'know, all the essential food groups – and he had a bottle, almost empty. Whatever rocket fuel sustained him, he reeked of it. And he kept laughing at me. It was a sinister laugh. He was mocking me because I was carrying a Bible full of Stick-It Notes. An array of these sticky notes – yellow, pink and blue – jutted from my Bible because that's the way I roll. I have this colour-coded system for the passages I think might be topical for our discussions. I explained all this to the old man and he told me: "Stick it where it fits, preacher man." I'm sorry but they were his words. What was I to do? I turned to Acts 9 and the story of Saul – the persecutor of early Christians – on the road to Damascus.

I began to read, but – blow me down – the old man spoke over me and quoted the same Bible story. He knew it by rote, the story of the risen Christ appearing to Saul – and Saul's conversion to become the apostle Paul, praise the Lord.'

'Praise the Lord!'

'And when the old man was done he sneered: "I should know. I'm the son of a preacher." Yes, his father had been a Baptist minister, but he said: "My father's gone to Hell." I wasn't sure how to respond, so I asked how he could be so sure. He answered – a language warning – "Because wherever that arsehole has gone, that's Hell. If it wasn't before, it is now."

'So I was thinking: This is a very damaged man, to hate his long-dead dad so intensely. What could a father have done – what could a man of God have done – to make his own son detest him all these years later? By now I was running quite late for my meeting, but I had to choose: go inside and talk *about* saving souls, or stay out here on the street and attempt to *save* just one soul. So what did I choose to do?'

'Street … you stayed on the street … one soul.'

'I stayed on the street. But this was going to be a hard nut to crack, so I asked God: "What in your name am I going to do?" And the Lord said to me, "Pat, this is not your moment for preaching. This is your time for listening." Listening? "Yes, Pat, listening." So that's what I did. I sat down with the old man on his swag, on the footpath, and I listened to his story. And what a story it was.'

An image appears on a big screen behind Pastor Pat. It is of a decrepit old drunk with a white beard, as Pat has described, sprawled on his swag.

'This is him, as I found him. His name is Brendan Buckley.'

This is outrageous. Seb cannot believe Pat's audacity. He has photographed a street drunk, made up a name for him and fabricated his whole story. It's fraud. This time Pat has gone way too far.

'But I'm not going to tell you Brendan's story,' Pastor Pat says. 'Brendan is.'

A collective gasp.

'That's right. Brendan has come to be with us today.'

A soft drum roll. The spotlight drifts from Pastor Pat and leaves him in darkness, panning to stage left. A lean, clean-shaven man steps into the light. He looks younger than fifty. The spotlight follows him as he walks to Pat, who says: 'Meet Brendan Buckley.'

Murmurs rise from the floor: 'No! ...Yeah! ... Hallelujah!'

'Oh yes it is,' says Pat. 'Our own small miracle.'

Seb doesn't know what to think. Should he be ashamed for questioning Pat, now that Brendan Buckley, transfigured, is preparing to speak? Or has Pat paid a drunk to bathe and shave and masquerade as a saved man? That might not be beneath him. The extra money in the plate today will cover this sideshow.

Brendan tells the story of a preacher who beat his wife senseless and his son, too, whenever the boy dared to intervene to protect his mother.

'My father beat Christ into me, then he beat Christ out of me.'

Seb listens in a fog of uncertainty, yet slowly he becomes convinced that Brendan is telling his story straight.

'I'm only here today because Pastor Pat gave me the time of day and listened to me say what I'm telling you now. Nobody's really done that before. I accepted Pat's kind offer of a shower and a feed, and for the past five or six days I've been cleaning up and drying out. I've come here to see what might happen next.'

If Brendan Buckley is a huckster, Seb is a dupe. So is Amber, who's wiping tears from her cheek. The remainder of the service is a blur for Seb. He watches Brendan watching what happens next: random convulsions in the mosh pit, the possession of the devout as they speak in tongues. They babble: 'Ala-ma-da-ka-shata, la-ma-shanda ...la-bada-soom-didi-da-la-shamba ...' Brendan is deadpan, just as Seb is determined to remain during these moments of the

Holy Spirit's purported domination of the willing. Seb once spoke in tongues. Now he abstains. He remembers submitting to it, and that possession feeling true, but now he believes he was acting and he considers it – at best – a kind of mass hypnosis. At worst, he believes, it's a contest between self-aggrandising fakers.

And yet Brendan Buckley is clearly grateful to be in this company, and sober. Who is Seb to question Pat in this particular matter? Seb hears this as God's direct admonishment. He must accept that Pat, on this occasion, has done something good and sincere.

The band plays its finale and Seb joins the slow shuffle out of the auditorium. He bumps into Robbie Watson, who says he'll be making a few edits on the funeral video and emailing it by early afternoon. Seb thinks how nice it'll be to crash on the couch and watch it with Amber and Mack.

Outside, he's not sure what to think when Amber asks Ant and Kerry and the kids to lunch. He is further confounded when Amber steps away from their huddle to clutch the arm of Brendan Buckley. She drags him into their circle and extends the invitation to Brendan.

'Too kind,' says the six-day-sober drunk.

Seb hears himself agreeing: *Too kind*. Once again he registers the Lord's reprimand. He takes Brendan's arm.

'We insist.'

★★★

'G'day, Dad,' says Connie. She's swivelling in Ted's office chair, from which she calls the nursing home at Tocumwal most Sundays.

'Val?' asks Mick Blunt.

'No, it's Connie. Your daughter.'

'My girl's Val.'

'That was your wife, Dad. Val was my mum. I'll show you the pictures when I come.'

'When?'

'Soon. What's news, Dad?'

'No rain, that's for sure.'

'Oh? On the news they said you'd had half an inch.'

'Likely story.'

'The nurse on the front desk said Clem was with you. Could you put him on?'

'Are you Clem?'

Connie can hear her brother confirming he is Clem.

Mick Blunt is ninety-four and has advanced dementia. Clem is seventy-three, Ted's age. He's recently retired from the stock and station agency he took over from his father, and handed it to his son, Matt, who's a couple of years younger than Seb. Clem has arrived to take Mick home for their ritual Sunday roast. He wrestles the phone from his father's grasp.

'G'day, Con.'

'Hiya. He sounds a bit off today.'

'He's fightin' fit, although it's raining even as we speak.'

'He knew me last week.'

'Comes and goes. When I came in today he asked after his son – Ted.'

'Oh dear, what'd you tell him?'

'I said he was well.'

'Shit. I'd better come down, like now-ish.'

'Don't rush it. Give yourself a break.'

'It'll be a break. I've got the locum at the surgery, so it might as well be now. I might get Gracie to come with me – girls' road trip.'

'That'd be nice.'

'Put Dad back on.'

'Hello?' Mick says.

'Me again.'

'That you, Val?'

'Hello, gorgeous. What's news?'

'No bloody rain, that's for sure.'

'What's for lunch today, Dad?'

'Mutton, roast potatoes, peas and gravy.'

Clem is probably stretching to lamb these days, but it's all mutton dressed as hogget to Mick Blunt.

'Sounds like heaven, Dad.'

★★★

Brendan Buckley sits in the back of the Range Rover with Mack, who interrogates him about life as a street sleeper.

'Is it really cold?'

'Can be.'

'Where do you keep your stuff?'

'I have no stuff.'

'Where do you go to the toilet?'

'Wherever I like.'

Brendan sniggers and so does Mack. Seb gives his son a pleading look in the rear-vision mirror: enough questions. Brendan sees this and changes the subject.

'It's pretty new.'

'What's that?' asks Seb.

'The car. Can still smell the leather, fresh off the production line.'

'Yeah.'

'Lovely. You've worked hard for it. You deserve it.'

*Bullshit*, Seb is thinking. He finds their guest's sudden smarm repulsive. As they roll down Bondi Road, Brendan asks Mack for their address, then requests that Seb drop him off.

'Just by the shops there'll do. Need to pick up a little something.'

'Don't worry,' says Amber. 'We have all we need.'

'I won't be long.'

Seb relents and pulls into the kerb. Amber flashes him a worried look, but he shrugs. What's he supposed to do? Activate the child lock? He gestures to it and she rolls her eyes. Brendan gets out and takes off at a trot.

'He's funny,' Mack says.

Ant, Kerry and their kids are waiting when Seb pulls up in Banksia Avenue. They ask after Brendan.

'He won't be long,' Seb says.

But he is. Forty-five minutes pass before the doorbell chimes. Seb answers and Brendan, grinning, is carrying a bottle of red wine in one hand and a bottle of white in the other.

'Something for the ladies,' he explains, thrusting the white at Seb. 'Nicely chilled.'

'You're on the wagon,' Seb says.

'Too right!' He hands Seb the red. 'This is for you.'

He's been drinking beer. Seb can smell it on him and wonders how much beer someone needs to drink so quickly to stink of it. A twenty-dollar note protrudes from Brendan's jeans pocket. As Seb approaches the kitchen with their guest in trail, Amber has her head down, looking into her phone.

'Oh look, honey,' she's saying, 'it's arrived from Robbie – the link to the funeral video. We can all watch it after lunch.'

'Who died?' Brendan asks.

Amber looks up, alarmed. It's clear to her, too, that Pastor Pat's reforming vagrant is half-cut. Seb puts the wine on the kitchen island. Amber notes Brendan's offering with an ambiguous grin, which Seb translates as distress.

'For the ladies,' Brendan says again. 'Pinot grigio.'

'Not for me, thanks,' Amber says.

Kerry indicates a small measure between her thumb and forefinger. Brendan cracks the screw cap, then makes a beeline for a glass-fronted cabinet containing the best crystal. He selects the biggest glasses and pours half the bottle into two of them.

'Anybody else?' he asks.

Ant and Seb decline. Brendan passes Kerry her glass, then takes a greedy slug from his.

'Just to wash down lunch,' he explains.

★★★

The study is glum, the curtains drawn to shield the computer screen from the afternoon glare. Connie sits at the desk, her thumb hovering over Simmo's number on her mobile phone. She's thinking she might call him, then that she might not. It might be wiser to proceed slowly.

Is that what he's thinking, too? Is it why he hasn't called?

She sees an email notification. It's from Robbie Watson, Seb's video guy, and he's copied in Connie. She reads the subject line: 'Ted's funeral video – link to early rough edit'. She clicks on the link.

Young Ted fills the screen. He's mid to late thirties, standing at the back of a surfboat, rippling muscle, glistening with sea spray. This is archive footage from the reels and videos Seb gathered in the days before the funeral. It's craftily intercut with mourners watching the same footage on the big screen in the church, and still more mourners spilling outside and onto the street.

Ted wields the sweep oar while his four oarsmen, young Simmo among them, propel the surfboat up and over unrelenting waves, horrifyingly big. The crew is competing against other boats. Calling the race are a couple of old Bondi clubbies but this commentary, as Connie recalls, was dubbed in some years later as a mocking tribute to mark Ted's twentieth year at the club, or some such milestone.

'It's a pleasure to watch Bondi's own Ted McCall at the helm, isn't it, Bill? At first glance, he's your textbook sweep, although that description doesn't quite do him justice. Just watch him: knees flexed, oar perfectly weighted, which gives him maximum balance and steering control. He's got options in this position.'

'That's right, Stan. Let's just watch how he takes on this next wave. She's a biggie, all right. Has to be a six- or seven-footer, but look how Ted's approaching it: he's called *easy!* and he's got his rowers digging in for the moment. He's going to bide his time. Whereas, if you look at the Narrabeen lads – just look at 'em – they're coming at it head-on, hell for the leather, not a second to lose. Oh no, you see, they haven't timed it right. The wave is sucking them in and it's already starting to break. Crikey!'

The Narrabeen boat glides up the almost vertical face. At the summit, for an improbable interlude, it is suspended ... until the entire crew abandons ship. They dive clear as the curling lip catches the bow and flips the craft.

'Ted sees the opening,' says Stan, 'and he's called *boat!* They're away again.'

While the Narrabeen boat is carried away, hull-up, on the same wave, the Bondi crew bursts through the combing wall of whitewash. For an instant the boat is airborne before they drop out of sight. When they reappear, over the next crest, the oarsmen are standing momentarily with Ted, levering the boat back to the surface.

'You see, Stan, Ted McCall – like all great sweeps – feels the vibrations of the surf through the soles of his feet, and that's how he anticipates its next moves. Not bad for a boy from the bush. Ted was eighteen before he'd seen the ocean, and over thirty before he'd stepped foot in a surfboat, but it's like he was born of the sea. Most of us who've grown up by the ocean have never mastered it. Ted somehow divines its temper, then he tames it.'

Connie recalls them cooking this up, and Ted's embarrassment.

The chatter of many voices, some instantly familiar to Connie, overlays the dissolving picture of young Ted on the high sea until it is replaced by mourners milling and taking their seats five days ago at St Luke's Anglican Church, which had become his preferred house of worship or song, or whatever it was to him. It had been Seb's church, too, until his late teens, when he defected to the tambourine-bangers. Yet Connie notes how at home Seb looks now, receiving wellwishers, directing the foot traffic, paying attention to the final details.

She leaves the video playing while she picks up the receiver on the landline and dials Ted's mobile. It's slow to connect. The mobile vibrates in the in-tray. She puts it on speaker and lays it near the keyboard.

'You've reached the phone of Ted McCall. Unfortunately, or fortunately ...'

She listens once again to Ted's goofy message.

'You realise,' she tells him without a hello, 'you should've died at Newport in 1984. I'm watching it now. Seb's happy-clapper mate, Robbie, has just sent us the video of your send-off. Was it Newport or Narrabeen? And was it '84 or '83? I think Seb was only in pre-school. Mainly I remember being terrified, and telling you, way back then, what might become of a human skull if it got in the way of one of your boats. How many big seas like that did you survive before your piss-ant paddle board finished you off – in a relatively piddling surf, too?'

Connie stops talking.

'It's gloomy in here,' she says at last.

She clicks pause on the video, goes to the window and tugs the curtain to the left. Light floods the room. She lifts the sash window wide-open. She checks the computer screen and is satisfied that the glare is tolerable. She reclines in the chair and clicks play.

'We can't plan it, can we?' she says. 'The manner of our deaths, I mean. Nor the manner of our living,' she splutters. 'Who'd have predicted I'd be screwing myself silly in my dotage, so soon after you toddled off?'

Connie listens to the opening strains of 'Amazing Grace'.

'Wait a second. It's the church choir. You'd have loved this bit. Probably not the solo, though.' Another splutter: 'They were missing their soloist, after all.'

She lowers the volume a little on 'Amazing Grace'.

'You don't get to sing the solo at your own funeral, Ted. Who is this, again? Brian Whatshisname. He made a gallant attempt, I suppose, but let's be honest: he's no soloist. I think there might have been some internal politics about who got to be your understudy for the occasion. I don't know for sure. That was Seb's department, sorting out all the churchy stuff.'

Connie leaves the call open but suspends her narration. The camera pans the aisles. She's interested in the who's who. And it's coming up to Seb's eulogy and she wants to see it in retrospect, to consider whether she was too harsh in her assessment on the day.

*... how sweet the sound / That saved a wretch like me ...*

'Cynthia Olivetti is magnificent, though, with her soprano part. She's a bit of a one-trick pony, I know, but she really can hold those high notes ... *a wretch like meeeeeeeee.* Silly Belinda Burrows was convinced you were shagging Cynthia. You and Cynthia! Hilarious! Poor Belinda. No bloody idea.'

The hymn goes for longer than Connie remembers.

'I always think of our Gracie when I hear this one. Amazing Gracie.'

The camera is angled on the pew nearest the altar. Seb sits closest to the centre aisle. Connie is further along the same pew, Amber and Mack and Gracie separating her and her son. The same angle catches Simmo watching Connie. She hadn't realised he and Vanessa were just a row behind, in the same pew as Clem and his wife, Shaz, and their son, Matt, his wife, Anna, and their kids, Wally and ... that's terrible. Connie can't remember the younger two's names.

A wider angle reveals Ted's coffin beneath the altar. Seb could almost reach it from where he sits. So could Lochie McCall, just across the centre aisle from Seb. Lochie is spitting distance from Ted, Connie's thinking. She gathers this is the closest the twins have been in thirty or more years. Age has been less kind to Lochie, or he's been harder on himself, and he's a long way from identical to Ted now. He's become heftier. Square-jawed and square-shouldered, he looks straight ahead, never glancing to the coffin, a sentinel to his extended family in the same pew. Closest to him is Tory, his wife and Connie's childhood bestie, later her bridesmaid. Then there's their adult kids, Lochie Jr, Alice and Sam, and young Lochie's wife, Tess, and their spoilt brats, Tim and Elle. They're still brats in their late teens, by most reports, which is possibly the only reason Connie remembers their names. She's never understood how Ted kept track. Despite his estrangement from Lochie, he never forgot the birthdays of his twin's offspring.

'Y'know,' Connie tells Ted's phone, 'I thought Lochie might've disgraced us at the wake, once he'd had a few complimentary beers under his belt. It didn't happen. Most disasters I imagine never happen.'

The choir is still going with the same hymn. It's epic.

*Through many dangers, toils and snares …*

'It's the disasters I don't imagine that happen.'

*T'was grace that brought us safe thus far*
*And grace will lead us home*

'Such a graceless prick, Lochie.'

It still infuriates Connie that it was Lochie who perpetuated the twins' separation when he was the one who inherited the earth. Lochie resented his brother getting even his thirty grand – the 'bugger-off money', as Ted called it, much later. Their alienation kept Connie and Tory apart. Even at Ted's funeral, they barely spoke. It saddens Connie they can't be close again.

The conclusion of the hymn is Seb's cue. While her son arranges his notes on the lectern, it occurs to Connie that he's becoming more handsome with age. More like Ted.

'Dad would be really annoyed to be missing this,' Seb announces.

The doorbell rings.

'Shit,' says Connie. She pauses the video. She goes to end her message to Ted but sees it's already cut off at the ten-minute limit. She strides down the hall and opens the door. 'Oh?' she says.

It's Simmo.

'I thought I'd, y'know, pop over.'

'I thought you mightn't.' Connie looks blankly at him.

'Sorry,' he says. 'I'll go.'

'No, don't do that. That's not what I meant.'

'That's good.'

'You're on the telly,' she says.

'The telly?'

'The computer, actually.'

Connie turns and walks back along the hall towards the study, leaving Simmo wondering on the doorstep.

'Are you coming?' she asks. 'Close the door behind you.'

He obeys and plods after her. He arrives at the study and she points to a second chair tucked under the back of the desk.

'Pull that around,' she says. Something possesses her to dial Ted's number again, and Simmo attempts to look unfazed by the sound of his dead mate's greeting and instruction to leave a message. Connie uses the mouse to rewind the video and replay the Narrabeen crew wiping out and the Bondi crew conquering the same wave.

'Hell!' says Simmo. 'It was all a blur at the church. Now I'm remembering it like it was yesterday.'

'Look at you: a boy.'

Connie watches it all again with Simmo, who mocks Bill and Stan's ode to the ocean tamer.

'That's it, Stan, he's the Messiah!' says Simmo,

Connie squawks: 'He walks on water!'

They have a good laugh until Connie sighs, and says, 'Oh dear. Imagine if poor Seb heard that?'

★★★

Seb did hear that. He's crouched on the narrow path outside the study's opened window. He can hear his mother's voice intermittently, whenever she raises it for emphasis above the ridiculous volume setting on the computer speakers. Seb can't make out the quieter voice of her visitor, who arrived only minutes ago. That voice reaches him in murmurs, soft and low, apparently male.

Ten minutes ago, perhaps fifteen, Seb excused himself from his lunch guests on the pretext of slipping down the back lane to fetch a lemon and a lime from his mother's garden. He was driven here by other impulses. He wanted to escape the oppressive presence of the born-again drunk Brendan Buckley and his co-drinker, Kerry, who'd become rapidly tipsy and flirty. Seb was also compelled to conduct a further reconnoitre at his mother's home.

Drawn to the side of the house by a racket, he heard her on the phone, discussing the funeral video as it played. The fragments he caught were unfeeling, macabre, deranged … 'what might become of a human skull if it got in the way of one of your bloody boats … that piss-ant paddle board finished you off … who'd have predicted I'd be screwing myself silly in my dotage … Silly Belinda Burrows was convinced you were shagging Cynthia … No bloody idea …'

To whom could she have been talking? Who might have indulged her like that? And who is this visitor who interrupted that call? Seb is tempted to take a peek, but he'd be caught. And Amber will be wondering what's become of him. He decides to retreat … except, just now on the video, Reverend Wallhurst is introducing him. Seb stops to listen to his eulogy.

'Dad would be really annoyed to be missing this,' Seb begins. 'He hated to be left out of a party. For all our sadness today, that's what we'll be doing: throwing him a party. Let's begin with the life of Ted McCall. It'll be heavily abridged. We'd be here for weeks if it wasn't, and Dad was never one to go on about himself. Anyhow, here goes: A paean to Ted McCall ...'

'A *pae-an*,' Connie scoffs, 'not a *pain*.' She hits pause on the video to allow herself a chuckle.

Simmo suggests: 'You say *pae-an*, he says *pain*.'

'I say a *pae-an in the arse!*'

Seb reels at his mother's insult and the back of his head strikes the weatherboard cladding.

Connie and Simmo hear the thud. Connie goes to the left of the window and presses her cheek against the architrave so she can see along the path. She catches sight of a hand and a foot. It's Seb. He's skulking there.

Connie thinks for a moment. She ends the call to Ted but she also grabs the computer mouse and clicks play, and Seb's eulogy resumes.

'Edward Clifford McCall,' he says, 'was born on November the seventeenth, 1949, the first of Cliff and Irene McCall's twin sons to see daylight ...'

Simmo goes to the window and looks along the path while Connie picks up her phone and leaves the study. Simmo follows her as far as the opened door and watches her as she stops in the hall and dials a number. When it answers with a recorded message, he is close enough to hear it.

'*You have dialled emergency triple zero ...*'

Simmo raises his hand – stop! – but she doesn't.

'Really?' she's sneering at the phone. 'I thought I'd dialled for an emergency pizza. You'd think they'd have a real, live human answering triple-0.'

*'Your call is being connected ...'*

A real, live woman asks whether Connie wants police, fire and rescue, or ambulance.

'Police.'

'Hang up!' Simmo pleads.

But a man answers. *'Your name and location, please.'*

'Connie Blunt, twenty-seven Banksia Avenue, Bondi, off Bondi Road. Would you like to know about my emergency, or would you prefer we complete my biography?'

*'Please, madam, describe your emergency.'*

'I have an intruder right outside my opened window.'

Simmo shakes his head: please, stop!

*'Madam, to your knowledge, are you in danger?'*

'I didn't think to ask him whether he was dangerous. Should I?'

*'No. Do you have reason to believe this man is a threat to your safety?'*

'Let's see: I'm a recently widowed seventy-year-old woman, alone in her home ...' She notes Simmo, aghast, but proceeds, '... while a stranger is lurking just outside her opened window. This may be wild speculation, but the widow supposes that the stranger intends to enter her house, probably via the afore-mentioned opened window.'

*'I see. Where is your front or back door in relation to that window?'*

'The window is at the side of the house. My doors are, as you have speculated, front and back.'

*'I suggest you exit the house via whichever door is closest, or whichever delivers you fastest to a neighbour.'*

'And the police? When might they arrive?'

*'We have a patrol car in the area. As soon as they can.'*

'Would it hasten things if you told them I was a little old lady?'

*'Please, madam, leave your home.'*

'Very well.' Connie hangs up.

Simmo steps into the hall. 'It's Seb,' he says.

'Are you certain? We can't be too careful.'

'Connie! It's your son.'

'And he's spying on me. A little jolt for him, that's all. Wait upstairs while I greet the police?'

Again Simmo raises his arm in feeble protest.

★★★

Seb is absorbed in the replay of his eulogy. It's sounding better than he supposed it might.

'Cliff McCall helped Irene deliver the twins on Burrabogie, their sheep, wheat and barley station out of Tocumwal, on the Murray River. It had been in the family for two generations and now the third was born all at once: Ted and Lochie ...'

Seb pays no attention to the car idling in the street until its doors open and he hears the chatter of a police radio. Then he hears the latch on his mother's front gate. Only now does he get it: they're here for him.

Seb runs for it. His shoulder catches the back corner of the house as he makes for the yard. He trips on the gum root and staggers, but recovers to keep running through the opened gate into the lane, where he collides with an unseen mass. Seb is instantly on the ground, beneath it. He's facedown, groaning. He is buried, it seems, under a large police officer. This officer has arrived via the dunny lane to cut off the absconder by crash-tackling him to the gravel.

'Got him!' the big cop declares.

Seb howls, which the officer interprets as resisting arrest. He applies a wrestling hold to keep Seb pinned to the ground.

'It's you,' Seb says.

'It's you,' says the officer, the same burly cop who manhandled Seb from the Tamarama cliff only two days ago.

His familiar sidekick, the skinny one, emerges from the back gate with Connie in tow.

'Oh,' she tells them. 'My mistake, officers. This is my son, Sebastian McCall.'

'Your son?' says the burly one. 'We've already met Sebastian.'

Seb hopes the big oaf won't elaborate. He sees that Amber is entering the lane from their backyard. She is followed by Mack, Ant, Kerry, Aaron, Luke and Jemimah, then Brendan Buckley. They've all come to inspect the commotion. Rollo Costa, too, is emerging from his yard.

'Honey?' Amber says.

'It's okay,' Seb tells her, finding his feet. 'A misunderstanding.'

'Yes,' Connie explains, 'we thought he was an intruder.'

'An intruder?' Amber asks. 'We?'

'Me,' Connie corrects the record. 'I.'

'But he was only coming to get a lime.'

'And a lemon,' says Mack.

'I wish I'd known that,' Connie says.

'It's okay,' Seb pleads. 'Couldn't be helped.'

'But you're bleeding,' Amber says. 'Your knees.'

The gravel has shredded his right trouser leg at the knee, which glistens maroon through the hole. The other knee bleeds into the cotton.

'Police brutality,' says Brendan Buckley, unhelpfully.

'Brendan!' replies the burly officer. 'I didn't recognise you with that haircut. What brings you to these parts?'

'They know Brendan!' Mack chirps, as if this is a happy coincidence.

An awkward pause is heavy with implication: Brendan is known to the police.

'Did you have a win?' the burly one asks, pointing to the hip pocket of Brendan's jeans, where a fifty- and twenty-dollar note are escaping. 'Nine days after pension day, must be a windfall.'

Brendan tucks the money back in.

'Look.' Connie sighs. 'I'm terribly sorry for the confusion. It really was a silly misunderstanding. Seb comes and goes as he pleases.'

The barb is intended for Seb's ears only. He hears it loud and clear.

Connie turns to head inside. She looks up to her bedroom and sees the curtain flicker, and she notes that Seb has seen it, too. But still Seb doesn't know who it is. He's exhausted with not knowing. Once his mother is inside, he steps into her garden and plucks a lemon and a lime to substantiate his alibi. He catches up with the others.

'What were you doing there?' Amber asks. 'I thought you must have been talking to her.'

The directness of her inquiry takes Seb aback.

'Seb?'

'I was ... I thought I heard something down the side.'

He knows it's flimsy. She rolls her eyes and walks ahead of him. Seb marks this as significant. It's perhaps the first time Amber has seriously doubted him. Everything has changed, he feels, in these moments.

Brendan sidles up to him. 'Spot of bother, son?'

'I'm not your son.'

'Go easy. I mean no harm.'

'I think you do.'

Brendan begins to move away.

'That money,' Seb asks, 'did Pastor Pat give you that?'

Brendan doesn't answer.

'He paid you for that performance this morning, didn't he?'

'I wouldn't call it a performance.'

'What would you call it?'

'An appearance.'

'For which you received an appearance fee?'

'No, I'd call it what Pat called it: a token of appreciation, something to cover my expenses. Look, I did it because he gave me the time of day.'

'And a hundred bucks, let's say.'

'Let's say a hundred and fifty. Do you think I bought you rubbish plonk?'

★★★

Connie finds Simmo sitting in the armchair by her bedroom door. It's only ever been used as a way station for laundry, never for sitting. This is unsettling. He's clearly unhappy.

'Come on,' she pleads, 'my own son – spying on me.'

'You shouldn't forget that.'

'What?'

'Your own son.'

'That's a bit harsh.'

'Who's being harsh? Who calls the cops on their son?'

'I called them off. I was always going to call them off. Anyway, you don't get to judge me all of a sudden, just because we're ...'

'What?'

'Y'know ...'

'Is that all we're doing? *Y'know?*'

'Of course not. I was joking.'

'I wasn't.'

She affects a silly grin, an attempt to cajole him. Simmo stands and moves to the door.

'Ted never did argue with you, did he? He always ran a mile from conflict.'

'You have no idea.'

'I think I do.'

And he does. She knows he does. Simmo is challenging her the way Ted never did, and never would. Now he walks out and Connie listens to his soft footfalls on the stairs, then along the hall to the front door, which he opens and closes gently, as might a gentle but angry man. It pisses her off, his dignified anger.

The doorbell chimes. Connie brightens. She hurtles from her

room and down the stairs and to the front door. She opens it wide, beaming.

'Yeah-Yeah?'

It's Gracie, who watches the smile dissolve from her grandmother's face. Connie attempts to recover it.

'Are you okay?' Gracie asks. 'I saw Simmo on his way out. He seemed ...'

'What?'

'I don't know. Is everything all right?'

'Yes. Come in.'

Gracie follows her.

'I was just watching the funeral video. I'll make us some Mum-tea.'

Gracie watches it from the start while Connie goes to the kitchen and puts on the kettle. As she waits for it to boil, Connie types a text message to Simmo: 'Sorry!' She looks at this single word on her screen and wonders whether it's enough. Or too much? She deletes the exclamation mark. Her thumb moves towards the send button, then back to the message field. She back-deletes. She puts the phone down, spoons tea leaves into her mother's teapot and brings out the matching cups and saucers and arranges them on a tray. The kettle whistles and she pours water into the pot, mostly. Her hand is shaky and she wets the bench. She doesn't bother to sponge it down. She finds shortbread biscuits in a jar on a high shelf.

'Yum!' says Gracie, as Connie enters. Gracie bites into a biscuit and immediately stops chewing.

'Stale?' Connie asks.

'Somewhat.'

It's adorable, Gracie attempting to be polite with her mouth full, but Connie can't focus on her granddaughter.

'I'll find something else.'

'No, let's just watch.'

Connie doesn't mention the drama of the police and Gracie's dad. Introducing that complication would be too exhausting now. Instead, as some kind of penance, she attempts to pay attention to Seb's eulogy and his rhapsodising about Ted. It's too good to be true, although none of it is untrue.

Seb, at the lectern, clicks a remote control and pictures appear of young Ted: chopping wood, on horseback, taking high marks on the footy field. A photograph of the young twins, arm in arm, offends Connie. With no context, it's a falsification, and Seb is far too kind to Lochie and his progeny, the fourth and fifth generations who keep Burrabogie in the family, as if none of that involved Ted's dispossession. 'They're all here today,' Seb says, and Connie hears his considerable craft as he moulds a McCall myth. She can't understand why he must. He could simply have left it out.

'It was during Ted's years at Sydney University that a life beyond the farm gate, beyond Tocumwal, beckoned. He muddled through most of an arts degree but his studies were incidental to the surf, musical theatre, the university reviews ...'

Various photographs appear of Ted the hammy showman.

'Then the big drought brought it all to an end. He abandoned his degree in his final year and returned to Burrabogie, where he was needed.'

Seb drones on. Connie is finding his delivery flatter the second time around, but she'll hear him out for Gracie's sake. It's a safe rendering of Ted's life: his exploits on the footy field, his wrenching decision to leave the family again a decade later (another airbrushing of history), his big New York adventure and Connie's part in it, which Seb dispatches in a couple of lines, and Ted's joining of the Bondi lifesavers, which was impetus to launch a business within walking distance of the club (he considered a surf shop and an ice-creamery before settling on the hardware business), and his recruitment to the business of oarsman Tommy 'Simmo' Sim, who Seb affords considerably more airtime than Connie, and

Ted's involvement in other clubs, business chambers, choirs, local charities, fundraisers …

'Ted was a joiner,' Seb says. 'He liked to belong. He belonged here, at this church. He had faith in God and faith in humanity. He believed in community. He liked people and people liked him.'

None of it, in isolation – even the God bit, at a stretch – is untrue. But Seb hasn't begun to tell the truer story of Ted McCall, mainly because poor Seb doesn't know it. Soon he will. Connie wishes she could be certain that he won't be the worse for knowing.

Old and recent photos hover, larger than life, over the altar, a rolling gallery on the big screen: Ted wielding a cricket bat in the back lane, Ted at the counter of Surfside Hardware, Ted the lifesaver, Ted surfing the longboard with the kids – Gracie then Seb then Mack.

'Children have their superheroes,' Seb says, 'but my hero was always Dad. Still is. He's always been the kind of man I've wanted to be. He was taller, more athletic, more handsome, wiser. He wore size-twelve shoes to my size-elevens. "See," I told him, not so long ago, "I'll never fill your thongs." I was joking then but I'm not today. I'll never fill your shoes, Dad. Each day, I can only strive to be a little more like you.'

Seb steps back from the lectern

'That was nice,' Gracie says.

'Yeah,' Connie agrees, and she wonders what kind of a mother could think otherwise. Of course it was nice.

A camera mounted on the altar follows Seb as he walks towards their pew. The same shot captures Connie standing and squeezing past their family and stepping into the aisle. She and Seb pass each other, either side of Ted's coffin, as she heads for the altar. He frowns.

'Pissed off,' Gracie observes.

Connie watches herself leaning into the microphone. She

notes her reptilian neck and regrets her years of neglecting to use moisturiser.

'I wasn't going to say anything today,' she begins. 'I didn't think I'd be able to. Seb adored his dad, as you've witnessed, so I was happy for him to speak for both of us. But now I feel a need to say something, if not on Ted's behalf, to let you know he would be grateful for all this attention. He'd be chuffed to be beatified by his only son, but also a bit embarrassed.

'Ted was dependable, decent, generous. And he was capable – at just about everything – and that could be aggravating, let's be honest. For the record, he never once beat me at Scrabble. But Ted would be embarrassed today because he was never self-assured, never smug. He could be unsure of himself, in fact, and vulnerable. This will surprise many of you, I know.

'He also lived in doubt about many things, including the idea of salvation. Ted loved coming to this church, but he came not so much to worship as to sing. He loved a tune. The mob down the hill, the Catholics, had a lousy choir, so he came up here instead. I think he was okay with doubt, though. He could live with it because he had so many certainties to compensate. The sun would always rise tomorrow, and he never missed a dawn.

'I've always detested that glib consolation: "He died doing what he loved." In Ted's case, though, it's undeniably true. He died surfing. His paddle board killed him. I wish I could accept that as a consolation. I can't.

'A nicer way to think of it is that Ted could have dropped dead at any moment on any old day, and still he would have died doing what he loved – because he filled his days with the things he loved among the people he loved and the people who loved him. He was expecting many more of these days. Yesterday I used the old calculator on his desk to work out the number of days he did have on this planet. He had precisely twenty-six thousand, eight hundred and two days. He'd be annoyed about not having thousands more, but hugely grateful for the ones he had. Thank you.'

Connie watches herself step back from the lectern.

'I was a bit glib myself,' she confesses to Gracie.

'You were not. That was perfect.'

Ted appears on the big screen over the altar and begins to sing, solo, the opening bars of 'Aba Daba Honeymoon'. He is surrounded on screen by his secular troupe, the Surfside Singers, who chant the chorus, and they sing it live in the church, too. The camera pans to them, but on the way it passes Seb, seething, in the front pew.

Gracie and Connie hum along as the camera arrives at these singers, halfway down the aisle, and it catches the church choir looking down on them from the loft. In the frame, just behind the Surfside Singers, is one unfamiliar face. Just one. He's tallish, thickset, sixty-something, with a full head of grey hair.

'Who's that?' Gracie asks.

'Don't know.'

That Connie doesn't know is noteworthy. Before the funeral, she had imagined it would be attended by quite a few strangers. As it turned out, she knew – or knew of – every face in the crowd, until now. This one might be the lone stranger. Connie wonders if he's one of the Rotary fellas, Ted's Tuesday night connections.

Connie tells Gracie: 'I'm thinking about taking a quick run down to Tocumwal – tomorrow even – to see Pop-Pop. Can you come for the ride?'

'How many days?'

'Not sure. Four or five? We could leave in the morning.'

'I have another summer physics tute – until eleven. I shouldn't miss it. Otherwise I'm clear until the year starts in earnest.'

'I'll pick you up there, straight after.'

'We're on,' Gracie says. 'Thelma and Louise.'

'Without the last bit.' Connie's clenched fist careens then

plummets: car over cliff. 'Kaboom!' she says, then spreads her fingers: car in flames.

'Spoiler alert!' Gracie protests. She kisses Connie's forehead. 'Hooroo,' she says.

'Hooroo yourself.'

The moment Gracie leaves, Connie types a text into her mobile.

You were right. I was wrong. I'm sorry. I'll tell Seb everything tomorrow morning before Gracie and I take a run to Tocumwal. Meanwhile, if you'd like company ...

She lip-reads it, decides it's okay and hits send. Within seconds ellipses pulsate on her screen: Simmo typing his response. The dots keep throbbing, suggesting a long reply. Can't he just type 'yes'?

The dots vanish. Nothing happens. Has he decided against answering? Connie tosses her phone – useless thing – to the desk. Then it dings with a new message. She takes one step forward to read the screen.

On my way.

# 6.
# SURPRISE

A feathery touch at the back of Connie's ankle stirs her from sleep. It crawls up her calf muscle. She smiles but keeps her eyes shut, happy to have Simmo in her bed.

'Tickles,' she says in faux protest.

She doesn't know the time but it's too early to be awake given the long drive ahead of her today. The tickling persists, however, and a creeping spatial awareness forces Connie to think: she was on Ted's side of the bed when they fell asleep last night, Simmo still preferring it that way. Yet this tickling is coming from behind her, from the sliver of space remaining on Ted's side. She opens her eyes and confirms that Simmo is still on her side. He's facing her, wide-eyed, worried. He casts a glance over her shoulder. Connie flips over and lifts the sheet.

'Mack?' she says.

Her grandson lies flat on his back at the edge of the bed, giggling. 'I tricked you.'

'What time is it?' Connie asks.

'Don't know,' Mack says.

'Barely five-thirty,' Simmo says.

Connie gasps. 'You came here in the dark?'

Mack is chirpy. 'You didn't know it was me.'

'How could I possibly have known? And at this hour?'

'You thought it was Simmo.'

Connie and Simmo say nothing.

Mack exhales, a world-weary sigh, pleased with the success of his prank. 'Yeah-Yeah?'

'Mmmmm?'

'Is Simmo having a sleepover?'

Connie turns back to Simmo. 'I suppose he is.'

Mack laughs heartily. 'Like kids?'

Connie looks sideways at Simmo. 'Something like that.' She's worried. No doubt Mack will report back to Seb. She strokes her grandson's soft hair. He's wearing the black ninja pyjamas she stuffed in his Christmas stocking. 'Love your jim-jams, little ninja,' she says. 'Your mum and dad don't know you're here, do they?'

'They're asleep.'

'I imagine they are. Why did you come?'

He doesn't answer, though she knows why. Mack witnessed the tensions yesterday and he's come as peacemaker.

Simmo tells Mack: 'Your dad'll wake up any time now, for our swim. He'll be really worried if he finds you missing.'

'I'll walk you back, Mack Mac,' Connie says. 'Just let me go to the toot first.'

★★★

Seb pulls on his togs and heads downstairs. He treads softly as always to Mack's opened door, careful not wake him.

His bed is empty.

Seb listens to the house for sounds of his son. There are none. He goes to the front door and confirms it is locked. He turns on lights and looks along the hall and listens again. He goes to the bathroom but Mack's not there, then to the kitchen, from where he surveys the family room. He steps into the pantry.

Mack is not in the house.

The back door is open but Seb can't see into the yard, it's

so dark. He turns on the garden lights and sees the back gate is ajar. He steps into the yard and slips into his thongs. Something possesses him to lift his towel from its hook and his goggles from the next hook. With these routine movements he's defying his trepidation. Mack will be at Yeah-Yeah's. He has no history of pre-dawn escapades to his grandparents', but where else could he be?

Seb walks towards his opened gate. It's black out there in the lane, moonlessly black. *Heavenly Father, let him be with Yeah-Yeah.*

A small dark mass streaks into the yard. It startles Seb. But – yes! – it is Mack.

'It's you!' he cries and sweeps his son into his arms.

'I'm sorry.'

'It's okay, it's okay. You're safe. Thank God!' Seb cuddles Mack and feels himself shuddering against him. 'You can't go running off like that, mate.'

'I know.'

'It's dangerous.'

'I'm sorry. Simmo said you'd be worried.'

The shuddering stops. 'Simmo?'

'Yes.'

Seb has to stop to think. This makes no sense. He lowers Mack to his feet and steps into the lane, where he sees his mother's shadowy figure pass into her yard, out of sight.

'You saw Simmo?'

'Yeah. Simmo's having a sleepover at Yeah-Yeah's.'

'Simmo?'

'Yes.'

'Simmo?'

'Yes, Dad.'

'Sleepover?'

'Yes.'

Seb processes it all. 'In the spare room?'

'No!' Mack huffs. 'You don't have sleepovers in separate rooms.'

'In Yeah–Yeah's room?'

'Of course.'

Of course … of course. Seb gets it now. Finally he gets it. It's been Simmo all along.

What a monumental fool Seb has been.

★★★

'Is he coming?' Simmo asks.

Connie is at the bedroom window, watching her gate. 'Not yet. I suppose he will.'

Simmo goes to his small backpack and extracts his Speedos and pulls them on. 'You two need to be alone for this,' he says.

Connie feels ill.

'Will you be all right?'

She nods, yes.

Simmo slips the backpack over one shoulder and heads for the stairs. Connie follows him onto the landing and watches as he flicks on the stairwell light and descends. Only as Simmo reaches the final step does she become aware of Seb storming through the house towards him.

Almost upon him, Seb dispenses with his towel and goggles. He clenches his fist. He swings his arm in a wide arc, a roundhouse punch that shatters the bridge of Simmo's nose. The sound is sickening. Connie screams.

Simmo bends over and cups his nose in his hands. When he comes back up, blood is gushing from his nostrils and through his fingers.

'That's for Dad,' Seb declares.

'Get out!' Connie says, taking the stairs at reckless speed.

Seb, still at swinging distance, stares at the gore of Simmo's face. Seb hasn't thrown a punch since primary school. This is the first he's ever landed and he's shocked by its force. It feels … good.

'How long has this been going on?' he demands.

'Out!' Connie says.

'Since Friday,' Simmo manages.

'You don't expect me ...'

'I expect you to get out,' Connie says.

She shoves Seb and he stumbles backwards into the mantlepiece.

'Stop it,' Mack cries.

They all turn.

'Stop fighting!' he says.

'I told you to stay home,' Seb says.

'I told you to stop fighting.'

Simmo is unsteady on his feet. He sits on the stairs and groans while Connie examines his injury.

'You've broken it, Seb. You've broken his nose.'

'It's okay,' Simmo says.

'It is not okay.' Connie continues inspecting the break. 'This is monstrous.'

'Stop!' Mack says, crying now.

Seb can't say what he needs to say, not with Mack here, but he turns to his mother.

'You have nothing to say for yourself?'

'Not at this moment, no. I need to get Simmo to hospital.'

Seb doesn't move.

'Just go, or I'll call the cops again.'

'Don't,' Mack pleads. 'Don't!'

Connie tilts Simmo's head back in an attempt to stem the blood, but it's coming in thick spouts. 'Take him home, Seb.'

Seb relents and takes Mack's hand.

Simmo asks: 'Will I get Vanessa to cover the shop this morning?'

Seb has no thoughts on this question.

★★★

Outside the emergency entrance, a stooped old man wearing a blue hospital gown has an unlit cigarette in his mouth and he's pushing his intravenous drip across the zebra crossing. Connie brakes and waits for him to cross. Simmo, beside her, already bruised under his eyes, has a box of tissues in his lap, but he's running out. At his feet are dozens of bloody gloops of discarded tissue. Connie is driving Simmo's Subaru because, in the rush, she didn't want to waste time looking for wherever Ted left the Mazda.

The patient has stopped on the crossing to light his cigarette. He repeatedly rubs the flint of a disposable lighter but it fails to ignite. Connie appeals with a friendly toot of the horn. The pedestrian gives her the middle finger. Eventually he gets a flame. He blows smoke in Connie's direction, smiles and proceeds, his bare arse hanging out the back of his gown.

'I'll have to park,' Connie tells Simmo. 'I could drop you here, if you like, but I really need to speak to the triage nurse. You don't want to be left too long in the queue.'

'It's okay. I'll come with you.'

In the bowels of the hospital, Connie finds a tight spot to park. It's a long haul for Simmo from here and he leaves a trail of viscid blood in the elevator and all the way to emergency. He bleeds some more on the waiting-room floor as they queue for the nurse.

It's an hour before Simmo is seen to. CT scans are arranged at Connie's urging. While they're waiting for the pictures, she takes him through the possibilities. Hopefully there'll be no need for surgery but she describes the bad-to-worst scenarios: a significantly shifted nasal septum, airway blockage, concussion, fractured skull, blood clots to the brain.

'Seriously?'

'Hopefully not.'

★★★

'Why didn't you wake me?'

Amber's inquiry precedes her arrival, still in her nightie, in the kitchen. She discovers Mack dressed for school but Seb still wearing only his togs. They are strangely quiet.

'It's almost eight,' she says. 'What's happening?'

Seb draws breath. Mack, attempting to remain staunch, says nothing.

'Guys?'

'It's Simmo,' Seb says.

'What about him?'

'I ...'

Mack can't hold out. 'They had a fight.'

'A fight?'

'It wasn't really a fight,' Seb says. 'I ...'

'What?'

'I hit him.'

'Hit him?'

'It was like a punch,' Mack explains.

'Whatever for? Is he okay? Where is he?'

It takes Seb too long to respond and he can see Amber's dread mounting. 'Hospital,' he says.

'Hospital? What have you done, Seb?'

'I'll drop Mack at school and put a note on the shop. I'll come back and explain everything.'

'Tell me, too,' Mack protests.

'It's school time, buddy.'

'It's too early.'

Seb goes upstairs and dresses in shorts and a T-shirt. He scrounges for tuckshop money on his bedside table. The short drive to school is a long stretch without conversation.

'If you say sorry,' Mack says in farewell, 'everything will be all right.'

Seb leaves a note on the shop door: 'Opening at 10 a.m.

today.' He keeps seeing his fist connecting with Simmo's face and experiences waves of revulsion and exhilaration. He expects he will feel remorse, but not yet. He feels righteous anger.

★★★

The scans give Simmo the all-clear. It's a severe break, but nothing more sinister. Surgery might be an option, but not today.

'It does look significant,' Connie tells him in the lift to lower parking.

Simmo checks himself in its mirror. His nose has swollen into a purple ball. He's black-eyed and blue-cheeked.

'I'll scare off the customers,' he says.

'No you won't. You can't work like this.'

'Not today.'

'Not for quite a few days. It was barbaric.'

'He had motive.'

'He was abominable. I'm so sorry. I should've explained everything sooner, as you said. I didn't know he was capable of this.'

It's a slow old lift. They listen to its hydraulics wheezing.

'Will you press charges?' Connie asks.

'Don't be silly.'

The doors crank open and Simmo inspects his face one more time in the mirror. 'I didn't see it coming, either.'

Connie can't quite remember where she parked Simmo's car. She looks up and down the rows until Simmo takes his keys from her grasp and presses the electronic button. The Subaru's lights flash and it chirps twice to announce itself. She arrives at the car to find it already unlocked.

'Will our car do that?' Connie asks.

'I should think so.'

'The things you learn. I drive so rarely I wouldn't know … Oh, shit!'

'What?'

'Clem. I forgot Clem. I need to call him to say we won't make it.'

'Why not?'

'I'm not leaving you like this.'

'Like what? I'm fine.'

'You'll be in the wars. You can expect terrible headaches. And I'm not leaving you with Seb.'

'Why? You think he'll have another crack?'

'He wouldn't dare.'

'I'd be ready for round two.' Simmo assumes a silly kung-fu pose and even sillier Chinese accent. 'The ancient wisdom of my ancestors. I'd kick the living shit out of him.'

Simmo discovers it hurts to laugh.

'See,' she tells him.

'Just leave me a script for some heavy-duty painkillers. I'll be fine.'

It's just after eight-fifteen as they pull out of the hospital carpark.

'Will you talk to Seb before you leave?'

Connie drives for several hundred metres before answering.

'I can't very well tell him and then leave town,' she says.

Simmo turns on the radio, just to do something. It's seventies pub rock. 'They're still playing this stuff,' he says.

'Look, I'll stay in Sydney and tell him.'

Simmo thinks about it. 'No, don't do that. You both need some cooling-off time. Tell him when you get back.'

★★★

'I wanted to tell you on Friday,' Seb tells Amber, 'but I was in a state and I didn't want to upset you.'

'Tell me what?'

He inhales and thinks.

'Seb? Tell me.'

'Okay. When I went to see Mum on Friday, there was someone with her.'

'What do you mean?'

'In her bed.'

'Oh?'

'I found her in bed with a man.'

'Oh my goodness! Simmo?'

'No. I mean yes, but I didn't know that then.'

'I don't understand.'

'I couldn't see him.'

'I still don't understand.'

'He was under the sheets.'

'Hiding?'

'No. He was …'

'What?'

'Y'know.'

'No.'

'He was … down there.'

Amber frowns.

'I mean,' Seb starts, 'he was …'

'Oh!' she says, suddenly comprehending. 'Simmo?'

Seb nods.

Amber is still processing it. 'Simmo?'

'As it turns out, yes.'

'Oh!'

'Yes, *oh!*'

Amber adds it all up. 'You still shouldn't have punched him.'

'No, probably not.'

'Absolutely not.' She leaves him to reflect on the distinction. 'But,' she says, 'you've just discovered this morning it was Simmo? How?'

'Mack.'

'What?'

Seb explains Mack's pre-dawn adventure.

'Oh my God. That's so dangerous.'

'I told him.'

Amber has so much to work through. 'How long?' she asks.

'Their affair? If I'm to believe them, since Friday.'

'Do you?'

'Not for a moment. I mean, how convenient.'

'But your mum loved your father.'

'So she says.'

Seb's cynical note upsets Amber, he can see. She always thinks the best of people. Even now she wants to think the best of his mother and Simmo. He can see the way her mind is working, that there must be some explanation.

He pulls out his phone and goes to his photo log. 'See,' he says. 'She was planning this.'

Amber takes the phone and studies his pictures of the contents of his mother's wheelie bins. 'What is this?' she asks.

'New sheets, see? Just for Simmo.'

'I think that's a bit wrong.'

'Of course it's wrong.'

'No, I mean you photographing your mum's rubbish.'

'Well, I ...'

'I don't know what to think. It's very ... it's not nice.' Amber starts to cry. She looks girlishly young when she cries. 'Where did you punch him?'

'His nose.'

'Is it bad?'

'It's broken.'

'Broken! That's not you. That's not my husband.'

'I was very angry.'

'I don't know you.'

'Yes you do. It was just this crazy situation.'

'But you couldn't even talk to me first. There's something very wrong with our marriage if you couldn't tell me.'

'Don't say that. There's nothing ...'

'There is. How long might you have gone on keeping it all from me?'

Seb doesn't know. He takes her hand and kisses it in lieu of an answer.

'Who did you tell? If not me, who did you tell?'

'Nobody.'

It comes out with conviction, but he instantly remembers it isn't true. He did tell somebody. He told Simmo. He confided the scandal of his mother to just one person: the man she's fucking. Imbecile. Seb is humiliated. He doubles down on the lie.

'I told nobody.'

★★★

Connie leaves Simmo at his front gate with a battery of painkillers.

'Go easy on the codeine or you'll get constipated,' she tells him.

'I know.'

'And make sure you eat with the ibuprofen.'

'Yeah, I know. What are you going to tell Gracie?'

'What?'

'It's a long car trip, just the two of you.'

He's right.

'I don't know,' Connie says. 'The truth, I suppose.'

'Before you tell Seb?'

'I see what you mean. I suppose not. I'll hold off.'

'Maybe you should just email him. You know, download everything. It's not ideal, but nothing will be.'

Connie thinks how that might go. No, she won't do that to Seb. She'll face him when she returns from Tocumwal.

She packs a little sports bag, plenty for four or five days. Connie prides herself on travelling light. Simmo's orange orchids are still in good shape but they won't be by the time she gets back. She wraps them in paper and leaves the house via the front door, where she finds another casserole, so she delivers it with the flowers to Mrs Visser.

Back at home, under the shower, Connie regards the aftermath of Seb's violence: the blood-stained hand basin where Simmo stood oozing from his nose and the glut of bloodied loo paper brimming from the toilet. She steps out of the shower, dries herself, goes to her wardrobe and selects a frock that will be cool and loose for the long drive. She slips into it and begins to return to the bathroom to clean up the blood when she hears her mobile ringing faintly. She's left it downstairs. It will be Clem. She moves quickly to answer it before it goes to message bank. Yes, she tells Clem, they should arrive by six-thirty or seven tonight. She mentions neither Seb nor Simmo.

It's tempting to go and see Seb now and tell him everything, but would she be doing that to hurt him, to punish him for his thuggery? Simmo is right. They need some space. And hanging around is pointless, Connie decides. She'll drive in early, fill the tank and stop at the fancy bakery on Bourke Street for coffee and cake. She ferrets in the kitchen drawers for keep-cups for herself and Gracie.

She moves towards the front door but has a thought: the condolence book from the funeral. She'll take it with her. From memory, it had a shiny, silvery cover, so it shouldn't be hiding. It is, though. She finds it at last on top of the dishwasher, in the tiny sliver of space under the bench. What possessed her to file it there?

She opens the book on the kitchen bench and begins flipping through it, scanning the first column on each of its left-hand pages, which contain the names of mourners written in their hand. Thereafter are columns for their phone numbers and emails and, on the facing page, their messages of condolence. For now, Connie is only looking at the names, and only for any she doesn't recognise. Six turns of the page in, she is yet to see one that doesn't ring at least a faint bell. There are hundreds more to go.

She'll try again in Tocumwal. She imagines she'll have little else but time there. She throws the book into her bag and finds the Mazda's keys on the hook where Ted left them. She hopes the car will be as easy to find. Halfway down the hall to the front door, she has another thought. She goes to the desk in the study and opens the drawer and rummages at the back among an array of loose keys. She finds a gold one. As she recalls, Ted's system went like this: a black key for the shop, a standard silver key for the front door of the house, blue for their window locks, and gold for the sliding door at the back. Ted never did get around to changing their fittings so one key would lock and unlock everything, as he relentlessly advised customers to do.

The gold key is stiff in the rusty old lock but Connie gives it a good rattle and shake and soon it engages with a satisfying clunk. She has to wonder: is this the first time in the history of the McCall-Blunt's occupation of this property that the back door has been locked?

On the footpath, she looks up and down the street to all the cars parked rear to kerb. She inspects the button on the key. She presses it and an electronic beep-beep sounds from a distance, in the direction of Bondi Road, behind her. She presses the button again and this time she sees the rear lights flash, fifteen or so cars away, on her side of the road. It's a revelation.

Gracie climbs into the front passenger seat and inspects the treats her grandmother has brought. 'You're the best.'

They wind through the roads within the grounds of the University of Sydney, past the old sandstone landmarks, the Manning Bar and the Fisher Library.

'I breastfed your dad under that tree,' Connie says.

'I know,' Gracie says.

'Of course you do, sorry. Enjoy the tutorial?'

'*Enjoy* is too strong a word. It's physics.'

'You're not winning?'

'Not yet, but I'll have to. Whether it's astronomy or climate, I'll need physics.'

They've discussed this often: what Gracie might do with a general science degree. It makes Connie proud that she wants a vocation, yet sad, too.

'You shouldn't have to live in dread, you lot.'

Gracie shrugs. 'I could just drop out and buy the cheapest, shittiest block of land in the country and turn it into a massive algae farm – to soak up all the carbon. That's a thing, apparently.'

'Really? Will it work?'

'Possibly not. Or I could switch to medicine and become a tropical diseases specialist, then beat the rush to Antarctica. Y'know, corner the market down there.'

'I hope you jest.'

'Me too.'

They riff on like this, which suits Connie. Anything but the war with Seb and Simmo's broken nose and the whole catastrophe.

'Oh!' Connie thinks aloud.

'What?'

She never did get back upstairs to clean all that blood from the bathroom. And from the stairs. It'll be nicely baked in by the time she gets home.

'It's okay. Nothing.'

★★★

His mother isn't answering. Seb knocks again on her back door, to be sure. He grabs the door handle and gives it a tug but it refuses to budge. This is unsettling. She hasn't suddenly secured the house against burglars, Seb realises. She's secured it against him. He walks home and searches in the second kitchen drawer, where he finds a gold key. He's almost at the back gate when Amber calls to him from their bedroom window.

'Seb?'

'Hi?'

'Who's at the shop?'

'No one for a bit. I'm just checking on something.'

The key is sticky in his parents' old lock but Seb jiggles it until it gives. He stands in the family room, breathing its funky, dead-flower air. He wonders why he's here.

He moves through the house, lifting the lid on the piano and playing a few chords before continuing on. He stops at Simmo's blood, congealed around the base of the stairs. A trail marks Simmo's ascent to the bedroom, where the bed is unmade but the sheets remain startlingly white. Seb touches them. They feel expensive.

He follows the bloody trail into the bathroom, where the basin is smeared with still more of Simmo's blood and the toilet is filled with magenta globs of tissue and loo paper. Why wouldn't she have at least flushed it?

Is that why he's here?

He turns back to the basin. There are three toothbrushes. Two are his mother's and father's, upright in their cup. The third – Simmo's, he must assume – lies on the edge of the basin, where a dribble of toothpaste has hardened to a scum.

Seb is here to clean up this terrible mess – his and his mother's.

He stands over the toilet and presses the flush button. The toilet slurps down the bloodied paper, but it chokes with a cough at the S-bend. He gives it another flush but it gurgles and regurgitates the paper, which settles into a scarlet clot at the bottom of the bowl. Seb flushes yet again and this time water floods the bowl until it is half filled. Filaments of tissue swim free of the clot, but the water fails to drain. He gambles on a fourth flush. The bowl fills rapidly until the tainted water and its tendrils cascade over the rim and flood the bathroom floor.

Seb steps backwards but the flood catches him. He heads downstairs to the laundry where he finds a toilet plunger, a mop and bucket, disinfectant spray and wipes. He is climbing the stairs with them when a *ding!* sounds from the study. He lowers the cleaning gear and goes to the opened door. In the in-tray by the computer, the screen of his father's mobile is lit with a new text message.

There can be no one from his dad's extensive sphere who does not know Ted McCall is dead.

He touches the screen and enters his father's password. Seb knows it well. It's the same password for their business account and for the safe at the shop: 4973. The first two digits are for Ted's year of birth, the second two for his age. The code was updated with his every birthday.

This text is from CB – Connie Blunt. It says:

Maybe Simmo was right.

Seb eases himself into the office chair and keeps reading.

I've decided I'll just tell Seb tonight, by email, when I get to Tocumwal. It sounds gutless, I know, but there might be too much to go through face to face. We're never good at that, Seb and me. I wish you were here to share this with me. Then again, it wouldn't be a discussion if you were still here, would it? We wouldn't be explaining anything.

***

At a truck stop, Connie fondles her phone and watches the amenities block in the rear-vision mirror. She places the phone under the dash. She knows it's a kind of madness, all this communication with Ted, but perhaps it equally keeps the madness at bay. Gracie, framed in the mirror, strides from the toilets and towards the car, eager to return to her grandmother's company. Gracie, solace for everything. For every shitty thing. She flings open the passenger door and collapses in her seat.

'Just made it.'

'Phew!' Connie says. Back on the highway, she accelerates past two trucks, then eases to cruise control. 'Where were we?' she asks.

'Graphene.'

'That's right. One atom thick.'

'Yeah, I'll send you the link,' Gracie says, 'but you can't even picture how thin that is. It's the first two-dimensional material ever discovered, but it's two hundred times stronger than steel and a thousand times better than copper as a conductor.'

'If there are no research positions, you could always get a job selling the stuff.'

'I'd be competing with a load of bloodsuckers on the stock market.'

'Is that a job description? Stock-market bloodsucker?'

'Better still, I'll become an influencer.'

'Influencer? Bloodsucker sounds more lucrative.'

'You'd be surprised. Remember Charlotte Hester from my netball team?'

'Think so. The gorky goal shooter.'

'Once was gorky, now is catwalk material. Anyway, that's what she does for a living these days: *influencing*. Just posts crap on social media – "go to this restaurant, see that show, wear this Zimmerman frock, walk in my Saint Laurent shoes" – and gets paid squillions. She's just bought a waterfront. Like, seriously, disgustingly rich.'

'How'd she get that gig?'

'Surgery.'

'What?'

'Surgery and injectables. Boobs and lips – definitely enhanced.'

'Makes me sad.'

'Makes her rich. She has to live with baboon lips, though.' Gracie leans across the console and pouts at her grandmother with baboon lips.

Connie pushes her away. 'You'll make me crash.'

★★★

The phone screen fades to black again. Seb re-enters the password and re-reads his mother's strange text to his father for the fifth time. Still it makes no sense. What is it she knows and Simmo knows and his father knew that they've all been keeping from him? How much worse could it be than what he's already discovered: this squalid business of his mother's and Simmo's affair? And why text Ted about it?

Seb scrolls and discovers it's not the first from his mother to his father since he died. There are two more, the first on Friday at 12:54 p.m. That, Seb realises, is within an hour or two of him catching his mother and Simmo.

'Actually,' it says, 'it's too complicated. I'll call.'

Call? So there are voice messages, too?

First things first. Seb goes to the second text, at 6:47 on Saturday night.

Simmo dropped in again today. Surprising. Lovely. Walking now to meet Gracie at the Pavilion. I googled around on shark attacks. You're seventy-five times more likely to be killed by lightning strike, according to some American study. I'd say that needs fact-checking.

It's bizarre: the widow reporting her affair in perfunctory memos to her just-dead husband. The texts are brief, in the kind of shorthand he remembers of his parents' conversations.

Seb goes to the log of voicemails on his father's phone. There are six since his death, three from CB's mobile and three from her home phone, all in the past few days. Seb studies the metadata.

The first call, from 5:23 a.m. on Friday, is just over eight minutes. The second starts at 12:56 p.m. that same day, immediately after she abandoned her text, confessing it was all 'too complicated'. Seb could cut to the chase and start listening there, but he'll need to hear them all. He presses play on the first and puts the phone on speaker.

It starts oddly. 'No I don't, Ted. I don't know what to do.' Then his mother breathes heavily. It drags on, her morose breathing and her perverse drollery.

'So here I am … lying in our dirty sheets … I always had that weird fetish for your sweat …'

★★★

Canola fields blaze storybook yellow either side of the highway. A dreamy pop ballad halts their conversation.

'Who's this?' Connie asks.

'Julia Jacklin.'

'Australian?'

'Yeah.'

'Reminds me a bit of Mazzy Star,' Connie says. 'Different, but you know, trippy.'

'Yeah.'

So Gracie follows up with Mazzy Star's 'Fade Into You'. She turns it up loud and they're wrapped in its stillness, its defiant quietness. It lulls them towards the next horizon where giant wind turbines barely turn, a sigh of breath through a still photograph.

'Take a pic,' Connie tells Gracie. 'I want to keep this moment.'

★★★

Seb moves to the second voice message, seven minutes and eight seconds. His mother doesn't bother with greetings. She opens by reporting: 'Seb walked in on Simmo and me this morning.' Seb awaits her elaboration. Presumably she will describe the scene he walked in on. Her voice shifts a gear. 'He caught us *in flagrante delicto,* as it were.'

She pronounces this exuberantly and titters at herself. She's unhinged.

'That makes it sound sordid,' she says. 'It wasn't. Not at all. It was sweet and tender, Ted, as I think you'd understand.'

Yes, unhinged.

'Poor Seb's in shock, of course.'

His mother describes what came next and Seb can quibble with none of the detail, but at no point does she attempt to explain to her husband what happened before Seb entered their room, or what led to her and Simmo occupying his bed three days after his funeral, as if that was all incidental background that wouldn't concern Ted.

She is co-opting her late husband as her confidant in the matter of her adultery against him.

But there's nothing here of use to Seb. It explains nothing. He hears the rest of this message in a blur of outrageous platitudes about wonderful Simmo and how much he's missing Ted. Seb wants to break something.

'So there you have it, Ted,' she says. 'We're not going to die wondering, Simmo and I.'

Seb goes to the third call, late Friday night.

'Me again. It's hot, Ted. Hooley dooley, it's hot!'

There's a sound close to the phone of swirling and chinking.

'I tried using that hammer thingy in the drawer to crush the ice, the way you do. The way you *did.* I keep doing that. Anyway, I squeezed the bejesus out of the lime and went easy on the tonic and I was especially reckless with the gin, the way you always say. Said. I don't know. I didn't bother zesting the lime, though. Maybe that's it. Could it really make that much difference?'

Seb listens to her crunching ice between her teeth. It might as well be cartilage and bone.

'I don't suppose Simmo and I would come as such a surprise to you. The timing, possibly. It certainly surprised me that it happened so soon, but not so much that it happened. Simmo was kind of awkward about it. Me too.'

A raspy, scornful laugh escapes from Seb.

'I'm mostly surprised by how wonderful it was,' she says. 'He really was something, our Simmo. I mean, frankly, he was pretty hot.'

Seb is sickened.

'It's been a long time between drinks, as you know,' she tells his father. 'What is it? Fourteen, fifteen years? It was all very well for you – you and your Rotary nights.'

What is she saying?

'Fourteen, I think it is, since the last of my Big Pharma junkets.'

She stops talking. Seb listens to her breathing until there's a sharp intake of air.

'Same time next year. Not sure why we kept that going, Will and I. Might as well call a plumber as a gynaecologist.' She sniggers. 'Remember? I actually made that crack to Will. Only teasing, but he took it to heart. He'd had a humour bypass.'

Seb is overwhelmed by nausea. He puts his mother on pause, scoops up the wastepaper basket from under the desk and heaves, but nothing comes up. She's suggesting that not only was she having an annual fling, but that it was an in-joke between her and his father. She's bantering on as if Ted were a winking advocate of her infidelities.

Seb dry-retches again, then returns the basket to its position under the desk. He touches the screen.

'Did you ever mention Will Masterson to Simmo?' she's asking Ted. 'I think you might've told me that you did. I can't quite remember. It doesn't really matter. I suppose I'll tell him at some stage.

'I really wish you'd told Seb, though. About everything, I mean. It's not fair it has to be me. I have no idea where to start. It would've been much easier if we'd done it when I said. If he was old enough to get Kimberley pregnant, to be a father – he wasn't, I know, but he insisted he was – then surely he was old enough to know our home truths.'

She stops talking. Her pauses are maddening.

'You know, Ted, I could still make you tell him. I had a distressing email exchange with Seb this afternoon. Then, this evening – I suppose I was seeking distractions – I did some more reading on this thing they're calling – what is it? – *augmented eternity*. I was telling you about the wacky widow turning her dead hubby into a chatbot, but it's going to get a whole lot spookier. If I was so inclined, apparently, I could collect every piece of data we have on you – your letters, emails, phone messages, all your favourite records and movies and books, all the videos of you surfing, and of your singalongs, and every bad joke you ever told, the whole kit and caboodle – and we could feed it into a super-computer and recreate your neural network. Effectively, it would be you, in mind if not body, but then we could create a hologram of you and it would be Ted McCall, resurrected, not just a robot regurgitating the kind of stuff you might have said, but a walking, talking character with a brain, developing its own ideas, evolving.'

She swirls the ice in her glass and slurps.

'Or so they claim. Maybe your hologram would grow a spine. You know, enough spine to tell your son the truth.'

There's a crushing weight in Seb's chest. He retrieves the basket from under the desk, but still he dry-retches. He clings to the basket.

What truth?

'I'm hardly going to resurrect you just to spite you,' she is saying, laughing theatrically. 'I'll leave resurrections to Seb.'

He realises how much his mother's low, scornful laugh sounds like his.

'I don't think you ever contemplated me having to do it, or how hard it would be. To tell him now, when he's going on forty, it'll be like telling him he's adopted.'

Another pause.

'Jesus, if I hadn't carried him to birth myself, I'd have to wonder.'

In this cupboard of a room, everything is magnified, especially the DNA in her smirking laugh. How much she sounds like him! Or he like her.

'Anyway, Ted, enough for now …'

Seb stares at the phone. She has to be kidding.

'It's late and I'm trying to stick to my routine – hit the water before the riff-raff.'

She sighs and knocks three times on hollow timber.

'Hooroo, my love.'

Seb glares at his father's phone. He picks it up. He puts it down. He knocks three times on the desk to confirm the echo of his mother, that she was sitting in this chair. Seb pitches forward and lays his head on the desk and rests before subjecting himself to her fourth and fifth calls. These, too, are an endurance.

She drivels on for ten minutes until she cuts out, then a further four in Simmo's company, but adds nothing of substance to the snippets he caught from outside her window yesterday – before she sooled the police onto him. Again he hears her disdain: 'A paean in the arse.'

He fears her sixth and final message, from late last night, will also yield nothing, but then he fears it will reveal all. He clicks play and his mother, as usual, dispenses with greetings.

'A change in the program tonight. I've got Simmo with me – under sufferance, I'm sure. He thinks I'm out of my mind, just for making these calls.'

'I didn't say that.'

'No, you're too polite. Say g'day to Ted.'

'It's okay. I'll just watch.'

She squawks. 'He *likes to watch*. He'll just sit here and watch me talk to my dead husband. And I'm the weird one?'

Seb hears a faint whimper from Simmo. He, too, must be tired of her relentless wisecracking.

'I was trying to explain to Simmo that I'm not calling for your benefit, Ted. These calls are entirely for mine, and they do seem to help. They knock my thoughts into some shape. Otherwise everything can swirl around in there for hours – because I'm not used to having all this time on my hands for stewing over things. I was doing a bit of that this afternoon. I'd called in the police on Seb when I caught him snooping on us. They handcuffed him, which was excessive. Simmo certainly thought so. I mean, he thought me calling the police was excessive, and fair enough.

'Anyway, I've agreed I'll tell Seb everything tomorrow morning. Everything. It won't make it any easier just because you're dead. Once I tell him, I suppose we'll tell everybody, and everything that anyone ever understood about our entire married life will change. Friends will stop calling – not because of what you were but because we deceived them. Not just you. Both of us. I went along with it and we lied and lied and lied, and now I'm the surviving liar. People will resent me for that or, worse, they'll pity me. That'd be much worse: the woman who lived in the closet.'

Seb feels a sudden rush of heat rising in his cheeks. At last she has said it. She's said the thing she was getting to. He's heard it now, but still he doesn't get it. He stands in a stupor. He sits back down.

'All these years in the closet,' she says, 'as the wife of a man in the closet. Who'd give two hoots these days if they found out you were gay? Nobody cares anymore, Ted. But they'll be intrigued about me. I'll be the talk of the town. Why would she stay with him? Or didn't she know? You wouldn't think a doctor could be so thick?'

She couldn't be more explicit, yet nothing is clear to Seb.

'Telling Seb will be hardest, of course. I'd sooner tell the world than tell Seb. I will tell him, though, tomorrow. Hooroo, Ted.'

But she hasn't told Seb. She's on the road to Tocumwal and she hasn't.

Seb reconnects the phone to the charger and returns it to the in-tray. He stands and walks from the room and becomes aware of a tingling numbness in his toes, a light-headedness. He's been sitting in the same position too long. He collects the mop and bucket and cleaning paraphernalia from the bottom step and wrangles them as he climbs to his mother's room. In the bathroom, he stands in a puddle and looks at the bloody mess – his and his mother's. He plunges the toilet. He mops up the flood. He disinfects all surfaces.

★★★

Gracie plays DJ. She's playing the divas, the young and the ageless – Angie McMahon, Nina Simone, Jen Cloher and Janice Joplin – and she plays some Bob Dylan and Paul Kelly because they're on the road and they always do, and they yak over the music because the highway devours conversation.

Connie introduces Gracie to the subject of augmented eternity.

'I thought you'd be amused.'

'Amused?' Gracie says. 'That's bonkers.'

Connie discloses she's been leaving messages on Pop's phone.

'Truly?'

'Is that bonkers?'

'Probably.' Gracie picks up Connie's phone and keys in the password – 5270. It's the same format as her Pop's: year of birth and current age.

'Don't read them,' Connie says.

'Why? Are they about me?'

'No, they're private.'

Gracie is disappointed. 'Then let me text him – from you. What do you want to tell him?'

'Nothing. I already did.'

'C'mon! This beats I Spy.'

Connie tries to think of something.

'I know,' Gracie says, and she starts thumbing her message into the phone, while singing the same treacly gibberish. She presses send and they listen to it slip into the ether with a *whoosh!*

★★★

Seb is in the laundry, watching the last of Simmo's blood drain into the tub, when he hears the *ding* in the study. What now might be possessing his mother to message his father? He goes and finds her text still on the screen.

Aba daba daba daba daba daba dab

These nonsense words irk him. They instantly evoke his father's arrival at his back gate on any given day. If the mood had ever carried Seb, he greeted his dad a third higher, *Aba, daba, daba …* But now he hears that stupid song with new significance.

It's so camp.

He swipes his father's phone and taps in the password. He types a three-word reply to his mother.

# 7.
# ROADKILL

Connie's phone goes *ding* under the dash and its screen lights up. Gracie frowns at her grandmother. Connie takes her eyes off the road while Gracie picks it up.

'It's Pop,' she says.

'Hardly,' Connie says. 'What does it say?'

Gracie stops the music, then lip-reads the message. Connie nudges her for the answer.

'Go to hell.'

'What?'

'It says: Go to hell.'

'Oh?'

'In capitals, with an exclamation mark.'

'Right.'

'Spooky,' says Gracie.

'It's your father.' Connie is livid. Seb is in the house, on Ted's phone. What is he up to? 'Call him,' she says. 'Put him through the speakers so I can talk.'

'On Pop's phone?'

'That's the one he's holding, apparently.'

Gracie resets Connie's phone to Bluetooth and calls Ted's number. After two rings, Seb's voice fills the car speakers.

'Yes.' He's loud.

'You're in my house,' Connie says.

'Yes.'

'I locked up.'

'I noticed.'

'You've broken in?'

'I used my key. You lied.'

'I beg your pardon.'

'You and Dad, you lied to me.'

Connie feels suddenly faint. She glances at Gracie, then back to the road.

Seb erupts. 'All my fucking life, you couldn't tell me.'

Connie brakes suddenly and the car jolts. Gracie glares at her: *What's going on?* Connie feels wretched. She should have stopped and called Seb privately. She checks the rear-vision mirror and finds a sedan swerving to overtake. Its horn blasts. Connie pulls into the shoulder of the highway and stops.

'Mum?' Seb asks.

'What have you done, Seb?'

'What have *I* done? What have you done?'

'You've listened.'

'Yes.'

'To his phone – to my messages. This is a gross invasion.'

'Gross? You and Dad lying, year after year, while you carried on your farce of a marriage – that's gross.'

Gracie, dumbfounded, says nothing. Connie needs to tell Seb that Gracie is with her, but first she has to answer this charge.

'Yes, we lied, but you're wrong about our marriage. I was going to explain it all to you.'

'But you didn't.'

'I was planning to write to you tonight and explain, so you could digest it all and then we could discuss it.'

'Explain now. We can discuss it now.'

He waits.

'Off you go then,' he says.

She falters.

'I'm almost forty, Mum,' he says, and keeps waiting. 'It's a bit late to be telling me our family is a sham.'

'It isn't. Please don't say that.'

'What should I say?'

Gracie gapes at her grandmother: *What is he talking about?*

'It was never a sham,' Connie says. 'Your father wanted a family, our family, more than anything. And that's what we did.'

'Was this some kind of deal between you two? Like ...' He is struggling for the words. 'Like, I don't know, like you gave up your womb to a homosexual?'

Now Gracie glares at Connie as though she's an alien. *Do I know you? Did I know Pop?* Connie feels hollow to her core. She keeps her eyes on the road while Gracie just stares at her.

'What was in it for you?' Seb asks.

'It was nothing like that.'

'Then what? Tell me.'

'I'm trying.'

Gracie covers the phone and mouths: 'Does he know I'm with you?'

Connie shakes her head, no.

Seb perseveres. 'How did you even, am I even ... am I even his?'

'Of course you're his.'

'Then why would you, knowing he was ...?'

'I didn't.'

'What?'

'I didn't know, not when we married.' Connie checks the mirror and realises they're on a blind bend. A road train looms behind them, too close. It thunders past, blasting its horn, and the car shudders. 'It's not safe here,' Connie says.

'What?'

'I need to get off this bend. Just let me get back on the road.'

'Why wouldn't you have left him?'

'I did, Seb, at first. I need to move the car. Please let me tell you, one thing at a time.' She starts the engine and waits for a break in the traffic, then pulls out. She accelerates to the speed limit and puts it on cruise control.

'Mum?'

'Yes.'

'When did you find out?'

'You were fourteen months.'

'He lied to you, too?'

'By omission, yes.'

They go quiet. Connie has been reciting this in her mind for years. It's not flowing as she imagined.

'He waited that long to tell you?'

'He didn't tell me.'

'I don't understand.'

'Tory told me.'

'Aunty Tory?' Seb says. 'Lochie's Tory?'

'Yes.'

This story – Tory's part in the story – seems so incidental, or at least as Connie considers what information Seb most requires and in what order. This is out of order. She had it planned, where she would begin, and that was not where or how she discovered Ted was gay. It was to be where and how Ted did.

But Seb is pressing her. 'Mum? What about Tory?'

So she starts from here, too late in the story.

'A couple of years after your dad and I married, Lochie and Tory had their wedding. I was her bridesmaid and so I gave a speech, a silly speech. I thought it was a funny story, that was all.'

Connie proceeds to recount it, in fragments, and to tell the part of the story left out of her speech at her own wedding. She's in such a fog, so muddled, she can't be sure which parts she is retelling and which she is merely remembering.

At Lochie and Tory's wedding reception, Connie had told the story about the old walnut desk in her childhood bedroom, where she had done her homework, and of the day when she and Tory were both thirteen years old, and Tory took her compass and used its spike to vandalise the desk with a declaration of their duelling infatuation with the same sixteen-year-old boy, Ted McCall. Connie described Tory engraving in the desk TD & CB ♥ TMac and how she helped her fill in the letters with blue ink and the heart with red ink.

'It's still there on that old desk,' Connie told the wedding guests. 'Tory teased me at the time: "You can have Lochie." Well, we were only kids, but how wrong she turned out to be. Here we are, ladies and gentlemen, if you'll be upstanding and raise your glasses: To Tory and her groom, the other McCall twin, Lochie.'

'It was just a cheeky wedding speech,' Connie is saying now. 'That was all.'

The teenage Connie and Tory had known Ted was unattainable. Both knew it was silly. Their lovesickness for the same boy became the self-mocking focus of the girls' inseparability.

'But what about it?' Seb asks. 'What's the point?'

The point?

'The next day, at their wedding recovery party out on Burrabogie, Tory cornered me. She was angry. She said, "Why would you humiliate us with that story?" And I said, "Humiliate you? It wasn't meant that way. It was for a laugh."'

Connie remembers it vividly, but is she retelling it so clearly?

'You knew,' Tory told her, 'that Lochie only married me once he knew you were definitely out of the question.'

'No, I didn't know that.'

'I think you did. You must have realised how mad he got when Ted announced he was marrying you. If you didn't, you'd be the only one.'

Connie told Tory: 'You know that Lochie tells Ted nothing.

225

If any of that's true, Ted and I would be the last to know.'

Connie had never had the heart or gumption to tell Tory what Ted had told her in Manhattan: that Lochie regarded Tory as the second-most marriageable woman in Tocumwal.

'Everyone at your wedding,' Tory said, 'could see how miserable Lochie was.'

He was a groomsman, but Lochie had declined Ted's invitation to be his best man, or to give a speech, so those duties fell to young Simmo, Ted's surfboat crewmate and, at this point, employee at Surfside Hardware.

'Lochie doesn't love me,' Connie pleaded with Tory.

'I didn't suggest he did. He just would have preferred you as a wife.'

'If you honestly believe that, why have you married him?'

Tory didn't answer. She merely asked: 'And why you Ted?'

Connie sensed something malignant in this, and that more was coming. She became instantly defensive. 'Because I love Ted. Because Ted loves me.'

'You sound so sure about that,' Tory said.

*She* sounded so sure that Connie was mistaken. Why would she question it?

'I'm sure,' Connie said.

'Even while he prefers men?'

Right there, the earth fell from under Connie's feet. Her head rang with those words: *prefers men.*

'Even while he what?'

'You knew that!'

'What?'

'You must have known.'

'Known what? What are you saying?'

'Ted prefers men.'

Connie reeled, as if concussed.

'So,' Tory asked, 'he didn't share that with you before you

married him? You must have heard something about that ringer.'

'The what?'

'Why do you think their old man told Ted he had to go. Someone caught him in the shearing sheds with the Kiwi ringer. They hushed it all up, but I thought you'd have heard. No one told you?'

'No.'

'I assumed your dad or Clem would have heard something. Anyway, Cliffy was having none of that business on Burrabogie.'

Ted, by now, was watching Tory and Connie from the veranda. He could see his wife was rigid with shock. She looked to him and he knew at once what it was.

Tory was still talking. 'You can understand why Lochie was so pissed off. You had your choice of identical twins, and you chose the queer one. The queer one got the girl.'

Connie says now: 'She wanted to hurt me. I suppose she had cause.'

Seb's breathing is heavy through the car speakers. No one talks. Somewhere in the back of her mind, Connie had wanted to hurt Lochie with her wedding speech – the one given as comic relief – but never Tory.

When Tory had left Connie alone in the garden, Ted went to his wife. He led her behind the hedge, out of sight.

'You're gay,' she said.

He sobbed instantly. The whole edifice of Ted McCall imploded. He crumpled before her eyes. 'Am I?' he said.

'You are or you aren't.'

'I don't have to be. I haven't been, never since you came along.'

'Never?' She wanted to believe that. 'But when did you know?' she asked Ted.

'I don't know. I still don't know.'

'What were you thinking? You married me.' She felt ill with rage and grief.

'I was thinking I wanted a life with you,' Ted said. 'You came to Manhattan when I was unsure, then you made me sure. You made me certain about what I wanted and what I didn't. I didn't want that life. I wanted you. I wanted a family.'

That life? What life? She insisted Ted describe it for her, his Manhattan sabbatical, his first prolonged experiment with homosexuality, until Connie intervened. He described the years of confusion that preceded Manhattan, a childhood of unbidden urges, of impossible crushes on boys.

'How old was he when he had these feelings?'

Seb's question jolts Connie from Manhattan.

'Eleven, twelve.'

Still it's a blur, the telling and the mere remembering. For Seb — and for Gracie, still speechless in the passenger seat — she relates Ted's recollections of his first inklings of an awareness. Of something. Ted told Connie he knew before he understood. His impulses spoke to him long before he comprehended there was such a thing.

'He couldn't tell anyone,' Connie says, 'because he thought he was the only one — the only one on the planet who felt that way. Whatever it was, he thought he'd invented it.'

Connie can still hear Ted, not yet thirty-five, using those words to explain to her what he felt as a young boy.

'I thought I'd invented it,' he said.

She fumbles through Ted's telling of it, that he was never much attracted to the girls who sought his attention. Sometimes he went with them. That seemed to be the thing to do. He believed his lack of interest in them would change, that his peculiar attractions would pass. They didn't. At boarding school he discovered there were others like him, apparently, because there was much discussion about fairies and poofters and faggots and speculation about who among them might be one. No one ever suggested Ted. He concluded this meant he mustn't be one. It mustn't be true. He was mistaken about himself. He wasn't a pansy.

Or if he was, he would change. He would choose not to be.

It was a rugby school and he played in the First XV. He rowed in the First VIII. He dated girls. He had proper girlfriends.

It wasn't until university that he met homosexual men who knew precisely what they were. He met quite a few there. In the theatre groups, in the reviews, some were open about it. Ted never was. He slept with some of them, but he was discreet. He never had boyfriends, never romances.

'I thought I'd grow out of it,' he told Connie.

'He thought it was a phase,' Connie tells Seb. 'It wasn't.'

Drought forced Ted's return to Tocumwal. His father and brother needed his labour and he abandoned university. It would be some months, they all agreed, but Ted was almost ten years back on Burrabogie with Cliff, Irene and Lochie. There were no homosexuals in Tocumwal, or none Ted knew of, or none he dared ask if he suspected. Local women placed themselves in his orbit and Ted, to please his mother, dated some of them. She wanted him to marry a local girl, to raise a family. He assured her that this was what he wanted, too. He had sex with some of these women. None of them lasted.

'When you were screwing them,' Connie asked Ted, 'did you imagine they were men? Just so you could?'

He faltered. It seemed he had to think about that.

'Sometimes,' he confessed, 'yes.'

'And me? Do you need to imagine I'm a man?'

He was slower to answer.

'No,' he said.

It seemed an equivocal 'no'.

'Certainly not at first,' he added.

'But now?'

Ted cried again. 'Sometimes.'

The truth was they had hardly made love since early in her pregnancy, but Connie had thought this normal, or not so abnormal, because whose sex life was ever invigorated by morning sickness, fatigue, constipation, postpartum infection, mastitis, the expressing of breast milk, soiled nappies? None of it was sexy. It was a phase.

It wasn't.

'You're homosexual,' she told Ted again.

'But I don't want to be,' he said. 'I want our marriage, our family.'

'But do you want me?' she demanded. 'I mean *want me.*'

'I love you.'

'That's not what I asked.'

'There's nobody in this world I admire more than you, Connie.'

'Fuck that, Ted. I don't want to be admired. I want to be desired.'

Connie is remembering now. She isn't divulging this exchange to Seb or Gracie. Gracie is still gawping at her. As if what Connie has disclosed already isn't enough for one day, she is yet to tell Seb that his daughter is with her.

'Mum?'

Seb is waiting.

'This is why Dad left Burrabogie?' he asks.

She's thinking: hasn't she already explained that? The swarm of memories refuses to coincide with the chronology and she can't be sure what she's left in or out.

'Yes. He was thirty-one before it happened again.'

'What happened?'

'The shearer,' Connie says.

'The ringer?' Seb says.

So she did tell that part.

'It was just a fling,' Ted told her. 'I would never have instigated it. I couldn't have picked him as gay. He picked me somehow. I don't know why he knew. He knew better than me, I suppose. He was more certain than I was.'

'Lochie caught them?' Seb asks.

'Almost certainly,' Connie says. 'Two sons were always going to be one too many for the property. It wouldn't split into two viable farms.'

The succession question was answered by natural selection. She remembers Ted putting it that way.

'The queer twin had to go,' she tells Seb.

She listens to him breathing. She awaits a question but none comes.

'By then your father didn't care,' she says. 'He didn't want the property and he didn't want a life with Cliff or Lochie. He left quietly and it broke his mother's heart, but nobody told Irene why he was going. The story never got out. The McCall name was safe.'

Connie is rambling. She's sure she is. Ted left with his bugger-off money – his name for it. He could take it or leave it, so he took his thirty grand and ran, first to New York, as far from Tocumwal and his father as he could get.

'Where he found men,' Seb says.

'He needed to go find out for himself. He was doing that – finding out, quietly, anonymously, with no one to judge him – when I flew in from London to snare him, with nothing but a childish conviction that he would be the love of my life. I was oblivious.'

Connie is exhausted. She hopes Seb won't interrogate her about Ted's adventures in Manhattan. By Ted's account they were torrid. Connie attempts to circumvent further inquiry.

'You'd understand what a very conventional young man your father was. He was conservative. I don't mean politically. He wasn't political, but he was socially conservative. He was a country boy and he was easily shocked, and he was astonished by what he found in New York, by how brazen they were. He might have found the same in Sydney but he happened to look in Manhattan.'

She won't elaborate on the cavalcade of queerness that confronted Ted: the line dance of promiscuity, the fake cowboys in their plaid shirts and ten-gallon hats, the mother imitators in their wigs, and the fetishists in their workboots and leathers. Over time, Ted described it all to Connie. The debauchery. At an underground speakeasy he found sadomasochists slung naked from the ceilings. He recoiled at the tweezering of their nipples, which was the least of it. He was horrified. Where was the affection, the love? He was still looking for it when Connie arrived.

'You confused him,' Seb suggests.

'I did. I was clueless and besotted and I marched right in. You have to understand the times, and the culture shock for your dad. It was outrageous and your father wasn't. It scared him.'

Gracie stares out her window. The canola fields are behind them and they're into hardscrabble sheep country. For her years of silence, Connie feels treacherous to Seb, but also to Gracie. And she feels she owes it to Ted to give them the kind of explanation he never did, and never would have.

'He'd always been popular. He didn't know how to be unpopular. But now he was presented with a lifestyle, if he chose it, that would undermine everything people understood about him and what he understood about himself. He saw what it might mean to adopt a gay life, and it terrified him. It was too dangerous. So when I landed, he was relieved. I was someone from home, someone familiar, though he didn't know me and I didn't really know him. But it turned out he liked me – really liked me. We were hilarious together and I think, yes, I confused him, and he did fall in love with me in his own way – I know he did – but I also presented him with an opportunity, a way out.

'Because what he really wanted was to continue living a very conventional life. He wanted a family, kids. Loads of them. He wanted a nice home to put them all in, and a solid business. He couldn't imagine any of that was possible as a gay man. Then I just fell from the sky, and I was the first woman he could picture himself spending a lot of time with.'

On Lafayette Street, Ted asked her: 'Could you see yourself married to someone like me?'

Someone *like me*. Someone *like a closet homosexual* might have provoked a different answer.

'Ted thought he could choose a heterosexual life. By marrying me, by starting a family, he thought he'd chosen.'

'He couldn't,' Seb says.

'He tried.'

'I can't understand why you stayed with him. Once you knew, why would you stay married?' The question hangs as condemnation: what kind of fool would stay married? Seb sighs, the speakers seething with his impatience. 'Why wouldn't you just leave?'

'I did leave,' she answers. 'Or I stayed.'

'What?'

'I stayed with you in Tocumwal. I told him it was over, that it was pointless, and that he'd have to return alone to Bondi, to the business, while I worked out what I might do next, where I could move with you, how we could pay for it, whether I could afford to keep studying medicine. He pleaded for us to come home with him. He kept saying he was choosing me, choosing us – that we were his life. But I told him, "You don't get to choose to be heterosexual."'

'I do,' Ted said. 'That's what I'm choosing.'

Left behind in Tocumwal, Connie told her father none of it. She told Mick Blunt she needed rest, that was all. One week became three.

'For three weeks I cried,' she says. 'I'm in grief now that he's gone – of course I am – but I'll admit it was a more unbearable grief then: coming to accept he could never love me the way I loved him. He loved me, but it would never be equal.'

Gracie is crying beside her grandmother. Still Connie can't cry.

Each night Ted rang from Sydney and Connie took the call on her father's enclosed veranda. Ted pleaded and Connie said no.

'Was he with men at this point?' Seb asks.

'He told me there were none, which I believed, and I still believe. But he also kept saying there didn't need to be any – at any stage – and I couldn't believe that.'

Connie, however, was due to commence the second year of her medical degree and needed to return to Sydney. She had no income and no shelter except for the one-bedroom rental flat currently occupied by the gay husband she was in the process of leaving. Ted had the fledgling hardware business, heavily mortgaged, with no capacity to rent her a second flat.

'You can't do it without me,' he said. 'Just come back, for now at least. We'll work it out.'

'No,' she kept saying.

Connie confided in her brother.

'You must have known, Clem. Tory thought you must have.'

'Why would I have known?'

'You'd seen him in New York. Wasn't it obvious?'

'You were with him in New York. Why would it be any more obvious to me?'

Connie hadn't had the slightest inkling. What might she have noticed? His gorgeous blue shirt? He wore no uniform, no denim and plaid, no black leathers.

On deadline to return to university, Connie relented. The marriage, in her mind, was certainly over, and she kept making that clear to Ted, but for now they could not afford to separate. As an interim arrangement, she returned to live with Ted, at least until they could find the means to divorce. This would involve sharing their only bed. Ted lived in the hope that, by the time it was financially viable to split, Connie would have changed her mind.

Upon her return, and finding Simmo alone at Surfside Hardware, Connie stepped into the shop, slid the bolt into the lock and drew the blinds. She wanted to hurt Ted. It is a detail that flashes in her mind now but she can't bring herself to share it. She attempts instead to follow the timeline.

Back at home with Ted, a month or more passed. Despite her grief, or because of it, Connie became fanatical about her studies. Ted, desolate with guilt, gave her all the time she needed. He relieved her of the burdens of home-keeping and especially of raising Seb. He was, in every respect except the one that mattered most to Connie, the perfect husband.

Their living arrangement, though peculiar, was better than any alternative she could imagine. At that stage. Connie kept working on the assumption that their divorce would follow her studies, which had years to run.

After several months, Ted attempted physical intimacy. Connie refused.

'I won't be mercy-fucked by my gay husband.'

She still wanted to hurt Ted, and this hurt him.

'It wouldn't be like that,' he said.

He wanted more children. Connie was adamant there would be no more, certainly not with her. She wanted him to stop pretending.

'Come out,' she said.

'No.'

'We can raise Seb together, but not while masquerading as a couple. Go public and I'll support you.'

Ted refused. There was too much at stake.

'I'm in hardware,' he said, as though the risk to their livelihood was self-evident. 'We'd be the faggot family. Seb would be the son of a poof. You'd be the doctor who married the fruit.'

'I'm not a doctor yet.'

'You may never be if we can't hold this together.'

It was expedient indeed to hold it together.

'Are there any men yet?' she asked Ted.

'No,' he kept answering.

She still believed him. His life, between running the business and keeping house and his commitments at the surf club, allowed no space for it.

'There should be,' she said.

It was difficult for her to acknowledge this, and to urge him to find male company, but she thought she should expedite the inevitable. She was living in a state of expectancy. Sooner or later, Ted would have to choose a gay life.

'Lie to the world if you must,' she said, 'but not to me, not to yourself.' Connie told him to pick a night.

'What are you suggesting?'

'One night a week,' she said. 'Make it a regular night.'

It took her months to convince him to even consider it.

'There never was a Rotary night, was there?' Seb asks now.

'Mmmm?'

'Tuesday nights. He never did go to Rotary Club, did he?'

Ted had declined several invitations to join Rotary. Rotarians, however, met on Tuesday nights, which best suited Ted and Connie's schedule. So Rotary became their euphemism. It became their code and Ted's alibi, should anyone ask. No one ever did.

'No,' Connie confirms, 'there was no Rotary.'

She can hear Seb's anger boiling. He erupts. 'Because his Tuesday nights were for cock.'

'Stop it, Seb.'

'Weren't they?'

'I'm with Gracie.'

This stops him.

'Gracie? What are you doing there?' She can't answer before he accuses her: 'You already knew all of this.'

'No!' she says. 'I'm hearing it now, with you, for the first time.'

They listen to Seb seething.

'So you don't know about Simmo?'

'Simmo? What about Simmo?'

Connie interrupts. 'My plan was to tell you everything first, Seb.'

'But you couldn't.'

'I was going to.'

'What's going on?' Gracie asks.

'Your grandmother and Simmo are *going on*.'

'Hey!'

Gracie rocks back against her head rest. 'Since when?'

'Since Friday,' Connie answers.

'This is so full-on!' Gracie says.

It is unbearably intense. Connie, though, feels she must speak on Ted's behalf.

'You need to understand what different times they were. It was still a crime, for heaven's sake. He was hardly the only man keeping this secret.'

She can hear Seb processing this. 'It wasn't a crime by the time I was old enough to understand. Still you both kept it from me.'

'I wish we hadn't. I'm sorry.'

'You're sorry?'

'Yes.'

'Ah well, never mind. She's sorry.'

Connie attempts a retreat. 'This is too much for now,' she says. 'You have every right to be furious. Let me call you tonight.'

'No.'

'No,' Gracie agrees.

'Who were these men?' Seb asks.

'I don't know. I never met them. No one in particular, which was the whole point.'

She won't describe Ted's Tuesday nights, what little she knows of them. In those early days he had ventured to the northern beaches where nobody would recognise him, where he met strangers in parks, on the headlands, in public toilet blocks. Connie will not mention the night Ted appeared at their door with facial wounds, livid with bruising, and told her that three teenagers had mugged him. This much was true. Days later he disclosed their apparent motive. They had assaulted both Ted and the man who occupied the same toilet cubicle. Like Ted, his companion wore a wedding ring. Many of the men who met this way were married, Ted told Connie.

'I have nothing left to hide from you,' he said.

It was a strange consolation, but she did want his honesty. She soon set some ground rules. She refused to lie awake wondering whether Ted was dead or alive. They discussed safer options than these gay beats in public places. There were bath houses. There were sex-on-premises establishments. Ted would need to budget for them.

'It's only sex,' he said. 'That's all it will ever be.'

'We'll see.'

She insisted they would review their living arrangements regularly.

'Which never happened,' she tells Seb and Gracie. 'We carried on raising you, Seb. I carried on studying and your dad built the business.'

Life was too busy for quarterly reviews. Ted invited Simmo to buy into Surfside Hardware. Soon afterwards, Ted arrived at the flat to announce to Connie that he'd found them a new home. Effectively he'd used Simmo's borrowed money as a downpayment on the house in Banksia Avenue.

'A real home!' Connie says now. 'I could have demanded we split then. We might have bought two flats instead of one house, but we never discussed that option. I don't know why, really, but I never raised it. Ted showed me Banksia Avenue and I fell instantly in love with it. I didn't think twice. This would be our home.'

'You could have had your own rooms,' Gracie says.

'We could have. We didn't discuss that either. I think it had crept up on me, but we were still husband and wife in our own way. I think we became the family we became, regardless of what was missing. Separate bedrooms would have been lonelier than separate homes. Much of our conversation had always happened in bed, and it still did. And there were other intimacies. He rubbed my feet. I rubbed his. There was no sex but we were great in bed together.'

Gracie's reaction to this is audible.

'You're not laughing?' Seb says. 'You can't be laughing.'

'No, not really.'

'There's nothing funny about any of this.'

'I'm sorry.'

'You are totally under her spell.'

Connie realises nothing she has said has broken through with Seb. He's still hostile. He's not even addressing her now.

'They've lied to me for my entire life,' he tells his daughter.

'I know, but ...'

'You expect me to forgive and forget?'

'No,' Gracie says. 'Only forgive.'

Connie intervenes. 'I don't expect that either, Seb.'

She drives on. For a long interval they don't speak. The paddocks have turned an insipid khaki. The monotony of the country grants no diversions.

Seb says: 'I wonder if you'd be so forgiving, Gracie.'

Connie knows immediately what's hidden in this remark. She assumes he will take it no further, but he does.

'If only you knew.'

Connie can hear the reprisal coming.

'Knew what?' Gracie asks.

'If only you knew what she wanted done about you.'

Connie braces for it.

'What she wanted us to do when we learned your mum was pregnant.'

Gracie turns to Connie. Connie glances her way then back to the road.

'She wanted us to terminate you, Gracie.'

Connie flinches.

'To abort you,' Seb adds.

Connie senses her granddaughter's scrutiny, but then Gracie says: 'Oh, that? Yes, we've already been through all that.'

Connie turns and frowns at Gracie. They have never discussed it.

'I would have told you the same, Dad. You were kids.'

'I don't believe this,' Seb says.

'I'm grateful you ignored her – of course I am – but you guys were crazy to have me.'

'We never gave it a second thought.'

'I know you didn't.'

'You wouldn't be here if we'd listened to Yeah-Yeah.'

'But I am here – and I know she's happy you didn't listen.'

Connie might cry now. She might need to pull over. She does neither.

'Of course I am,' Connie says.

'Oh,' Seb says, 'so you're happy?' They listen to him laughing cynically. 'Well, as long as you two are happy.'

The car speakers go quiet.

'He's hung up,' Gracie says.

★★★

Ted McCall's phone is a dead weight in his son's hand. Seb drops it on the desk. He needs air. He goes to open the window.

'Seb?'

'Amber?'

She is at the study door.

'Have you been there long?' he asks.

'Quite long.'

'You heard?'

'You had it on speaker.'

'I'm in shock.'

'Me too,' she says.

'I was about to come and tell you.'

Amber holds Seb's gaze. 'Were you?'

Seb has to think. Was he? 'Yes,' he says. He is unused to seeing her so grave, so doubting of him. 'I should get back to the shop,' he says.

She begins to move away, then stops to say something, but doesn't.

'I don't know what to do,' Seb pleads.

'No,' she says, 'you don't.'

'What do you mean?'

'Why would you talk like that to Gracie?'

Seb is perplexed by the question. It provokes him. 'We've just discovered my father was a closet homosexual and you're asking me about Gracie?'

'You're hurt, of course you are, but why would you want to hurt Gracie?'

'I don't.'

'But you did.' Amber leaves.

Seb leaves too, then doubles back. Wherever he's going, he's taking his father's phone.

★★★

Connie wishes Gracie would say something. They've travelled in silence since Seb ended the call.

At last Gracie speaks. 'Want me to drive?'

'Yes, please.'

Connie pulls over. Gracie leaps out and walks around the front of the car. Connie goes via the back. Gracie drives for a good stretch, some kilometres, before Connie speaks.

'You didn't have to do that.'

'What?'

'Cover up for me.'

Gracie shrugs.

'It's true,' Connie tells her. 'I did want them to terminate.'

She's aware that she has left out the critical word: *you*. Terminate *you*.

'I'm sorry,' Connie says.

'Don't be. I meant what I said.'

What did Gracie say precisely? It's a blur.

'If he'd been my son,' Gracie says, 'I'd have told him to do the same. I can't suddenly go all right-to-life just because it was my life.'

'That would be reasonable,' Connie says.

Gracie sets the speed to cruise control.

'Your dad never listened to a thing I said. I'm glad in the case of you – yes, I certainly am. But he's never forgiven me for that.'

'I won't either,' Gracie says.

Connie turns to her. What is she saying?

'Because there's nothing to forgive.'

Now Connie could finally cry. Yet again, she doesn't.

'Your turn to choose the music,' Gracie says.

Connie types a search into her phone. 'We've lost the internet,' she realises. She fishes in the glovebox for CDs. 'I can't choose.'

'Joni?' Gracie suggests.

'Too sad.' Connie opens a CD case. 'Remember this?' she asks. She slips the disc into the drive.

Gracie waits and then it's loud, jump-start rock'n'roll. From the opening bars there's a wanton backbeat, gritty guitar riff, screaming lead vocal. Gracie frowns.

'You don't remember?' Connie asks.

'No.'

'The Easybeats. You and Pop danced to this one. So cute.'

'When?'

'You might have been two.'

'And you expect me to remember?'

'I'm sure he filmed it. Didn't we ever show you?'

'I'd remember if you did. We'll have to find it.' Gracie listens. 'Turn it up!' she says.

It's so remorselessly fun. It stakes its claim on two minutes of highway and when it ends the letdown is immense. The scenery is dull here, the receding horizon hazy. There's no definition between land and sky, just the world dilating before their eyes.

'You must have more questions,' Connie says.

'Loads.'

★★★

Seb doesn't return to Surfside Hardware as he told Amber he would. He goes instead to Bondi Hardware, their one-time competitor, now a fashionable bar. He perches on a high stool at its big, wide-open bifold window that overlooks the street and the tables with bench seats on the footpath. A draught beer in a tall, frosted glass has arrived for him on the ledge under the window frame. He must have ordered it but he has no recollection of a conversation with a waiter or waitress. He is not much of a drinker but Seb is here, nonetheless, to drink. The beer slides down easily enough but he knows he won't stomach much more of it. He orders a bottle of pinot noir because, upon inquiry, a waiter suggests this will go down easiest.

Two glasses later, this seems to have been sound advice.

Also propped at this window, a couple of metres along, is another solitary drinker. He is old and white-haired, calcified and miserable. In front of him are three full shot glasses. He lifts one of

243

them, sips from it, and winces. He throws it down and that seems marginally less painful than sipping.

Seb is a third glass into his bottle when he is struck by a morbid realisation: God is not here. It is a moment of terminal lucidity. God is not here with Seb. All at once, the Lord's absence is colossal. There is no divine breath, no enveloping light. God has leached from Seb, from his bone and marrow. God's assurance is gone.

For a moment, Seb considers whether it is the alcohol. No. He knows he is already drunk but he cannot blame intoxication for the instant evacuation of his soul. Seb, like the old drunk beside him, is utterly alone. It is a frighteningly clear-headed realisation, this sudden emptiness, this voiding of his faith.

It compels him to dwell on the origin of that faith, on its substance. He does not trace it, as his mother always has, to his lightning teenage awakening at a Christian youth camp. Rather, Seb knows it was the gradual and unerring example of his father. All of Seb's faith, in fact – in God, in humanity, in anything he thought worthy of his implicit trust – was founded on a particular aspiration: to be more like his dad.

Seb had been the wayward teenager, the prodigal son. He had returned to the bosom of his father and found in Ted's example all the framework he needed to assemble himself as a better man. Ted had provided the human hardware. Seb's endeavour to be like Jesus had been, in truth, an attempt to be like Ted. Seb's true devotion had been not to his heavenly father but to his earthly one, the unassailable, rock-steady Ted McCall.

The liar Ted McCall.

All along, his father had no faith in Seb. Ted could never entrust Seb with the truth of himself. He could never tell his son what stirred him or what made his pulse race and his heart skip – that it was other men.

This alone is shocking but it is not the worst of it. The worst is that Ted was never going to let his son any nearer.

Amid this awful epiphany, Seb notices Brad Wiseman, his fellow Odd Sock, is dining at an outside table. He is sitting opposite a woman whose back is to Seb. It is an extraordinary back, and her dress is so daringly backless that Seb, from this vantage point, can follow the tattoo of a gleaming metal bike chain that runs the full length of her spine, from the nape of her neck to the cleavage of her buttocks. What little of her dress he can see is a dazzling turquoise, which complements her bronze skin.

Momentarily Seb thinks of Beth, his tattooed barista. He has this thought for no other reason than Beth, too, being tattooed and bronze. He attempts to make eye contact with Brad rather than dwell on the woman's back, but Brad seems to be assiduously avoiding Seb while he puts in his spadework. Seb turns away from them and extinguishes this train of thought because it is frivolous and he came here not for distractions but to wallow in his lifelong betrayal by his parents.

The white-haired drinker growls to himself. Two empty stools separate them, for which Seb is grateful. The loner might be seventyish, about his parents' age but not so well preserved. Like Seb, he is drinking with purpose. He's one of those long-familiar Bondi faces who remain total strangers. Another Surfside Hardware customer, perhaps. Whoever he is, Seb decides he has a degenerate look about him, and that he too is fixated on the tattooed back of Brad's companion.

Seb takes his father's phone from the right pocket of his shorts. There are no new messages. He takes his phone from his left pocket. He must have bumped it to silent because there are six missed calls. Most are unknown numbers. They'll be customers or suppliers wanting to know why the shop is shut. Seb will keep them wondering. There are two missed calls from Amber. He'll keep her wondering, too.

'Seb!' says a voice from outside.

He looks down and finds that the woman in the backless dress – now that she's turned around – is none other than Beth the barista. He has only known her facing the cafe counter, so until now he's never seen her most spectacular tattoo.

'Beth!'

'Hi.'

Seb notes Brad's keys on the table. He swivels on his stool and sees Brad heading for the toilets. When he turns back to Beth he makes a point of focusing on her face rather than the smaller of her tattoos, the florets on the crescents of her breasts.

'Hot date?' he asks, and instantly thinks he shouldn't have.

Beth seems to blush a little. 'I wouldn't go that far.'

'Brad would.'

Beth balks. 'You know him?'

'Yeah.'

'And?'

'Watch him, that's all.'

'Why do you say that?'

'He'd root anything that moves.'

'Oh?'

It dawns on Seb that this remark was gratuitous. He doesn't know how to back out, or whether he should. He's taken by the way her turquoise halter neck shows off her florets. Her breasts are like decorated eggs in cups.

Beth is clearly unsettled.

'Sorry,' he says, 'I realise how insulting that must have sounded. I wasn't suggesting for a moment that you are *anything that moves*. You're way out of his league, if you ask me.'

Beth really blushes now. 'I didn't ask you.'

'No, sorry.'

'But it's nice of you to say.'

'I'm actually a bit drunk,' Seb says. 'I might say, *disinhibited*.'

'You managed to say that quite well, considering. *Disinhibited*.'

Seb senses a tingling at his temples, an agreeable fuzziness. He refills his wine glass until the bottle is empty.

'Only four glasses to the bottle?'

'Depends how you pour them,' Beth says.

'Into the glass, ideally.' He flags down a waiter and gestures: same again.

'Are you okay?' Beth asks.

'Do I look that bad?'

'Sorry?'

'*Are you okay*? The last time someone asked me that, they thought I was about to neck myself.'

'Jesus, no!' she says. 'Are you?'

'No!'

'Good, and I didn't mean to suggest you were. And, sorry, I shouldn't have said ...'

'Said what?'

'You know, *Jesus*. You being ...'

'Being what?'

'Um, religious.'

Seb recoils at this encroachment. Why would she know the first thing about his being religious?

Beth seems to detect his irritation. 'I'm sorry' – she says it again – 'but when you work in a cafe you get the goss on the regulars.'

'Right,' Seb says, defensive. He shifts a gear to confrontational. 'Did you also know I'm married?'

'Yes. You *are* wearing a ring.'

'Yes, I am. That's good.'

'What's good? That you're wearing one or that I noticed?'

'Both, but that you noticed, yes. I didn't want you to think I was, y'know, flirting.'

Beth laughs. 'You mean you weren't?'

Seb falters. 'Was I?'

'I was taking the piss,' she says.

But Seb wasn't. His question – was he flirting? – was a genuine inquiry because he's so unaccustomed that he does not recognise his flirting for what it is.

'Oh,' she says. 'You're serious?'

He confesses: 'I've had two girlfriends in my life – and married them both.'

'Really?'

'Really. So I don't know much about it.'

The waiter arrives with Seb's second bottle.

'So where's my hot date?' Beth says, standing to look past Seb into the bar.

Seb turns and finds Brad Wiseman standing over a table where two young women are drinking. They're considerably younger than Beth.

'Chatting up the locals,' she says.

'I couldn't possibly comment,' Seb says.

'I'm not fussed.'

It seems she isn't. She changes the subject.

'You should take it easy. It's been a really tough time. Just horrible, your dad going the way he did. So random. People just adored him.'

Seb forces a smile to suggest he appreciates the thought, but he really doesn't want to hear more platitudes about his father. He drinks.

'Nobody had a bad word for Ted,' she says.

'Nobody really knew him.'

'What?'

'Never mind.'

'That sounded bitter.'

'I suppose it was.'

Beth is startled.

'Families!' Seb says. 'We never know a fraction of the shit that goes on, especially in our own.' All of Seb's instincts tell him not to say any more, but she's frowning at him. 'Do you want me to tell you?' he asks.

'Only if you think it'll help.'

'I can't imagine how.'

She frowns again. 'Don't worry then,' she says.

But he does. He worries. He asks her: 'Would you have picked my old man for a poof?'

Beth gapes at Seb.

'No?' he asks. 'Me neither. He fooled me, too.'

'That's awful.'

'I thought so.'

'No,' she says, and she seems quite flustered now, 'I mean it's awful that you'd choose that word. You're in shock, obviously, but … I don't know.'

Seb turns away and sees the loner is looking at them. Was he listening? Did he even know Ted? Everyone knew Ted. If he's heard it, there's nothing Seb can do about it. It's out now. His father is out now. Seb looks back to Beth.

'When did you find out?' she asks.

'Today.'

'Well, no wonder you're in shock.'

'Yes. We're talking about my father, the husband of my mother.'

'It must have been hard on her.'

'Oh, I don't know. She was in on it.'

Beth looks puzzled. 'It's probably not a great idea to do this drunk,' she says.

'I tried sober. It was no better.'

'What wasn't?' asks Brad Wiseman, sliding back into the bench seat opposite Beth.

She remains standing at the window. 'Seb's just a bit upset,' she says.

'Do you know Seb?'

'I make his coffee. I made Ted's.'

'Ted McCall,' Brad says. 'Legend!'

'Legend!' Seb echoes him, his sarcasm clear.

'Can we get the bill?' Beth asks Brad.

'Don't worry. I've already fixed it.'

'That was unnecessary. Thanks.' She reaches for Brad's hand and shakes it.

He's not expecting this.

'Look after yourself,' she tells Seb.

They watch her departure – her magnificent back. The old loner watches too.

'Ah well,' Brad says, then heads inside.

Seb swivels on his stool and watches him join the table with the two young women. The loner is still following Beth's long exit. He lifts a glass, throws it back and winces again. Seb is wondering what the miserable old perve is drinking – double shots of balsamic vinegar? – when the loner speaks to him.

'If you asked me, mate, I'd never have picked your old man for a poof.'

Seb scowls. 'I didn't ask you. And you're not my mate.'

★★★

Gracie, at the wheel, has questions, so many questions, and they have nothing but time.

'You said so yourself, at your wedding. Pop looked at you the way your dad looked at your mum.'

'I was wrong. I was just caught up in the moment, wanting to say something lovely about Mum, for Dad's sake, and I suppose for mine. I think I believed it, or wanted to, but I was wrong.'

'That's so heartbreaking for you.'

'It was. And for Pop, too.'

Gracie's wistful smile is a comfort. It somehow heartens

Connie, this shared sadness. She's had enough talking now and she's happy just to sit and watch the road, but Gracie keeps going.

'Wednesday mornings must have been torture.'

The brevity of this observation is devastating. Connie, at last, cries.

Gracie, her eyes on the road, hears the sound of her grandmother attempting to stifle her sobbing. She turns and Connie's cheeks are wet and instantly Gracie cries in sympathy.

'Look at us both!' Connie says.

She's always marvelled at Gracie's sensitivity, but she wasn't expecting her to so readily imagine the agony of her Wednesday mornings. Connie had only ever shared that particular torment with Miranda, well before she'd introduced her to Simmo. In the first months of Ted's Rotary nights, Connie hardly slept. When he came in, after midnight, she'd be awake but pretend to sleep. Then she'd watch him sleeping, soundly. He was spent. She'd envisage what had enlivened him, made him eager, worn him out. They were dreadful fantasies. She'd attempt to imagine his excitement, and she'd attempt not to.

Connie discovered it was better to make Ted describe it, to demystify it. He didn't want to, but she interrogated him. He was embarrassed and humiliated to give her the answers, but he did and it helped, and soon she'd heard enough. She didn't need to put him through it again.

'I've dealt with a lot of marriages in the practice,' Connie tells Gracie. 'Few are that honest. But you're right: it didn't stop the torture of my Wednesday mornings, not for quite a while. I took to waking up stupidly early on Wednesdays so I could leave home before Ted woke. I'd just walk and walk and walk. It was on my strolls that I met Miranda, who'd be heading for the pool. It was Miranda who got me swimming. She was the only one I could share it with – all of it.'

They're coming into Albury. It's still an hour and forty to Tocumwal.

'I'll keep driving,' Gracie says, 'but I could do with another coffee.'

'We need to fill up. The servo coffee was barely drinkable last time.'

'It'll do.'

'Not for me,' Connie says.

They pull up to a bowser.

'I need to make a call,' Connie says. 'Can you do the honours?'

She hands her credit card to Gracie, who fills the car while her grandmother crunches the gravel and talks to Simmo. It's a long call. Simmo takes it all on board with little comment while Connie watches Gracie watching her in the mirror. When she returns to the car, Gracie is finishing her coffee.

'Reliably bad?' Connie asks.

'*Nostalgically* bad.'

'That's what I said last time?'

'Yeah. All my best lines are yours.'

Gracie pulls back onto the highway. Connie notices the grease-paper wrapper of a Chiko Roll in the console.

'You didn't?' she says.

'I did.' Gracie picks it up and takes a bite. 'Yum! Pop always loved a sneaky Chiko Roll.'

'Did he just?'

'You know, he'd say: "Don't tell Yeah-Yeah."'

'No wonder. It's nothing but batter, salt and fat.'

'Yeah, perfect! It looked a bit shrivelled in the bain-marie, like it'd been there since 1955, so I got her to pop it back in the deep-fryer. You'd never know the difference.'

'From 1955? I doubt there is any, nutritionally.'

'Want a bite?'

'No, thank you.'

'There's cabbage in there, too. Don't forget that.'

Connie howls. 'You sound so like Pop.'

Gracie glances sideways. 'What about you?' she asks her grandmother.

'What about me?'

'You were only thirty or so. What did you do? You know, for sex?'

Connie blushes. 'Now there's a neat segue. We were discussing Chiko Rolls.'

'What did you do?'

'Not a lot.'

'But something. Tell me.'

'Do you really want to know?'

'Why not?'

Why not?

In Connie's university years, she explains, it wasn't so difficult.

'Nobody at uni cared that I was married, or especially noticed. I did have some nice, uncomplicated things.'

'*Things?* You mean *affairs?*'

'No.'

'Boyfriends?'

'No, not boyfriends. *Bed friends.* I was mature-aged so they were mostly younger.'

'And Pop knew?'

'I told him, yes.'

'Was he jealous?'

'In his way, I think he was. I think he was mainly worried.'

'About what?'

'That I'd fall in love.'

'Did you?'

'Never.'

They watch the river on their left.

'When you say *some*,' Gracie asks, 'how many?'

'Let me see.' Connie counts them on her fingers. 'Four,' she says. 'No, five.'

'At uni?'

'Yes.'

'Those were the days,' Gracie says.

'They were and they weren't.'

One bed friend might have been nicer than five, but Connie didn't want a complication. She wasn't looking for love.

'I already had love, as complicated and compromised as it was,' she says.

Connie sees how happy that makes Gracie, and how sad, all at once. Gracie gets it all in a blink. They let the river carry this thought.

'It was harder after uni,' Connie says. 'It's not like we had dating apps. Where was a married mother in her mid-thirties – or a Bondi doctor who happened to be a woman – supposed to go to find a discreet encounter?'

'So what did you do?'

'Nothing. After uni, absolutely nothing until my early forties.'

'And then?'

Martin Varga became her first locum at the surgery. He ran the practice for fortnightly stints, twice a year, while Connie and Ted took Seb on holidays.

'The first time, I had to work with him for a few days to show him the ropes. I suppose there was a spark. He wasn't married, which made things easier, and he had a flat in Darlinghurst, not too far away, so it was plausible, and it suited me for a few years. We got together quite often.'

'Until?'

'Until he asked me to leave Ted and marry him. I shouldn't have been surprised, but I was. I didn't hesitate to tell him no. Understandably, he finished it, and soon enough he found someone and they made a lovely family.'

Connie tells Gracie about her only other *thing*, her same-time-next-year arrangement with Will Masterson, the gynaecologist, which lasted until Will, like Martin, asked Connie to make it permanent.

'I don't think he ever loved me. He was hopelessly out of love with his wife, that was all.'

'Did he leave her?'

'No.'

'That's so depressing.'

'Did you get napkins? You've got grease on the steering wheel.'

'Sorry.'

'Better there than in your belly.'

Connie finds wipes in the glovebox and hands them to Gracie, who keeps talking while she rubs the wheel.

'I'm still unclear about Simmo – how you connected and when.'

'I left that out,' Connie says.

'Well?'

'You're relentless.' But she tells her. 'I'd always sensed Simmo was attracted to me. Just a look my way, nothing more. I was older. I thought that added to it, the allure or whatever, but I was his best friend's wife. He was never going to try anything.

'By the time I found out about Pop, I was thirty-one to Simmo's twenty-three. I'd agreed with Pop to come back from Tocumwal, but I was still angry. I wanted to get back at him, I suppose. I was also wondering about Simmo. What made the two of them so close? I wondered if I'd misread Simmo. God knows I'd misread Pop. So I had to ask myself: were Simmo and Ted, you know, lovers?'

'No!' Gracie says.

'I went to the shop when I knew Ted wasn't there, when Simmo was alone. I locked the door behind me and flipped the sign to closed. I shut the blinds. I went to the counter and asked him: "Are you fucking my husband?"'

'Wow!' Gracie says.

'He was horrified. For the record, no, he wasn't.'

'But did you know?' Connie asked Simmo. 'Did you know he was gay?'

He hadn't known. Ted had only disclosed it to Simmo in the past weeks, when he'd needed to explain Connie's absence.

Connie stepped behind the counter and moved close to Simmo and asked: 'Ted's never tried it on with you?'

'No,' Simmo said.

'Like this,' Connie said. She put her hand to his crotch.

'No,' Simmo said.

'If anything,' Connie told him, 'you'd want me, not Ted.'

'That's so steamy,' Gracie says. 'What if Pop had walked in.'

'I think I wished he would, but he didn't. I told Simmo, "I know you want to. It's okay. We can."'

'And?' Gracie asks.

'And nothing.'

'Nothing?'

'He said no. I said, "What do you mean, no?" And he said, "Even if I want to, I mean no."'

'Why?'

'Because you don't really want this,' Simmo said. 'You want revenge.'

Connie thought about his charge. 'What if I want both?'

'He still wants you – your marriage,' Simmo said. 'He's not leaving you.'

'But I'm leaving him. He knows I will.'

Connie kissed Simmo. He drew back from her.

'You were so hot,' Gracie says.

'Of course I was hot. The man was a saint.'

Gracie laughs.

'No,' Connie says, 'there was too much at stake, too much on the line for Simmo. They were already talking about him buying into the hardware shop. There was the business, the friendship, everything.'

They pass Lake Mulwala, where platoons of ghosts are wading as always – all the river red gums drowned by the damming of the Murray. On most trips they discuss their perverse beauty, but not today.

'Do you regret not leaving Pop?'

'No,' Connie says. 'As I say, I see a lot of marriages in the practice. Plenty of them are loveless. Ours was never loveless. Sexless, but never loveless.'

Gracie rubs Connie's shoulder.

'Both hands on the wheel,' Connie says.

'Music.'

Connie finds Springsteen in the glovebox. She slips it in the CD drive and the opening piano rollick is an instant balm. Springsteen growls sweetly and Connie loves that Gracie knows every word and precisely when to roll down her window and let the wind rush through her hair. Connie does it, too. They do it on this road every time. They let the hot wind rush in while they drive due west into the setting sun. A ceiling of cumulus clouds is mottled pink by the last blush of daylight.

'No bloody rain, that's for sure.'

Connie can hear her dad's refrain under Springsteen. It makes her oddly eager to be there, home in Tocumwal, yet a bigger part of her doesn't want this road to end. Just her and Gracie, true as can be.

Connie's ring tone blares through the car's speakers, supplanting the music. Her phone's still on Bluetooth and Seb's name is alight on the screen. She answers and Seb launches in as though their last call hadn't ended.

'What I don't understand,' he says, 'is the marches.'

The marches? Gracie is puzzled but Connie knows what he's saying.

'Mum? Why would you let us proceed with our rallies while you went off on your own?'

He's slurring his words, but he keeps going. 'Wasn't that your cue to say: "Seb, there's something we've been meaning to tell you."'

They had joined rival street marches in the lead-up to the national vote on marriage equality. Ted was not interested in protesting, so Connie recruited Jean Amos to march alongside her in the YES rally. Seb and Amber marched with their congregation and affiliated churches on the NO side. Seb carried Mack in a baby sling that doubled as a placard: 'NO! to gay marriage,' it said. They made the evening news and the front page.

'I didn't know until you were in the paper,' Connie says.

'But you could have spoken up then.'

'I didn't want to raise this today,' Connie says. 'You're upset enough.'

'Didn't you and Dad even discuss it? "Here's our chance to tell him." You didn't think of that?'

'Yes, we discussed it,' Connie says. 'Seb, have you been drinking?'

'Quite a lot.'

'I'm concerned, that's all.'

'I'm concerned that you and Dad ignored this obvious opportunity to come clean with me.'

'I wanted to.'

'But you chickened out.'

'Your father refused.'

'Dad chickened out? How convenient, now he's not here to defend himself.'

'He didn't chicken out. I'm not speaking against him on this – because we all know he was a great father. He was the natural parent. I never was. You adored him for it. In all honesty, I think I resented him for it sometimes.'

'You're blaming me for adoring him?' Seb asks. 'I was a kid.'

'I'm not. I blame me, mainly.'

She always knew a child couldn't be impartial in the apportioning of its love. A child loves who it loves, and Connie never had any illusions. Ted was the more lovable.

But Connie is off-track.

'Look, I wanted your father to march with us. There was no way he was coming out as gay, so I said, "Fine, march as though you're straight – like me, like all the other straight people marching for equality." He just wouldn't. "I am what I am," he said. "It's not political. It's just me." I thought that was a cop-out. Everything is political, I told him. But your picture in the paper, that confirmed it for him. He saw no point. You seemed so dogmatic. He didn't chicken out. He just saw no point.'

'I don't understand that.'

'Your picture, alongside all that talk of marriage being exclusively for a man and a woman, as though his being gay made him unqualified to be a parent. There were nutjobs alongside you in those rallies who reckoned the Lord rained down fire and sulphur on Sodom and Gomorrah and all the rest of it. What was your father meant to say? "Well, Seb, as a matter of fact, I'm gay. I should have known that disqualified me from being your dad. Sorry we ever had you."'

'No. If he'd spoken to me, I would never have marched.'

'But it is what you believed, isn't it?'

'You don't know what I believe, and you'll never know what I might have been willing to believe if only you'd told me the truth. You didn't, and I have no idea what to believe anymore.'

Seb ends the call.

★★★

He stares into his phone.

'Seb?'

He looks up. Beth has reappeared at the window at Bondi Hardware. She is squeezed between the bench seats that separate the tables on the footpath. She is still in her turquoise dress, its colour so vivid she seems deep-etched against the night. Yes, night. Seb sees it's suddenly dark out. Beth is barefoot. She's carrying milk in one hand and teabags in the other.

'You should get home,' she says. 'You'll only get more miserable sitting here.'

'Makes little difference where I sit.' He drinks again.

'I'll call you a taxi.'

'I'm fine.'

'You're not fine if you don't know what you believe anymore.'

'You were listening.'

'Not especially. You were kind of loud.'

'Let me buy you a drink.'

Beth waves her hand – no. She looks at his bottle. 'Is that your second or third?'

Seb's eyes roll to the ceiling. 'Not counting,' he says. He stands abruptly and sings: *Aba, daba, daba, daba* … 'You know that one?'

She doesn't. Seb keeps singing … *daba, dab / Said the Chimpie to the Monk. Baba, daba, daba, daba daba, daba, dab / Said the Monkey to the Chimp.*

'It's about a monkey and a chimp who get married,' he says. 'It's a children's song but it's quite unnatural, don't you think? They're two different species.'

'It's just a silly song.'

'It is indeed a very silly song, and my father sang it every day to my mother. Don't you think that's unnatural?'

Beth seems uncomfortable with the direction of the discussion. 'It's probably not the time for a debate about sexuality, Seb.'

'What debate? I'm not debating any of that. I'm only saying it's as unnatural for a homosexual man to marry a heterosexual woman as it is for a monkey to marry a chimp. Wouldn't you agree?'

'I don't know. I don't know the circumstances.'

'I just told you the circumstances. Pretty fucked up, hey? You'd have to agree with that much.'

She offers no opinion. She moves to leave.

'One more question, Beth. Are you a believer?'

It takes her aback. 'Mostly not,' she says. 'Sometimes.'

'That's cheating.'

'Fence sitting?'

'Yes. Of course, you know I was a believer.'

'Yes.'

'I believed in the whole shebang – the Father, the Son and the Holy Spirit – but now I realise I only ever really believed in the father and the son. You know, Dad and me.'

'Seb.'

'And it turns out my father couldn't be believed about anything.'

'Seb.'

It's another voice. Seb looks into the night.

'Amber?'

She's on the footpath, behind Beth. She appears to be examining Beth's tattooed back. 'What's going on?' Amber asks.

He's slow to respond.

'Your phone wasn't answering,' she says. 'It was well after closing time, so I went to the shop, and I found Simmo locking up. He had to go in and work with his broken nose because he got a call saying nobody was there.'

'Simmo? He shouldn't have done that.'

'No, you should have.'

'I know, I know. I'm a bit ...'

'You're drunk.'

Beth smiles uneasily at Amber. 'I work at the cafe next to the hardware.'

Amber scarcely acknowledges her. 'Come home,' she says to Seb. 'Mack's waiting for his dinner.'

Seb hands a credit card to a waiter. The bill says three bottles. He waves to Beth and follows Amber to the car.

Once there, she demands: 'Why can't you talk to me like that?'

'Like what?'

'Like you did to that woman.'

'Beth? No, I hardly know Beth.'

'That's what I mean. Why can you talk to her like that, but not me?'

'That was the wine talking.'

'No, it was you.'

Amber cries. She unlocks the car and gets into the driver's seat. Seb gets in and tries to console her but she blubbers over him.

'This is serious, Seb. You can't talk to your wife about the things that matter.'

'I can.'

'But you don't.'

'I will.'

'Maybe you should get drunk more often, if it makes you say what you're really thinking. But say it to me, not that stranger. You were so honest with her.'

'She's just the barista.'

'She's beautiful.'

'You're beautiful.'

'I'm your wife!'

Her nose is running. Seb can't find a tissue.

'I'm not a kid,' she says. 'Is that it? Do you think I'm too young to hear those upsetting things?'

'No. What things?'

'Tell me what you told her – that you don't believe anymore.'

'No ... I ...' He doesn't know what to tell her about what he does or doesn't believe. 'I just ...' He knows he sounds hollow.

'Don't change it,' she says. 'Tell me whatever's in your head. Upset me.'

'I never want to upset you.'

'That's the problem.'

Her breath stutters with her crying. He's never seen her so distressed.

'Pray with me, Amber. I didn't mean what I said. I want you to pray with me.'

'I don't want to pray with you. I want to talk to you. I want you to talk to me.' She keeps blubbering. 'Sometimes,' she says, 'I think God comes between us.'

'Don't say that.'

'He's all we've had in common from the beginning. If we take him out of it, what do we have?'

'You don't need to do that – don't take him out of it.'

'Just for a moment, so we can talk – just you and me.'

He can't believe he's reduced her to this desperation.

'Would we have anything to talk about?' she asks.

'Of course we would …'

'Go on then.'

Seb falters.

'Just talk to me,' she says. 'If God is here, he can listen.'

'Of course he's here. Please don't doubt him, Amber. Not you. I didn't mean all that.'

'Stop it, Seb. You did mean it. Just tell me the truth, God or no God.'

★★★

The last of the sun flickers, faint as a distant porch light, in the west.

'Not far,' Connie tells Gracie. 'Watch for roos.'

'I am.'

'Don't mention anything to Clem.'

'You won't tell him?'

'I will, but tomorrow. All I can manage tonight is a stiff drink and some loose talk.'

'Pop.'

Yes, that's what Ted always said. 'How about a stiff drink and some loose talk?'

# 8.
## OLD HOLLOW

Seb wakes from a strange dream about a desperate quest for a toilet. His bladder is indeed full and he has the hangover he deserves. He reaches for his phone and sees he has half an hour until the alarm. He switches it off. In the dark he finds the toilet. His flow is so long and loud he fears it will wake Amber. He returns to the bed and sits on its edge. It seems Amber's sleep, at least, is undisturbed.

Seb's forehead pulses with a dull ache. He anticipates an upwelling of anxiety, but it doesn't come. He has an eerie sensation of being suspended. This is a little unnerving but not altogether unpleasant. He remains sitting but plants his feet firmly on the floor.

'You're wobbly,' Mack told him when he arrived home last night.

The last time Seb was so drunk he was seventeen, when he and his mates drank with the singular ambition of stupefaction. It's that long since he's been – what did they call it? – *munted*. Yes, he was categorically munted last night. But this hangover is different. The thing he recalls about his teenage hangovers is the forgetting. He'd get so smashed he remembered little of the trouble he made. But Seb remembers everything about last night: his flirting with Beth, his outing of his father, his public doubting of God, his making Amber cry, and his making Amber doubt. He remembers her saying: 'I think God comes between us.'

And yet he didn't make her say those words and he didn't make her think them. That was all Amber and it frightened him, and excited him. She's always been thoughtful, as in kind, but Seb has never known his wife to be troubled by thinking so deeply. Last night she thought deeply enough to disrupt the entire foundation of their marriage. She was prepared to sideline God, to disqualify Him if needs be. This continues to frighten Seb, and excite him.

Vertigo. Seb might be suspended over the end of his marriage or, just possibly, a better version of it.

Something is hissing and flapping against his foot. Seb looks down and finds a cockroach, trapped on its back and flailing. He reaches down and slips a fingernail under its back and flips it onto its feet. The critter scurries under the bed, possibly to live another day, more likely to die of whatever toxins the pest controllers sprayed last month. They claimed their arsenal was benign to every living organism except the cockroach, which sounded far-fetched to Seb. Whatever, he'd prefer this one died on its feet.

The lightest touch on Seb's back sends an ecstatic shiver through him.

'Hi,' Amber says.

'Hi.'

'Aren't you swimming?'

'Actually, I think I will.'

'Good.'

He turns to look at her. 'You need more sleep,' he says.

'No, I slept just fine. Maybe I'll wake Mack and we'll follow you down.'

'Great.' He stands.

'You're earlier than usual,' she says.

'A crazy dream woke me.'

'Tell me about it.'

'Oh, it was nothing.'

'You said *crazy*.'

'Weird. Silly.'

'Tell me. We have time.'

So Seb returns to bed to tell Amber of the dream, or what he can recall of it, in which he roams an unfamiliar city in quest of a public toilet. He somehow becomes aware he is in Melbourne and that he has flown there today so he can drive somewhere south of the city limits, where his father has apparently taken up residence. Ted needs his help. Why is unclear, but Seb knows he must relieve his swollen bladder before he can be of any use to his dad.

'You could have gone to the toilet at the airport,' Amber suggests.

'I know, but that's not the dream.'

This is the dream. Seb wanders into a grand sandstone building which must surely contain a toilet, but once inside it becomes something else, a war ruin, and he follows a crumbling corridor lined with forlorn men and women, their faces covered in a white dust as fine as talc. They are all too shell-shocked to offer directions to a toilet. Seb passes through an opened door and is transported instantly underground, where he stumbles in the dark over dirt and broken rocks. He stops to urinate but is accosted forthwith by small-statured people, or are they creatures? Just when he fears all hope is lost, a small aperture of daylight opens in the distance. He goes towards the light, a jagged hole, at chest height, through which he can see the feet of pedestrians passing. Seb clambers towards them and is almost out when a hand tugs at his leg. He kicks violently. A little voice yelps. Seb turns and finds a wide-eyed urchin, a boy of perhaps Mack's age, pleading voicelessly. The boy's face is a mask of dirt and for all Seb knows it is Mack, or it could be a child from the Subcontinent. Seb reaches in to give the boy his hand, to hoist him from his netherworld, but another hand emerges and snatches the child, whose frightened face recedes into the dark.

'Then what happened?' Amber asks.

'I woke up.'

'But what happened?'

'I got up and went to the toilet.'

'But what happened to that boy.'

'Nothing. It was only a dream.'

'But didn't you feel you should climb back in for him?'

'Yes, but I don't think you have any control over your actions in a dream.'

Amber falls quiet for some time.

'It's probably just as well,' she says.

'Why?'

'If you'd gone back down there, you might have wet the bed.'

They laugh at her joke. It surprises them both because Amber isn't a joker. Seb climbs out of bed.

'I'm sorry,' he says, 'for last night. For everything.'

'I know. You should say the same to Simmo.'

'I will.' He collects his togs from the chair.

'Seb.'

'Yeah?'

'I'm still a bit scared. For us.'

Seb wishes he could reassure her. 'Me too,' he says.

'There's lots we need to talk about.'

'We will.' He slips on his togs. He goes to leave.

'Seb.'

'Mmm?'

'That was nice – to hear your dream.'

'Nightmare.'

'Still, it was nice to hear you tell it.'

He smiles and turns to go, but yet again she says his name. He turns back.

'Now that we know all about your dad,' Amber says, 'I think you should try to be happy for your mum and Simmo.'

Seb balks. 'Happy?'

'Yes.'

'I don't know. That might be a stretch. I might need some time.' He moves towards the door.

'Is it because you saw what you saw? You know, the way you found them – Simmo and your mum?'

Seb frowns. 'I don't think it's that. I think it's about the whole deception thing. All three of them deceived me.'

'I understand that, but the part about Simmo and your mum, that doesn't trouble you at all?'

Seb has to think. 'I wouldn't go that far. Yes, it troubles me.'

'Why?'

'Nobody expects to find their seventy-year-old mother like that – having that done to her.'

Amber laughs. 'Half her luck.'

'What do you mean?'

She waves him away, still laughing, but he persists.

'What do you mean?'

'Well, I'm twenty-eight and you've never done that to me.'

No, he hasn't. Her observation ricochets with connotation.

Seb asks: 'Do you want me to?'

She's suddenly embarrassed. They don't really talk about sex. They do it, but they don't talk about it.

'Do you?' he asks.

She huffs: 'If the moment ever took you, at some stage, why not?'

Seb moves towards the bed and Amber shrieks.

'Not now! You'll be late.'

'I'll be quick.'

'You might be,' she says, 'but I might not.'

She is, though. She's rather quick.

★★★

These old lace curtains never could stifle a dawn. Connie has woken in her childhood bedroom, in the same lumpy single bed to which she progressed from her cot. The bed has newish sheets but otherwise the room hasn't changed in sixty or more years.

Clem and Shaz have renovated the kitchen and opened up the enclosed veranda but they've done little else to update the place since they moved into town six years ago, when they shifted Mick Blunt to the nursing home. They expected Mick wouldn't see out the year, and they've been expecting the same every year since. He's still on his feet. It's his mind that grows feebler by the week.

Connie heard Clem and Shaz's reports on his decline over a few grogs last night. He's becoming especially fuddled on the events of moments ago, yet he still has flashes of staggering clarity about the distant past. He'll name Clem without hesitation on one visit then have no idea who he is on the next.

Connie hoped to sleep in this morning, there being little sacrificed in having fewer waking hours in Tocumwal. It wasn't to be. It must be sixish now. Connie's travel bag is open on the floor and the day's first light is glinting off the condolence book's shiny cover.

Connie swings out of bed and plucks the book from the bag. She takes her mobile phone from the bedside table and goes to the old walnut desk under the window where she did her homework until she moved to boarding school. She pulls the chair from under the desk and sits. Its front right leg jiggles as it always did.

She runs a finger into the declaration engraved on the desk: TD & CB ♥ TMac. The blue ink has faded from the initials but most of the red ink, remarkably, remains in the well of the heart, fifty-seven years after Tory's handiwork. The compass she used remains in the pewter mug on the window ledge, along with assorted pens and pencils from the era. There's a protractor in there, too, and a wooden imperial ruler. It's a museum piece, this bedroom.

Connie uses her phone to take a snap of the desktop.

'He's a bit old for you, Connie,' she recalls her mother saying when Val found the desk vandalised. It was months before Valentina succumbed to cancer. Connie has long wondered whether Val might already have known something about young Ted. Might Cliff McCall have confided it to Mick Blunt – 'He's a bit different, that one' – and did Mick pass it on to Val? Yet Connie can't picture Cliff ever being so forthright about it. He and Mick had been mates for most of their lives, but only in the way so many country blokes were mates. They were affably aloof.

And if Mick did know anything, he needn't have heard it from Cliff. Her father kept his ear to the ground. Connie still finds it implausible that he'd heard no rumours by the time Ted asked him for his daughter's hand.

'You don't need his permission,' Connie had told Ted.

But her husband-to-be was old-fashioned that way.

She can also imagine how charmed Mick must have been to be asked. If he'd heard any scuttlebutt he might have pushed it from his mind, there and then.

Connie hears the tinkering of cups and saucers, of tea in the making, in the kitchen. She'll join Clem shortly and bring him up to date with the whole shitshow in Sydney. She'll need to distil the shit, she's thinking, or it could take all day.

She opens the condolence book on her desk at its first double-page spread. She reads half a dozen messages on the right-hand page. Most are well-meaning but hackneyed. Two are quite elegant. The trite and the true. She takes the ruler from the mug and uses it to scan past each name in the first column on the left-hand page. She continues, a slow scan of the names on the next three spreads. Once again, no unfamiliar name leaps out. It is not until the seventh spread, halfway down, that she finds one: Mark Romero. This name is entirely new to her.

There is no address or number listed, but Romero has penned

an oblique message: *To rise thither with my inebriate Soul! … Count many a year of strife well lost.*

Which is evocative – of something. Of what, Connie isn't immediately sure. Clearly these words are code for some deeper understanding between Mr Romero, whoever he is, and Ted. Connie picks up her phone and thumbs the name, Mark Romero, into the search bar. Only last night Clem was boasting that the internet connection was much improved. True enough, the information superhighway delivers the likely Romero to Tocumwal in a flicker. Professor Mark Romero lectures in twentieth-century American literature, with an emphasis on modernism, at the University of Sydney. Connie clicks another link and Romero's official university portrait appears. This confirms he is the stranger from the funeral video.

He has fair-to-greying hair, thick and unkempt. He wears plain reading glasses, unfashionable, and a collared shirt, its colour indiscernible. He is bookishly pallid. He is jowly enough to suggest he might also be plump, although Connie only has his head and shoulders to go by. He's hardly trim, taut and terrific.

He is not what Connie ever imagined as Ted's type.

Alongside the photo is a brief bio and an email address and even his mobile phone number, apparently for the convenience of pestering students. Connie could go on supposing. She creates a contact and types his details into her phone.

She takes the ruler again and continues scanning to the end of the condolence book. There are many names that mean little to Connie other than some memory of their existence. It surprises her that she can know, or know of, several hundred people, but after four decades in the neighbourhood there are the hardware regulars, the clubbies, her patients, Ted's two choirs, the local chamber of commerce, the sundry locals – and all these names are, as it turns out, stored in her memory bank. She arrives at the last entry on the final spread and concludes that Mark Romero is, without question, the only one who is altogether unknown to her. She expected to find more.

Where are the rest of the 'Rotarians'? Where are all the Tuesday boys? Connie has always imagined younger men. Not boys, but considerably younger than Ted.

Romero – what is he, five years younger than herself? – does not scrub up to her expectations. He has let himself go. Yet Prof Romero, it seems, was Ted's only fuck-buddy to declare himself at the funeral. Why should he be the only one? It's possible others snuck in late or slipped away without signing the book. Perhaps they, too, had their reasons to be discreet. But Connie had been looking out for them. She'd been curious. Who wouldn't be?

She types again into her phone's search bar, this time select words from Romero's mysterious message in the condolence book: *rise thither inebriate soul strife well lost.*

Because she can. Because the planet can no longer withhold its mysteries. It will be one poem or another, Connie assumes. In fact, it is two short poems. The first is Walt Whitman's 'One Hour to Madness and Joy', the second Sara Teasdale's 'Barter'. Connie reads the first and finds it both bleak and beautiful. On a second reading it is less beautiful, but she is seized by its defiant lines: *One hour to madness and joy! O furious! O confine me not! … To escape utterly from others' anchors and holds! / To drive free! to love free! to dash reckless and dangerous! … To ascend – to leap to the heavens of the love indicated to me! / To rise thither with my inebriate Soul! … To feed the remainder of life with one hour of fulness and freedom! / With one brief hour of madness and joy.*

Connie is hurt. She is wounded by the insinuation that she was the 'other' who confined Ted, whose anchors and holds he needed to escape – and that she allowed him no freedom. The fuck she didn't! And she is insulted by the implication that she and Ted shared no hours of madness and joy of their own. The fuck they didn't!!

And what's with all those gratuitous exclamation marks, Walt Whitman? We're receiving you loud and clear, Walt fucking Whitman!!!!

Connie prefers Teasdale. *Life has loveliness to sell … Spend all you have for loveliness, / Buy it and never count the cost; / For one white singing hour of peace / Count many a year of strife well lost, / And for a breath of ecstasy / Give all you have been, or could be.* Connie can read into these lines what she may, and she does. She reads and re-reads them. They are rallying cries. They might even be hers and Ted's – mottos for their uncustomary marriage.

But they aren't hers and Ted's. They are Ted's and his fuck-buddy Mark Romero's.

★★★

Everything is the same. The Odd Socks are in their daybreak huddle, their conversation typically animated, although the injured Simmo is not among them, of course. Seb, running late, trudges across the sand towards them. When they see him coming they step apart and greet him with too much deference.

They know. He knows they know.

Nothing is the same.

Bertie van de Boor bluffs: 'I was just telling them about Dim's nose – how he tripped in the aisle and faceplanted. Smack!'

'You spoke to him?' Seb asks.

'Yeah, I called in to the shop yesterday. Poor bastard's black and blue, and he says: "You should see the other guy." Funny bugger!'

All but Seb laugh. Brad Wiseman – who likely heard everything Seb said at the bar last night, and who has likely reported it to the crew this morning – avoids eye contact.

'Let's go,' Marty says, and they begin to jog.

On the return lap, Seb thinks of stopping them. 'It was me who broke Simmo's nose,' he could begin – then explain it all, properly. He doesn't. In the surf, he swims well out in front of the pack. Ted always kept just a few body lengths ahead of the others. But Seb isn't leading them, he's thrashing them.

'You should get on the turps more often,' Marty tells him as they leave the surf. Then he blushes horribly.

Only Brad knew Seb had been on the turps. This is confirmation that he's reported back to the Odd Socks.

Of what consequence is it, anyway, that they know? Seb won't be surprised if they never raise it with him. And yet, if they never do, from this day forward they'll think differently of Ted – and of Seb and his mother – and the family will only be discussed in light of its scandal.

Amber and Mack are waiting in the shallows at the north end. She has brought Seb's softie and Mack has his.

'They all know,' Seb whispers to her.

'Does it matter?' she asks.

'Word will get around. It might affect the numbers for the paddle-out. It was looking like a couple of hundred.'

The ceremony to dispense with Ted's ashes off Bondi is scheduled for Sunday, just five days away.

'They'll still come,' Amber says. 'Why wouldn't they?'

'I don't know.'

Amber watches Seb and Mack surfing the two-footers. Mack hustles his father for the take-off on the best of the sets. Seb rides in on a lesser wave. He stands knee-deep with Amber and watches Mack.

'He's ripping it up,' Seb says. He tells her about his swim this morning. 'It was like I was possessed. I'm a bit embarrassed about it. I mean, I left them for dead.'

'Them? Or your dad?' Quick as a flash. She's smirking, happy with her black joke.

'I shouldn't laugh,' Seb says.

'You should. Mack is so much more competitive against you than you were with your dad.'

'I know. We're different like that. If I could've beaten Dad, who would I have looked up to?'

★★★

By the time Connie showers she has missed Clem.

'He still goes in most days,' Shaz says.

'So much for retirement.'

'Matt's tied up with property sales and rentals. There's not enough stock-and-station work, so he leaves what's left to Clem.'

While Gracie sleeps until after nine, Shaz shows Connie what she's done to revive the stone-fruit orchard and citrus groves that Val planted.

'She'd love it,' Connie says.

When they go inside, Connie finds Gracie in her bedroom. She is inspecting the graffiti on the walnut desk. Connie leads her granddaughter to the lounge room and a gallery of old framed family portraits. Gracie dwells on one. Val is pregnant.

'She's about your age,' Connie tells Gracie, 'or a little younger. That's Clem in her belly.'

★★★

At the nursing home they find Mick on an enclosed veranda where he and four fellow residents seem grafted to armchairs. No one is talking. Mick brightens at the sight of Gracie.

'Val,' he says.

'It's Gracie, Dad. Your great-granddaughter.'

'Hi Pop-Pop,' Gracie says and kisses his forehead.

'Just like Val. Good thing she's not here, too. I'd never pick you apart.'

'And I'm Connie.'

'Of course you're bloody Connie.'

She supposes he does know.

'Gorgeous day,' Gracie says.

'Better if it rained.'

Same old conversation starter. They fall into a long silence and Gracie watches the garden with Mick, as if it's a point of interest.

'Cuppa?' Connie asks.

'If you can get their attention,' Mick says. 'They'll never come and ask – not this mob.'

'We can do it ourselves, Dad. They've got teabags in the kitchenette.'

'Teabags! That'd be right. And someone keeps hogging all the Scotch Fingers.'

They sustain this kind of talk for a good while. Mick is right about morning tea: no one comes. Gracie finds the kitchenette and returns with three cups, teabags still in, on a tray. It also bears five biscuits, three Milk Arrowroots and two coated in sugar with the letters NICE etched on them.

'No Scotch Fingers?' Mick asks. 'Bottom of the barrel.'

Mick chooses one of the sugary biscuits, dunks it in his tea and swallows three-quarters of it.

'Stale. They've got some cheek calling 'em Nice.'

'What about me, nurse?' an old woman protests to Gracie.

'She's not a nurse,' Mick says, drooling biscuit. 'She's my Val.'

Gracie is yet to sip her tea. She forfeits her cup to the woman, who selects the remaining Nice biscuit from the tray. Mick grins knowingly at the three unclaimed Milk Arrowroots.

'Who'd want 'em?'

Gracie leaves again in the direction of the kitchenette. Something moves Connie to seize this moment alone with her father. Against her better judgement, she goes fishing.

'Tell me about Ted McCall, Dad.'

'Cliffy's boy?'

'Yeah.'

'Got a boot on him, that kid. Sure can kick a footy.'

It seems Ted is not, for the moment, Mick's son-in-law, let alone his son as he was yesterday. He is merely Cliffy's boy. Connie dives straight in.

'It turns out he was gay,' she says.

'Who?'

'Ted McCall. Cliffy's boy.'

Mick looks vacantly into his teacup.

'You know what I mean?' she says. 'He liked the fellas, not the ladies.'

Now Mick looks confused and Connie regrets mentioning it. He looks again into his cup, as though it might hold the answer.

'You never heard that?' she asks.

'What?'

'That he liked the fellas?'

'Who?'

'Ted.'

'Cliffy's son?'

'Yeah. Did you hear he liked the fellas?'

'He was a fairy?'

'Yeah. Did you ever hear that?'

Mick shakes his head.

'Did Cliffy never tell you that?'

'Tell me what?'

'That Ted was a fairy?'

'No! Cliff McCall's a cagey bastard. Tells nobody nothin'.'

Especially now he's dead. Thirty or more years dead. Connie wants to scream – at herself as much as her father. Why didn't she do this thirty years ago. Now she'll never know whether Mick Blunt, too, was a cagey bastard who told his daughter nothing about the fairy she was about to marry.

Still, Connie perseveres. 'You never heard about some funny business out in the sheds?'

'Which sheds?'

'On Burrabogie, the McCalls' place. You didn't hear anything about Ted McCall getting caught with the ringer in the shearing sheds?'

'Don't think so.'

'You wouldn't forget that, would you?'

Because it was more than talk. This was Ted's account, as told to Connie. She keeps leading her witness.

'And that's why Cliffy sacked Ted, remember?'

Mick only shakes his head.

'And yet Cliffy didn't sack the ringer,' Connie says.

Her father looks at her open-mouthed. 'Nobody sacks their gun shearer,' he says.

'No, I suppose not. So, none of this is familiar to you, Dad?'

'What?'

'This talk about Ted McCall.'

'Talk of the town, that lad.'

'Oh yeah?'

'He's got a boot on him, Ted. Ever seen him kick a ball?'

Connie gives up. 'I have indeed,' she says. 'I have indeed.'

Mick picks up a Milk Arrowroot, dunks it in his tea and bites it in half. It takes some chewing.

'Like eating soap,' he says.

'Try one of these,' Gracie says.

She's returned with an unopened packet of Arnott's Scotch Finger biscuits. She rips them open and hands one to Mick.

'I skipped across to the shop,' she reports. 'This is the trick: never buy the assorted ones. Just buy whole packets of Scotch Fingers.'

'Won't last long,' Mick says. 'Not around here.'

★★★

'Should we go in search of something stronger?' Gracie asks Connie. 'Those teabags were insipid.'

'It's a bit early for gin.'

'And I'm right out of crystal meth,' Gracie says. 'Coffee?'

Connie is anxious to catch up with Clem, but she won't desert Gracie so soon. They go to a cafe in Deniliquin Street where they talk about the nursing home and agree they don't want to die in one. Then they drive out to the cemetery to visit Val's grave. It is overgrown with long grass and weed, but under the gravestone there are flowers fresh enough to suggest Clem has come here in recent days.

'Tell me that thing about the chops again,' Gracie says.

Connie repeats the story of Val, rake-thin, standing over the dinner scraps at the kitchen bench, chewing any gristle or fat left on the chops.

'She'd gnaw them to the bone before she wrapped them up in old newspaper. Couldn't bear the waste. I can still see her licking the greasy newsprint off her fingers. She'd be horrified to know this is my most enduring image of her.'

Back in town, Connie parks outside the stock and station agency.

'Won't be a moment,' she tells Gracie.

Inside, Connie finds her nephew at the counter and Clem at a desk. Clem smiles.

'Got a minute?' she says.

His smile vanishes; he's read her uneasiness. Clem tells Matt he won't be long. They step outside and Connie is aware of Gracie watching them from the car, so she leads her brother up the street, in and out of the shade of shop awnings. When the foot traffic around them eases, Connie stops and faces Clem.

'Seb caught me in bed with Simmo on Friday.'

Clem isn't the expressive type, but Connie can see he's floored.

'Simmo?' he asks.

'Yeah.'

'You and Simmo? How long?'

'Since Friday.'

'I see. I thought, maybe …'

'No. Not when Ted was alive.'

It's brutally sketchy, but Connie has other matters to confront.

'Rightio,' Clem says. 'You've explained everything to Seb?'

She nods. She doesn't want to go through all that again.

'How'd that go?'

'As you'd imagine.' Connie looks up and down the street, then back to Clem. 'You knew all along, didn't you?'

She doesn't need to spell it out; he knows what she means. But Clem doesn't react. He doesn't move a muscle, which is just like him.

'Before New York, you knew.'

Connie notes a twitching in her brother's upper lip.

'I've let you off the hook until now,' she says, 'but Ted told me way back that he'd told you everything. I never believed you didn't know, so I extracted it from him.'

'He told me not to tell you,' Clem says.

'I know he did. And he told me not to tell you that he'd told me that. And I haven't, until now.'

Clem is stripped of his composure. He surveys the street.

'Why did you stop over in Manhattan?' Connie asks.

'Because Ted was a mate. Why not?'

'But you already knew he was gay. Were you curious?'

'What are you saying?'

'Did you want to find out for yourself – how it felt? Dip a toe in the water?'

'Stop it. That's ridiculous.'

'Why is it? How would I know?'

'We were friends, Connie. He'd been run out of town by his father, so I was worried about him – as a mate. Gay men do have straight friends.'

'And straight wives.'

281

Clem bows his head. Connie is surprised by her anger. For more than half her life she has known what Clem knew but she's respected Ted's confidence.

'This is precisely how a gay man ends up with a straight wife,' she says. 'The bride has no idea her groom is gay because his best man – her brother – conspires to keep her in the dark.'

'It wasn't like that.'

'What was it like?'

He proffers no alternative.

'I know what it was like,' Connie says. 'You didn't want your little sister left on the shelf. Better she marry a queer than never marry at all.'

Clem shakes his head. 'You were in love and so was Ted,' he says. 'Would you prefer I'd wrecked it before it started?'

'Possibly. How could you be sure – that he was in love?'

Clem turns to the traffic, then reels back to Connie. 'I asked him.'

'You asked him? Ah well, you sorted that out.'

'No,' Clem says, 'I told him. I told him, "You'd better be sure." And he said he'd never been surer about anything in his life.'

This stops Connie for a moment. 'And you believed him?' she asks.

'Yes, I believed him.'

'Or was it wishful thinking?'

'Possibly, but I believed him.'

'You thought he could just flick a switch?'

Clem takes some time to think about it, then admits: 'Yes, I did. That might sound stupid now. At the time, that's exactly what I thought.'

They become aware of locals watching them from across the street.

'We're making a scene,' Connie says.

'Don't worry.' But he looks worried.

Connie keeps going. 'You thought I'd somehow cured Ted of his gayness.'

'I suppose I did.'

'He never did tell you of our arrangement?'

'What arrangement?'

'That I allowed him to be with men?'

'No.'

'Because he never brought it up with you again, and you never asked. Weren't you curious enough to ask him: "Whatever happened to your predilection for men?"'

'I was curious enough, yes. Bold enough, no.'

'Or didn't you wonder what he was up to when HIV exploded? That came only a few years later.'

Clem nods: he did wonder.

'But you just hoped for the best?'

Again, he nods.

'Well, just so you know, I never did just hope for the best. I never was a wishful thinker. I insisted he take every precaution.'

Clem is listless with guilt. She can see he is.

'I imagine you did,' he says.

'I was never at risk anyway.'

Clem frowns.

'We never had sex again.'

'I'm sorry?'

'Never. It's remarkable – isn't it? – what we conceal from each other.'

Clem steps towards her. 'Jesus, Connie, I'm sorry. I really am.'

'Don't be too hard on yourself. Ted's the one who made us all tiptoe around it. But I do wish you'd come to me before my wedding and said the same as you said to Ted: "You'd better be sure." You could have armed me with the same information you and Ted had. "You're marrying a homosexual, little sister, so you'd better be bloody sure."'

Clem thinks about this. 'Would it have made any difference? You adored him. Wouldn't you have married him anyway?'

Connie, too, has a think. 'Quite possibly, but I'll never know.'


Connie drops Gracie at the house without explanation, then drives the fifteen minutes out of town to Burrabogie. The dirt road to the homestead is much improved but the cattle gates remain a chore. She must get out of the car and back in three times to open and shut the gates. Gracie might have been a useful companion but Connie needs to do this alone.

The Mazda rumbles over the bridge that crosses the irrigation channel and Connie can see this has alerted Tory. She's wiping her hands on a tea towel as she steps onto the veranda.

'I'll put the kettle on.'

'No need.'

Tory does anyway, tea being a prerequisite for conversation. While she's busy in the kitchen, Connie sits on the veranda watching the irrigation channel. It had been discussed as a potential dividing line for the farm, were Lochie and Ted ever to split it. She's glad they never did. Connie notes the old punt, still tied up in the channel, as Tory arrives with the tea and home-baked biscuits on a bone-china plate.

'Is Lochie still using that to move stock?' she asks.

'Not for decades. He takes it for the odd spin, drops a line in.'

'Catch anything?'

'Carp if he's lucky.'

Connie sips her tea then puts down the cup. 'There's something I never asked you.'

So much for pleasantries. Tory smiles stiffly.

Connie proceeds to ask: 'Why do you think you only told me about Ted after your wedding and not before mine?'

They haven't spoken of it since the day after Tory and Lochie's wedding.

'You'll remember I was angry with you,' Tory says.

'I could hardly forget. But, if not, would you ever have mentioned it?'

Tory thinks before answering. 'Probably not.'

Connie looks to the wall clock, which they've always kept out here, strangely, on the veranda. It was Cliffy and Irene's wedding gift to the couple – faux antique, inexpensive. It's still keeping time.

'Yes, I was angry, but I'd wanted the best for you, Connie. And we didn't want to interfere with Ted's chance to, you know ...'

'Go straight?'

Tory thinks again.

Connie presses the point. 'You too? You thought I'd managed to turn him?'

'I don't know. I think we hoped so, yes.'

'For my sake? Or was Lochie just glad his queer twin wouldn't go public?'

Tory looks across the channel, into the middle distance. 'I think both of those things can be true,' she says. 'I'm sorry. I've never felt I could bring it up.'

'Me neither.' Connie takes an orange zest biscuit and bites it. 'That's divine.'

Tory smiles.

'Remember when we had no secrets?' Connie asks.

'I do.'

'I've missed that.'

'Me too.'

Connie takes out her phone and brings up the picture she took this morning of her desk. She hands the phone to Tory.

'Oh my goodness.'

'Still there,' Connie says.

'Can I have a copy?'

'Of course.'

Tory forwards the image to her number.

'Will you show Lochie?'

'God no.'

Tory takes her first sip of the tea. Connie takes another. It's tepid. They drink it regardless.


As Connie drives out, an approaching vehicle trails a stream of dust. It will be Lochie. Who else?

He stops on the other side of the channel to let Connie take the bridge first. As she nears his ute, she sees it is improbably shiny for a working truck. She notes the three-pronged star emblem on its grille. Who needs a Mercedes for a ute?

Wanker!

He winds down his window, expecting she'll stop, but Connie drives on, not so much as a wave.

She decides to head out to Horseshoe, to see what's left of Burrabogie's little beach on the Murray. On her way she passes the shearing sheds. They're ghostly quiet when nobody's shearing.

At the river bend, erosion has taken most of the beach but it's still a pretty nook. The water has a silky sheen to it. Connie's thinking it's a pity she didn't bring her togs.

★★★

Seb is alone at the counter of Surfside Hardware. It's been an especially quiet morning. The bell sounds to announce a customer. It is not, however, a customer. It is Pastor Pat, whose arrival at the shop is a first. He is entering with purpose and in the crowded moments it takes him to reach the counter, Seb concludes he must have received intelligence. Amber likely confided in Kerry Waldren and Kerry felt compelled to report it to Pat, or she shared the news with her husband and Ant relayed it to their preacher.

'Seb.'

'Pat.'

'You're leaving us,' Pat says. He's not asking.

Seb had planned to go to Pat himself, to attempt some kind of exit discussion, an explanation of his and Amber's intentions. It's galling to be ambushed like this.

'What have you heard?' Seb asks.

'Let's see. It's confusing. On the one hand I've heard you're thinking about going out on your own – starting your own church.'

Seb doesn't answer.

'Look, you wouldn't need to do it all alone, Seb. Why not think about setting up as a satellite to us? That would make you viable from day one.'

Seb still says nothing.

'No rush,' Pat says. 'Think about it. There'd be benefits, synergies, as they say.'

'And on the other hand?'

'Sorry?'

'What did you hear on the other hand?'

'Oh, well, I'm not sure how to put it. On the other hand it's suggested that you've had a crisis of faith.'

Seb stares blankly at Pat.

'Which seems very sudden. So, in one breath you want your own church, in the next you're doubting there's any point.'

Seb offers no explanation.

'So I've come because I'm worried for you.'

'No need.'

'It sounds more to me like some mid-life crisis.'

'That's a bit condescending.'

'It wasn't meant to be.'

'Can you have a mid-life crisis before you're forty?'

'And I've heard you've been drinking.'

'Have you?'

'Yes. Which might explain the crisis of faith.'

'Your spies have got that back to front.'

Pat frowns.

'First came the crisis of faith,' Seb says, 'then the drinking.'

'You seem to think that's funny.'

'No.' Seb dispenses with any attempt at civility. 'Your being here, Pat, is what I find funny. As if you'd be the one to save me.'

Pat is suitably insulted.

Seb keeps going. 'I had doubts about you long before I had doubts about God. Your shameless vaudeville show.'

'I beg your pardon!'

'You turned our church into your vanity project.'

The doorbell chimes and startles Pat. A young man enters and heads for the aisles.

'You might as well know, Pat, that I'd been planning my church for quite a few years.'

Clearly Pat is surprised. 'Where?'

'Here.'

'Here?'

'Yes.'

'In this little shop?'

'Yes.'

'But you've changed your mind?'

'It would seem so.'

'I should hope so.'

Seb looks towards the customer and feigns interest. 'Is it wood glue you're after?'

'Yeah.'

'The Gorilla should do the trick.'

The customer takes his advice and brings it to the counter. Seb rings up the sale: $10.95. He notes Pat smirking at the old cash register as the customer leaves.

'A church might be an easier way to turn a dollar,' Pat suggests.

'You'd know all about that, Pat. How's the Tesla running?'

'Like a dream.'

Ted's phone dings under the counter.

'I need to get that,' Seb says. He doesn't but he's glad for the interruption. He places the phone on the counter and taps the screen. It's a text message.

> I've come out to Horseshoe. It's remarkable – Old Hollow's still there, tempting as ever. I might risk the swim to Victoria and back, for old time's sake. One drowning's probably enough for this family in one week, but I'm a much stronger swimmer these days. Just as well. I've come without my togs and I wouldn't be a pretty corpse in the bollocky.

Seb looks back to Pat. 'What else did your spies tell you? Did they mention my father?'

'Your father?'

'Yes, the news that he was gay.'

Pat drums his fingers on the counter. 'Nobody mentioned that. Is that what this is all about?'

'What divine punishment do you think might befall my old man?'

'That's between your father and God.'

'Is it? I recall you telling us about the vile affections of men who burn in their lust for other men – how they'd surely burn in Hell.'

'I might have quoted the scripture.'

'You attempted to. I thought at the time you'd misquoted Paul, so I went back to Romans to check. You got it quite muddled. Paul actually said God was so furious that people were descending into idolatry and other sin that, for their punishment, he gave them up to their lusts. He abandoned them to their free will – to their debauchery – which doesn't sound like much of a punishment.'

'I'm not here for a theological debate, Seb.'

'Just as well for you.'

'If this was only about you, I'd give you up now. I'm here for your family. You're taking Amber and Mack with you.'

'Amber has her own mind.'

Pat leans across the counter, his face indecently close, his breath metallic and sour. 'And Mack? Can he make up his mind?'

'He will, when the time comes.'

'They'll lose their friends, their community.'

'Only if you command it.'

'I'll do as the scriptures command me.' Pat lays a hand on Seb's shoulder and recites Corinthians: '"Be separate from them, and touch no unclean thing."'

'So stop touching me,' Seb says.

Pat walks to the door. He turns back and appraises the shop. 'I can just see it, Seb: the Church of Doubters and Unbelievers.'

★★★

Connie stands ankle-deep in the river, self-conscious about her nudity yet conscious that she needn't be. She has this quiet stretch of the Murray to herself. The last and only time she swam this particular crossing was the day after her wedding, when Ted dared his new bride to swim to Victoria and back.

It had been an initiation rite that Cliff McCall set for his twins, to be completed – or not – on the occasion of their tenth birthday. Cliff stood on Horseshoe, on the New South Wales side of the Murray, and watched the twins, in contest, set off for Victoria. It was only fifty or sixty yards from bank to bank. The real challenge was Old Hollow, an ancient redgum that had toppled into the river from the Victorian bank. Once they reached it, the boys had to dive down and feel their way to the underside of the submerged gum and find a small cavity through which to enter the cavernous trunk, then swim through it and exit via the widest opening at its roots. They could see little until – unless – they emerged. Then they'd swim home to their father, a state away in New South Wales. If they made it back, they passed Cliffy's test.

Ted did, so Cliffy let him swim in the river, unsupervised, from that day forward. It would take Lochie three further attempts to complete the test unaided. On this first go, he emerged much later than Ted from the trunk, alive but crying and blubbering.

'Go back,' Cliffy told Ted, 'and get your sooky brother.'

A few years later, when Ted was impertinent enough to raise it, he asked his father: 'What if we hadn't come up?'

'You did,' Cliff said.

'But what if we didn't?'

'Then I'd have known you couldn't have been trusted alone at the river.'

Seb was ten years old, too, when initiated at Old Hollow, although Ted swam alongside his son and guided him through the trunk. Ted had done the same for his new bride, although Connie surfaced frightened and gagging and coughing up water.

Now she plunges in and swims hard at an upstream diagonal to counter the current. She opens her eyes but sees nothing. It's so different to the ocean pool, where she's secure in the warp of things, where the saltwater in that chamber is buoyant and Connie is suspended and so is all time and care. Here she's already in a contest with the river, its water heavy, pulling her down. At the Icebergs, she knows it's the reaching of her arms that propels her, yet she prefers to imagine herself yielding to the pull of the pool, the black line on the bottom bearing her from end to end while she succumbs to its obliviating constancy. Here she is fighting for every stroke and every breath.

Nearing the southern bank, she stops for air, then dives down three metres, beneath Old Hollow. Given the hopeless visibility she is surprised by how quickly she finds the portal on the underside of the gum. Hoping her lungs are up to it, she feels her way inside the tree and strokes towards the other end.

But there is no glimmer of light to swim towards. She reaches into the murk and is stopped by a wall of wet sand. Her way is blocked. Old Hollow is no longer hollow. It has silted up.

Connie retreats and feels beneath her for the cavity she has just entered, but she overshoots it and for some inflated seconds she cannot find the hole, her only escape. The resulting panic depletes her reserve of oxygen. She has time enough to imagine her death, until her thrashing right hand locates the fracture in the tree. She claws her way out and swims for daylight, up and up, and when she breaches the surface her chest aches with the inrush of air.

Her ears pop. She is dizzy.

Somewhere, a motor is gargling water. A houseboat rounds the bend.

'Look, Dad, she's in the nuddy.'

A young boy on deck is delighted with his discovery. His father, at the helm, honks his horn and the whole family comes to inspect the skinny-dipper. Connie raises a middle finger to them. She waits for them to pass, then swims back to Horseshoe.


She is about to drive away when her phone rings. Jean Amos's name appears on the screen. Connie turns off the engine and accepts the call.

'Jean.'

'Connie. Is everything all right?'

'Let me think. *Everything* is quite a lot.'

'Are you okay?'

'I'm fine.'

'Good. It's just something Keith said, but it's probably nothing. He was drunk.'

'Oh? What did he say?'

'It was something Sebastian said, actually, or something Keith says he heard Seb say.'

'Last night? They were in the same bar?'

'Yes. I gather both were hammered, which sounded unlike Seb. No doubt Keith's got it mixed up.'

Connie takes a few moments to respond.

'Possibly not,' she says. 'What did he hear?'

Jean takes longer to respond.

'Keith thought Seb said ... I know it sounds silly ...'

Connie completes her sentence: 'That Ted was gay.'

'Yes, that's what he said.'

'Jean, if there was one person I could have told – should have told – it was you.'

'You're saying he was? Ted was gay?'

'Yes. I haven't been a good friend.'

'Don't be silly, you're ... I'm just ...'

'You're shocked,' Connie says.

'I am. I'll confess I am. You were so good together. I mean, I can't think of anything that might have made me suspect.'

'Nobody ever did. Ted was so firmly in the closet, he needed his wife to stand guard.'

'Huh! Oh sorry, I don't mean to laugh.'

'Why not? Ted laughed, too, the first time I said that. I was his decoy.'

'I'm just, it's just, I mean you were more than his decoy. It was more than a marriage of convenience.'

Connie bellows: 'I'll have you know, Jean Amos, it was a marriage of considerable inconvenience.'

'Aren't they all?' Jean says.

They sigh in allegiance. A loud bird call – *ya-hoo* – interrupts them.

'Where are you?'

'By the river.'

They talk for half an hour about marriage.

'I suppose,' Connie says, 'so much of any marriage is the

administration of living, isn't it? Food on the table, bills paid, leaky roof sorted. I don't want to diminish any of that – just getting through the procedural stuff is a feat – but after all that, if you still like each other, if you're still in the habit of making each other laugh, it's probably not a bad marriage. Or so I keep consoling myself.'

'So you should.'

'No, I wasn't just a decoy. It's lovely of you to say so.'

Connie sits watching Old Hollow, for how long she's not sure. Another houseboat gulps its way past. She thumbs an email to Trish Mayer, her bridesmaid, in London. They lost contact after the wedding, but they've conducted the occasional email back-and-forth in recent years. Connie has never told Trish about Ted's secret. Now she does. It feels absurdly cursory in the telling, yet it fills four screens. Trish, no doubt, will bombard her with questions when she wakes on the other side of the planet.

Connie should get back to Clem, Shaz and Gracie – they'll be wondering. But she flicks through the clips of Ted's singalongs and plays one, then another. It's her way of eternalising him.

She finds herself conducting searches on the phone for emails containing hers and Ted's joint bank statements. They shared a single bank account for what remained after their respective business expenses – and while neither was silly with the kitty, they became comfortable and there was no decreed limit on their run-around money. Not once in their married life did Connie feel the need to pore over their accounts to check on his spending. It's weird to be doing it now, she realises, but she scrolls through successive monthly statements to examine the details of his Tuesday night debits.

Connie scours every Tuesday in the past seven statements. The restaurant, as recorded on these ledgers, never varied. It was always

Da Nonna, Glebe, and the bill was an even eighty dollars every time. She presumes that was Ted's share. It must have been his and the professor's practice to go Dutch, if Connie is to allow – and she does – for a beer to start, two main courses, one entree and one dessert to share – because Ted never wanted three courses to himself – and a middling bottle of wine between them, and a tip to round it up. That's how Connie and Ted always did it. Their bills were tediously in the same ballpark, about $150 for two.

Ted made no attempt to conceal this trail from Connie. He was clearly confident it would be of no interest to her. Only now is it so. Its very tedium is what intrigues her. Ted was hardly running around with his run-around money.

Connie is assuming Glebe, an easy stroll from the university, is Prof Romero's neighbourhood. The point being: Ted has been seeing the same man for some time. For how long? She could keep mining the bank statements. Instead, she brings up the contact for Romero she stored this morning. She thumbs the call button and it connects.

He answers promptly. 'Mark Romero.'

'Hello.'

'Hi. Who's calling?'

'This is Connie Blunt.'

Seconds pass.

'Ted McCall's wife,' she says.

'Yes, I know. Sorry. Hi.'

'Hi.'

'I wasn't expecting you.'

'I suppose not. I was hoping we could meet.'

He hesitates.

'Of course. What were you thinking? Coffee?'

'Dinner.'

'Dinner? Did you have somewhere in mind?'

She doesn't mean to keep him in suspense. She's considering how presumptuous she might be. After pausing for too long, she decides: quite presumptuous.

'I was thinking Da Nonna.'

She waits.

'When?' he asks.

'How are you placed tomorrow?'

'Tomorrow night? I'll have to check.'

'It's a pity it couldn't be tonight – it being Tuesday – but I'm in the country.'

'Tocumwal?'

'Yes.'

'I'll book us in. Seven-thirty?'

'Perfect,' Connie says.

'Ciao.'

It can sound so pretentious – *ciao!* – but the way he says it is unaffected, as if he speaks the language. His name is Italian, yes, but perhaps he was born there, or his immigrant parents spoke it in the home, unlike Val. Connie so wishes she had.

Prof Romero is at least polite.

What was she expecting? Someone ill-bred?

★★★

Seb knocks on Simmo's front door. Soon it opens. His face is worse than Seb expected.

'Who's got the shop?' Simmo asks.

'I'll be back in ten. The bruising – it's really bad.'

'Looks worse than it is.'

'Are you using heat on it? It'll get the blood flowing under the skin.'

'I'll give it a go.'

Simmo steps out and leans against the veranda rail. Seb leans there too.

'Should hold both of us,' Simmo says. 'Can't promise.' He rocks a little to test its resistance.

'I'm sorry,' Seb says.

'I know you are.'

They absorb this quietly. There's mint growing in a pot hanging just over Simmo's head. He breaks off a little bunch, rubs into his palm and gives it a whiff.

'I might've done the same,' he tells Seb.

'No you wouldn't. It's just, you were the last person I'd have thought of.'

'You weren't to know.'

'Which makes it worse – to discover the three of you did know ...' Seb pauses, to give Simmo some space.

'That's the way it goes with friends,' Simmo says. 'You keep their secrets.'

'Aren't we friends – you and me – after all these years?'

'Yes, but your dad came first.'

Seb can smell the mint. He breaks off a bunch and takes a whiff. 'I think that's been my mistake – never having a friendship like yours and Dad's. I got kind of waylaid.'

'You've got loads of time.'

★★★

The Mazda rattles over the cattle grid. Clem and Gracie are on the veranda, and Connie sees she has their attention.

'All good?' Clem asks as she climbs the steps.

'All good,' she says. 'We'll have to pack up tonight though, Gracie. I need to leave first thing in the morning.'

'Already?' Gracie says. 'That's a quick turnaround.'

'At least rest one more day,' Clem says.

'Thanks, but I can't.'

# 9.
# RIGATONI

Mark Romero is at a window table. The Professor, as Connie thinks of him, has his back to her as she enters. On her approach she has time to notice a slight balding at the crown of his head, and to wonder whether this was his and Ted's regular table. Perhaps the Prof has made a point of moving tonight, to deny her even that small insight.

'This is nice,' she tells him as she sits.

'Yes,' he says, 'you're in Ted's chair. He liked to watch the foot traffic coming up the hill. It's my neighbourhood, so I'm not so fussed.'

Straight in. No handshakes, no introductions, no stuffing around.

Which suits Connie.

'Is your place close?'

'A few doors down.'

'So this is your kitchen?'

'Only on Tuesdays, normally.'

'For a long while?'

'Oh goodness, yes.'

What is that supposed to mean? Connie sizes him up. The Professor catches her smirking.

'Am I not what you imagined?' he asks.

Connie attempts to think of something inoffensive to say. 'No,' she admits, 'I suppose not.'

'What did you expect?'

'It doesn't matter.'

'I can take it.'

'Okay then.'

But still she hesitates. He is impatient for the answer.

'Well, frankly,' she says, 'I was expecting someone a little younger.'

The Professor grins.

'And slimmer,' she says.

'Ouch!'

'Sorry, that sounded bitchy.'

'I was younger when we met – and not so plump.'

'And when was that?'

'Wine, signora?' A waiter has arrived at Connie's shoulder.

'Yes, please,' she says. 'What's that you're drinking?' she asks the Professor.

'Just the house Trebbiano. Ted liked it very much.'

'Why not? You do it by the glass?'

The waiter nods to confirm, then goes to a sideboard to fetch an opened bottle and returns to pour.

'Cin cin!' she says.

'Saluti!' says the Professor.

They clink glasses and Connie takes a greedy gulp.

'Delicious,' she tells the waiter. 'I think we'll need a bottle, or maybe I'll need my own.'

The waiter winks and goes to get a bottle.

'You're not driving?' the Professor asks.

'No, enough driving today. That might explain my inelegant thirst.'

'No need to apologise.'

'I wasn't.'

He has lovely manners, Connie concludes, and she wonders about hers, but she barrels on.

'Now, when you say *a long while*, how long is that?'

'Sorry?'

'You said you'd been coming here a long while.'

'Twenty, no, twenty-three years.'

Connie's chest is instantly heavy and tight. She coughs. 'You and Ted?'

'Oh no. That's just me.'

The weight lifts.

'And you and Ted?'

'Let me see. That'd be eighteen-ish ...'

'Months?'

'No! Years.'

'Oh?'

'You're surprised?' he asks.

'Well, yes.' She can see he's surprised that she's surprised. She adds: 'Quite fucking surprised, actually.'

The waiter arrives with the bottle and an ice bucket.

'Fill 'er up,' she instructs him.

'Me too,' says the Professor.

They both drink eagerly.

'He didn't tell you?' he says.

'No.'

'But you knew he was gay? I'm sure he said ...'

'Of course I knew he was gay. I didn't know about you, that's all. I didn't know you were a single entity.'

The Professor frowns.

'I mean, of course you're one person, but I thought his Rotary nights were many people, not one.'

'Rotary nights?'

'He didn't share that with you?'

'No.'

'Tuesday night was Rotary night. That was our little joke, our euphemism, but the point was that Rotary nights were for Ted and his assorted fuck-buddies.'

'Assorted?'

'Not all at once. One at a time, I mean.'

'Oh?'

'That was our understanding from the very beginning. I'm talking forty-ish years. His fuck-buddies would be many and various and, preferably, anonymous. It was never meant to be the same person, week in, week out.'

The Professor is devastated. 'He really never mentioned me?'

'He really never did.' Part of her wants to hurt him, but she's already feeling his pain. 'I suppose that's because you weren't a fuck-buddy,' Connie says. 'Eighteen years! That's a husband.'

Mark Romero shakes his head – *no, no, no!* – but Connie repeats her pronouncement: 'You were his husband.'

'I wasn't. I wish it were true, but he always made it clear he had only one spouse, and that was you.'

A little bread roll has found its way into Connie's hands. She is squishing it between her thumbs and fingers.

'He insisted you were his wife.'

'Did he?'

'He did.'

'Am I supposed to be chuffed?' she asks. 'I *was* his bloody wife.' Connie breaks some bread, puts it in her mouth and chews. 'I'm a bit light-headed, sorry. I need to eat something.'

The Professor picks up his bread and breaks it. He drops the two halves on his plate.

Connie asks: 'Did he mention that his wife – his one true spouse – had surrendered her conjugal rights?'

'Not in so many words.'

'But in enough words that you understood. You, his one and only Tuesday night thing, were privy to our marital secret.'

The Professor blenches at her hardness.

'You were allowed to know all about me,' Connie says, 'but I wasn't allowed to know even of your existence.'

'Are you ready to order?' asks the waiter, who has reappeared at Connie's side.

'I'll have what he's having,' she says, deadpan.

The Professor laughs involuntarily, painfully. He gets her movie joke. She clutches the table with both hands to mimic Meg Ryan.

'I'll spare you the full orgasm scene.'

'Ted always said you were funny.'

'I'm a riot.'

The waiter shuffles uncomfortably. 'So,' he declares, 'the usual: rigatoni alla Genovese for two.' He collects their menus and leaves.

'What a prick!' Connie sighs.

'Gino?' asks the Professor, looking to the waiter.

'No, Ted!'

'Oh?'

'Eighteen years, you say?'

'Yes.'

They both eat bread.

'I'm sorry to press you on this,' the Professor says, 'but did he specifically lie about it? Did he ever say it wasn't the same person each week?'

'No. He didn't need to. I never asked. Why would I interrogate him about it? When you have an understanding with your husband that he can fuck anything that moves, what secret can he possibly need to keep?'

The Professor has no response.

Connie answers herself. 'That he's in love. That he has just one lover.'

'Is that so terrible? Would you really prefer he was fucking anything that moved?'

Connie gives this question her full consideration. 'Yes. I really and truly would. Fuck whoever you like, Ted, but *love* me.' Connie senses the irritation of a tear on her cheek, the second time she has cried since Ted's death. She is annoyed it's happening in public, and especially here, before her rival for his love. 'I once told Ted he was the great illusionist and I was his accomplice,' she says, 'but he was so good he fooled even me, the accomplice.'

The Professor is shaking his head again. 'He did love you. First and foremost, I'd say.'

'Would you just?'

'Yes. I'm not saying it to make you feel better. I'll be honest: I wanted to take him from you. I wanted him to leave you for me, but he wouldn't hear of it. You had the marriage; I had Tuesdays.'

His voice breaks on 'Tuesdays', and it provokes Connie to cry more. His pain resembles hers. She has a sudden urge to be tender and she clasps the Professor's hand. As a reflex to her touch, his lip quivers.

'You must be pissed off,' she says.

'Yes. Thank you.' His hand is shaking under hers. 'That's what hard feelings feel like,' he says.

Connie asks: '*One hour to madness and joy* – was that a reference to your Tuesday nights?'

'Walt Whitman. I suppose so.'

'I read your entry in the condolence book. That's how I found you. I rather resented it – *confine me not,* or whatever it said – the suggestion that I held him back.'

'Not at all. Ted never suggested that, not for a moment.'

'But you did.'

'Possibly. Okay, yes, but it made no difference.'

Out on the street, a woman laughs. Her frivolity is jarring. The Professor releases Connie's hand.

'Pissed off doesn't begin to explain it,' he says. 'I used to describe us as *monotonously monogamous.* He liked that. He thought it clever. But now I feel that our eighteen years have been struck out. He never uttered my name to you, so I didn't exist.' He takes back Connie's hand.

She asks: 'Did he ever tell you that he'd mentioned you to me?'

'I'm trying to think. Perhaps not. No, I don't think so, but I think he let me assume that he had. I don't know, but my whole life with Ted is only my memory now. We never had mutual friends we caught up with, who could be witnesses to our time together. He was steadfastly uninterested in the gay scene. He met none of my circle, gay or straight. Never even a sneaky dinner in my apartment. There's nobody to vouch for my life with Ted McCall.'

'I'm sorry, Mark,' Connie says. It feels right, at last, to call him Mark. 'I hadn't considered this possibility,' she says.

'What's that?'

'Of you having cause to be so aggrieved.'

A cluster of six people outside moves by the window. It's only twenty minutes' drive from Bondi but the people here seem different. More European. Worldlier. It's probably not true but, whatever the distinction, Ted's other life seems exotic to Connie.

'It's his capacity for casual dishonesty that shocks me,' Connie says. 'He didn't lie, as such, but he failed to disclose. Ted and I kept his big secret, but my great consolation was that at least we had absolute honesty between the two of us, that there was nothing we needed to keep to ourselves. We had to fib to the world, and to our son, but I never thought I'd discover Ted was lying so breezily to me.'

'Didn't you ask him for details about his Tuesdays?'

'Not for the sordid details, no. I have an imagination. It was meant to be rumpy-pumpy, so I hardly needed it described blow by blow.' Connie sniggers at her grubby joke.

'It was typically less eventful,' he says.

'Well of course it bloody was. You were a couple. Ted probably settled for a mutual foot rub while he farted and fell asleep in front of the telly.'

'That could happen, yes.'

'Don't I know it! Which is far more painful to imagine, that he needed two foot-rubbers. Neither of us was enough.'

Mark Romero looks to the street. 'He did have a foot fetish,' he says. 'Sadly, I have the most unattractive feet. He mentioned yours – how lovely they were.'

Connie doesn't want to be flattered or humoured.

'Was he deceiving you,' Mark asks, 'or protecting you? Perhaps he was protecting us both – the lives we separately had with him? I think you're right: neither of us was enough. He wanted and needed us both.'

'But only he got to have the best of both worlds. He should have introduced us. The three of us could have had dinner occasionally. Why not? I think I could have dealt with that, if only he'd told me, but to learn now of this sneaky double life. It's so shabby.'

Connie drinks and refills both their glasses. They sit listening to the buzz of the restaurant.

'Now I wonder,' she says, 'whether there were others – whether he had other long-term lovers before you.'

'Yes,' Mark confirms.

'For fuck's sake. Who?'

Connie awaits the detail.

'I met Ted at John's funeral, in fact.'

'John? John who?'

'Oatley.'

'How long were they together?'

'Seven years.'

'Seven!'

'John was HIV-positive when they met. That's what finally killed him.'

Connie doesn't react to this disclosure.

'Of course,' Mark adds, 'they were safe.'

'I have no doubt,' she says. 'That's hardly my concern. Let me think about this. John Oatley was his husband, too. Till death did they part.'

'If you like.'

'No, I don't *like*. Ted had another double life, then he went through all that grief and never felt the need to tell me, to cry on my shoulder. Now I'm the one feeling invisible.'

'The more I think of it, I do think he was protecting you. He was protecting his marriage, his family, from all of those complications.'

'Don't make excuses for him. It was cowardly.' Connie's proclamation is loud enough to turn heads. She lowers her voice. 'He was a coward. He loathed conflict. His whole life was an avoidance of confrontation. He did it with his family, with his bollocks of a brother. He couldn't bear the thought that anyone might think less of him.'

Mark doesn't disagree.

'Did he tell you that I wanted him to come out?' Connie asks.

'No.'

'He should have.'

'Yes, he should. I did, too, of course.'

'But there was no way he was coming out. He had to be adored by everybody. He was addicted to it. He couldn't risk it.'

Mark nods, yes.

'Did he tell you that other men's wives envied me?' Connie asks. 'None of them had a husband as perfect as mine. I could never tell them what they had that I didn't.'

They stop talking for too long. Mark has nothing to say to console her. Connie makes an effort to relaunch the conversation.

'So, you're saying that you and Ted hooked up at his partner's funeral?'

'Not quite. We met there, but started seeing each other much later.'

'I'm not judging. Who am I to judge?' Connie tells him about her and Simmo in the aftermath of Ted's funeral.

'I had no idea,' Mark says.

'What do you mean, no idea?'

'That Simmo might, you know ...'

'Simmo? Why would you have any idea? You know Simmo?'

Mark is suddenly flustered. 'Not really. I mean, we met once –
no, twice – quite a few years back.'

'Did you?'

'Briefly, yes. Oh dear, I've dobbed him in.'

'You have.' Connie considers leaving the table to call Simmo,
to have it out with him immediately. Why wouldn't he have
mentioned Mark Romero? 'How did you learn Ted had died?
Simmo?'

'No. He wouldn't have had my number. I got it from that
night's news.'

'God no! Your mobile's on the internet.'

'Simmo wasn't to know that. Look, don't be too hard on him.
It's my fault. I pushed Ted. I needed to meet someone, anyone,
from his life, but the options weren't really there. Only you and
Simmo knew.'

'And I wasn't an option.'

'No. It was always me who had to take action, never Ted. Life
just came to him. He never had to make the moves – not with
John, not with me.'

'Not with me,' Connie says. She tells him of New York and her
Transatlantic plot to snare the man with whom she'd been secretly
smitten since her infancy.

Their meals arrive during this long story. They are hungry. It
is honest provincial cooking.

'Ted always ordered the same,' he says.

'We'll need another bottle. Are you okay with red?'

'The Sangiovese's good.'

'Do they do it intravenously?'

Detail flows with the wine. A year after John Oatley's funeral –

after a respectable period of mourning – Mark tracked down Ted.

'I pursued him.'

'You and me both.'


After dinner, out on the street, Connie asks to see Mark's apartment. He is momentarily affronted.

'Sorry, I won't intrude,' she says.

'No, it's all right. It's a mess, that's all.'

He leads her upstairs. His door opens to a large combined living room and kitchen. The available wall space is floor-to-ceiling bookshelves. There is a ladder on wheels to reach the highest books, as in a public library. On the dining table are two books, and papers he's apparently marking.

'This is what you call a mess?' she says.

Connie is drawn to the ladder and, absentmindedly, she pushes it. She's impressed by how noiselessly it rolls on the shiny parquet floor. She stops when she arrives at a shelf that carries not books but framed photographs. There are four of Ted and Mark, one recent, the others over their years together. The first must be from their earliest days, when Ted was already in his mid-fifties but looking forty-something. Mark was indeed slimmer then, and handsome enough.

On the next shelf is a picture of Mark at a similar age, with two young girls.

'Nieces?' Connie asks.

'Daughters.'

'Sorry, that was presumptuous. And their mother?'

'We were married.'

'When did that end?'

'About the time I met Ted.'

'After?'

'Yes.'

'I don't mean to cross-examine you.'

'It's okay.'

'Do you still talk'

'With their mother? No.'

Connie doesn't push him for detail. She leaves him space to decide what to do next, and he elects to give her more.

'Talk about a double life!' he says. 'That was mine. I'd been fucking men anonymously all through my marriage, long before I acknowledged this probably meant I was gay.'

His self-mockery makes Connie laugh.

'I'm sorry,' she says.

He brushes the air. 'It is laughable.'

His self-derision is appealing. He's looking quite dashing, suddenly, here in his domain. Connie thinks he'll probably wrap it up now, but he carries on.

'It was a free-for-all out there, an absolute fuckfest, for any married man who wanted some man action. The internet, when it came, made it even easier. Hooking up would never be a problem, had I wanted to continue that way – a married man, dabbling. Seriously, I think most of the men on those sites were married to women.'

Connie is not surprised by this. Ted had explained this much. She can only gather now that he did so to provide cover for his fidelity – his monotonously monogamous years with John Oatley and Mark Romero.

'When Ted came along, I couldn't lie anymore, not to myself, not to anyone. I told my wife everything, and that was that.'

'What?'

'Finished,' he says.

'The kids?' Connie asks. 'Do you see the kids?'

'The younger one, all the time. The elder one, not since I left home. She was eleven then, almost thirty now.'

'I'm sorry.'

He shrugs.

'You still have time to fix that,' Connie says.

'I hope so.'

She can see through opened doors to the two bedrooms, the smaller of which has a single bed but is otherwise furnished as a study. It has yet more bookshelves and a workstation that looks untouched in recent time, apparently abandoned for the dining table.

The main bedroom is spacious and tasteful. Streetlight pours in through a tall, three-panelled federation window. The bed is a queen and it looks cosy compared with her and Ted's king. The branches of an old fig lap at the windowpanes, their shadows dancing on the bedspread. It reminds Connie of Manhattan.

'I won't keep you up,' she says.

'I'm a night owl.'

'Ted must have been a bore. Early to bed.'

Connie heads for the door and he follows her.

'I'm glad I intruded,' she says.

'Me too.'

'You're not invisible, Mark. I'll vouch for your life with Ted.'

On the street, while she waits for a passing taxi, Connie calls Ted's number.

★★★

His father's phone dings faintly and stirs Seb from the beginnings of sleep. He remembers he's left that phone in the kitchen.

'You need to go to his settings and turn off sound alerts,' Amber says.

Her voice, close to his ear, is startling in the dark.

'Sorry,' he says.

'It's okay. I was awake.'

'Worrying?'

'I'm okay.'

How okay? Seb has to wonder. The dark amplifies the quiet. He speaks to fill the void.

'It's not really my place to change the settings. It's Dad's phone.'

'He won't mind.'

Seb grunts at her joke. Another one! Just the way she says it, it's surprising, flirtatious. Everything about her is new. She's worrying, and that worries him, but she's also more casual with him, less deferential. It's as if he's having an affair with his wife.

'You didn't tell me Pat came to the shop,' she says.

'Pastor Pat? Did he call in here, too?'

'No, Kerry called to warn me. She felt bad because Ant went and told Pat everything. And I felt bad because I told Kerry everything.'

'Don't feel bad. I'm the one ... Pat reckons I'm tearing you and Mack away from your community – that he'll have to tell everyone not to see you if you choose to stop going to church.'

'It's not Pat who worries me.'

'Who then?'

'God.'

That word, *God*, still carries its awe for Seb.

'He's always just been here, with us,' Amber says. 'It's like he's suddenly outside, that he's not living with us anymore.'

'You don't have to choose, you know, between God and me. I still don't know what I believe.'

'But while you don't, I don't either. I can't help it. And everything feels – I don't know – less.'

'Less?' This word, too, is awesome. Terrifying. 'Between us,' Seb says, 'I honestly feel everything is more, not less.'

'Between us, me too. But God, if he's still there, is so much bigger than us. I've never questioned him until now.'

'Then don't.'

'If you do, I can't pretend not to. But then I think our life will be missing the most important thing.'

Amber is right to worry. Seb knows she is. Their marriage is reborn, and it's never been so precarious.

'Aren't you going to listen?' Amber asks.

'Mmmm?'

'To the message on your dad's phone?'

'I probably will.'

'Of course you will, but aren't you going to listen now? Aren't you curious?'

'Here?'

'Don't you want me to hear it?'

'It's not that. It's ...'

But it is that, and now Seb has to wonder why he wouldn't want Amber to hear it. Does he really need to vet it before she can listen? He goes downstairs to get his father's phone. When he returns, he finds Amber sitting up in bed, eager.

'Okay,' he says.

Seb clicks on the message and discovers it's on FaceTime, so his mother appears on screen. She's on a footpath, apparently somewhere in Sydney. Back from Tocumwal so soon?

She begins with an odd declaration: 'We had your usual, Ted – the rigatoni.' She looks up and down the street, then continues: 'Actually, Seb, I gather you'll be getting this. This is for you.'

There is a hum of traffic, the tooting of a horn, a brief gust of dance music.

'I think I told you that your father's Tuesday nights were for meaningless flings. I was wrong about that. I've just had dinner in Glebe with Professor Mark Romero. It emerged that he was your dad's partner for the past eighteen years.'

The dance music escapes in squalls as a door behind her opens and shuts.

'It's a strange thing, at my age, to suddenly discover you've been alone for much of your married life. I mean – stuff you, Ted – you couldn't even be true to our lie. Taxi!'

The bonnet of a cab enters the frame and stops. Its engine idles. The camera jumps from gutter to night sky while Connie gets in.

'Banksia Avenue, Bondi, please. You were gutless, Ted. Excuse me, driver, I was in the middle of something. And, Seb, sorry, this *is* for you. I suppose I'll cool down, but that's the way I'm feeling for the moment: that your dad was too gutless, too piss-weak, to tell me there was someone of consequence, that he was in love. It was never going to be equal between us, but I made my sacrifices because I thought he was making his. He never did. He sacrificed nothing. He had his husbands.'

*Husbands?* Plural. Seb and Amber don't understand. Connie says nothing for a long stretch. The camera in her lap frames her head at an odd angle, her chin jutting out. It makes her look severe.

'If he'd only told me about John Oatley. That was before Simmo was married, before I even introduced him to Miranda. That might have changed things, had I known.'

Connie unwinds her window for air. The traffic gathers volume. Her voice is cracking. Seb has never seen her so brittle.

'I suppose you were right, Seb. It was a charade, after all, our marriage. I thought it was at least more honest than so many ho-hum marriages. Turns out we were pretty ho-hum ourselves.'

Amber nudges Seb. She chews her lip.

'I've had a few drinks,' Connie says. 'I'm angry.'

'Next right?' the driver asks.

'Yes,' Connie says. 'Actually, no, next left. Could we go to Francis Street instead?'

★★★

There are no lights on at Simmo's. Connie's been sitting alone on the fence outside for a good while, debating whether he deserves to be woken. She decides now that he does. She goes to the door and rings the bell. The light comes on in the front bedroom, Vanessa's room.

'Shit.'

Vanessa must be staying over.

The door opens and she squints at Connie, puzzled. 'What's happening? Is everything okay?'

'It's nothing, sorry. I didn't think ...'

'Connie?' Simmo says, emerging from his bedroom along the hall. He's pulling a T-shirt over his gaping boxers, which he adjusts on approach. His bruising is more startling than when she left him.

'Sorry,' Connie says. 'It can wait until tomorrow.'

'No,' he says, 'come in.'

Vanessa is confused but she returns to her room.

Connie follows Simmo along the hall. As she crosses the threshold into the kitchen, she announces: 'I've just come from dinner with Mark Romero.'

'Oh?'

'Yes, oh! You knew him.'

'Not well.'

'But you knew all about him.'

She can see he's scrounging for an answer.

'Simmo?'

'I couldn't really tell you.'

'That's the best you can do?'

He goes to the sink and takes a teacup and a glass from the dish rack and fills them with tap water. 'Ted confided in me,' he says. He hands the glass to Connie while he drinks from the cup.

'Ted's been gone for – what is it? – almost two weeks. Haven't your loyalties shifted somewhat?'

'Of course. I would have gotten around to it, but things have been moving fast. I suppose I still felt conflicted.'

'Ted's dead. I'm not. No contest.'

'I know.'

All the wine Connie drank is clammy in her mouth. She's

315

dehydrated. And quite drunk. She drinks most of her water. 'Are there any other bombshells?' she asks.

'I don't think so.'

'Think hard because I'm getting too old for this shit.'

'Wait,' Simmo says, 'there is one other thing.'

'Yes.'

'Soon after I met Miranda, long before we married, I spoke to Ted.'

'Yes?'

'I told him I loved you.'

'You what?'

'I wanted to know whether he planned – whether you both planned – to stay as you were.'

'Married?'

'Yes. I wasn't going to wait my whole life for you, Connie, but I didn't want any regrets. I didn't want to find out too late that you and Ted were finished, that there may have been hope for me.'

'This is what you call *one other thing*? What did Ted say?'

'He begged me not to.'

'Begged you not to what?'

'He begged me not to do anything, not to say anything to you, not to even think about it. He had no intention of giving you up.'

Connie follows the second hand moving around Simmo's wall clock. It's a noisy contraption and it seems implausibly slow. Connie is attempting to put a rough date on Ted's plea to Simmo. Miranda married Simmo in late 1998, so some time before that. But this was still fifteen or more years after Simmo had rejected Connie's advance in Surfside Hardware.

'That's a long time after, you know ...'

'I know.'

'You kept thinking about me?'

'Never stopped.'

'Jesus, Simmo.'

'I can't remember a day when I didn't.'

'You didn't tell me that.'

'I couldn't. It was hopeless, but it didn't stop me thinking.'

'Why was it hopeless? You gave me up without a quarrel?'

'I quarrelled, all right.'

'How?'

'I told him it was unfair. I said he was using you.'

'And?'

'He said if I believed that I could fuck off.'

'And?'

Simmo shrugs.

'You didn't fuck off. You put up the white flag. You could have discussed it with me.'

'I wanted to.'

'But you didn't.'

'No.'

'I could have done with any ally,' Connie says.

'An ally? Is that what you wanted? I wanted much more than that. Ted said you'd never leave him for me.'

'Did he just?'

'He did. And I had no reason to believe he was wrong.'

Connie looks away to the noisy clock.

'Was he wrong?' Simmo asks.

She doesn't answer.

'Was he?'

'Probably not.'

'So I was right not to tell you. If I had, I'd have lost you both.'

Connie refills her glass with water. 'Does it make you despise him?' she asks.

Simmo thinks.

'No, I can't despise Ted.'

Connie drinks more water. It will be an almighty hangover. 'Me neither, which is infuriating.'

'I need to ask something,' Simmo says.

'What?'

'Do you think you'll ever love me the way you loved Ted?'

The clonking of the second hand exaggerates her delay in responding. At last she does.

'No.' There, she's said it.

Simmo bows his head.

Connie takes his hand. 'I can only love you the way I love you.'

He looks up.

She brushes his hair with her fingers. 'It's still so black. Sure you don't dye it?'

'Positive,' he says.

It's a strange diversion.

'I've been thinking,' Connie says, 'we should tell Seb it's time.'

'For the shop?'

'Yeah, that he can buy us out – as long as you've had enough.'

'I've had plenty.'

'I'm going to scale back at the surgery. I'm thinking two days a week might be enough. Penny's been pestering me for years to let her take over.'

'Good plan.'

'I'll let her do it gradually, pay me out over the next couple of years. Then, if she can't afford the real estate, I'll collect a little rent until she can.'

Simmo still has Connie's hand. He lifts it and kisses it.

'I should go,' she says.

'No, stay.'

'You should tell Vanessa first.'

'In the morning.'

'She'll be protective. She'll think you deserve someone younger. You spent enough years nursing Miranda to her death.'

'That did cross my mind,' Vanessa says.

She's at the entrance to the kitchen.

'You were quiet,' Simmo says.

'I was quiet? You've been pretty quiet yourself. How long's all this been going on?'

'Since Friday,' Simmo says, 'but it's a bit more complicated than that.'

'So I gather.'

# 10.
# THE DIY CHURCH OF
# DOUBTERS AND UNBELIEVERS

It is just after nine the next morning when Connie, on her approach to Surfside Hardware, encounters a strange scene. Seb steps out of the shop and onto the street. He weaves between cars in a long line of slow-moving traffic, then stops on the median strip. He pivots there and, looking back to the shop, he raises his hands, shoulder width apart, palms facing each other. Connie can only assume he is praying.

She stops outside the shop, beneath the awning. His focus, through the frame of his raised hands, is above the awning. He is mouthing words. She hopes her son isn't losing his mind.

He looks down to street level and finds her, waiting. He crosses back to the footpath.

She asks: 'Can you take ten minutes for coffee next door?'

'I wish I could say I was too run off my feet. Slow morning.' Seb flips the sign on the door and locks up.

★★★

There's only one free table inside at Reggie's. As they take their seats, Seb realises he has never before, in all his years as a Reggie's customer, sat down inside. This only clicks because he is observing Beth from this angle for the first time, and so he is seeing her splendid tattooed back. She sees him in the reflection of her angled overhead mirror and she smiles, her everyday greeting. Seb is embarrassed, less that she's caught him looking than for what she must be thinking about his drunken carry-on the other night.

Something else comes to mind.

'We've never done this before,' he tells his mother.

'Had coffee here?'

'Had coffee anywhere.'

'Heavens,' Connie says, 'I think you're right.'

Beth leans over the counter. 'I've got your usual, Seb. What's your mum having?'

For introductions, he says only: 'Beth, Connie.'

'Is it ink?' Connie asks her. 'The tattoo?'

'God no. I can't do pain. It's henna.'

'I love it.'

'Thanks. I'm so sorry for your loss. We all loved Ted.'

'Thank you.'

'I've signed up for the big paddle-out. Will you be paddling, too?'

'Uh, no,' Connie says.

She raises an eyebrow to Seb and mutters, as an aside: 'The festival of Ted McCall.'

Seb grins. It's an oddly conspiratorial joke between them, at Ted's expense.

'Just make me Seb's brew,' Connie tells Beth.

'And I think I'll get a piece of crumble,' Seb says.

Beth turns to face the espresso machine.

'Did you check out her back?' Connie asks.

Seb senses instant heat in his cheeks. 'Did you notice me checking it out?'

'Who wouldn't? It's riveting.'

This attempt at playfulness between mother and son feels

awkward. Neither is relaxed about it. Seb catches Beth looking at them in her mirror, admiring their apparent shared amusement, and he's strangely heartened by her casual blessing.

'You got that message on your dad's phone?' Connie asks.

'Yes.'

'Good.'

Seb says: 'I didn't know know you could record a FaceTime call then share it.'

'Me neither. It's one of those tricks Gracie showed me once upon a time. I thought I'd never remember it, but it was late and I gathered you wouldn't be taking calls – and I really needed to make sure you got it.'

They sit quietly. Connie becomes suddenly solemn.

'He was very easy to be with, your old man,' she says. 'We did find our own way to be married.' She looks to the wall with the big framed aerial photograph of Bondi Beach. She studies it and something about it troubles her.

'I'm sorry he put you through all that,' Seb says.

They both know instantly the enormity of these scant words. It is the first utterance of sympathy, for anything, that either can recall Seb offering his mother. Connie smiles in gratitude but looks away, once again to the photograph. Seb's crumble arrives, then their coffees, and he senses his mother is as relieved as he is by the interruption.

Connie sips her coffee. 'That's good. Not so milky.'

Seb spoons apple crumble into his mouth. Caramelised crumbs stick to his lower lip and remain there. Connie wants to tell him, but she doesn't want to seem too motherly. That might annoy him, so soon. The crumbs, though, are stubborn on his lip. They make him look boyish and this provokes a memory of watching him eat in his infancy. Connie was never much of a doter, but she had her lapses.

'I actually came here to tell you something,' she says.

'Oh?'

'If you're ready to take over the shop, Simmo and I are ready to sell up.'

'Hey?'

He clearly hasn't seen this coming.

'You knew?' he asks.

'About your church? Oh yes, sorry, your dad told me. I know he wasn't meant to. He didn't keep too much from me – apart from the small matter of his husbands.' Connie chortles blackly, unsure what's possessed her to make light of it.

Seb is bemused.

'I've decided you may as well have your dad's share now,' she says. 'There's no point waiting till I'm gone. I plan to be around for a ridiculously long retirement.'

Seb appears overwhelmed. 'The longer you're around,' he says, 'the more you'll need that money.'

'I'll be fine.'

'It's just that ...'

'What?'

'I don't know anymore.'

'You don't know what?'

'That I'll go ahead with the church.'

This stops Connie.

'So I'll need to resolve that question,' he says.

'What question?'

'What I believe and what I don't.'

'This is very sudden.'

'I know. I need some time.'

He's so earnest that Connie can't bear to watch the crumbs sticking comically to his lip. She points to her lower lip and swipes it with a finger. Seb gets it. He wipes his lip and dislodges some of the crumbs, though not all.

'I thought you'd be happy,' he says.

'Only if you are. Only if you're certain.'

'I'm afraid not. I'm not certain about anything.'

'And I'm afraid that's because of me.'

'No,' he says, 'it's because of Dad.'

This stings Connie. Is she so inconsequential?

'I don't understand,' Seb says, 'why he'd raise me in a faith he had no faith in.'

'He had some. He had a bet each way.'

Seb clears his throat. 'Story of his life, it seems.'

Connie notes the resentment in this crack. She surprises herself by leaping to Ted's defence. 'I think it's impossible for us to appreciate how hard it was for him to be himself. There's so much I still need to tell you, but in the weeks and months after he came out – after Tory outed him to me, I mean – he prayed and prayed to be straight.'

Seb dwells on this until saying: 'Prayers unanswered.'

Connie agrees. 'Not a peep out of God on that subject.'

Seb finds this funny, so much he convulses.

'Good grief!' Connie says.

*Good grief!* It's a Tedism. It's such a Ted thing to say that it makes them both laugh some more. In the process, Seb dispenses with the last of the crumbs on his lip.

'We haven't been especially good at it,' Seb says.

'What?'

'The grief thing.'

'No,' Connie says.

'This is an improvement.'

They sit with this thought. Connie looks again to the drone photograph over the beach, the identically sized rectangles of surf and sand, the sunbather in canary-yellow bikini and the lone surfer, on the gem-blue water, with matching canary-yellow togs and longboard.

'What is it?' Seb asks.

'Too good to be true.'

'Sorry?'

'It's staged.'

'I suppose it is. I hadn't thought too much about it.'

Connie changes the subject. 'Do you remember the superb fairy-wrens in our garden?'

Seb frowns. 'The blue ones?'

'Everyone remembers the blue ones, the breeding males. The brown ones – the females and the non-breeding males – nobody talks about them. Anyway, they're back.'

'That's nice.'

'The first time I connected with your father, in New York, he was wearing a blue shirt, and when the fairy-wrens first arrived at our place, twenty or more years later, I thought: They're the same stunning blue. And I teased him about it.'

'How?'

'I pointed out that fairy-wrens are socially monogamous but sexually promiscuous.'

'Sorry?'

'They stay with one partner for life but all the while they play around. "Just like you, Ted." That's what I told him.'

Seb spends some time digesting this. 'But you were wrong,' he says. 'He wasn't.'

'Sexually promiscuous? No, as I discover. He was socially monogamous with me and sexually monogamous with Mark Romero.'

'He should have told you.'

'He should.'

Seb finishes his coffee. 'If I'd known all this about him,' he says, 'I could've told him that I never had a problem with gays, and I never really believed God did. It was just our church allegiance, and I went along for that ride. Marriage was for a man and a woman – for raising kids. But when the vote came back and they changed the law, and men married men and women married women and the sky didn't fall in, I knew we'd been wrong. That I was wrong. My church would never have pushed that barrow.'

'If it went ahead.'

'I wish I could have told Dad that.'

'I wish we'd given you the chance.'

Seb's hand is within easy reach. Connie doesn't want to risk taking it in hers lest he recoil and she spoil the moment.

'If there's to be no hardware and no church,' she asks, 'what will you do with yourself?'

Seb doesn't seem to know.

'I don't see you as a property mogul,' she says.

'I'll leave that to Amber.'

'What then? You're too young to put your feet up.'

He tells her about Pastor Pat's visit to the shop, and his sarcastic parting shot about the Church of Doubters and Unbelievers.

'I've been wondering: is that such a silly idea? Might it actually work?' he says. He makes an invisible banner with his hands: 'Surfside Hardware – the DIY Church of Doubters and Unbelievers.'

'You're serious,' she says.

'Not overly. It's a thought.'

'That's what you were doing when I arrived. I thought you were praying.'

'I was seeing how it might scan as a hoarding.'

'It fits?'

'Yeah. Look, I'm probably not serious, but why shouldn't doubters and unbelievers have somewhere – some place to congregate, to talk about right and wrong, to do some right, some charity, whatever? Or we could just sell the shop and be done with it.'

'We could do that, too,' Connie says, 'but let's not rush it. Give it all the thought it needs.'

'If nothing else,' Seb says, 'it could be a place for people to come and sing. We could expand the Surfside Singers – build the troupe. And then, maybe, I could do some more study.'

'What?'

'I don't know. Charles Darwin's first degree was in divinity. There's hope for me yet.' Seb looks at the wall clock.

'You need to go,' Connie says, but she needs to say one last thing. 'You know, I was probably trying to punish your dad by making him do all the heavy lifting with raising you. He over-compensated so much for my absence, I always thought you were just fine. I'm sorry if you weren't. I think I punished myself, really. If you didn't miss out, I certainly did.'

This is too much for Seb. He wishes they weren't in public. He stands. 'I'd better get back.'

'Or we could go and find the fairy-wrens,' Connie says.

# 11.
# IT HAD TO BE YOU

The woman in the frock shop called it 'electric lilac'. Amber had her doubts until Seb coaxed her to try it on. She's wearing it well this evening. She's standing by the kitchen island, waiting for him, as Seb walks through the back gate and beholds his wife aglow in her birthday frock. He slides shut the bifold doors and takes a key from his pocket and inserts it in the lock. He gives it a good jiggle to make a show of locking the door, though he doesn't.

'Okay?' Amber asks.

'He's settled down. I promised we'd bring him a doggy bag.'

Only ten minutes ago Mack put on a wingding performance, an overacted tantrum at not being allowed to join them for Amber's belated birthday dinner. It was Mack's little contribution to his father's ruse. Amber fell for it and suggested cancelling their booking at Flavio's and telling Kerry and Ant to come instead to their place. Seb told her it would be unfair to cancel so late on a Saturday night, and Mack promptly backed off and allowed his father to walk him to Yeah-Yeah's.

To complicate matters, Seb has just received a text from Kerry, apologising that Ant has pulled out. He breaks this news to Amber.

'It'll only be three of us. Kerry just messaged.'

'Pat got to him?'

'Yeah.'

'Why wouldn't she call *me?*' Amber asks.

'She's embarrassed. She was worried it'd spoil your celebration. I told her it won't. We'll have more fun without him. No boring bits.'

'You didn't tell her that?'

'No, I'm telling you.'

Amber smiles but Seb knows this is a blow. Her estrangement from their fellowship is becoming painful for Amber. Only last night she told Seb: 'Even if God was never there, I still miss Him.' How can Seb compete with a god who was never there yet will remain eternal?

He closes the front door behind them. He has a one-word text message to his mother pre-typed on his phone's screen. While Amber gets into the front passenger seat, he hits send. 'Go!' it says.

At the top of Bondi Road, Seb exclaims: 'Oh no!'

'What?'

'I've left the iron on.' It's a desperately lame excuse but he could think of nothing better.

'Are you sure?' Amber asks.

'Pretty sure,' he says.

'We'll be late. I'll call Mack to do it.'

'He didn't take a key. I'll swing back. If you jump inside and switch it off, I'll turn the car around.'

When Amber reaches the front door, Seb slips out of the car and follows her in. He arrives at the opened door when she is halfway along the hall, outside the bathroom where he ironed his shirt. She looks inside and sees there is no ironing board still standing and no iron plugged in.

A thud in the back room startles her. She panics and runs towards the front door and into Seb's arms.

'There's someone in there,' she says.

'Yes.'

Seb turns her around. A mob carrying balloons and streamers

is pressing into the narrow hall to greet Amber. 'Surprise!' Mack cries, and they all echo him. There are twenty-six of them moving down the hall, led by Mack and Connie. Kerry is at the front, without Ant. Alongside her is Amber's father, Des, who has flown in at short notice from the Gold Coast with Maryanne, his third wife. They all reliably followed Seb's instructions to assemble at his mother's and proceed up the lane when he gave the all-clear. It's all gone to plan, but now Seb can see Amber's bewilderment and he fears surprising her was a mistake.

Mack runs ahead of the ruckus to hug his mother. 'Surprise,' he says again.

'Thank you, my darling. Thank you, everyone.'

Amber is struggling to break a smile. She turns to Seb, to kiss him, because that's what a wife should do now – affirm her love for her husband, for all gathered to witness – but she looks lost, apologetic. *I don't deserve this.* Yes, you do, he's telling her, in the way of the telepathy between husbands and wives.

In the crush of these seconds, while the mob moves in on Amber, she's signalling that she's not ready tonight to celebrate their marriage. They may be marking her birthday but these celebrations are always meant as testament to the marriage. She can't be sure yet about theirs. It's too soon. She may yet choose God, and that might be an irreconcilable difference. This is what she's thinking, Seb knows. He doesn't know why he knows. He just does.

Amber's father hoists her into a bear hug and mistakes her tears for joy. The mob jostles her down the hall, through the family room and into the yard. Seb follows the tumult. Corks are popping in the kitchen. The caterers have arrived on cue via the back lane, and they are filling glasses with fizz and passing the canapes. Coming through the back gate now is the audio-visual guy, delivering the big screen and speakers. It's too late for Seb to call him off. Seb will have to sing.

'Nice work, Dad.'

Gracie has arrived at his side with Vanessa, and now Simmo completes the circle. The girls have done a marvellous makeup job on Simmo's face, though not enough to mask all evidence of the assault. What was black and blue has faded to a jaundice-yellow and brown.

Conversation is a whirl, much of it about the big paddle-out for Ted tomorrow. Seb can't be sure how little or how much time has passed before he's on his feet with a microphone in his hand, introducing the late, great Ted McCall, who appears on the big screen at his piano, his son standing by his side.

Connie watches this phantasm of father and son, larger than life on the screen, the two of them dwarfing the real-life son in the foreground, Seb in the flesh, who leaves his father to sing the intro.

*Why do I do just as you say*
*Why must I just give you your way ...*

Seb, off-screen and on, chimes in for the chorus:

*It had to be you*
*It had to be you*
*I wandered around, and I finally found*
*The somebody who*
*Could make me be true*
*And could make me be blue*
*And even be glad*
*Just to be sad – thinking of you*

Connie must have heard Ted sing these lines a hundred times. Tonight she hears them anew.

Seb can see that Amber's anxiety is melting. His audacious party trick is working, for now. If only for now. It's no cheap trick. It's the best he has. It's all his defective love – a kind of prayer to the god who isn't there – and he hopes it's enough.

# 12.
# THE PADDLE-OUT

It's windier than they hoped, the sea choppy, the waves fluky. Close-out breakers spit a white mist towards the horizon. Two hundred or more paddlers have come with their surfboards to the Bondi shore, in their bikinis and boardshorts and budgie smugglers. They are massed around a surfboat, which is wedged on a sandbank in the shallows.

Connie crosses the beach, carrying a porcelain urn. She's wearing a pristine-white shirt with a grandfather collar over her bathers. She bought one for herself and one for Seb, who's wearing his over his budgies. He looks pastoral as he natters with the crew by the surfboat.

Twenty metres away, Mark Romero stands alone in a grey windcheater. His attempt to be inconspicuous, perhaps, sets him apart from this gala of flesh. Connie thought he might not come. She wouldn't have blamed him. She notes the mob trying not to stare.

Simmo, already stripped to his budgies, ready to row the boat, breaks from the crowd and approaches Mark. Connie lets them talk for a minute before she joins them.

'You've come more sensibly attired than the rest of us,' she tells Mark.

'The weather hasn't turned anyone away.'

'Ted should be seeing this. He's out and nobody cares.'

Mark scans the crowd. 'They'd care more if he were alive.'

Connie shrugs: possibly, probably.

Simmo heads back to the boat, but now Seb is approaching.

'Seb,' Connie says, 'this is Mark Romero.'

They nod.

'I've heard all about you,' Mark says.

'I wish I could say the same.'

'I wish so, too.'

Marty Ratcliffe arrives wearing only his budgies and holding a loudhailer at his side. 'Ready to roll, Mzzz Blunt?'

'Ready as I'll ever be,' she says.

'You're paddling?' Mark asks Connie.

'Hell no, but they are putting me in that boat. Marty, this is Mark Romero, Ted's other partner.'

While everybody knows, it is her first public outing of Ted. It's easier this way: to confirm it incidentally.

'Okay,' Marty says. He fumbles the loudhailer from his right hand to his left so he can shake Mark's hand. 'Do you need a board, mate?'

'No. I'll be the cheer squad.'

Marty nods and moves off.

'Thanks for that,' Mark tells Connie.

'For what?'

He smiles. It is also the first public confirmation of Mark Romero, Ted's other partner.

'Wish me luck,' Connie says, then follows Marty to the surfboat.

At the shore, she stands ankle-deep by the boat. Erratic waves slap the gunwales.

'You'll be fine,' Seb tells his mother. 'Hop in.'

He gives her a boost. She sits on the rear platform where Seb, in Ted's place as sweep, will stand and steer. She looks back to Mack and Gracie, at the front of the pack of boardriders, with floral wreaths around their necks. Her grandkids look divine; they're champing to chase the boat. Beth the barista is behind them with a longboard nearly twice her height. Amber has joined Mark Romero behind the phalanx of paddlers. Connie watches Simmo and Marty and their fellow rowers in the ritual of pulling their budgies into their bum cracks to expose their buttocks, so they'll slide on the boat's seats with a little seawater for encouragement.

'You might as well wear G-strings,' Connie tells Simmo.

The loudhailer crackles and whistles with the wind and Marty barks into it: 'Okay, you lot. The conditions are less than ideal. It'll be a long paddle because we'll need to get out near the point, well past the breakers. If anyone reckons they won't make it, please withdraw now because all the lifesavers will be preoccupied, sending off one of our finest.

'And before anyone on a surfboard starts the paddle-out, give us blokes in the boat a good head start – let's say fifty metres – in case we scuttle the bloody thing.'

'Is that likely?' Connie asks. 'Should we come back on a calmer day?'

'Everyone's here now,' Simmo says.

The rowers, two either side of the boat, push it off the sand at an even canter. On Seb's command they leap aboard as one and heave on their oars. Seb is last on, straight to his feet. They scoot over swells and crash through whitewash. Salt spray stings Connie's face and soaks her shirt. She's squashed between Seb's toes and the handle of Simmo's oar, which looms at her face. She twists around to look up at Seb. His shirt, like hers, is drenched. From this angle he could be Ted. Calves, thighs, forearms, pecs – the surf casts them in the same mould. Seb's legs are akimbo and through this frame she watches the boardriders make a howling cavalry charge into the waves.

The boat rears up and Connie shrieks. It's near vertical, bursting through a breaker, and she fears Simmo and the crew might topple on her, but the bow falls and the horizon reappears as the hull wallops the surface. They forge on and in quick time they're out to sea. The shoal of paddlers catches up and disperses to encircle the boat. The riders sit up, straddling their boards, and link hands in an unbroken chain.

While Seb's long oar steadies the boat, the four oarsmen raise their blades to the sky, a sculptural flourish, and a drone buzzes overhead to capture it.

'Let's act fast, Mum,' Seb says. 'Stand up here, with me.'

Connie, hugging the urn, clambers to her feet, precarious, the boat rocking. Seb lays down his oar and clasps her shoulder. Both are wringing wet.

'Ready?' Seb asks.

Connie unscrews the lid from the urn. Seb looks to the drone to check it's got them covered.

'Okay,' he says. 'Let him go.'

'You do it,' Connie says.

'No, you.'

'Both of us,' she says.

So Seb holds the urn with her.

'On three,' he suggests.

They count it down and on three they upend the urn over the edge. Ted's ashes spill from its spout in a singular convulsion, as though he's still intact. It's a slow stream. One man makes a lot of ash.

A squall picks it up and blows it back at Connie and Seb. It showers them, their sodden white shirts becoming black with Ted's ash. They're wearing his remains.

Laughter erupts from the boat crew and the great ring of paddlers.

'You'll have to jump in,' Simmo says. 'Both of you – to wash him off.'

'You can't be serious,' Connie says. 'I won't put a toe in. You know that.'

'Just this once.'

'No.'

'Come on, Mum,' Seb says. 'Let's rinse him off.'

'No!'

Seb takes hold of her hand. Connie resists.

'This is madness,' she says. 'We could be eaten by sharks.'

Seb agrees. 'Possibly.'

Connie lets her hand go limp in submission. Seb tightens his grip and, together, they jump. Their flight is brief. They surface among the ashes swirling in the froth, the specks of Ted slipping from their matching shirts.

# ACKNOWLEDGEMENTS

It was a long time between books for me – decades off the fiction tools. This novel could not have happened without the wise counsel of many generous and sharp-eyed readers. Throughout every draft, my wife, Donna, was my first set of ears. I dragged her from our shed, her studio – the she'ed, we call it – and read aloud to her the latest instalments. She listened patiently and her painterly fingerprints are in these pages. Thanks to our daughters, Jess and Kate, for their enthusiasm for this project.

The advice of all readers was indispensable, from medical expertise to questions of worship to knowledge of surfboats and social history. I thank:

Fellow writers Tracy Ellis and Malcolm Knox; *all* my siblings, Bill, Michael, Alannah, John, Stephen and Rosanne, and the doctors in Alannah and John's houses, their partners Philip Barraclough and Mellisa Riddle; Nick and Jane Lush, Julie Lewis, Ron Harmer and Kurt Poniewierka, Pamela Kelly, Chris Rands and Myrto Schaefer, Michael Beach, Philippa Sandall, Alan Morrow and Annelise Grey, Katherine Osborne, Nick and Margo Efrossynis, Sue Joseph, Eric Gailloux, Steve Larnach, and the author of *Crew*, Tony McGowan. And, for her unforgettable wedding speech, Lara (Gilmour) Ferguson.

I thank Courtney Barnett for letting my characters relish her song 'Avant Gardener' as much as I do (© Copyright Native Tongue Music Publishing. Print rights administered in Australia and New Zealand by Hal Leonard Pty Ltd ABN 13 085 333 713 www.halleonard.com.au. Lyrics used by permission. All rights reserved. All unauthorised reproduction is illegal.) And Australian band WAAX for mention of its belter 'Holy Sick'.

My special thanks go to my agent, the brilliant and thoughtful Fiona Inglis, and her team at Curtis Brown, and to Juliet Rogers and Diana Hill at Echo Publishing for giving this story their love and attention, and to Lauren Finger, most graceful of editors.